The Night's Gift

by
Sarah Hersman

A MISCHIEVOUS MUSE BOOK

MISCHIEVOUS MUSE

The Night's Gift
by Sarah Hersman
A Mischievous Muse Book / Mar. 2018

Published by
Mischievous Muse Publishing Arts Alliance
Los Angeles County, California

Library of Congress Cataloging-in-Publication Data
Hersman, Sarah
The Night's Gift/ Sarah Hersman.
Fantasy/Young Adult Fiction

Mischievous Muse
ISBN: 978-1-938208-26-3

"In a twist on YA urban fantasy, Alvara has always known she was special: her ability to grow wings every night, only to have them disappear at sunrise. What she needed to know was why. Alvara's feeling that the world is off-kilter should resonate with teenagers everywhere."

> – Jeff Blyth
> Screenwriter of the upcoming film, Blue Lights

"Imaginative and tightly crafted, The Night's Gift is an action packed novel brimming with fantasy and humor, with an inspiring affirmation of growth and soulful connection at its core. Its endearing protagonists, Alvara and Jake, come to terms with their shared special gift as they brave ordeals in intriguing settings. A thrilling tale that keeps you engaged with surprising twists and turns, and unexpected character revelations. Its deftly rendered interplay of reality, memory, and dream is rooted in psychological insight, offering young readers a compass to navigate a world of uncertainties as a spirit of agency and responsibility is affirmed."

> – Romy Sutherland, Author at Senses of Cinema
> UCLA Professor of Comparative Literature

"Hersman asks her readers heavy questions: What are the consequences of past failures? Can purpose endure a crisis of faith? How can we navigate a world where misguided, morally ambiguous actions have terrible effects? Honestly, I couldn't put it down."

> – Deborah Hoover

Other Books You May Enjoy

The Wish
The Cloverfield Chronicles
by E. V. Jones

The Fairies of Feyllan
by Cat Spydell

The Secret Half
The LightBridge Legacy Series
by Elayne G. James

Flight to Andolin
Journeys of a Reluctant Heroine
by Roe Jewell

For Nancy, Mike, Katie, Megan, and JJ
for loving and accepting the weird.

If the Sun & Moon should doubt
They'd immediately go out

- William Blake

Chapter 1

Wind caressed her cheeks, and the stars were high and cold. The moon, a small sliver tonight, shone like a peephole into heaven.

Her wings beat the air, carrying her ever higher.

Alvara would never be used to it, not ever. The night was her companion, at once enfolding her in a cocoon of darkness and opening a thousand starlit paths for her to discover. Flexing her arms and feeling her wings compensate, she reveled in the sensations of flight.

Closing her eyes, she allowed herself to spin into a dive, daring herself to continue falling, to keep her eyes closed for as long as possible. The vertigo of freefall made her stomach lurch. Wind whipped through her hair and tears leaked out in the rush of speed. When she couldn't take it anymore, her wings snapped open as she opened her eyes. She laughed at how far she still was above the lines of houses and businesses below.

The whole city snaked out beneath her like a circuit board from one of her physics labs. The lights on the sides of buildings, the regularity of streetlamps, and the slow winding of cars on the freeway all leant themselves to the illusion. The school's college counselor constantly repeated her advice to use their college essays to illuminate interesting connections in everyday life. Alvara had a few months left until she had to submit college applications, but the essay kept giving her trouble. *My Winged Life*, she thought. Too bad it was more likely to get her into a government research facility than into college.

She could control her wing muscles down to the individual flight feathers, and she made nearly unconscious adjustments for stability as she climbed again. The moon's light chilled her exposed skin. Despite the exertion, Alvara shivered.

Leveling out, Alvara blinked the wetness out of her eyes. She then directed a course towards the cluster of skyscrapers poking through the flattened suburbs.

As she neared her destination, her thoughts kept coming back to the dream of the night before. It haunted her.

In the dream, she had wings, but it was day. She wore a cream dress, rather than her standard white turtleneck and pants, and her dark hair whipped across her face as she flew. Alvara couldn't see her arms, for wings encased them; wings consisting of wax and feathers rather than muscle and bone. Overwhelmed by a desire to soar higher, she flew closer and closer to the brightness above. Her father's voice, which she scarcely remembered, warned her to stop. A face flickered within the brilliance of the sun's light, beckoning her nearer. She continued to climb, though the heat threatened to consume her. As she beat her wings, wax dripped off her arms, and her fingertips emerged. Terrified, but powerless to halt her ascent, Alvara screamed. Wax leaked out of her eyes and mouth and her wings turned to scattered feathers as she plummeted to the ocean below. She awoke just before striking the surface.

As her strong wings beat to gain altitude again, she followed the curve of the freeway, imagining what it would be like to fly around the world. The oceans were the problem, she thought. The story of Icarus and the sun . . . she shivered at the memory of the dream. She could never cross the ocean in one night, and with the rising of the sun she'd suffer poor Icarus' fate and tumble to her death; not due to wax facsimiles of wings, but because her wings depended on the night. By day, she was earth bound, but by night the sky was hers. Still, one could wonder.

The closest she had come to being truly alone had been during an aunt-enforced bonding vacation she would never forget. Some latent maternal instinct had compelled her aunt to rent a cabin up in the mountains for just the two of them, but her aunt had spent the majority of the time watching reruns of old shows through flickering static. At night there, as Alvara glided over the empty forest, it felt as if the trees below her were part of some hostile ocean, lightless and devoid of warmth.

Alvara refused to be daunted by the tragedies of her life. She had never known her mother; she had given birth to Alvara as her last act. Since her father had died, leaving her an orphan, she experienced joy through a veil. She felt strongly that something was not right, that her life was off-kilter somehow and couldn't be fixed. The truth that God loved her had helped her to cope, and the proof of her wings that assured her the stories of Him were true. In her day-to-day life, she was often alone. Yet Alvara never quite felt alone while flying. Each night she prayed, and each night the wings bloomed from her shoulder blades. She was secure in her belief that God had given her wings. Even now, she knew God watched over her; she could feel it best when using her gift.

Nearing her destination, she began to descend. Flying on cool nights like this was a challenge; there were few updrafts to keep her afloat as she approached the roof. Many times, she had been grateful for the soft edges to her wings. Like a snowy owl's, they made no sound as she descended. She couldn't help but feel that it was all part of the plan, her white wings and outfit—in the light-polluted sky, she blended in with the gray background, whereas a sneaky black superhero outfit would have stood out against the city night. Not that she hadn't considered a bit of spandex.

Once or twice. It was classic heroine, especially in comparison to her ratty pants and turtleneck. *Perhaps if I ever get an allowance*, she thought.

Beating her wings once, twice, she landed on the roof, keeping her wings extended for balance. The industrial building's flat roof made it an easy landing, but multiple near-disasters had taught her to be cautious. The night smelled of jasmine flowers, a scent she much preferred to some of the smells that often permeated this place.

She walked along the ledge, leaning over and counting windows as she walked. Finally, she found the one she sought. With a practiced motion, she swung herself over the lip of the roof to rest her feet on the windowsill below. Pain shot through her forearm as she scraped it along the metal sill. She maneuvered her wings to squeeze through the open window without damaging them, hissing at the stinging pain.

She found herself in the children's division of a hospital, the walls full of color, covered in self-portraits made by the children who lived there. To the right of the window in the room she had entered, she saw a sink and washed her arm with soap and water. The cut wasn't as bad as she thought.

"Hello there," Alvara heard from the doorway. Startled, she turned toward the sound.

A nurse in a blue uniform leaned into the room, squinting into the darkness before she turned on the overhead light. "Hello miss, are you lost?" she asked in a gentle voice.

"Um, yes," Alvara stammered, praying that her wings would go unnoticed. "I can't remember how to get to my room. 514?" she asked, remembering that she was on the fifth floor.

"That's no problem, dear, straight down this hall and make a left at the second turning. It will be on your right. Do you want me to walk with you?" the nurse asked, though she seemed anxious to continue her rounds.

"That's all right, I can make it. Thanks," Alvara called, and let out her breath when the nurse continued down the hallway and out of sight. Score another point for her outfit, she thought. The nurse had just assumed she was a patient. And who else would she be, on the fifth floor of a hospital in the middle of the night?

The nurse's obvious ignorance of her wings didn't surprise her, though each possible discovery still made her nervous. Most adults couldn't see them, as if something more important always kept their attention. As an experiment with her aunt, she had moved her wing to brush her aunt's arm. Alicia had reached up to scratch her head to avoid it, though she didn't seem to realize why she had done so.

Alvara knew she shouldn't take it for granted that they would go unnoticed. Once, as she had flown around soon after she had discovered her gift, a man walking home had glanced up at her and stared as she flew by. She never knew if he had seen her wings or just the figure of a girl floating through the night, but it reminded her to be cautious.

After leaving the room, she read the signs to remind herself of where to go, and walked down the hallway to her left. She passed closed doors on either side, wondering where she should stop tonight. She'd visited the hospital every few nights over the past month, so she was beginning to get the hang of the place – she had visited with her father once before, when she was much younger. It turned out she had only had a short case of pneumonia, but she had always remembered the hospital, wondering how she could help those who had a long-term home there. She loved flying, but was compelled to share her wings with others, for whatever solace or hope their beauty could provide.

Her soft shoes making no sound, Alvara stopped by the door numbered 526. The name on the card by the door read, "Jonathan Venesta." She knocked, and a young voice answered, "Come in." She checked both ways down the hallway, but all corners and turnoffs were visible in the dim automatic lights, and no one was in sight. Her heart beat with anticipation as she crossed the threshold and turned to close the door.

She heard a gasp from behind her, and turned to see a young boy gaping wide-eyed at her as he sat up in bed, rubbing the sleep out of his eyes as if to return to reality. She smiled at him, and said, "Don't be afraid, I won't hurt you."

"Who are you?" he asked, clutching the covers with his small hands.

"I'm just a friend," she explained. "My name is Alvara, what's your name?" She thought he was about ten years old or so, with the dark hair and olive skin of a mixed heritage like her own.

"Jonathan," he said. He blew out his breath as if getting down to business. "Why are you wearing wings? Halloween was months ago." He tried to sound matter-of-fact, but his voice shook slightly. She didn't want to frighten him.

"We'll talk about them in a sec. Mind if I sit down?" He nodded, so she sat at the end of the bed, folding her wings as best she could parallel to her back. She adopted the mannerisms of a tough mob boss, with shifty eyes, and complete with the invisible cigar. "So eh . . . ", she pretended to take a long puff, "what are you in for, eh?"

He frowned and said, "Lung cancer." She was horrified and started to apologize for her tasteless joke, but he broke into a laugh. "Oh man, that was such a funny face! That would suck. But I'm actually here to see if chemotherapy can get rid of a lump in my brain." He sighed.

"So, how's it looking?" she asked, fearing his answer.

"Not too good," he replied. "My father and the doctor were talking the other day, and I heard a bit." He shrugged. "Nothing much more to do here but watch TV and see my friends sometimes." He played with his blanket, not looking at her. Then he whispered, "If you're an angel, could you give me a bit more time? If you wouldn't mind."

His eyes met hers, but Alvara didn't know what to say. On her previous visits, she had visited short-term residents, some recovering from surgery, others for illnesses or mild psychiatric problems. She didn't know how to cope with this.

For the girl who needed surgery on her knee after a soccer fall, Alvara knew she probably just wanted some company, so they talked about soccer, she let her feel her wings, and she told her God loved her. Another older

4

guy thought he saw things that weren't there, and so his parents had checked him in for a week or so for some diagnostics. He told Alvara that he knew gnomes lived in his backyard, so Alvara traded stories of her nights of flying, saying that sometimes grownups just couldn't believe in things like that anymore. Those two cases had been almost fun, filling Alvara with warmth that she could make others' lives better. What did she have to offer to a child who thought she had come to take his soul to Heaven?

He broke her introspection with a touch on one arm. "Don't worry," he said. She realized she was crying, and felt ashamed, wiping her eyes dry. "Come on, no te preocupes. My mama always told me there was a better place, pearly gates and heavenly angels and all, and she wouldn't have lied to me." Alvara stared in wonder at the small boy, who was somehow comforting *her* now, wondering where she had gone wrong.

"I'm not," she began. "I'm not an angel. I'm just a girl with wings. Sorry to scare you." Determined to at least be as strong as he was, she tried a smile. "So, what would you be doing right now if you weren't stuck in this hospital?"

"Um, sleeping?" he said, and Alvara laughed in surprise. Jonathan stared into the distance as he continued. "Though after school, I used to play shortstop. Baseball was my thing."

"Wait, but doesn't that sport have a lot of standing still? Slightly boring? That one, are you sure?" she teased.

"Don't knock it, chica," he said. "Sure, sometimes you stand still. But when the pitch comes, you have to move. It's all about instinct."

"Fine, maybe I haven't fully experienced baseball's deeper mysteries," Alvara replied. "Do you even like school, or would you prefer baseball 24/7?"

"Hey, don't share this with my friends, okay? But school is actually pretty great. I really like math, and when I grow up," he stopped.

Alvara's heart ached for him, but she tried to keep her face impassive. "When you grow up," she prompted.

It took him a minute, but he continued. "When I grow up, I want to be a doctor. You know, help people and stuff like that," he mumbled.

Alvara smiled. "Sounds like a pretty sweet goal. I mean, I'm about to write college applications and I'm still not sure what I want to study, or what comes after that."

"So," Jonathan asked, shifting his weight on the bed. "You're going to college, so you're not an angel. So why," he asked, pointing to the wings loosely furled on her back.

Alvara traced her hand along a wing, reveling in the soft brush of her feathers. "Every night, ever since I was little," Alvara began. "I prayed to God to allow me to serve him by helping others. My dad taught me that prayer," she added, the memory of her father almost overwhelming her. "And God granted my request by giving me wings. They are a sign of His love, a truly precious gift."

"Wow," Jonathan said. "So, kind of an angel."

Alvara snorted. "Sure," she said. "And for a while now, I've used them to spread hope, if I can, by bothering little boys when they're trying to sleep."

Jonathan smiled, and seemed to be working up to a question.

"Would you like to touch one? I'm pretty sure it won't kill you," Alvara said, trying to keep a straight face.

Jonathan touched one, disbelieving, tracing the edges of feathers and feeling the muscles at the base of her wings that melded into her back. His touch was gentle, and she tried to keep from giggling when it tickled.

"Um, do I get a request or anything?" he asked, almost shyly.

"Sure, whatever I can get you, in," she checked her watch, "approximately half an hour. I'll need to get home soon."

He glanced away, embarrassed. After a few seconds of waiting, it all came out in a rush, "Can you take me flying for a bit?" He tried not to appear too eager and failed.

Relieved to have a gift to offer him, she smiled, jumped off the bed, and bowed, saying, "I'd be delighted. You'd better get dressed, it's cold outside."

On her way home, she saw their flight though his eyes, and laughed at the memory. She had hugged him close to her body as she launched them both from the window. Her strong wings flexed to carry the added weight, and she worked on climbing higher and higher. She drifted over the city, pointing out his hospital below. He remained silent, and she wondered if he was all right. Once she got to a suitable height, she asked if he wanted to dive. She had to shout a bit to be heard over the sound of the wind. He yelled back, "Yes!" and she let her weight fall forward, pulling her wings into an 'M' shape behind her body, making sure to hold the boy tight around his middle.

It had been a good thing she had him in a death grip, because the squeal of laughter that erupted from his body might have caused her to drop him otherwise. As she negotiated the fall, adrenaline filled her system, and her ears filled with the sound of wind blended with his whoops of joy. She pulled out of the dive with the practice of years, and watched as his arms released his hold on her, reaching to each side as if they were wings of his own. The words, "worth it, worth it, worth it," echoed in her heart through the rest of the flight, through the kiss on his forehead as he wished her goodbye, the curl of his skinny fingers around the white feather she had given him as she leapt into the black night.

She negotiated the early morning sky, flying lower to be able to see the ground through the thick layer of fog that enfolded the city. Her watch told her it was about 3 a.m., and she was happy that tomorrow was Friday. She could last until the weekend, with a bit of coffee. She couldn't keep getting by on these few hours of sleep or she would most likely go mad. And that could lead to doing something stupid, something she couldn't afford.

Her homeward trip forced her to remember what awaited her there, and she felt her easy peace melt away. This afternoon, when she should have been working on her homework, she had returned again to her research on winged humans, with such titles as "Early History of Flight,

Ancient Flying Myths and Legends", "Daedalus: The Long Odyssey from Myth to Reality", "Surgeon's Flight of Fantasy", and "Human Evolution. What changes would we have? Wings?" She had read ancient tales of human flight, and along with Icarus and his father Daedalus, there had been Bladud, who had perished during experimentation with wings covered in feathers. In addition to these early failures, modern scientists had deemed the possibility of humans ever evolving wings "virtually nonexistent", with no vestigial structures to develop.

Her aunt Alicia had interrupted her research, and proceeded to remind her exactly how welcome she was in her own house. Alvara frowned as she remembered the conversation.

"What do you work on?" Alicia accused, and her thick Puerto Rican accent nearly obscured her words.

"Work for this week's Bible Study," Alvara lied, realizing too late that she should have claimed schoolwork. She prepared for the worst.

"What happened to some history today? You said that you will have a test on Friday?"

"Yeah, I was about to get to that, I—"

"You know how I feel about this religion of yours. It is one thing to be a good Catholic and say confession, but this much time, it makes me uncomfortable. I just think you should be taking more time for work that is getting you far in life, like homework."

"Tía, I'm working as hard as I can—"

"Alvara, you can work more hard on school. Your mother was a smart girl, but you have a head in the clouds; missing assignments, doing bad on exams, and, oyes, Ms. Barton called me yesterday to tell me that she catches you sleeping!" Her aunt shook her head, and her hoop earrings flapped back and forth to punctuate her disappointment. "If the time you are making for this church is distracting to you from what is important, maybe you need to think of your priorities: doing good in high school so you can make your own way in the world." That phrase, to 'make your own way in the world,' was her aunt's favorite advice. It was a slap in the face that while Alvara might live here now, this wasn't, and would never be, her home.

Alvara had wanted to scream at the image of her aunt standing there with her satisfied, red lipstick-saturated smile. Sometimes, Alvara believed that she could just leave this half-life, this pretend family story that her aunt kept spinning for the both of them, and go. Even in her anger, she always held her tongue, as she considered her nights spent on the wing. She couldn't tell anyone; not even her best friend Max, about her secret.

But it was never a struggle to keep from 'fessing up; her aunt would just laugh, or worse, think she was mentally unstable and send her away. If she left her aunt, who knew if she would ever again have the freedom to use her gifts; at least while trapped in this façade of a home, her time was her own. So she always swallowed her anger and the desire to do anything drastic. This afternoon she had just smiled and promised to work harder at school.

Alvara sighed in resignation, tipping a wing to choose her house out of the series of identical roofs on her street. She landed with a soft thump, and listened to make sure the house was silent. She walked over to the side with her bedroom window, and swung over the side, exhausted and anticipating the night's sleep ahead of her.

Alvara caught a glimpse of movement in the darkness of the room, and swung a fist. She felt the edge of her fist brush feathers and gasped, her wings beating once to keep her from falling out the open window.

"Ouch! At least her aim is as terrible as her interior decorating," a female voice grumbled. Alvara searched for the source. The dark bird that had nearly hit her began to preen its feathers as it sulked, glaring at Alvara with flinty eyes.

"You're real," a man's voice croaked from her desk chair. Alvara prepared to dive back out the window and escape from whomever had found her out when he yelled, "Wait!"

She glanced back at the old man in her chair, one foot out the window. Eagle wings stretched from his back to drape over the sides of her chair, and his face crinkled into an excited smile as he saw her notice. "I'm sorry we scared you. We didn't mean to, and we're not going to hurt you or turn you in." The moment stretched, and Alvara hovered on the brink of diving out the window, unsure of whether to go or stay.

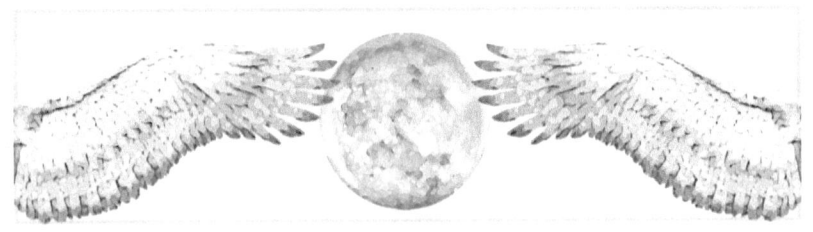

Chapter 2

A young girl tracked sand into the store, flip-flops slapping the smooth concrete flooring as she walked. She began to peruse the odds and ends of the little shop called A Siren Symphony. The girl moved past the green tea herbal remedies, incense burners, ancient texts and medieval sword replicas towards the bird figurines that dangled from the ceiling just out of reach. When he heard her laugh, the old man behind the counter asked her which one was her favorite.

"That one is a crow," she explained in solemn tones. "She looks kind of sneaky. I like being sneaky and not getting in trouble. I like her a lot."

"More tricky than sneaky, I'd imagine," said the man, attempting to mirror her solemnity but breaking into a smile. "Ravens are very tricky birds. In the Native American tradition, sometimes the Raven's tricks would help people, and sometimes not. Mostly I think he just liked to trick them for the fun of it."

She nodded, satisfied, her sunburned nose wrinkled with concentration. The raven's wings extended and curved to one side, as if she changed direction in midflight. Her eyes smirked with hidden knowledge. The girl continued to stare at the bird, even though many more above and below her were forever frozen in their dance across the air. Yearning flickered across her features, and the man felt his heart swell.

The man moved out from behind the counter and walked toward the raven. He plucked the raven from her string and placed her gently into the hands of the girl. "Make sure you take good care of her," he cautioned. He added, "Leave her on the windowsill at night, so she can remember the sky." The girl stared up at him, and her eyes gleamed in the light. She nodded once and walked from the store and along the sandy path; Jake could see her through the window, pigtails swinging back and forth, eyes fixed on her treasure.

It's no wonder I barely make ends meet, he thought, watching as a group of teenagers in bikinis biked past his store without glancing in. But his good mood lasted for the rest of the day.

Jake Coughlin closed the shop early and walked home, the first leg of his path along the concrete course at the beach's edge. The crash of the surf drowned out any other sound, and Jake let it fill him up and carry him out to sea. He wore a short sleeve shirt and slacks, which caused him to perspire as he walked, though the breeze was cool. His tired eyes and graying brown hair announced his transition from the image of a responsible father to a doting grandpa, but he had no children of his own to notice the change. He turned inland.

His feet led him along a walkway next to the canal, and a row of extravagant waterfront mansions watched his passage with silent faces. The water in the canal was low at this time of year, and many of the miniature canoes and paddleboats lay beached on the algae-covered banks. After a few minutes, he turned off the walkway, traveling the back alleys to reach his street.

As he entered his apartment, his smile slipped from his face. Evening had almost arrived, the sun just passing through to take the daylight somewhere else. Even the nightfall and bright moon could bring him little joy, though in the past they had been a balm for his heart. All around him, families sat down to eat, couples watched the television, and friends met at fancy restaurants to laugh and watch their evenings melt into nights spent together. These moments were not for Jake; he did not deserve such peace. Should the pang of his self-imposed sentence ever dampen the guilt that dwelt within him, the rising of the moon would bring with it a nightly reminder of all he had lost.

As a child, Jake had loved mysteries. Though he could see that the refraction of light was a logical explanation for the blueness of the sky, to his nine-year-old mind it did nothing to explain the depth of its promise.

One August evening in his tenth year, as the moon rose above the tree line behind his house, he encountered the best mystery of all. He felt an itch in his shoulder blades and the rip of his tee-shirt, and staggered to compensate for a sudden weight on his back.

Jake yelled and began hitting whatever had landed on his back, clawing at the immense feathered beast, surprised at the pain that radiated through his body when he did. He reached shaking fingers over his shoulder and gasped, feeling large feathery wings poking through the remains of his shirt.

But he was just young enough that the phase of disbelief soon passed, and he struggled to free his wings from the entangling fabric. They burst from their captivity, spreading twice his height in each direction. He simply stared at them; the regions he could see, at least. Smaller brown feathers rounded the forward edges, but large stiff flight feathers stretched off the back of the wings. At the very tips, he could see flight feathers as long as his forearm, but he couldn't quite reach them to touch. They rustled softly in the wind.

Jake found he could flap them up and down just by thinking about it. They were connected by bone and muscle to his shoulder blades, and even when he closed his eyes he could feel them. The wings were a part of him. At his first attempt at flight, he ended up flipping himself over onto his back, and laughed as he tried to right himself. When he managed to stand, his mother's voice caused him to jump.

"Honey, do you have some explaining to do?" she asked him, wearing the frown he thought of as you're-in-trouble-mister. Her nut brown hair was up in a bun, and she still wore her skirt and tan shirt from her job as a secretary. He hung his head and prepared to say he was sorry. Jake hadn't known that growing wings was against the rules, but his mother knew way more rules than he did.

"I'm sorry Mom; I don't know what happened." He watched her, wincing. Her expression didn't change. "I didn't mean to—"

"Didn't mean to? That's a funny way of explaining how your sister came to be locked in the closet. She told me that you two were playing hide-and-seek." She sighed, shifting her weight and crossing her arms firmly.

Jake was speechless, peeking from his wings to his mother and back again. He moved them up and down, wafting a soft stream of air towards his mother. It may not have been the wisest course, but some part of him couldn't believe that she hadn't commented on his transformation. Yet with the gust, his mother moved a stray hair out of her face with one hand, and didn't seem to notice that anything strange had happened. Was it even possible she couldn't see them?

He decided on the safest course. "I'm sorry, Mommy, I just forgot."

"Well she could have been trapped in there until bedtime. You need to be more careful, honey," she finished.

He shouldn't have forgotten about the game, but had just wandered outside to be alone. But he took his mother's advice very much to heart. He did need to be more careful. He wasn't thinking about his sister when he replied, "I know, Mom. I will."

"Good," she said, as if it was all settled. His mother smiled, and told him he had a half hour before he needed to come inside to bed. He agreed. A half hour, he repeated back to her, and watched her walk back across the grass and into the house.

When she was gone, he ran and launched himself into the air. He laughed as his new wings carried him over the trees at the end of the yard and into the cool night sky.

Every night since, or at least every night with a moon, Jake had grown a new set of wings. Sometimes he grew songbird wings, sometimes those of a hawk or an eagle, and once an albatross. In school and in his free time, he used to study the various types of birds, so that he could recognize each set of wings. He used to fly almost every night, whenever he could sneak out of his front door or through his open window. Though there were a few close calls, his mother worked every spare moment, and his sister went away to boarding school. They never discovered his nighttime wanderings.

As he grew older, he realized that his wings must be magic, as no one but he could see them, and as, no matter their size, they could lift him into the air. But wings were as much a part of him as hands and feet, and their appearance each night became a different kind of normal. Each morning, he would slip into bed before the sun rose, and wake to find his shoulders bare as before. Even as a kid, he knew that it would be dangerous for him if someone ever found out about his wings.

Jake sat down to eat his macaroni and cheese alone in his apartment. Sometimes thoughts of how happy he had been as a child troubled him. He used to think of his wings as a treasure, a forgotten gift that was his to enjoy. Yet they had let him down . . . but he refused to let his mind tread that beaten path tonight. Not after the little girl had made his day.

Jake stifled a yawn as he turned the doorknob to his bedroom. He was pushing 65, and had begun to notice the signs of age in his slower pace and declining energy levels. After cleaning up his dinner, he prepared for bed. A framed photo of a smiling middle-aged woman sat next to a Polaroid camera by his bedside, but he barely glanced at either item. He kept an eye out for the rise of the moon as he changed into his pajamas; he'd ruined too many good shirts to allow himself to get distracted, even though he could usually feel it coming. Sitting on his bed, he commenced to watch the moon crest the horizon, displacing the setting sun with its quiet beauty.

The familiar itch returned, and a small smile snuck onto his face. He had the wings of a bee hummingbird, the smallest bird in the world. He could feel their soft hum against his back. Reaching behind him with one hand, he felt their musculature, their tiny but tireless strength. He grabbed his Polaroid from its position and turned away from the full length mirror on one wall.

This was his token gesture to the magic that gave him wings. It had been years since he had flown, but each night he had photographed the wings. He kept all the pictures in a shoebox underneath his bed. He had never figured out how the camera could see his wings when people couldn't, but it didn't matter. He glanced past the strong muscles still visible along his upper back and admired the bright blue wings emerging from his shoulder blades. He snapped a picture and put it in the box.

The ritual completed, Jake turned to the window, feeling the moonlight on his skin and the almost silence of a weekday evening. He didn't notice until his feet began to leave the floor that his hummingbird wings were a purring blur behind him.

He breathed deeply, and allowed his feet to rest on the ground again. After running his fingers along the tiny feathers once more, he climbed into bed. Fighting back his sorrow and his guilt, he tossed for an hour before his exhaustion overcame him.

As Jake approached the door to his shop, he saw the girl from the day before waiting outside the door. She saw him coming from far off, and ran to meet him, wrapping her arms around him as soon as she was close enough and thanking him over and over again. Feeling a bit awkward, Jake waited until she had broken away from him before looking down at her, more than a little puzzled.

"Thank you so much!" she exclaimed again, beaming up at him. She was missing a front tooth today.

"Uh . . . you're very welcome" he answered with a small smile. "It was my pleasure, I'm glad you liked the figurine."

The words came out of her in a rush. "No, for the birdie, my birdie! You told me to leave her by the window, and my Mommy did it when I asked her to, and then when I woke up in the night she was gone and I thought she'd fallen out the window so I went to the window to find her but then she flew back in and landed on my hand and it was amazing! I told my mom but she said I had just been dreaming but I wasn't dreaming. My birdie flew!"

The little girl gushed over her gift. For his part, Jake smiled and nodded, with pleasant nostalgia for childhood days of make-believe. And so he listened and asked questions. As he entered his shop, the girl followed him in, tracking in sand from the beach outside, and describing with words and gestures the night she had spent with her bird companion.

Her story finished, the girl thanked him a final time and left, skipping with joy. *Would you look at that,* Jake thought to himself. *Nobody knows happiness like kids do.* He spent the rest of the day hiding a smile.

Every few days thereafter, the little girl returned to his shop. He learned that her name was Jenny, and she often swooped into his shop with another tale of her adventures with her new best friend Winnie. At Jenny's insistence, her mother waited outside the store as she talked with Jake, but once entered to thank Jake for humoring her little girl. He told her it was his pleasure.

Jake took solace in these visits: to him, Jenny and her stories were the best thing to come his way in a very long time. By the end of the week, Jenny had spent many nights with her bird, but her stories made a degree of sense; it sounded as if the bird had mostly watched from a corner, only rarely nuzzling Jenny or speaking to her.

As Jake watched her leave the shop, he considered that her stories might be more than a flight of fancy, no pun intended. Perhaps a bird had taken to visiting her at night. Certainly a bird figurine coming to life was in the same realm of belief as a man who grew wings.

He glanced at the other figurines hanging from the ceiling of his tiny shop. They dipped and swung on their strings, clearly fashioned of plastic and lacquer paint. He shrugged and cleaned up the store, curious in spite of himself to see whether the bird would reappear.

A few mornings later, Jake opened shop as he often did: he let in the soft California sunshine, wiped the sand from the porch of the store, and breathed in the cool salty air to invigorate him for the day ahead. He had found the night before another difficult one to bear. It had been a new moon, and that meant no wings. He'd experienced it for more than fifty years, yet their absence still left him feeling hollow, unwanted, and ordinary. Even the knowledge that his wings would return the following night, as they always did, was not enough to quell his discomfort.

The customers trickled in, as they tended to on an average Thursday morning in early summer. A small boy salivated over the miniature knight's joust in a corner, but his mother entered to retrieve him and left, leading him by the hand. A group of school-age girls entered, giggling, but were more concerned with their conversation than the store. Jake knew that, to them, his store lacked magic; it was just a place for them to be together. He didn't begrudge them their secrets and laughter, and smiled with polite unconcern as they left just the same.

Lunch had passed before the girl returned. Her enormous smile made the events of the previous night apparent, but he let her explain anyway. He could see her mother through the door, and waved. The woman shrugged, as if to say 'what can you do?', and smiled at Jake. He returned his attention to Jenny. She was breathless with excitement.

"Jake, Jake, she came back again!" It wasn't just an aphorism then, Jake thought, as he watched her literally jump up and down as she spoke. "She doesn't really talk to me out loud but she said she was sorry but she had to take a few nights off. I said I was afraid that she was gone forever but she just hopped onto my shoulder again! Jake, she's so wonderful and funny, and she's my best friend and I want you to meet her!" Jake considered how to reply.

"Honey, I don't think your Mom would like it if I came over at night to watch for the bird. But I'll tell you what. How about I borrow her for one night, and get a chance to meet her and talk with her, and then I'll return her to you tomorrow. Is that okay?"

"Sure," Jenny agreed. "Let me go get her." She ran outside to tug on her mother's shirt. Her mother produced the bird from her purse, and Jenny ran back inside to offer her to Jake. He accepted her with solemnity, and waved to mother and daughter as they continued ambling along the walkway.

Jake pulled some packaging from beneath the counter to wrap the bird for her journey. Though he appraised her with a practiced eye, she seemed as lifeless and unmoving as the rest of the birds in his shop. He shook his head at his own whimsy. *You've been too long alone, Jake old boy*, he chided. He slipped the box with the bird into his bag and greeted the next customers with his characteristic smile and nod.

Massaging his hands, Jake entered his apartment. After reheating leftovers from the night before, he brushed his teeth and got ready for moonrise. Shirtless, he sat holding the bird. His rough, careworn hands were so different from her smooth, lacquered wings. The window outlined the sky, and starlight lit his room. He watched as the moon rose, and sighed as he felt the sleek wings of a falcon unfurl on his back.

The bird remained still in his hands, though moonlight bathed her. Jake stared at it a bit longer, and then placed it on the bedside table. Try as he might, he couldn't stop from feeling bitter disappointment that nothing had happened. He chided himself for an old fool. At least Jenny had a heck of an imagination.

Bending down, and leaning on the bed for support, Jake removed the box of photos from under his bed. He had turned on the lights and turned away from the mirror, holding his camera, when he heard a few sharp taps on the window.

Knowing that his wings weren't invisible to everyone, Jake switched off the light and prepared to make up an excuse. The opportune ones ran through his mind; props for a Halloween costume, genetic experiments, a pet bird perched on his shoulders that made it appear as if he had wings. None were that plausible, but they didn't have to be. People craved reassurance that their understanding of the world was correct. They would accept even silly explanations in order to hold on to this belief.

He had just settled on the pet bird idea when he saw a dark shape flapping against his window. Bats could get turned around, he thought, and waited for it to reorient and disappear into the night. Though it flew back and forth, it stayed near his window. He cracked the window, preparing to shoo it away. It was huge for a bat.

No, it was a raven or crow, he saw, wings glossy as they beat to maintain altitude. Odd coincidence.

"Goddess, you're thick! Let me in, fluff for brains! It's not as easy to hover as I make this look." Jake scanned his surroundings, searching for the source of the voice.

The bird let out an exasperated squawk and managed to nudge the window far enough with her beak so she could squeeze into the room. Jake could do nothing but stand back and watch. Sure, birds didn't typically speak, but Jake could adapt. Old guys didn't typically grow wings either.

"Um, hello," he blurted. As she preened her rumpled feathers, she glared at him with unblinking eyes. He felt like a child. "You must be Jenny's bird."

"Nope, I was undercover actually," she replied, the feathers of her chest puffing outward. Her voice sounded harsh, with chirps and whistles and long clacking tones, and he realized he heard the human-sounding voice only in his head. "My first assignment. Jenny's a sweet girl, and knows how to treat a house guest," she added, her feminine voice thick with sarcasm. "Reminds me of my sister," she finished, her voice softer. So Jenny hadn't imagined her adventures; it wasn't her fault she had missed a couple details.

"I didn't mean to offend," he added. "So, this may be obvious to you, but you're not related to the figurine from my store?"

She cackled, her glare gone for the moment as she cocked her head at him. "I can see how that would be confusing, fluff for brains," she smiled. "It was just the entrance point for my cover. It made a good story for Jenny."

"Right," Jake said, his thoughts muddled. "And assuming I'm not going gradually mad in my old age, I can understand you."

The bird put a wing to her head, shaking it in the universal gesture of resignation to dealing with thick individuals. "So you've noticed. I can only speak with you when you've got wings, see, and most birds don't bother with it at all, but there's a bit of a situation. I'm only glad I found you in time. I was going gradually mad with doll houses and dress-up at Jenny's place."

She then jumped off the shelf to swoop onto his forearm. He barely kept from dropping her when she landed. She was lighter than she appeared; the scientist in him stirred, wanting to inquire about her flying habits, how she had learned English, and where she had picked up human mannerisms. He shook his head to attempt to focus his thoughts.

"Does this have to do with my wings?" Jake asked in a low voice, though it was the only explanation he could imagine. Even in the privacy of his room, with a talking bird, he feared revealing his secret. "How did you find me? I've never shown my wings to anyone." His heart twisted at the white lie, but it was as good as true now.

"Well, I've been searching for you for almost a year; I was lucky to stumble onto Jenny. You give off a kind of aura I can sense, like a magnetic field. And with the current situation, that field sort of spreads to people you interact with. So I found myself orienting towards Jenny, and I hung out with her until I figured out that you were the culprit. With your residual field, I could even speak with her on days she spoke with you. I was lucky; you're the last one on the list." She fluttered her feathers in excitement.

"List?" he asked.

"You know. Of others like you," she replied.

It took a few seconds for her response to make sense. Others like him. He had been solitary for most of his life. He had always believed that he was a quirk of nature, a mistake some unknown experimenter had made and then forgotten. All children are told that they are special; to Jake it had always been a favorite inside joke. He enjoyed and accepted that his wings would always set him apart.

Jake had wondered if there were others with his ability when he was in college; in a few bouts of loneliness, he had even put cryptic ads into some local newspapers. If they did exist, he had never found them. He considered the implications. He could be part of a community, with people who loved flying as much as he did, who could maybe understand some of his past. His eyes flicked to the photo by his bed and then away. Maybe he could even fly again.

Seeing the excitement in his eyes, the raven forestalled his attempt to speak. "Sorry for not clarifying," she interrupted. "There's no lost civilization of flying people that you somehow couldn't find. As far as I and others of my kind know, there is one like you in each generation of humanity, and when one dies another is born. Three at a given time seems to be about it. Like I said, lucky to find you. There is a ridiculous amount of humans these days to sift through, and I didn't have forever."

So there were two others out there, Jake thought, a younger adult and a child. He prepared to ask the question he had avoided all his life, the question of who or what had given them this power. But with the raven's words, it clicked into place.

"And the power comes from the moon," he guessed, halfway between an answer and the next unfathomable question. She nodded, and they both glanced at the thin crescent hovering outside the window. "How? Or why?" He asked, but she shook her head.

"Who knows, fluff? The birds just know it happens; some can feel it when another like you is born. But our prayers to the Moon have been in vain. She just sits there, silent and smug."

"Wait a minute," Jake said. He massaged his temples and took a deep breath. "You sound like you think that the moon is somehow alive?" Just because he accepted the fact that he had wings every night didn't mean that he had to discard scientific certainty in other areas. The moon was a dead rock that orbited the Earth.

But the raven stared at him with what Jake would swear was sympathy. "You can't see her, can you?" She asked. Jake shook his head, his brow furrowed. "You know the way most people can't see your wings, even though they are obvious to you?" Jake nodded.

"Well don't you think the one who gave you that power would be an expert at it herself? Walk over to the window, look up at the moon, and thank *her* in your heart for your wings. Don't thank *it*, the glowing shape that you see floating above you. Thank her, and you should be able to see her too." He must have looked skeptical, because she cajoled, "Come on, fluff. You could at least try. "

Highly doubtful, Jake left the raven on the bed and walked to the open window. He let his wings rise and fall, their sleek feathers whispering in the still air. Admiring the crescent of the moon, he tried to imagine something else, and thanked that person for the gift of his wings.

After a moment, the moon flickered, and a smiling woman appeared. Her face was pale, radiating moonlight, and her long dark hair filled the sky from horizon to horizon. Each bend of her hair flickered with a small point of light, and they were the stars in all their glory.

Jake took a moment to recover from his shock. When he blinked, the rock had reappeared, resolute and immovable in its silver dominance over the night sky. He turned to the raven, and a shiver passed over him as he asked, "Who was that?"

"She is the Goddess of the Moon," the raven replied, as if this were self-explanatory. "And she's the reason a monkey like you can fly each night, and of course why you can't during the day. Your loss. This night flying sucks. Try to remember how that felt and you will see more of her. But now you should get some rest, it's late." She shook her wings, preparing to leave.

"Wait," Jake said. He needed time to think about this.

The bird in front of him had answered many of his questions, the oddness of which he still needed to consider, but he had many more. The one that popped into his head seemed irrelevant as soon as he spoke. "Why do I need to get rest?" he blurted. "I mean, we could just talk all night. There's so much I'd like to know about you."

She flew to the window. "I'm off to say goodbye to Jenny. And you need rest so that tomorrow we can go and meet another like you." She prepared to jump, but paused on the sill. "My name is Laerik, by the way." She winked and soared into the night, and with a few wing beats she was gone.

Chapter 3

She was just a kid, he thought; a scrawny Latina who could be somebody's grandchild, her fierce demeanor at odds with her angelic wings. The girl remained crouched on the windowsill. "What are you doing here? How do you know where I live?" she demanded, her eyes narrowed.

"We'd like to be friends," Jake offered, raising his arms to reassure her. "Maybe a bit of a dramatic entrance, sorry again. I know it sounds absurd, but this bird helped me find you. Your wings are beautiful. I've never met another person who had wings like me. Before tonight, that is." He didn't know why he was babbling, but couldn't think of the proper thing to say.

She kept her eyes focused on him, not relaxing one bit. Waiting in her room had seemed a grand plan; now he just felt silly. She cautiously stepped into the room, but remained close to the window.

"I want you to go now," she said.

"I'm sorry, maybe I should explain—" Jake began.

"Hey," she cut him off. "Just because you grow wings, that doesn't necessarily make you one of the good guys. Whose side are you on?" she asked.

"Side?" he repeated. He was lost.

"Your wings," she retorted, like he was an idiot. "They come from someone. Mine are from God, and you're either on His side . . . or someone else's."

Jake spotted an ornate wooden cross on the wall to his right. He tried to resist, honestly he did, but the girl's strange accusation put him in a weird mood. As his fingers curled over the cross, he pretended to thrash in agony.

She responded with a gasp and a shout. It cut off abruptly when she realized he had been kidding.

Her anger was a near thing. "That's not funny," she snarled. It took a moment for her demeanor to soften as she accepted the joke. "Thanks for the litmus test," she said, and made no move to enter farther into the room.

Jake cursed himself for his poor timing. "Look, I'm really sorry about that," Jake replied, spreading his hands in apology as he set the cross on the desk. "Sometimes I can't tell when a tense moment needs a joke or not."

Her body remained tense. "Who are you, and what are you doing in my room?" she demanded again.

"I'm Jake, Jake Coughlin. I run a specialty shop in Venice Beach, not too far to the north of here." He gestured. "I found out that you had wings; don't worry, I'm not going to tell anyone," he added, "And I wanted to meet you. That's the main idea."

She met his eyes and gave a small nod. "I'm Alvara," she said. She finally stepped inside and stuck out her hand, and he stood up partway to shake it. Her palm was still cold from the night air outside. "It's good to meet you, Jake," she said, but she didn't smile. She stepped back toward the window, but no longer looked as if she would leap out of it.

"Likewise, Alvara." He saw her cast a furtive glance toward Laerik, who preened her wings on a shelf. "And this is Lay-rik or Lah-rrick or something similar, though it sounds like halfway between a chirp and a caw when she pronounces it. And, well . . . " Jake scratched his head and flexed his wings, so the feathers ruffled the research papers on her desk, "you noticed I have wings."

"Um, yeah," Alvara blushed. "Well, since you were nice enough to prove you're not a demon . . ." she shrugged. "What kind of good works do you perform with your wings?"

"Uh, well. Good works? I run a shop that sells pretty odds and ends; and it seems to make some people happy enough. I do well with kids, I suppose. Though none like this little girl; I bet she's missing you, Laerik. It's funny how a kid you barely know can turn your whole world . . . " Jake sat on the bunk, lost in thought.

Alvara sat on her windowsill, and seemed a bit more at ease. "You seem to care a lot about that girl. She probably misses you too. I bet you're like her guardian angel."

An image and a sound and a smell assaulted him at once; the sound of her voice over the edge, the smell of wet dirt leisurely, lazily giving way, and the blinding bright of a raging sunset, his fear and helplessness not making it set even a millisecond earlier.

The ferocity of the memory destroyed the simple serenity of the moment, and he broke out in a cold sweat. It took him a moment to remember what she had said. "Thanks, she's a sweetheart."

He took a breath to steady himself, and soon he relaxed again. He wanted to tell her about his experience with the Moon Goddess, but he figured it could wait; she was sure the wings were from God, and he was having a hard enough time believing in the mysterious woman himself.

"So I only found out yesterday that there were others like me. You've noticed certain rules that I think we have in common; some nights, when there's no moon, you don't get wings; most people don't have what it takes to see your wings; your wings are the size and shape that you wish and hope them to be." At a hesitant nod from her, he continued. "So I've just learned, with the help of Laerik here, that the birds know a bit more about this than we do."

"Wait, she can talk?" Alvara said, skeptical.

19

"Sheesh, are all humans this slow? Read my beak: Yes, I can talk. I spoke to you earlier when you almost punched my wing! I am a noble raven and I've trained for this mission. And almost all birds know where you live, Alvara; you fly almost every night. Did you think we wouldn't notice? And there's a bit of a situation. Jake, explain so we can get to the good stuff, please. And use small words," she added, causing Alvara's expression to darken.

Before Alvara could respond, Laerik flapped across the room, cackling with glee when she uncovered Alvara's beanie baby collection. She reduced each beanie baby to white stuffing and shreds of cloth as she fashioned herself a cozy nest on Alvara's desk. Beans dropped from the wreckage to scatter on the carpet. Alvara let out a soft cry as Laerik grasped a raggedy dolphin; the bird paused for a moment and set the dolphin to one side, a small peace offering.

"No problem, help yourself," Alvara muttered. She took a deep breath and looked at Jake expectantly.

"All right Alvara, so here is what we've learned. About one human in every generation is born with this ability to grow wings at night; this gift comes from the moon, which is why it begins at sunset and leaves by dawn. Birds have always been able to sense people like us somehow, and they try to keep tabs on us all over the world, though Laerik hasn't told me why yet." Jake tried his best to explain, though it sounded crazy to his ears as well.

"Wait a second, you say your gift comes from the moon?" she asked. Jake nodded. "That doesn't make sense; mine is a gift from God." Jake wasn't sure what to say in reply, and she continued before he could speak.

"Look, you can think what you like. I know what I've felt. God gave me these wings to help others, and that's what I plan to do." She finished with calm assurance, and he knew it wasn't worth the debate.

"It makes as much sense as anything else I've heard," Jake replied with a shrug. "Honestly, I've never been much of a believer. Laerik seems to think our wings come from a moon goddess, and I might have seen a beautiful woman instead of the moon in the sky the other night . . . " He shrugged, at a loss. "But I can't say there's much I fully understand about our wings or where they come from." She seemed mollified, and he tried to remember where he had stopped in his explanation.

"So the birds are well informed, see, and more attune to the shifting of the natural world than humans have been for a long time. And they've noticed this situation; certain locations feel wrong and unnatural, kind of sweaty and uncomfortable, like preening and preening but the feathers never quite smooth into place . . . that was the closest description I could get from Laerik." Laerik nodded, unsmiling.

"And so when a messenger came to her flock and asked for volunteers to find one of us in the vicinity—"

"I volunteered, of course. No one can track like I can, and look, proof!" she exclaimed, pointing at Jake and Alvara with each wing.

"So Laerik found me . . . well I mean us, you know, she wants both of us, you can come along, um, when we sort of go to find out what was going on. It seemed reasonable to me; what do you think?" After one of the longest speeches in this decade, Jake shut up to give her time to think it over.

He knew it hadn't worked as she stood to walk toward the bedroom door, her head in her hands. "This is just too weird. I can't think about this right now. I have school tomorrow! Today!" she clarified, glancing at the clock on her bedside table. She looked back at Jake from where she stood by the door. "I've been up all night, I'm too tired to think about all this. I can't . . . You should go."

"Of course," Jake agreed after a moment, trying to hide the disappointment in his tone. "I'm sorry to have bothered you. Look, how about I give you the address of my shop, and you can come visit me there if you like." Jake patted his pockets until he came up with a rumpled business card. "Here. Hope to see you soon."

She took the card as he opened her bedroom door. He looked back once, and saw her staring at the card, her face unreadable, before he made his careful way out of the house.

"We should be heading home to talk to my aunt, it's getting late," Alvara said as she moved to grab her backpack. Max remained sitting on his rock, staring towards the city. Ignoring her. "Please, Max! I really need a favor this time."

He finally looked at her, and his normally pleasant features were tight with anger. "Oh, so this is different from those ten thousand other times I've heard those words, usually alongside ideas about how I should lie to your aunt or my parents about needing to gather bugs at night for a school project . . . or map star charts with you until the wee hours of the morning! We never do anything like that, Alvara. I mean, it would be cool if we did, it would be fun, but these are just cover stories for you and your 'alone time' wandering around the city at night."

Alvara felt herself getting angry in response. She barely remembered how a full night's sleep felt, her aunt wouldn't leave her alone, she was struggling in her classes, and now Max wanted a piece of her too? Before she could retort, Max continued in a calmer voice. "Come on, Al. We've been best friends for years. You know I respect your privacy and all, but you should also know that you can trust me. I mean, I tell you everything about my life, and, well . . . I'm here if you ever want to talk, I guess."

A gentle breeze wafted across her brow, and her anger dissipated. Max didn't deserve her biting his head off just because she was cranky. And maybe he had a point.

She and Max had been inseparable since they were both in first grade, when a bee had landed on her arm and he had held her hand and told her not to move until it buzzed away. He knew about her father, her faith, nearly everything in her life that mattered. And she had repaid his trust with obvious untruths, and they both knew it. For the first time, Alvara felt ashamed of herself for hiding this part of her life from him. He had never given her reason to fear, to doubt. He wouldn't turn away, no matter how weird it might be at first. And, in a tiny, selfish corner of her mind, Alvara really didn't want to go it alone anymore.

"Ay," she conceded, and met his gaze. "Okay Max, you win." She sighed and lifted a few strands of hair past her ear with the tips of her fingers. "A fair warning that you may be getting more than you've bargained for with that little speech. It will just be another half hour or so until the sun sets. You may have noticed you never see me after sunset; we just talk on the phone."

"Uh, yeah, but I thought that was just some strange rule of your Aunt's." Max looked at her with an odd expression.

"I, well . . . something happens to me after sunset. I've always prayed to God to be better able to help people with their problems, and to have a physical reminder of my faith. And He actually answered my prayer! A real, physical answer, and I want to show you. I know you can't really promise not to freak out, but . . . promise not to freak out?" She grimaced and waited.

"Hmm. So you're definitely a werewolf. Am I in danger?" He looked left and right like he was searching for an escape, but Alvara couldn't laugh. "Seriously Alvara, I'm not really sure what you're talking about. But I am something of a scientist," he said, sitting up straighter, "so I'll promise to try to understand. Is that enough?"

"Yeah, that should do it. All right, about 25 minutes to go."

So began twenty-five of the more awkward minutes of her life. More than once, Alvara was close to explaining what was about to happen. But she kept coming back to the fact that Max might not be able to see her wings. She still didn't know why some people could and some couldn't. And if he couldn't see them, he might think she was crazy, and she wasn't sure she could deal with seeing that look in his eyes.

At first, Max looked like he wanted to ask her more questions, but he didn't. Then his brow furrowed, and he was lost in thought. Alvara surreptitiously watched him, out of the corner of her eye. His face had lost much of the roundness she remembered. He had started wearing his hair shorter. Each glance was like a Polaroid, burned into her retinas and slowly coming to mean something more. She found herself blushing, and scolded herself, forcing herself to turn away. Alvara stared at the distant streets and buildings of her city, which seemed to change shape as the setting sun gave them strange shadows.

As the sun disappeared, leaving the hilltop in a bright twilight, Alvara prayed soundlessly. She felt her wings spring forth under her shirt, and then unfortunately rip through it. She managed to hold her shirt in place as Max glanced up at the sound.

Alvara couldn't breathe and her heart thundered in her chest as Max stared at her, the seconds passing in silence. He tilted his head and squinted, looking past the end of her shoulder, where she hoped he could see her wings. His eyes widened suddenly, and she felt a smile.

22

"You are so beautiful," he said. He was staring into her eyes, not at her wings.

Alvara felt herself blush. "Um . . . thanks, Max. So I guess you can see them? You're not freaking out."

He blinked. "Yeah! Yes, I could. Can. You have wings. Well, I mean it took me a minute, but then they just sort of shimmered into place. I guess they were there all along, but, you know, it took me a while to see them there. I thought it was the sunset. Silly, tough to confuse the two now, but well. Surprise was my first thought, and then . . . yes. You have wings."

Alvara laughed. He was processing, out loud, which was a good sign. "Yup, these are them." She flexed them, keeping ahold of her shirt. "They come every night that there's a moon since I was young. I've had all kinds of crazy adventures with them, stuff you wouldn't believe, Max! You remember that one time for Halloween when I decided to go trick-or-treating just that once; you convinced me, remember? I focused really hard when the sun was setting and instead of being big and useful, my wings came in small and scrawny, and with that white dress I could pull it off as an angel costume. It was such freedom, just walking around in the open like that. That night almost everyone could see them," she said, remembering how wonderful it had felt to experience the night without the fear of discovery.

"But most nights, sometimes with you covering for me and sometimes not, I was going flying, and these past few weeks I've gone to the Children's Hospital down on 23rd Street. And the kids, their faces just make all the sneaking around so, so worth it." She remembered her night last week with Jonathan, and felt her eyes fill with tears. He had been so brave, and he might not live to see the summer.

"Hey, it's okay, don't cry. I can see how much this means to you–" Max began.

Alvara pulled away, blinking rapidly. "I am not crying. Where'd you get that dumb idea?" She turned her back on him and sat down on her rock, her wings wrapping around herself until she could get her emotions under control. It was harder than she thought, even after showing Max her wings, to let him in. There was so much that wasn't fair about the world. And she couldn't put off thinking about those midnight visitors forever. She had brought Max into this, and he was coping somehow. *God, I don't deserve him. But thank you,* she thought.

"Max," she said, and he turned to look at her, his eyes serious. "I'm sorry. I didn't mean that. A lot has been on my plate these past few days. When I got back to my house last week, there was a guy in my room, and he had wings too. It scared me, at first."

"As well it should! What was he doing in your room?" Max sputtered.

"I thought he was going to turn me in or something. It was strange seeing wings on someone else." She was silent for a moment, staring into the distance. "He told me a lot about what he knew of what we could do." She looked over at Max.

"Hey," Max said. "When I said I was in, I meant it. I'm still super pumped that you're not a werewolf. Wings are way cooler and less likely to take a violent turn." Alvara snorted with laughter. "So go ahead, what did the winged stalker have to say?"

"Well, there was also a talking bird, a raven I think. No one explained why." And she had been too tired to ask.

"Of course there's a talking bird, why wouldn't there be?" Max mumbled. "Okay, leaving that aside. What did the man and/or bird talk about?"

"The man, whose name is Jake, seems to think this gift comes from some moon goddess; he couldn't explain much better than that, though he seemed to think that there was both the physical moon and a Goddess of the Moon, and that she was responsible for giving us wings." Alvara shrugged. "I don't think he's right, but if that's his faith, then who am I to question? And the Lord works in mysterious ways; if He wants to just give me this gift when the moon is in the sky, who am I to argue with Him?" she asked.

Max shrugged. "Well, this goddess person could exist too, you know; God doesn't have to be the only one in the sky. Though, it could still be him, like you said, mysterious ways and all that," he added. "So what's the point of the gift, according to Jake?"

"I don't know." She bit her lip. "I kind of told both him and the bird to leave. It was maybe four in the morning and I needed to sleep."

"Yeah, good for you," Max said. "If he really wanted to talk, he could have picked less questionable circumstances. Do you want to talk to him again?" he asked.

"I think so. No, definitely. He gave me his card, and I was thinking about going to see him at his shop tomorrow."

"No you were not," Max countered. "You were thinking about asking me to come with you."

"Max, you don't need to—" she began.

"I accept!" he struck a gallant pose, and she broke into a smile as well. Though the sky was darkening in earnest now, she could still see his grin in the faded light.

"Glad to have you on my team, Maxy," she said. She gave him a hug, and it was warm and solid and real. Despite Max's arms pinning her wings, Alvara felt that she might lift off the ground.

Chapter 4

The sun was high as Alvara and Max made their way to Venice Beach on the public bus. The California weather had flirted with the idea of summer for weeks now, with days of foggy gloom following others of hazy warmth. Alvara wished that the weather would just get on with it. Summer was almost upon them.

It was a day like today that guaranteed it. The sky was empty of clouds but full of promise, and they weren't the only ones who had turned out to enjoy the gathering heat. Alvara and Max disembarked near the beach, and Alvara had to shade her eyes to shield them against the brightness of the sun reflected off the sand. Heavy beach bags weighted them down as they walked. They intended to spend a whole day at the beach, but the crowds were a bit daunting.

"I think it's this way," Alvara said after a moment, and they shuffled with the crowd along the path by the beach. They had both been to this part of the beach before, so the variety of people and sights didn't faze them.

Families corralled their young kids on tricycles. Teenagers zoomed past on roller blades, while body-builders struck poses on the scattered patches of grass along the path. Women in long flowing sundresses exclaimed at the displays as they walked in their wide-brimmed hats and designer sunglasses. There was even a group of men gathered in a drum circle, surrounding two or three dancers moving to the rhythm, their hands making shapes in the air.

But mostly there were shops. On both sides of the road, garish displays of discount sunglasses or tie-dyed T-shirts or original works of art drew the eye, reducing the pace of the crowd to a slow crawl.

"Baaaaah," Max bleated, darting his eyes around like a hapless sheep in a herd. Alvara rewarded him with a chuckle and a punch on the shoulder.

She noticed the store peeking out of an alley that led off the beach. A Siren Symphony was a small shop sandwiched between a pipe and hookah store on the right and yet another sunglasses kiosk across the alley to the left. The name of the shop was in green, with an elegant drawing of a mermaid curving around the lettering. She and Max stepped inside together.

Alvara had to wait a moment for her eyes to adjust. She could hear the sound of an air conditioner, and sighed in relief at the temperature change. Her eyes wandered the shelves and exhibits, and she saw beauty everywhere. There were dragon figures woven out of paper, and unicorns made of glass, and an impressive array of bird figurines dangling from the ceiling. A fleet of small fountains gurgled in the corner. A raven, maybe the same one that had showed up at her room, looked up from the handmade roost near the front counter and squawked, flapping its wings once. So, not the same one, as Alvara was pretty sure the one in her room could talk. The raven went back to preening. The whole store had a relaxing and magical vibe, and Alvara decided she liked it.

"Hello?" she called out.

"Just a second!" a man's voice yelled from the back room. Jake emerged soon after with a stack of boxes that he rested on the counter. "Alvara, so good to see you!" His grin was infectious, and she couldn't help a small smile.

"Hi, Jake. This is my friend Max." They nodded at each other. "How . . . have you been?" she finished. She was afraid it would be awkward, considering their first meeting.

"Oh, pretty well," Jake answered, gesturing to the store. "Fantasy films have been big this year, which even gets teens and adults excited about the kind of stuff I sell here. It's always popular with children, so business is pretty good." Jake scratched his head and broke into a smile. "Actually, a kid is what started me on my path to visiting you. This little girl wanted a raven figurine and didn't have any money, so naturally I let her have it. Then she's back in my store telling me these wild tales of how her raven came to life and spoke with her. I admit I entertained the notion," Jake said, half smiling. "Who was I to question?"

At this similarity to her own thoughts, Alvara found herself warming up to Jake. It was hard not to; the man never stopped smiling. Alvara checked to make sure the store was empty. "Jake, you seem like a nice guy. But you do understand how weird this all seems, right?" she gestured to the room and meant the situation. "I snuck home and saw a strange winged man in my room, and all of a sudden this secret I've held in for my whole life was just out in the open. Why didn't you call me or come to the door?"

"I know," Jake admitted. "But if I came up to you on the street and knew about your wings but had none of my own, wouldn't that be even more frightening?" Alvara hesitated, but nodded once. "I didn't consider how odd it would be to meet me like that, and apologize again."

"Hey, I'm new to all this growing-wings stuff," Max said, "but how did you find out where Alvara lives?"

"I was just getting to that part of the story," Jake replied. "Max, say hello to Laerik. She told me what she knew, and led me to Alvara's house." He gestured to the raven by the counter, and Alvara tried to see similarities to the raven the other night. But her room had been pretty dark, so she gave up.

"Right, the talking bird," Max said. "Um, hello, Laerik. How are you?" Max shook his head in disbelief.

The bird in the corner inclined its head before returning to preening. "She can't talk with us during the day," Jake explained. "It's related to our gift. It's the only possible explanation for her keeping her beak shut for so long," he jested. Laerik squawked and turned her back to them in a huff.

Jake massaged his temple. "Like I said, I didn't want to scare you, Alvara. I just couldn't wait to meet you, and see your wings, instead of battling our joint skepticism and attempting to believe all this in daytime." He spread his hands. "It's a lot to swallow."

"Understatement much?" Max muttered.

"Tell you what," Jake said, pointing at them both. He reached under the counter and pulled three ice-cold root beers out of a mini-fridge. "Let's go for a walk."

Alvara accepted the suggestion and the root beer with a polite nod. Jake offered Laerik a shoulder, which she took with a dignified caw, and the group walked outside. Jake flipped a sign over that told potential customers he would be back soon, and the two kids, man, and bird strolled along the beach.

A tanned guy was making full use of speakers on his bike, blasting music at unwilling pedestrians and generally adding to the chaos of the path. Alvara winced and tried to enjoy the sunshine.

"Yo, Alvara!" she heard, and turned to look behind her. A pretty redhead with a sunburn rollerbladed up to the group and executed a perfect ice hockey stop. Alvara couldn't quite place how she knew her, though she looked familiar.

"Hey," Alvara said. "Sorry, I'm blanking on your name." The girl mimed crying before waving her hand.

"Nah, it's cool," she drawled. "I'm Tess, you know. And where are your wings, anyhow?"

Alvara had a moment of pure terror before she realized how she knew Tess. "Tess, from the hospital!" she exclaimed. The last time Alvara had seen her, Tess had been preparing for some heavy-duty knee surgery. "I'd appreciate if you keep that on the DL, Tess. I only have them at night."

"Omigod, I'm so sorry!" She exclaimed, putting her hands over her mouth and looking from Jake to Max and back. "Holy crap, I mean, of course they're secret, duh. But hey, I just wanted to say thanks again for your visit. Seriously cool!" She wrapped Alvara into a hug.

"You're welcome," Alvara replied, glowing with warmth. "And how's the knee?"

"Dude, it's insane!" Tess effused. "The surgery went perfectly, and look, not even a real scar!" She gestured down to her left knee, and Alvara could barely make out a few thin crisscrossing lines. "Physical therapy was a cinch! I knew my parents were full of it when they yammered on and on about how long it would take. I'm back to playing soccer already," she grinned.

"That's so great, Tess," Alvara beamed. "It's so good to hear from you."

"Yeah, glad I saw ya," Tess winked. "Laters!" She rollerbladed down the street and was lost around a curve of the path.

"Well that was cool," Max proclaimed. "You made a difference, Al!" Alvara blushed and continued walking, sending God a thank you for the encounter. They weaved through the crowd.

"So you hinted at a trip," Alvara prompted Jake, changing the subject.

"Yeah. Laerik said the birds know of a woman with wings in China. Shanghai, specifically. So we might want to go and meet her, if we can find her. And of course, there are those places that felt wrong that she talked about . . ." Jake trailed off, glancing at Alvara out of the corner of his eye.

She snorted. "Seriously Jake? That's your pitch? You tell the heroine of the story that she must go on a quest to save the world?" She shook her head. "And then the heroine whines, 'why me?' or 'I don't believe in magic.'" Alvara shrugged a shoulder in an almost unconscious gesture of adjusting a wing. "I guess we can skip that part at least. I'm kind of primed to accept a bunch of strange circumstances, including talking birds. No offense, Laerik."

The raven on Jake's shoulder seemed pleased, and hopped onto Alvara's shoulder to peck her on the cheek before taking flight. "Ouch," Alvara winced, rubbing her cheek. "What was that for?"

Jake chuckled. "I think it was just for getting her name right. I have the hardest time making it sound harsh like that." They strolled, sipping their root beers. A break dancer was drawing a crowd to their left, and they stopped to watch. He convinced members of the audience to crouch down in a long line, and backed up for the dramatic leap he would make over all of them. Alvara's chest constricted with the rest of the audience as he leapt, landing safely on the other side. Gravity, she thought, made for high entertainment when you didn't have wings.

"I have started thinking about it, though," Alvara added. "I still have a few more weeks of school before summer vacation, and I don't want to go yet; traveling to China is a big deal. It would be neat to meet another person with wings, but . . . I don't know. There's no rush, right?" She shrugged. "It's a lot of money, and wouldn't I need a passport and visa and stuff?"

"Yeah, I looked into that," Jake said. "I have a little saved up; I don't want to pressure you or anything, but if you decide to go I could cover you for the ticket, passport, and visa. Though we should start your passport application soon if you want it by the summer. Sheesh," Jake said, seeing Alvara's chagrin. "I keep forgetting we just met. I don't want to seem forward, but it really is a pleasure to meet you, Alvara."

"It was lucky you found me, Jake, though I would have appreciated a less clueless way of introducing yourself." She smirked.

He returned her smile. "I'll work on that."

"One thing I was wondering about," Max began, as she watched Laerik settle onto a nearby tree, "was what you would tell your aunt. If you decide to go, I mean."

"Fair point," Alvara remarked, "but I have an idea on how to deal with that when the time comes; remember that favor I was begging of you yesterday, Max? I was thinking we'd go on a 'camping trip'." She made quotation marks in the air. "That way, if I took a week-long vacation, you could just pretend to be gone too and my aunt won't have to worry. This would mean a lot to me," she finished.

"As if I could say no," Max conceded, though he didn't seem thrilled.

"Thanks, Maxy," Alvara replied. "If you want, we could go on a real camping trip later this summer!" She flashed him a thumbs up. "I hope we can talk soon, Jake? I sent you my email." Everyone stopped walking to part ways.

"Well then I guess there's just one thing you've missed," Jake said, "and I'm surprised it got past a smart girl like you."

"Yeah," Alvara asked. "And what's that?"

"Oh nothing much," Jake replied, with a twinkle in his eye, "just that you assume you're the hero in this fairy tale." Alvara punched him on the shoulder for his trouble, but he didn't seem to mind one bit.

After they said goodbye to Jake, Alvara and Max slipped past a drum circle and nearly got hit by a gang of skateboarders before arriving at a stretch of more upscale shops. The noise fell, and Alvara could finally hear the noise of the surf, waves just visible across the wide stretch of sand. She noticed that Max wasn't saying much.

"Hey Max, what's up? You seem quiet."

He sighed. "Just puzzling."

"Care to share?" she asked.

Max finally met her eyes. "I'm just trying to figure out a way to come with you, and coming up with nothing."

"Max, I don't even know if I'm going to go," she began.

"Look, Al, you have to. These wings are a part of who you are, right to the core. If there's some chance for you to find the last person who shares them, and discover what they really mean, you should take it."

Alvara dodged around a man with dreadlocks on rainbow rollerblades, and they walked in silence for a while. "I want to go," she murmured. "I want to go meet that Chinese woman, and share my gift with her. But I've never been anywhere other than here, you know? My aunt would never let me just go. And then there's Jake; I just met him. Literally, two days ago we met, and I'm thinking of flying halfway around the world with him. No pun intended," and Max looked confused. "We would go by airplane," she clarified.

He laughed and they left the path to find a good spot on the sand. They unrolled their towels and sat in companionable silence for a bit. She saw that he was smiling with his I-need-to-ponder face, so she let him think. It was nice to just relax, letting her gaze roam over the glistening surf and toward the horizon. Her toes dipped into the warm sand, and she watched the facets shine as they tumbled past each other. Alvara didn't spend a lot of time just enjoying the sunshine, and decided it was an experience she needed more often.

"It seems to me that you just need to decide whether or not to trust your instincts or common sense," said Max.

"What do you mean?" she asked.

"Well, common sense says no way in hell should you go traipsing around the world with an older man who you just met; he could do all sorts of unspeakable things to you." She didn't even punch him this time, just scoffed, but he looked serious.

"Come on; get to the part where I start listening to what you're saying."

"And then there are your instincts. You trust him, don't you?"

She thought about it for a minute. "It's weird, but I kind of do. Today it didn't feel like I was just getting to know him, it was more like catching up with an old friend. I don't know Jake that well yet, but if I know anything, I know he would never hurt me."

"That's really cool, Al," Max said. There was a new glint in his eyes, indiscernible and strong.

"Well, talk more with Jake about this China thing. And let me know how it goes," he continued. She thought he would bring up coming to China with them again, but he didn't. He just looked at her. "I don't know what I'd do if something were to happen to you."

"You'd find someone else to bother," she said lightly, unable to meet his eyes. "Honestly, you sound like an old man. I'll be fine."

Chapter 5

Three weeks later, Jake climbed the steps to Alvara's front porch. It was a gorgeous afternoon, and the sky was light blue and cloudless in the carefree manner of Southern California. But Jake couldn't dismiss his unease, both with what they'd managed to learn about their wings, and what they still didn't know. Every time he considered the webs of causality and where they might originate, his thoughts felt like those pennies you race around the flat, plastic vortexes in museums; orbiting round and round, increasing in pitch as they chase each other into the whirring black hole of the center. He knew he would have to let the pennies fall eventually, but he was in no hurry to examine that hole in himself. He knocked on the door and waited.

A Latina woman answered the door. She was middle-aged with short dark hair tending to grey, and a mixed expression somewhere between harried and tired. "Hello," Alvara's aunt said. "You must be Jake. Alvara has told me so much about you."

"Yep, that's me," he replied, "Pleased to meet you, Alicia."

"Come in, Jake. Would you like a drink?" Her Spanish accent was thick, but after a second he could parse the words. Jake nodded, and she left to fetch the glasses.

Jake walked across the tile floor to settle himself on the stiff, beige couch. The protective plastic barrier crinkled as he shifted his weight. A large, gilt-edged mirror topped the fireplace, but the gilt was more than half gone. A fake palm tree leaned toward him from one corner of the room. Another corner sprouted a small figurine of the Virgin Mary, surrounded by lit candles.

Alicia returned with two glasses of water and joined Jake on the couch. Jake took a few sips of water, and then ran his fingers over the glass, wiping away the condensation. He had a hard time relating to adults. She spoke first and relieved his tension.

"I would like to hear how you and my niece met. Can you tell me this?" Her tone was polite, and less confrontational than her words. Jake, relieved that Alvara hadn't shared the truth with her aunt, launched into the tale they had agreed upon.

"Sure. A few weeks ago, Alvara and Max were wandering around Venice when they stumbled into my shop. I run a little shop on the strand, sells fantasy knick-knacks. Small objects," he explained, when he saw her frown at the colloquial word. "Anyway, we got to talking a bit. Seems they were interested in going hiking together, but had never done that sort of thing before. I told them I was planning a camping trip, set for a few weeks hence, and offered to help them get settled with equipment and such. You must have seen her running around with stuff," he said. Alvara's aunt nodded.

"Truth be told, it's been a heck of a fun time helping them plan, so we figured we may as well camp in the same campground; my kids and I could give them a ride and be there and all, but they'd have the freedom to have their own trip." Cover story complete, Jake stopped for a sip of water. It had just enough truth to it to be plausible, and Jake hoped her aunt wouldn't give him a hard time. She surprised him by doing the opposite.

"That's so nice of you, Jake. Alvara's been talking of this camping for many days, and she may really be loving such a fun vacation with fresh air. But I don't want her to make trouble for you . . ."

"Oh, no. Not at all. We get along well, actually. She's a sweet girl."

Her aunt seemed to chew on his words, and then burst into a disconcerting smile. She had lipstick on one of her front teeth.

"She is very sweet," her aunt gushed. "Also so smart. Did you know she leads her own Bible Study groups on Sundays?" She shifted her weight on the couch, staring at Jake to see how he took the information.

"Ah, well, that's great," Jake agreed.

"It seems to me that you are being friends, Jake," she continued, sipping her water.

"You could say that," Jake answered, shrugging. "Like I said, we've had fun planning this trip."

"You said you have your own kids?" Alvara's aunt exclaimed. Jake was having trouble keeping track of her sudden shifts in conversation.

"Yes," Jake replied, wishing he could have glossed over that white lie. "Two, a girl and a boy. The boy, Michael, is eight, and the girl, Cathy, is 14."

"Two children, it must be so difficult, no?" she winced.

"Difficult?" Jake asked, confused. "I wouldn't say that. My children are great." This cover story had transitioned from uncomfortable to painful.

"Oh, of course they are, of course," Alvara's aunt cooed. "You seem to be a man who knows what *is* really being a parent; I can see this. I have just found it a difficult . . . what word . . . transition. I lived alone for many years, and then when Alvara's father died," her aunt shook her head as if to imply deep sadness. "She did not speak of this to you?"

"No, we've mostly talked of the trip. I wouldn't expect someone to bring that up very often." Jake had shared the secret of his wings with Alvara, but family tragedies were a horse of a different color. He should know.

Alvara's aunt stared intensely at Jake, and spoke with clear diction to make herself understood. "Well, it was very hard, you see. She lost her mother when she was born, and what to do? Her father and I, we had our differences, but she was family, of course, and if I did nothing, she would have been in that foster home forever. But the problem is, it is hard for me, keeping up with a teenage girl. I just want her to be happy and make her way in the world, you know?" she asked, sipping her water.

"Of course," Jake answered, unsure of where she was going.

"And you, you have two children already. Alvara, she loves children," her aunt said nonchalantly, and Jake suddenly realized what she was implying.

"Now, wait a moment—" he began.

"Oh, please do not say what you are still thinking, Jake," her aunt said, anxiety written on her features. "I only want what is best for Alvara, and this situation is very hard. Please be still thinking. Jake, we were talking of the camping trip, yes?"

"Never mind that—"

"More water?" she pounced. Jake shook his head.

"Look, Alvara is a swell girl." He didn't know how to reply to her bald-faced proposal, so decided to ignore it. "My family and I will do our best to watch out for the two of them. Now, is Alvara home? I wanted to talk with her about some more specifics of what she should bring for camping with Max. I figured we could walk up to the bluffs and talk."

"I'll get her." Alicia met Jake's eyes and offered up a small smile before leaving to search for her niece. Jake tried to dismiss her suggestion. As far as her aunt knew, he had just met Alvara a few weeks ago, and she was suggesting that he somehow adopt her? She couldn't know that his intentions were good. Alicia didn't seem like the most attentive parental figure, but he never expected that she would be so ready to hand off her niece to a stranger. Jake wondered what it was like for Alvara to live here, more as a burden than as a member of a family. The sound of mournful voices in Spanish issued from the kitchen, where Alicia was presumably occupying herself with Latin music.

While waiting for Alvara, Jake rehearsed the checklist for their trip in his mind. Passports and visas, check; hooray for expedited processing. Plane tickets to China, check; one week to go. Sanity of the trip: to be determined.

Jake's eyes caught a row of pictures on an ornate bookshelf to the side of his couch. Alvara and her friend Max, he recognized, though their much younger faces were difficult to see behind the enormous gum bubbles they were blowing in the picture. A second picture showed Alvara and Alicia standing in front of the Hollywood sign. Alvara was smiling, but Alicia had a neutral expression. They weren't touching.

A third and fourth picture held Alvara and what must have been her father. In the first, the man held a dangling, screaming Alvara upside down while facing the camera and grinning from ear to ear. In the other, he leaned over her as she stirred a pot on the stove. They were both wearing Burger King crowns. Jake smiled as he looked at her father, wondering what it might have been like to be in a picture like that.

"Hey Jake!" Alvara said as she wandered in. "What's up? I thought we were gonna talk about the trip later tonight?"

"Yes, we still can. I had a favor to ask now, but we can still finish last minute plans on the computer later."

"Um, let's head out to the backyard. I have a swing set," she said with false enthusiasm. She pointed towards the source of the music and mouthed, "My aunt is listening." This made Jake feel uncomfortable all over again.

They headed across the patchy yard, and each picked a swing. It had been most of his life since Jake had sat on one, and it was comforting. Jake wondered whether or not to bring up what her aunt had said.

While he was still considering, Alvara spoke. "By the way, thanks again for offering to pay for this trip. There's no way I'd be able to afford the flight, much less the hotel and everything else."

"Don't worry about it. I've been saving for a long time, like I said. I'm glad it's going to a charitable cause," Jake replied with a small smile.

Changing the subject, he asked, "So, how is life here, with your aunt?"

"It's all right, I guess," she answered, kicking the dirt. "So you must have heard from her about my parents? She can never let a conversation pass without using that story to turn my life into some tragic telenovela." Alvara rolled her eyes. Jake just nodded, and she continued with a sigh. "It was really good of her to take me in. And she lets me have a lot of freedom, which I take full advantage of," Alvara said, though it sounded more like a rote recitation than something she actually believed. Jake decided not to bring up Alicia's other comments.

"That sounds pretty good," he said instead.

She half-smiled but didn't meet his eyes, and kicked at the dirt below her swing. "So, what's the favor? I figured it would be difficult to convey in code, with my aunt snooping and all."

"Thanks, it would have been. I have to confess that I haven't flown in a few decades or so."

"What? Decades? Why not? And didn't you fly into my room a few nights ago?"

"I climbed up from the ground level," Jake smiled sheepishly. "It was a bad idea from the start. I guess the answer to that first question is a bit complicated. But I think I'd like to try it again, get back into practice, and was hoping you could help. Tonight, maybe? I wouldn't want to go all the way to China just to embarrass that poor woman by flying straight into a power line and ending up barbequed. Would you mind coming out with me and reminding me of the ropes?" Jake kept his request lighthearted and tried to ignore the twist of guilt that he would fly again soon.

She brightened. "Oh, sure! I've never flown with anyone else. Well, you know why. Tonight will be great; my aunt will be working late, so she'll be sound asleep pretty early. Wait outside my window about half-past midnight?"

"If I miss the appointment, will your carriage turn back into a pumpkin?" Jake asked.

She rolled her eyes. "You bet, so don't be late."

You are getting sleeeeeeepy. Alvara could hear her aunt having what sounded like a spring cleaning session in the other room; she wasn't responding well to Alvara's telepathic hypnosis. It was 12:28 p.m., and Alvara had somewhere to be. She had called Max earlier, and had begun to reveal the parts of her life she had kept secret for so long. It was still a bit surreal that he supported her completely, and had accepted her strange ability as if he had always known about it. In such a short time, their friendship had reached new levels of trust, as they laughed together for hours about mortifying moments of near discovery that she had barely escaped and future plans for midnight missions.

It had taken some convincing, but Alvara thought he was finally all right with not coming with them to China. He kept telling her to be careful, as if she had actually been about to flap her wings across the Pacific Ocean herself. It was both sweet and aggravating, him wanting to protect her, but she was glad that someone staying behind knew what they planned. And her aunt was *still* cleaning, how long could it possibly take?

After what seemed like about an hour, her aunt quieted and turned off the light. Nine minutes had passed.

Alvara's wings got in the way of everything, as they did around this time of night, and she was anxious to meet Jake. She peered over the window edge, and saw him sitting against the house wrapped in a lumpy cloak and looking like a bum. She bent down to pray, thanking God for the gift of her wings, and they grew. Wearing her white outfit, she leaped out and glided down to where he was sitting, touching down lightly on the damp grass.

"Hey, Jake. Ready for some flying?" He sat up, and she could see that his shirt had holes in the back, and that instead of a cloak, his massive golden eagle wings had provided warmth. He flexed them a bit as if he had sat there for a while, and lurched to his feet.

"Ready as ever, I guess. I'm glad our wings are about the same size tonight; it'll be easier for me to learn when I'm watching you do it." *No pressure*, she thought, and tried to explain flying as she explained it to herself.

"So in some sense it's you versus the wind, but if you're fighting it, you'll have a hard time getting anywhere. It's more like swimming, and how the ocean will keep you afloat as long as you work a bit not to drown. Does that make any sense at all?" It was more difficult to explain than she had expected.

"As I've said, a bit out of practice. It could be ringing some bells, but I think maybe learning by doing will be the best."

Alvara placed her feet nearly parallel to the walls of her house and explained. "Okay, so from experience I know that the wind hits my house and comes off at this angle, and so the best way to take off when you're not coming from the window is like this," and she pointed her arm to demonstrate. "Follow me, and we'll meet on the roof, as long as you can land like a ninja."

Flashing a grin, she jumped into the air, and with two downbeats of her wings appeared to be on a collision course with the side of the house. Knowing it was a cool effect, she flared them just in time, soaring up the side and curving around to land neatly on the roof. She flapped her wings a few times to steady herself, and left them extended for balance as she walked to the edge to watch Jake. It was funny, she thought. His expression was almost guilty as he prepared to take flight.

Less nimbly, but with smooth motions, he took off and headed toward the house. With a graceful arc, he swooped to land where she had on the roof, not even requiring the extra few wing beats for balance.

"Not bad, for an old-timer," Alvara laughed.

"Okay, so it comes back pretty fast," Jake ceded, his face flushed with emotion. "Let's get flying, then, shall we?"

Alvara flashed a smile, and dove backwards off the top of her house, curving her wings to allow her to complete the spin and fly off into the night. Alvara glanced over her shoulder to see Jake opt for a gentle push off, and heard the beat of his wings as he caught up to her. She settled into a smooth breathing rhythm, and flew with her arms and legs slightly bent, allowing her to relax most of her body while her back and shoulders worked to keep her moving forward.

She loved this, absolutely loved this; in her deepest thoughts, she believed that this gift was worth it for its own sake, for the rush and the glittering magical moments that would always be hers. Her nightly hours of freedom allowed her time away from her aunt's financial problems and snide remarks, her satisfactory progress at school, and even her best friend Max. It wasn't anything she owed to anyone else, nothing she would ever have to repay.

Though she did try, in a sense. She gave of herself and her gift whenever she could, because she knew how it felt to believe that nothing would ever be right in the world again, and hoped that seeing a girl with wings might make people believe other things were possible, too. She quoted her favorite Bible verse to herself: Those who hope in the Lord will renew their strength. They will soar on wings as eagles; they will run and not grow weary, they will walk and not be faint." Isaiah 40:30-31. It never failed to inspire.

Lost in emotion more than in thought, she felt the city spreading beneath her, and her wings took her to the place where her nights always ended: the roof of the Children's Hospital. She stretched a bit after the exertion, running her fingers through some of her flight feathers to smooth them into place. Then she folded her wings and turned to search for Jake.

He was half a minute or so behind her, giving her room but keeping up well enough, and came in for a standard landing, flaring his wings to stall before touching down. He stretched as well, but with a bit of a grimace.

"You all right?" she asked.

"Yeah, I'll be fine. I hate to repeat myself, but it's been a while, and I was plenty younger the last time I flew. It'll just take a bit of time to get endurance back." He was smiling though.

"Jake?"

"Yeah?"

"Why was it you stopped flying in the first place? I don't mean to snoop, but I love this, and can't imagine wanting to stop."

Jake's smile fled. He finally admitted, "It's my experience in life that all good things have a dark side, yin and yang, inseparable. I used to think the magic of my wings could make anything possible. I was wrong. I didn't deserve to keep my wings, but the best I could do was not use them." Alvara wanted to know more about it, but knew they were just starting to be friends. She didn't want to mess it up.

"So," she changed the subject, "any idea where we are?"

He tried to smile a bit. "No idea, I was busy avoiding power lines and keeping one of my shoes from falling off and smacking some poor innocent bystander on the head. Care to enlighten me?"

"You said you liked children, right? Well this is one of my favorite places in the whole world, crammed to the brim with messed up, sick children who would just love to meet you." She smiled.

He frowned in worry. "But, you know that kids can almost always see our wings, right?"

Alvara laughed. *This was going to be such a great night.* "We're counting on it."

Chapter 6

"G'night, Jake. See you tomorrow." Alvara was exhausted, but the memory of Jake with three-year-olds dangling off his wings as they both attempted to keep the kids quiet made her smile for the thousandth time that night.

"All right, we can meet for lunch and talk more about packing for China. And sleep well." She groaned and waved, turning to shut the window behind her and almost colliding with a frantic Laerik.

"We have to talk! Jake, come up here!" Laerik's voice carried a note of panic, and Jake turned from his walk to his car. With a few powerful wing beats he headed for the window, and stalled to land on the edge. But he misjudged the ascent and twisted one foot, reaching to try to grab the upper half of the window as his wings beat to keep him there. Alvara grabbed his hand and helped him through the window. "Watch your wings, that frame is sharp," she warned.

"Thanks," Jake said, sitting on Alvara's desk chair and massaging his ankle. "Still a bit rough."

"We have a serious problem." Laerik chimed in, her eyes wide in obvious agitation. Alvara sat on the bed and furled her wings as best she could to keep them out of the way.

"What's the matter, Laerik?" Alvara asked. Jake turned on the desk lamp so they could see each other, but the directional spotlight gave Alvara's beanie baby collection the shadows of wild beasts rather than children's toys.

"I just heard from some birds near where you live, Jake. They saw some men and a woman searching your store and then your house." Alvara turned to look at Jake, and even with half his face in shadow it looked pale.

"There shouldn't be anything for them to find," Jake said. "They shouldn't have found any indication that I haven't led a normal life."

"An owl saw a man leave with a shoebox, Jake. When I met you, I saw what was in there."

Jake frowned. "I hid those under the floorboards."

"What did he find?" asked Alvara.

"I used to take a picture of each set of wings I grew," Jake explained, "because each night they were different." He addressed Laerik. "But that doesn't guarantee that they would even see the wings in the pictures; I never asked if anyone else could."

"Jake, I don't think you realize how bad this is," said Laerik, shuddering.

"What do you mean? Who were those people?" Jake asked.

"They left you a note." Laerik held out one leg, which clutched a small roll of paper. She shook out her leg as if it were stiff while Jake read the note aloud:

Jake Coughlin:

Our files indicate that you possess a singular ability that you have neglected to use for many years. It has come to our attention that you have recently resumed use. In regard to this change, and to the delicate balance of power currently at risk, please be informed that:

a) *You must discontinue use of your ability.*
b) *You must discontinue association with others of your ability.*
c) *You must register your ability in our proprietary database.*

You have one week to comply with provisions b) and c), though provision a) goes into effect immediately. Please be advised, that although we wish to take no direct action in this matter, if you refuse to comply with these provisions we will be forced to take measures against you, or if necessary against your young friend. The choice is up to you.

Regards,
Mr. Robert Noon
Legion of the Light

Please report your ability through email at this address: Robert.b.Noon@gmail.com

Alvara felt the beginnings of fear, but under it was annoyance. "Someone found out. And he's threatening both of us! Who does this guy think he is?"

"No idea. Wait, there's a post-it note," Jake continued, flipping over the sheet, and Alvara saw the scrawled script as Jake read:

There's nowhere you can go that we can't find you. Listen to Robert, and things will not have to get messy. -I

Alvara crossed the room and took the note from Jake, flipping it over and back, but the rest was blank. Just that email address and the chilling warning. Messy. "These people were at your house, Jake," she whispered.

"You guys need to get out of here!" Laerik shrieked, and Alvara jumped at the outburst. Laerik was having a hard time sitting still; her wings twitched back and forth and her dark eyes were wide.

"What haven't you told us?" asked Jake.

"The birds, the ones who told me about this," Laerik gasped between rapid breaths. "They described the woman they saw the same way other birds have described those places; as making their feathers itch! The owl I spoke to was nearly out of his mind with panic. I think this woman, and maybe others like her are at the heart of those places, which makes her very, very, very dangerous. This is the core of my mission, Jake! I have to keep you guys safe."

"I'm sorry about those birds, Laerik. This guy does sound serious," Jake admitted, re-reading the letter, "though not as serious as that extra note from this 'I'. Perhaps she is the woman the birds saw? But I think Laerik's right, Alvara, and we should treat them as if they were dangerous."

"What if we go to the police?" Alvara brightened. "People aren't allowed to break into places and send threatening letters."

"And tell them what?" Jake asked. "That a man is threatening us to stop using our wings or else? I wouldn't know how to spin it to even give them a hope of taking the case. I think we're on our own for this one." They sat for a moment, Alvara staring at the sprawl of a seashell collection she had been meaning to get rid of. As Alicia hadn't ever taken her to a real shell collecting beach, most of the shells were broken. But they were still hers.

"Jake, this woman could be at my house tomorrow. If I get a similar message, or worse, something happens to my aunt or Max, I won't be able to live with myself."

"You're right. I don't think we can risk meeting with these people, nor respond to their threats," Jake continued.

"Wait, why not? What if we just register in his database?" Alvara asked. The requests hadn't been too unreasonable.

"Don't you dare! They'll find you!" Laerik squeaked, flapping to land on the desk and burying her beak under one wing.

"Shh, it's all right," Jake said, stroking Laerik's feathers. He turned to Alvara. "You saw the letter, Alvara. We can't assume that would solve anything. Do you think that's really what he's after?"

"No," she said with a small voice. "And we just found each other. We can't let some lawyer make threats to force us into line." She took a deep breath as if to settle herself, but as a thought struck her, her eyebrows shot up in surprise. "Wait a minute. That's creepy! Didn't you just start flying tonight? How did he find out?"

Jake looked thoughtful, and then frowned. "I'm not sure, but he is very well informed. You're right, we should stick together."

He came and sat next to her on the bed. Laerik's claw tapped on the desk; she held the rest of her body still by force of will.

"Alvara, I'm worried," Jake said into the near silence. "This trip can't just be a pleasure trip to visit someone else who has wings. If it is, we shouldn't go at all. It's too much of a risk. But for me, it's always been more than that." He paused, but Alvara waited for him to continue.

"Have you ever had the feeling that something was somehow . . . off about the world? It's always seen as the age we live in, and I've attributed it to . . ." his face darkened, ". . . other things, but it's been there for years."

"Jake, I know what you mean," Alvara admitted, surprised to find her eyes full of tears. She blinked them away. "Sometimes it's like I can't be happy, or shouldn't be, or . . . " She balled her hands into fists so hard she could feel her nails cut her skin. She had never tried to explain it to herself like this. "Like you said, like some part of the world was teetering on the brink of falling down . . . I don't know. I've felt it. My faith has gotten me through." She tried to smile. "I thought everyone felt that way sometimes. What about it?" she asked.

"I think it has to do with us, and our wings. I feel like it's up to us to figure out what it is that's broken and fix it." Jake smiled as he shrugged and ran a hand through his hair. "It sounds crazy to say it aloud," he apologized. "But I feel like that woman in China may be the key; maybe she'll know more than we do. We have to find her to find out. Even with this man who doesn't want us to use our wings, and whoever the other person is. Maybe especially since we know he's out there. I've talked enough for the both of us," Jake concluded. "What do you think?"

"I know what you mean, Jake. Something does feel like it's slowly breaking. It scares me, that feeling. But you're right, we have to figure out what it means." Alvara let out a breath. "We have no choice but to go." Jake nodded, and glanced down to read the note again.

"It says here that we have a week until we violate Robert's requests. If I lay low and don't use my wings, these guys have no reason to bother either of us. Our tickets are for a week from now, so let's keep everything as planned. Are you okay with that?"

"I guess," Alvara said, though the thought of waiting a whole week unsettled her. "At least that way I can still finish school. Joy," she added.

"A week, then, and we'll be off. Stay safe, and let me know immediately if you see any hint of these people in the meantime." Jake sighed. "I hope this woman we are looking for isn't too difficult to locate."

"Oh, have a little faith! I tracked you guys down, didn't I?" Laerik challenged. She seemed to have forgotten about her fear of minutes before.

"That you did," Alvara encouraged. "See you tomorrow, Laerik."

"No you won't," Laerik retorted. "If you guys are really going to China, I have to leave now so I can meet you there."

"Laerik," Alvara said, exhaustion making the words come out condescending. "You know the ocean is really big, right? You can't just fly across."

"Won't, you'll see," Laerik promised, leaping into the night.

Alvara sighed, deciding that Laerik could take care of herself, and too tired to worry about particulars. "Have a good night, Jake."

"See you soon, Alvara. Be careful."

Jake walked back down the street toward his car. He put the key in the lock, and turned it. He opened the door, and eased into the seat, shutting the door behind him. His previous concerns about the origin of the letter were far from his mind.

So they were finally going to China. He was glad of it. The deafening silence in the car pressed down upon his skin from all angles and directions, and the pressure froze him in place. It had been beautiful, the time with Alvara and the children, and he didn't want to spoil it by thinking of the future or the past. He thought again of letting all the children play with his wings, and their squeals of laughter. So beautiful.

He turned the key, and the sound of the engine brought him back. He put the car in gear. He made his way to a freeway, drove an hour, and then two, with the thoughts filling his mind too numerous and overlapping to make a degree of sense.

Jake drove, and drove, his wings cradled around himself to fit in the driver's seat of his small sedan, until he reached a place to leave his car. He grabbed the flowers from the passenger seat and walked across the gravel path. With a few soft beats of his wings, he vaulted the wrought iron fence, and his feet tread the path toward the end. He recalled his promise to Alvara not to use his wings, but figured an extended leap shouldn't count. He walked a few minutes, and arrived at his destination.

It was a smallish stone, worn smooth by many years of salty ocean breezes. Rory would have liked the location, shaded by a tree and topping a low, grassy hill. It read, as it always had, "Aurora Coughlin, wife loved more deeply than even she knew." And below that, her favorite book, "I know why the caged bird sings." That was all. There. It never felt like enough, not for his Rory. If only there could be a shining monument, surrounded by laughing children and dancing birds. She had been so full of life; a rock was almost a joke.

He could see her, one eyebrow raised, holding up the stone, saying something like, "Yeeeeah. Thanks Jakey. This is a really swell rock. If there were ugly rocks out there, well, this one would make them feel pretty, that's how nice it is." She was never far away, especially here. His hands shook as he knelt before her grave, placing the bouquet of wildflowers he had gathered that day on the ground. He could feel it coming, the memory, as it did every year without fail. He embraced the pain, and was thrown backwards, until–

"God that was awful. I'm sorry, I know you've been planning this date for, like, ever, but Jakey, you've got to admit; was that not the worst food you've ever eaten?" He would have felt insulted, but her eyes were dancing. He could see that she wasn't annoyed, just amused by their utter failure of a dinner.

"I'm crushed, my darling, utterly shattered that my best laid plans have fallen short of your supreme Highness. How many lashes will it take to teach me my lesson in humility?"

"Wow, hold your horses honey, no bedroom talk until later. We have this one, last opportunity to save this date before I attempt to bury it in my memory forever. Are you ready for my proposition?" She raised an eyebrow.

"All ears, sweetness."

"Well that's unfortunate, as I had plans for the rest of you later." She smiled wickedly, and her dark eyes made Jake's heart beat faster. God, she was beautiful. "So to save this very regrettable date, I propose that we go for a walk on the bluffs and watch the sunset, and then you fly me away to a romantic bedchamber of your choosing. Preferably ours, but I'm not picky." He grinned and turned the car onto the road leading up to the bluffs. He saw a thought occur to her as her forehead crinkled.

"What is it, Rory?"

"It's been twenty years. We've been married for twenty years." He waited for her to go on. "I used to worry about this very moment. Nothing personal to you, 'course, but I've seen marriages go bad, as if time diluted their bright colors until there was nothing left to be happy about." He knew she was thinking of her parents. "But it hasn't happened to us. Your dopey nice-guy smile and ridiculous chivalry has somehow made this thing work." She reached out and ran a hand through his fluffy hair, and Jake smiled but kept his eyes on the road. "I just wanted to mention it, in all seriousness, in and among all the love I have." She kissed him on the cheek. "Okey-doke, you can relax, I'm all done with the sentimental." He knew she wasn't, and was glad of it. "Let's stroll like young lovers."

They made their way along the bluff, a cliff that ran a few hundred yards along the coast. The setting sun imbued the bleached grasses and muddy path with magical hues, and they walked hand in hand through the dusky light until they reached a spot to sit with a perfect view. It had rained the day before, and the ground was still damp, but Aurora insisted that they owned a washing machine for a reason. So they sat together on the soft ground. He smelled wet earth, and as she leaned her head on his shoulder, the floral smell of her shampoo. He put an arm around her, and kissed the top of her head. Life was beautiful.

In the present, Jake tried to keep them there, the two lovers with no warning, no preparation, no knowledge. But memories are made of time, and time moves forward.

Jake had most of his weight on the ground, while she was resting on him, so maybe he had a bit more warning. He felt the wet ground start to shift, and only had time to throw himself sideways before the whole cliff face slid toward the ocean. He had a firm grip on his wife's arm, and held tight while she screamed as the ground slid out from beneath her.

"Rory! Are you okay?" he managed to yell. He was pressed flat to the ground, legs and arms splayed for balance, when he was finally able to peer over the new cliff edge. His wife had streaks of dirt on her dress and cheeks, but held onto his hand with all her might, it felt like.

"Not really," she managed to gasp, her grip tense with fear, "help me up?" Jagged rocks poked through the turbulent ocean almost two hundred feet below her dangling legs.

"All right. Hold on." Jake did his best to pull her over the lip, but both their hands were slippery with dirt. He began to sweat with the effort of holding her. "Aurora, can you see anything to grab onto? I can't get a good enough grip to get you over the edge."

"Um, yeah there's a strong-looking root over here; can you move your hand to the left a bit? Like that. Yeah. Right, ouch, I'm holding onto that and you now. Now just the root. See anything you can use as a rope?" She was now too low to reach with just his hands.

Jake searched the immediate area, but could only see grass, and their car some distance away. "No, there's nothing here."

"So go get the rope in the car trunk! I can't hang here forever."

"Aurora, can you hold on for another minute? The sun will set before I can even get to the car, and then I can fly down and grab you."

"Jake, just go get the rope! If you run you can get it fast and I CAN'T HOLD ON! Jake, run!" She had both hands around the root, and one foot braced against the cliff face, but she was right; she couldn't hold on forever. In the setting sun, he saw the length of his shadow stretching toward the car. But somehow, Jake couldn't leave her dangling there, even to help her. He physically could not do it. Fear froze him in place. But he didn't know how to explain that to her. So he got angry.

"Just hold *on*, Rory! You can do it; you're a damn strong woman. I can feel it, less than a minute to go now."

"Jake, you and your damn wings! What if you're wrong?" She sang a folk song, her words quavering with fear. Her voice wafted over the edge of the cliff, and it helped him focus. He took a breath, re-estimating the distance to the car. If he ran, he'd make it with the rope in about thirty seconds, before he grew wings. He turned to run.

But they didn't have thirty seconds. The root Aurora held pulled loose from the soil. Out of the corner of his eye, he saw her fall. She screamed, and he yelled her name, and there was a flash of light as the sun set. She was gone.

Jake sought frantically for a glimpse of her along the stretch of coast below, but all was tranquil; the waves crashed undisturbed against the rocks. He dug his hands into the earth as large, black vulture wings grew from his back, and he wrapped them around himself, swaying as his unblinking, frantic search for her blurred with tears.

Jake knelt before her grave. His eyes were dry, as they were most times he traveled here. Every year was one more year he could have spent with her, had he been less proud of his wings, or a stronger man– able to leave his wife to run to get the rope. He had had enough time.

That night and the next morning, the coast guard and volunteers had searched in boats and dive teams for her body, but it had never been found. This stone was just a figurehead, a symbol of his empty life covering an empty grave. He hadn't flown since that night, the night he had flown not with joy but with ferocity, howling his rage to the moon like an animal. Until tonight, he remembered, and the guilt rose up again and threatened to overwhelm him. How could he have lost something so precious?

"Rory, I miss you." The whispered words escaped his lips, having come straight from his heart. And in his grief, in his delirium of loss, he could almost hear her answer.

You moron, don't you dare, he heard in his head. *Don't give up now. There's a way out of this; you can figure it out. Trust yourself, trust your friends, and take everything else with a grain of salt. And use your damn wings! I forgave you long ago, it's time to shake it off and forgive yourself. I love you, and–* but that was all. He waited for more, but nothing came.

It felt so real, like she was behind him, arms around his waist, whispering into his ear. *You've gone off the deep end, old buddy,* he said to himself. He realized that he was crying. He didn't feel sad, but more like a weight had lifted from his shoulders; his own personal albatross had come to life, kissed him on the cheek, and flown away. He laughed, realizing that no matter how he knew it, it had been real. His wife loved him and had forgiven him for everything.

Tears ran down his rough cheeks, dripping off his ears and wetting the collar of his shirt. His back hurt with his prone position, so he jumped to his feet with joy, which sent a twinge through one leg. It was tough getting old. He smiled, and imagined Rory smiling with him. He kissed his fingers and touched them to the top of the headstone, resting them there for a moment. He felt twenty years younger as he leapt into the air and flew back to his car. He had a lot to do before they traveled to China, and only a week in which to do it.

Chapter 7

There was just no getting around it; the airplane seat was uncomfortable. As tired as she felt, Alvara couldn't get back to sleep. It had been an exhausting week. She had stayed alert to and from school, questioned Alicia about any strange visitors, and kept what felt like one eye open for intruders every night. However, neither Robert, nor the mysterious "I", had turned up, either at her place or at Jake's. Jake and she had boarded the flight to China without a hitch. Alvara had come to realize that extreme sleep deprivation often paralleled the mystical periods of her life, but that didn't help her cope now when her only wish was for a comfortable horizontal position.

Unlike the car ride to the airport, Max's farewell had a surreal clarity to it. She remembered the fierce hug, and being about to grumble about it when he leaned toward her. His mint Chapstick lips had turned aside at the last moment and brushed her cheek. He whispered that she'd better be safe and keep in touch, his breath warm against her skin. She had been frozen for a good five seconds while he held her gaze. Then he had nodded, returned to the car, and driven off into the early morning fog.

When had an absolute lunatic replaced her best friend? She had thought about calling and asking him to explain the kiss when they touched down, but she would likely die of the resulting awkwardness between them. Better not to think about it too much.

The icing on the sleep-deprived cake was the three-hour flight delay at the airport, ensuring that the sun would set well before they landed in Shanghai. That last would make these airplane seats a bit more than uncomfortable, to say the least. Jake had gone over with her, multiple times, a way to make her wings smaller, but it just seemed so wishy-washy; she had kept asking what they would do if it didn't work, and each time he had said that they'd figure it out. Typical.

Alvara tried to turn over and sleep sideways, hoping to get some rest before her wings made it impossible, but it was no use. She couldn't find the right position, and no matter the angle, the sun managed to slant in from a window across the aisle and bore through her shut eyelids. She settled down to being miserable, eyes closed in defiance even though she was wide awake.

"Alvara?" She was so frustrated at his interruption that she pretended to be asleep. But he, delightfully, paid no attention to her ruse. "Alvara, time to wake up. We need to talk about sunset again. It will be here soon."

She groaned and tried to stretch, but the seat was too small for it to be satisfying, even sticking one leg out into the aisle. She hated flying in planes. "Jake, we already went over this like twenty times; I get it." She glared at Jake, who was composed as always. She could see he wouldn't be swayed, so she toned it down to a mild sarcasm. "Fine. All right, Jake, go ahead and explain. I always say, twentieth time is the charm."

He kept his voice down, so she had to pay close attention to hear him over the roar of the plane engines. "You know that you can't grow your angel wings here; you wouldn't fit in the seat, not to mention that someone might notice."

"No kidding. But I've told you before that I've always grown the same wings, ever since I was a little girl, no matter that sometimes I've wished for them to be smaller or less obvious a few times. Once for Halloween I made them a bit scrawnier, but that's not what you've been asking." Alvara had experienced no breakthrough understanding in the past couple of hours. Worry finally gnawed its way through her exhaustion.

"I know. That's why I'm going to try to explain again how to grow hummingbird wings, just in case you need another refresher. I used to use them when I needed to go out after sunset, because you can keep them hidden underneath your clothes. That way, no one will even notice we've been here. Ready to try?"

"Uh, yes. Remind me how it works?" Her mind was working in slow motion, but she tried to focus.

"So when you feel the sun starting to set; you can feel it right?" She nodded. "You have to feel yourself growing hummingbird wings, despite any evidence to the contrary. You will imagine a hummingbird, so light you almost couldn't feel one land on your back, except for the tiniest feather brush. Instead of the gush of power I feel when larger wings sprout, I feel a contained energy; these tiny wings have the power lift me off the ground, just like all our wings can. And then they grow. Make sense?"

"Well, when you say it like that, it sounds so easy," Alvara muttered. She couldn't exactly practice. What if it didn't work? She tried to brush aside her worries. "In a few minutes, I'll try it for real."

Jake seemed satisfied with that response, though Alvara noticed he kept glancing down the aisle to where the blonde and brunette female flight attendants handed out drinks first to the left, and then to the right, heading toward their row. Alvara knew just how much was riding on this, and rehearsed her memories of hummingbirds. The minutes ticked by, and the flight attendants were almost upon them. So was the sunset.

Alvara felt the tingling of wings, and thanked God in her head for the gift. Then she imagined a hummingbird perching on her back, and how the wings would feel light and energetic.

But her wings had already started to grow, and when the reality differed from her imagining, she panicked. With the conflict in her mind, the wings that grew were unique; they were about half the size of her angel wings, and the bright green of a hummingbird. She didn't have time to marvel; they had split the back of her T-shirt and forced her to lean forward into her lap to make space for them. She glanced right as one nearly hit Jake in the face and ended up squished against the window, and left at the other wing, which exploded out into the aisle. A man reading a magazine a row back leaned out of the way to avoid it, without seeming to notice that he had done so. Thankfully, the wing hadn't hit anyone, but the older, blonde flight attendant on the far side of the cart was peering at it with a glazed expression, as if she could almost see it.

"Jake!" Alvara gasped, "What can I do? I can't stay like this." She tried to fold up her wings, but there wasn't enough space. She could see recognition dawning in the woman's eyes. It wouldn't be long now.

He pushed her wing forward a bit, so he could see her. "Alvara, try to imagine the hummingbird wings now, more clearly than you've ever imagined anything. Maybe they will shrink."

"Have you ever changed your wings once they grew in?" Adrenaline surged through her, and she tried to focus.

"Once, I think . . . but now's the time for you to get it right. Try, before that woman gets here and we're really in trouble." They both looked at the older woman, who had stopped serving drinks and was staring at Alvara, brow furrowed. "Now."

Alvara took a deep breath and closed her eyes. She thought of flower nectar, and the humming sound that wings make when they move too rapidly to see, and the lightness and beauty of hummingbird wings. With excruciating slowness, her wings began to shrink, folding in on themselves until they were two small hummingbird wings tucked flat against her shoulders.

"Jake, did you bring an extra shirt? I think mine is kinda shot." Alvara smiled with pride as she sat up. She glanced left, directly into the wide blue eyes of the flight attendant, who was standing next to their row, her face a mask of fear and confusion.

"What in the hell was that?" she asked.

"Mary, what are you talking about?" the other flight attendant asked. "Oh, this young girl has a ripped shirt, poor thing. Must have caught on the chair, aren't I always saying how these seats are ancient? Honey, don't worry, the airline will pay you for the damage; I'm terribly sorry." Her eyes had passed right over Alvara's back when she noticed the shirt, even when she had readjusted the edges to reveal the hummingbird wings as she spoke. Though the blonde woman Mary had flinched, this woman hadn't batted an eye.

"No, Teresa, I'm not asking about the shirt; you didn't see her back? Oh." Recognition dawned as Mary must have realized Teresa couldn't see the wings. "Never mind, you're right," she said. "Would you mind finishing with the drinks? I'll follow up with this young lady about her ripped shirt." Teresa nodded, gave Alvara one more consoling smile, and continued on her way.

Mary waited until she had passed a couple rows, and then hissed, "Now answer my question. You know what I'm talking about. What in the hell was that?" She crossed her arms and refused to budge, and Alvara had no idea what to do.

Jake saved her. "All right, ma'am, let's not get carried away here. Just let's go into the back of the plane and we can all talk for a minute." He motioned for Alvara to get up, and she cast a glance at the woman. Mary seemed about to speak, but instead nodded once, turned, and walked to the back of the plane. Alvara held the back of her shirt together as they followed, trying to calm her breathing when she felt like running away. But here, there was nowhere to run.

When they reached the empty rear of the plane, Mary closed the curtains and spun to face them. Her expression was angry, but Alvara could see tears in her eyes. "Start talking, girly! What the hell was that?"

"Um," said Alvara, "I don't really know what you mean."

"Don't you play those games with me!" she exclaimed. "I saw your wings, don't think that I didn't!"

"Sure, all right, you did, just please try to calm down," Alvara said.

Jake stepped in. "It's okay, we'll explain," he said, resting a hand on her shoulder. "There is a lot in the world beneath the surface; you just got your first taste of it today. This girl has wings; you can wrap your mind around that, can't you?" Mary hiccuped.

"No, not really," she blinked back tears. "How do I even begin?"

"It's just made of two normal ideas, a girl and a pair of wings, that don't normally go together, is all." Mary sniffled, and Jake handed her his handkerchief.

"Is she some sort of genetic experiment? Or is it some sort of magic? I don't know what to think about this. This doesn't make any sense! It's just not rational." She blew her nose.

"It isn't so hard to believe that for every couple of things we know about the world, there is at least one we don't. Isn't that right?" Though she was surprised to be addressed, Alvara nodded in agreement.

Mary began to calm down. She handed the handkerchief back with a small 'thank you', and Jake smiled. "Wow, some speech," she breathed. "Woo. I guess the initial shock is starting to wear off; it's not impossible to believe." She wiped her nose. "I assume there's some sort of explanation, but I don't want to hear it. Can you fly?" she asked Alvara, and Alvara nodded. "Ha, that's amazing. Do you have wings too?" Jake frowned, but nodded. "My stars, really? I wouldn't want to be rude, or anything, but can I see?"

Jake paused for a moment, but lifted his shirt. Alvara thought that Mary seemed surprised, but if it was because of his disrobing or the two green wings that danced on his back, she couldn't tell.

"Can I touch?" Mary whispered. Jake turned. She reached up one hand, and with her fingertips, briefly touched his wings. Jake shuddered at the contact. Both of them seemed to grow uncomfortable, thought Alvara, as Mary withdrew her fingers and he dropped his shirt.

Jake adjusted his shirt and met Mary's eyes. "I hate to ask, but we don't want to become common knowledge. Can we trust you to keep from mentioning us to anyone?"

"Oh, of course, of course," Mary said, sounding flustered. "I know I've asked a lot, but I'd like to know your first names. It's all been so . . . strange and wonderful. I'm Mary. Of course." And she gave an old-fashioned curtsy that made her appear younger than she was.

Jake looked to Alvara, allowing her to choose whether to answer or not. She really appreciated it. "My name is Alvara, ma'am, and we appreciate your confidence." Jake smiled, and she knew she had chosen correctly.

"And mine is Jake," he said. He extended his hand, and Mary reached out to shake it for a long time. "It's been a pleasure."

"Oh dear, I must return to work. I just . . . thank you for speaking with me. I hope you both have a great flight, and, well, an excellent vacation in China." She said the last part in a hurry, smiling at Alvara, and beaming at Jake, before disappearing through the curtain.

Jake held open the curtain for Alvara, and said, "That went well." Alvara could only let out a held breath in agreement, causing Jake to chuckle, as they walked back to their seats.

As Jake settled down to sleep for the next few hours, he found himself musing on the events of the day and night. They had had a close call with the flight attendant; he feared that most people would have wanted to use their wings for personal gain. But he had felt a spark with her . . . and that had him worried almost as much as becoming a science experiment. Her soft blue eyes and bleached blonde hair were different from the smiling dark eyes and dark hair of his beloved, but they still pulled him; he could tell she had suffered a loss, as he had, in that ineffable way two lost souls had of connecting with another. And when she touched his wings . . . he had become so afraid that his bond with Rory was disappearing, he had shied away from any kind of connection with women for years. He could never allow Rory to be eclipsed by another.

Jake was jolted from his thoughts when Alvara's head landed on his shoulder. He tried not to move and noticed she was finally asleep for the first time this flight. Her dark hair had fallen across her face, and she was in danger of sliding forward. He reached up and pressed her head back, so that she rested against his arm and shoulder. *Would you look at that*, he thought, and settled back to get some sleep.

Even still nights are not as still as this night. The crickets and bullfrogs are absent. As is the distant hum of traffic, the sighing of young lovers, the slamming of screen doors, and the barking of dogs at little nothings. There is only the small stretch of sand enclosing the playground, and it is silent.

Wait. Hush now.

Listen.

There it is again, the smallest sound. But upon listening, even the breath of a whisper can seem to fill up the silence until it is the only sound in the world.

Creeeeeeak. Creeeeeeeak.

A little girl sits on the swing. Her hair is long and dark, or perhaps of middling length and light, but it hangs across her features, obscuring them. Her pale arms grasp the chains. They stick out of a pale dress, though the color is indiscernible in the moonlight. She sits on the swing, her bare feet first in front of her, and then bent behind her, as she continues to swing back and forth.

Creeeeeeak. Creeeeeeeak.

She rises and falls and rises again, alone in the moonlight. Most little girls would get bored, stop the swing, and maybe try the slide. Or better yet, call out for their mothers to take them home, wrapped in the warmth of family. But she doesn't. Her swinging never falters, and the height she reaches never changes; it is more like a video clip of a little girl on repeat than a little girl swinging. But this fact does not bother her, and she continues to swing.

She screams. Nothing has changed in the still night, but the little girl screams and falls from her swing. Her hair pools around her head and her arms wrap around her shoulders as she shakes on the ground. There is hair and sand in her face, and she continues to cry.

No one comes running.

She reaches behind her back to scratch at her shoulder blades. She continues to cry as she scratches and scratches, until she finally breaks the skin with her tiny nails. Blood that looks black in the muted night stains her dress in two spreading pools over her shoulder blades, and she stops scratching. She simply grasps both shoulders, arms crossed across her chest as if holding herself together, and her shaking subsides.

The girl pulls herself into a sitting position and brushes the sand from her skin. She glances around the playground, as if seeing where she is for the first time. She gets unsteadily to her feet, but spasms and falls to the sand again.

'No no no no,' she whispers under her breath. 'Not again, I'm not ready, no please!' she has her arms curled around her belly, this time, as she lies in the sand. With what seems an intense pain, she screams and rolls over onto her back, and her face shines in the moonlight.

It is a child's face, heart-shaped and delicate. It is streaked with blood and tears, and wracked with pain. She stretches her hand out, grasping for another hand to hold, and clutches sand instead. She screams again, and opens her eyes for the first time. Her eyes are silver, and reflect the light of the moon exactly. Finally, she lies still, breathing hard on the sand, staring up at the moon with fear, and sadness, and a wild joy battling in her eyes.

She lies on the sand, staring up at the moon, and the silence of the night reigns once more. She almost seems to be waiting for someone.

No one would come.

Chapter 8

As Jake stepped off the plane and into the terminal, he collided with a wall of sound. He and Alvara wove through harried families dragging unbalanced luggage and teenagers exclaiming over shared music videos, with airport employees struggling to be heard above the din. Just as they successfully navigated into the stream of people heading toward the baggage claim, a squeal of laughter reverberated through the large terminal chamber, announcing a little girl in a blue jumper before she darted across Jake's path. When the girl glanced back at her mother, one intense moment of eye contact was enough to calm her frenetic progress. The girl stopped and smiled at Jake before her mother led her away through a mix of neon-lit stores and more somber displays.

The girl's hair, Jake thought, reminded him of something. The way it fell was familiar, though the hair he knew was lighter and drooped to hide a face . . . and Jake remembered his dream from the plane: the girl on the swing. She seemed so alone. Jake wasn't one to put much stock in dreams, but this one felt different; the emotions from the dream persisted into waking, and he recalled a sensation of clarity his dreams usually didn't possess. And it concerned the moon, too, he thought. He couldn't quite remember what the girl looked like. She was screaming. Jake shuddered. He couldn't afford to dwell on it now.

Customs was another sort of nightmare. Their customs official, who reminded Jake of a body builder, flexed his muscles and frowned when Jake said he was Alvara's family friend. But after a moment, he shrugged and let them pass. Boredom could certainly be convenient, though it made Jake uneasy that he and Alvara might draw unwanted attention.

As they got nearer to the exit, the press of humanity increased. Jake saw the bus stop through the doors, and prepared for the pushing and shoving throng the tourist guides had warned about.

However, despite the insanity of the airport, the Airport Shadow bus system defied expectation with its ordered tranquility. There were eight different buses headed to specific destinations within the city; travelers made polite lines behind each of the routes. After seeing the correct line a little ways down the sidewalk, Jake nodded towards it and began walking.

Alvara followed behind, seemingly distracted. They took a seat on the empty bench by the stop.

Something brushed Jake's head, causing him to flinch and cry out. A dark shape banked and came back for another pass, and he prepared to smack it away. He realized just in time what, or who, it was.

"Laerik!" Jake said, as the raven landed on the back of the bench between Alvara and him. "You actually made it. How did you get here?"

Laerik let out a loud squawk and turned to preen. "Oh, right," Jake said. They'd have to wait for sunset to hear Laerik's story.

For now it was simply cloudy, but Jake could feel that it wouldn't be long until the sun set. Again. With the fifteen hour time difference and the ten hour flight, they had lost a whole day in the air. The street where they sat was calmer than he expected from such a busy city, though some travelers were still catching cabs and dragging suitcases to friends waiting in cars. Though the sun was already hidden behind the terminal building, the heat was oppressive and sticky.

"Not to sound like a kid or anything," Alvara began, "but I had this creepy dream on the plane. I'm still kind of freaked out." She peered sideways at him past her hair.

Now it was Jake's turn to be uncomfortable. "Uh, what kind of dream?" It couldn't be the same dream.

"It's hard to remember, but it had this little girl with a silver dress in it, swinging on a swing. It was weird because I've never dreamt about anyone I don't know; it was like I was just floating there, watching her." Alvara's feet swung a bit on the bench, unconsciously mimicking the girl's movements.

"I think I had the same dream," Jake whispered.

"Really?" Alvara gaped.

"Yes, I think so." He could still see the little girl swinging back and forth, over and over. "It must mean something. She was looking at the moon, after all, remember?"

"I don't remember that part. But she was crying out, I felt so bad just watching her and not being able to help." Alvara ran her hands through her hair and pushed it behind her ears. "I mean, but what can we do about it? It was just a dream."

"I'm not sure it was 'just' anything; I've never had the same dream as anyone else before, and like you said, it felt different. But we can just file it away and figure it out later. Does that work?"

Alvara slammed her fists into the bench, her face contorted with frustration. "No, Jake, that doesn't 'work' for me. You just take all this stuff at face value, Mr. Calm and Collected when confronted with weird coincidences and strange quests. I mean, we're in China! Someone saw our wings on the plane before we even arrived! A man is chasing us, and has threatened to hurt me if you didn't follow his instructions! What are we supposed to be doing here? Meeting a random Chinese woman, just because a bird told us to?!" There was a loud squawk, and Alvara yelled, "NO OFFENSE LAERIK!" Laerik took flight, coasting out over the traffic and alighting on a street lamp.

"Come on, Jake, at least think out loud with me for a sec. We are letting the fact that we don't know anything give everybody a chance to tell us what to do. I know what you've said on the topic, but I already *know* why I have wings; it's a gift from God, in order to help me to help others. I'm guessing something bad happened with your wings, and you don't want to talk about it, and whatever. But we need to trust each other. We don't know what we're going to find here." She sighed and looked away.

Jake was silent for a moment. "Don't forget, hummingbird wings," Jake said as he felt the sun begin to set. His shoulders tingled as his own wings poked through his shoulder blades, barely touching his loose polo shirt. With their arrival, Jake felt somehow more capable of dealing with the problems they had accumulated. It was as if wings added another dimension to their potential choices; now, if need be, they could literally overcome their problems.

Alvara's wings didn't burst through her shirt this time, so Jake figured she was getting the hang of fine control. Neither said anything for a few long minutes. Jake watched the people load into and out of buses and taxis, a constant arterial flow that was both busy and healthy. He sighed with relief as a cool breeze ruffled his hair, signaling a drop in temperature.

All that had happened was a lot for Alvara to take in. Jake understood feeling overwhelmed. But somehow, he had always been waiting for an adventure to happen to him. Ever since he first grew wings, he had had this instinctual knowledge that there would be more to it than just getting to fly around at night, some greater purpose. He had never told anyone but his wife about that feeling, though. It had seemed a bit childish, even for him. And once Rory was gone, and he stopped his research to open that fantasy shop, well, he just let that feeling slip away into an old man's dusty dreams. And yet, here he was.

"You're right," he said.

"About what?" she asked, and he saw a dry humor in her snooty refusal to meet his eyes.

"Everything. Also smart. And wise," he added, and she turned around. "You're right that we don't know who to trust, nor do I have a satisfactory explanation of why we grow wings in the first place. I'm glad you brought all this up. As you can see, I'm pretty gung-ho about adventuring. Must be my youth."

She chuckled. "If you're going to blame it on anything, Jake, youth is pretty far down the list. Let's go with 'boy*ish* curiosity' with an emphasis on the '*ish*'."

He chuckled. "Fair enough. But you're right about us needing to be careful. Laerik was beside herself about that woman, and the letter sounded serious; life's not safe for us right now. Let's see if we can locate this woman here, and decide after that if we want to get more involved in this. Does that work? I mean—" he tried to think of a different phrase to use in the context.

"Sure, Jake. It 'works'," she said, making quotation marks in the air as she did. "So what's the plan once we reach the city center? Before she left to do whatever it is got her to China, Laerik mentioned finding a park so she could talk to some birds. It seems a bit open-ended. What if the birds speak Chinese or something?"

"Sorry to break up all the bonding going on over there, but it seems I must chime in," Laerik called as she settled on the bench. "Now that you and fluff-for-brains here have worked out your issues." She ruffled her feathers as she settled. "The birds will not speak 'Chinese'. All birds can communicate with each other, because we, unlike you, have maintained contact and information transfer for our whole existence. And besides, you should be able to understand them all at night anyway. Furthermore, it doesn't matter *which* birds we locate. They will take us to the highest authority in the area, who will know where this woman lives, as she should be a high priority."

"That's all super-fascinating," Alvara said. "But I have to know how you got to Shanghai. There's no way you could have flown, no offense of course, but did you stow away on a ship?"

"Ugh it was horrible," Laerik lamented. "Worst idea I have had in my whole five years. But a friend of mine suggested it, and it sounded fun," she buried her beak in her wing. "An albatross carried me."

"Whoa," Alvara said.

Jake had some questions. "Laerik, sure a wandering albatross can make the journey using dynamic soaring, but I'm not at all sure that a raven is streamlined enough to – "

"I have suffered greatly," said Laerik.

"Jake, you're a bird nerd, big surprise," Alvara said, but she was smiling. "Just let it go for now. Laerik, you poor dear," Alvara continued, and scratched her neck until Laerik's eyes closed in pleasure.

Jake sighed and tried to tamp down the vestiges of his professional curiosity. "Glad you're okay, and thanks for the info, Laerik. Do you want to meet us in the park downtown?"

"Yes yes yes please! No buses. Albatross was bad enough. You showed me that park near the hotel on the map? Get to that park and stay put, and I'll find you."

"Please be careful."

"Bet I can get that guy's toupee without him catching me."

"Laerik, no!"

"Kidding, sheesh." And she flew off into the descending night.

Their bus arrived. After Jake swiped his credit card, they slipped into their seats. And then they were off into Shanghai.

The bus was a rickety and close-packed place, and Jake rubbed a section of window with one sleeve in order to see out. The first aspect of the skyline Jake noticed was the profusion of high rise apartment buildings and corporate sky scrapers. With the sun setting, the city was ablaze with light, reminding him more of Las Vegas than a standard metropolitan city in the US. The streets the bus took to reach the city center were well-made and passed through the more affluent areas, but Jake could still smell the odors of the real China beneath: diesel, charcoal, dust, and the tiniest wafting of sewage.

Jake pressed his nose into the window, grinning with eyes wide open so he didn't miss a single detail. He had always loved traveling, which was pretty constant with his research and Rory's singing career. China had always been on the list of places they had wanted to visit in their spare time, and there it had remained. Like Alvara, he wondered what China had in store for them.

The bus shuddered to a stop a few times along the route, and Jake and Alvara got off at the fourth stop. They dragged their bags a couple of blocks through the city streets, with no street signs in view, and somehow managed to find their way to Wanping Hotel.

After checking in and dropping their bags, they asked the manager behind the counter how to get to the park where they would meet Laerik, Jing'an Park. She spoke excellent English, and directed them to a spot a few minutes' walk to the west. They set off, carrying coats, as the mild day was becoming a chilly night.

A few minutes passed, and Jake caught a glimpse of the park. A green corner broadened into a wall of foliage, and they made their way to its edge.

Upon entering, it was a different city. The sounds died down to a low hum as they walked along the paved pathways. Jake had the blanketed feeling that night had fallen, though the city lights were still visible through gaps in the trees and shrubbery. There was an artificial lake ahead, and he and Alvara made their way around its edge, searching for a bench. They found one, and took a seat to wait for Laerik to catch up with them. But she wasn't the first to arrive.

A bird flew down and landed not far from where they sat. Jake recognized it as a spotted dove. It blinked at them with deep red eyes and dipped its head toward them, before flying up to rest on a branch behind them. Soon a red-billed starling, a common moorhen, and what Jake was pretty sure was a hwamei, with its distinctive white painted eyebrow, had joined the throng. Each bird that landed bowed in its own way, and removed itself to a nearby tree to observe the others. In a group, a kingfisher, a light-vented bulbul, a Eurasian tree sparrow, a blackbird, and a magpie landed as well, though they waited for each other to bow before taking part. They flew up to the tree as a unit.

Alvara glanced at him with one eyebrow raised, as if to question whether he was seeing this as well. Jake shrugged, and they watched as a black-crowned night heron, a white Wagtagtail, and a soft-feathered little grebe, which seemed quite flustered as it bowed, all flew up to join the others. Jake and Alvara passed a few awkward minutes examining the different species of birds lined up in the trees behind them. The birds stared right back. Finally, Laerik showed up, out of breath.

"I'm here, I'm here, thank Goddess," she said. "Sorry I'm late, but I see you've met the leaders, more or less, of their respective flocks here in Shanghai. I would introduce each of them to you personally, but I think you would spend all your time trying to get their names right, and frankly we have other business here." She fluttered her wings in excitement. "As a first step, they'd like to see your wings. They can feel their presence, of course, but they haven't seen someone like you up close in a while; it seems this woman is pretty secretive about it. Does that 'work' for you guys?" She made parentheses in the air with her wings and cackled with glee.

"Fine with me; not like enough people have seen them yet today," said Alvara, and lifted the back of her shirt, fluttering her hummingbird wings. The birds responded with a chorus of coos and twitters, and then, as one, turned to stare at Jake. He lifted his shirt with a performer's flourish. The uproar was identical, and was cut short once more. Jake caught small snippets of murmuring speech in the response, but the birds didn't attempt to make themselves understood.

"Nice, great, thank you," said Laerik. "Now, we need to figure out where the woman lives." And she cawed and chortled, turning her head and wings in distinctive patterns.

The moorhen warbled and cocked its head at her. This time, Jake heard him say, "Though we were polite to your guests, why exactly should we assist a fledgling who disobeyed the authority of her flock?"

Laerik bristled. "I am on an assignment–" she began.

"–of your own making," the heron boomed. "Your flock sent a transoceanic messenger ahead to warn us, as soon as they knew your destination. You have no authority here."

"You have broken no laws," the sparrow chirped, "so we can only highly recommend that you return to your flock, young fledgling."

Laerik didn't even cringe. Why did she lie to us, Jake wondered? "Elders," Laerik cawed, "how can you be so blind to what's been happening all around you? I had to act; my flock was talking themselves in circles with endless debates! They sent delegations to our friends in the sparrow and seagull communities, but each group was only waiting for the others to move first!" she flapped her wings and flew to a closer branch.

"I've felt it for over a year, and I couldn't wait any longer. Maybe you believe me, maybe you don't, but some natural thing is askew, and it's wrapped up with these winged Children of the Goddess. I know how to track, and even though I can barely feel her, I believe I could find the woman here myself. But we could really use a break; we don't have the time to be flying up and down the streets of Shanghai. People are after us!" Here she shivered in fear. "So come on, just lend us a wing on this."

The branches of the tree swayed in a light breeze. The hwamei spoke, lifting an eyebrow. "Laerik, I too have felt these . . . imbalances. My heart is gladdened that you have brought the others here to meet with our own winged child. I am in favor of helping you, as no other bird has come forward for this mission."

The heron huffed in distaste, but other birds chimed in. They expressed disapproval of Laerik's method, but were in favor of helping as they could. Jake shook his head, but didn't speak. As an ornithologist, he would have given anything before for the strange glimpse into bird society that unfolded in front of him, however unlikely he would have been to publish his observations. Tonight, though, he just hoped the birds would be willing to help.

The blackbird flitted to a lower branch. "We don't know her name," she apologized in twitters, "But she lives in the top window of an apartment near my nest. I can show you."

Laerik bowed deeply, "Thank you, Elders," she intoned, wry sarcasm in her voice, "for saving me the trouble of tracking. Owe you one!" she saluted.

Some of the birds grumbled, but the hwamei glided over to her and they touched foreheads. "Good luck, little one," he whispered. Laerik, who was sobered by his gesture, simply nodded her goodbye as he flapped off. Alvara and Jake bowed to the gathered birds, though Jake felt silly. One by one, the other birds dispersed, and the tree branches swung back and forth with the removal of the weight. At last, only the blackbird waited.

Jake turned to Laerik. "So you lied to us," he stated. She shifted her weight from foot to foot on the branch and wouldn't meet his eyes.

"Well, it sounded better if I was on an official mission. You know. And I would have been!" she cawed. "I wasn't lying when I said I trained for this. I was about to graduate, and I asked for this mission. I was polite and everything. But the elders just stared until one of the chicks squeaked 'Nevermore'." She sighed. "I don't have to explain to you guys what a cheap shot that was. The rest of the flock burst into laughter and returned to discussion. So I said screw it and left."

She finally looked up at them both. "I'm really sorry I lied. You guys didn't care if it was official or not, and I really do want to help. It is my mission," she finished.

Alvara smiled first. "It's okay, Laerik. It was pretty cool how you argued your case in front of those impressive elders."

"I know, right? Thanks, fluff!" Laerik beamed. "So I'm about to meet up with that blackbird and find out where the woman lives. You guys want to come meet her?" Laerik was instantly excited, and flew from tree branch to tree branch. It was exhausting to watch.

"Laerik, not tonight," Alvara sighed. "It's getting late for house calls, and we'll have a lot to talk about. That's assuming she can understand English. I think I can speak for both Jake and myself when I say we need sleep to return to full sanity." Jake gave a tired nod and yawned for effect.

"Let's spend the day in Shanghai, and visit her tomorrow at sunset. Laerik, you should catch up with the blackbird and find the woman's address before heading to sleep. 'Work' for everyone?" Jake asked, raising his eyebrows and smiling as he made the quotation marks that were now a running joke.

"'Works' for us," the other two said in unison, solemnly raising arms and wings and following suit.

Chapter 9

"Come on, we don't want to miss it," Jake said around the toothbrush in his mouth. He leaned out of the bathroom to see Alvara still sitting on her hotel bed, which was decorated in cherry-blossoms on a white background and identical to his. She was staring at the autumn mountain water color on the wall without seeing it, sipping the coffee he'd brought her from the lobby. She blinked slowly, and Jake worried that she would fall asleep sitting up.

"Is this really necessary?" she mumbled, but she downed the coffee and added her cell phone to her side bag.

"Quite," Jake said, and held the door open for her on the way out of the hotel room.

They made their way to the park from the night before, but how different it appeared in the bright morning light. Eddies of wind ignited flashes of light on the ripples in the lake, the flowering bushes were in full resplendent bloom, and early risers thronged in the paths. Many jogged in pairs or groups of three, but Jake was fascinated by the individuals, and even one large group, performing Tai Chi.

The men and women danced from one pose to another, never ceasing as they balanced and extended, manipulating unseen balls of energy. The movements were simple and graceful, the activity deceptively easy. Jake could see some of the participants beginning to sweat, even in the crisp morning air.

"I have half a mind to join in, you know," Jake teased Alvara. She had been watching the men in fascination, but turned to him in horror.

"I'm likely to die of embarrassment as it is," Alvara shuddered. "We're staring at a bunch of old people working out. Not my idea of a standard tourist activity."

"Well, I have some options of those, if you'd like," Jake offered.

Alvara shrugged, and asked "How about a tourist breakfast?" Jake nodded his agreement.

After an interesting breakfast of pot stickers, tea, and some fruit juice, Jake was ready for some exploring. Alvara vetoed the majority of his touristy ideas, so they finally settled on walking along the Bund.

Jake tried not to feel disappointed as his careful plans were tossed aside. Alvara's heart just wasn't in it, and Jake couldn't really blame her; everything felt like it hinged upon the meeting tonight. Would they have another friend to share gifts and secrets with, or just a stranger who wanted nothing to do with them? And there was still the unspoken worry that the man from the Legion would catch up to them.

Once Jake stopped trying to entertain Alvara, they both began to have fun. The Bund was great for people-watching. A bleached-blonde photographer was taking shots of a lady in a feathered bridal dress from a bunch of angles. She didn't smile in any of the pictures. Slow barges floated past the Shanghai skyscrapers visible across the water. A couple of young Chinese tourists took turns taking pictures of each other in dramatic poses that made Alvara snort with laughter.

They bought some noodles for an early lunch and relaxed on a bench. A group of teenagers danced to live jazz a little farther around the curve of the broad avenue. Though it was still early, the sun seemed to target Jake in particular; Jake was already sweating profusely.

"So, what about spending the afternoon visiting the Jade Buddha Temple?" Jake asked, airing his shirt in what he hoped was an unobtrusive manner in order to generate some breeze. "I read that it was beautiful. And then maybe renting bicycles to get to the woman's apartment?"

"Sure, Jake," Alvara replied. They sat in silence for a bit, watching the dancers appear and disappear through a line of flowering trees. Fluorescent orange umbrellas spaced at intervals announced the sale of dumplings, or bao buns, or various meats grilled on a stick.

"My dad would have loved this," Alvara admitted. Jake turned to look at her. "He was a handyman, and could repair almost anything electronic; he always said that the greatest and worst electronics came out of China. He got this travel book for China for Christmas one year. He used to read it to me to help me fall asleep, and talked about the Great Wall, the terra cotta soldiers, the walled gardens, the palaces. We never had enough money to go, but he would plan out these elaborate trips with me just the same." She smiled sadly. "Sometimes we decorated the living room like a particular part of the country, just with cutout decorations. Then we'd make a dish, like kung-pao chicken, and imagine all the terrific sights we could see from our restaurant."

Jake ate his noodles in silence. He understood now why his exited account of his tourist plans for the day had upset her. They reminded her of her father.

"He sounds like he was an amazing guy," Jake finally said.

Alvara shook her head. "Ridiculous," she said, "and amazing. I just wish I could have shared my wings with him; I didn't get them until after the accident. I know he would have loved them. He would probably have used them for a different purpose though," she finished, and chuckled.

"What do you mean?" Jake asked.

"Oh, for pranking!" Alvara laughed. "He would have seen their potential immediately. There was this one time that a group of kids egged our house three nights in a row. The third night, do you know what my dad did? He hid out in the bushes with Ziploc bags of flour and water, and when they showed up, he pelted them! I was hiding with him, and their faces, of course dripping with white paste, were fantastic."

Jake nearly snorted noodles through his nose as he laughed; Alvara's father had a long list of noble pranks, and Alvara told one story after another. Once, Jake felt a twinge of guilt that he hadn't told Alvara about Rory. But the moment passed, and the conversation traveled new paths.

Their noodles finished, Jake brought out his Polaroid to take pictures of Alvara in front of the view of downtown Shanghai. A random Chinese man tapped him on the shoulder, and asked in clear English if Jake would take a picture with his family. So, to the amusement of Alvara, Jake posed with strangers, and when the picture came out Jake realized they wanted to take it. He handed it over with reluctance.

It shouldn't have been so difficult to part with, but his camera had done nothing but photograph the nightly appearance of his wings for years; seeing one of its pictures in the hands of strangers was an awkward, discomfiting feeling. Jake frowned as the couple strolled away.

"I can't stop thinking about her," Alvara said suddenly, leaning out over the railing to look across the water at the Shanghai skyline.

"Who?" Jake asked.

"The woman with wings," Alvara whispered, though no tourists were close enough to overhear. "This city has 14 million people in it, I looked it up. China as a whole, over a billion. And she's alone here. That's sad, but the strange part?" Alvara said, leaning against the railing. "The only other two people in the world like her live a few miles apart. Jake, the odds are unbelievable."

"I didn't always live in Southern California," Jake said, frowning.

"That just adds to the idea that maybe you moving there wasn't random chance," Alvara added excitedly. "Maybe we were supposed to meet. That's got to be it. So finding her, maybe it's part of God's plan for us."

Alvara bowed her head, as if in prayer, but then turned to look at Jake with a slightly sheepish expression. "You don't mind if I pray for us, do you?"

"Be my guest," Jake said. "Every little bit helps, I've heard." As he watched her pray, dark ponytail flopped to one side and lips moving soundlessly, Jake felt a profound tenderness for Alvara. If she thought they'd get some assistance with this strange quest they were on, he hoped like hell she was right.

A few hours later, the Jade Buddha Palace visited and dutifully documented with Jake's Polaroid, Jake and Alvara turned their bikes toward Zhabei. Laerik had told them that the woman's apartment was in that district, and they had the address on a slip of paper. The sun was just beginning to set, casting the city streets into shades of gold and grey, temporarily blinding Jake as he passed in and out of its beams. Jake felt a rising anxiety about what they would find when they met with the woman that evening.

They biked along streets in the Zhabei district, searching for Laerik.

Jake's anxiety rose as cars and bikes packed themselves into the narrow streets at rush hour. The traffic signals and lanes were polite suggestions at best. Jake regretted his choice of bikes.

Jake finally spotted Laerik perched on a small tree across the street. Alvara waved, and she took flight, leaving the two of them to follow her trail among the now twisting streets. They had left the tourist district behind, and the change was becoming more noticeable, like a modern coat of paint peeling back at its edges to reveal older layers beneath.

The traffic lights had disappeared, and in their place were short militant men standing on boxes and yelling to direct traffic. Bicycles swarmed across every available bit of road, but locals, rather than tourists, pedaled them all. Men in suits on bicycles dodged piles of trash and spat into the gutters at the side of the street. A boy and a girl ran past, flying a dragon-shaped kite and shrieking with joy. The smell of charcoal swept over them, carried on the breeze, and Jake wondered what it was from.

"Jake, look at that," Alvara pointed, and he turned to see one of the slew of automobiles drive by on that road; it had a mesh-covered truck bed filled with chickens. With each bump in the road, chickens slammed into the enclosure, their feathers being yanked loose to drift into the ruts in the road.

They continued following Laerik until she swooped down to land on a lamp post. She had stopped in front of a four-story apartment complex. It was an off-white boxy stucco structure that was a relic of the 50's, with a sign declaring its name in Chinese to any who could read it. Jake and Alvara parked their bikes against a tree, and walked across the street and up the front steps.

"Third floor," Jake muttered to himself, and saw the buzzer. The blackbird had told Laerik the woman was named Zhu Biyu. He hesitated, wondering what else he and Alvara might find inside. Laerik made the decision for him by swooping down and pressing the buzzer with her beak.

A man's voice asked a question in Chinese, and Jake replied. "Ni hao, is this Mr. Zhu?"

"Yes," the man said, "and who are you?" Mr. Zhu's English was comprehensible, though accented with rising and falling tones in odd places.

"My name is Jake, and my friend Alvara is here as well. We are here to speak with your wife, Zhu Biyu. We have some exciting news for her." He and Alvara had agreed that this was the easiest way they could gain entry without revealing too much of their true purpose. Jake hoped it would be enough.

The intercom went dead. They waited to be let in, but after a few minutes realized that no one was coming.

Jake frowned. "Maybe she doesn't live here anymore," he said, leaning against the stucco wall, "and it seems he won't let us in, anyhow. Let's see if we can pick up her trail somewhere else."

"Hold on, you can't be giving up?" Alvara asked. "No way; this is crazy, we're in China for this exact reason. And anyway, I have an idea."

"I'm all ears," Jake said.

"It takes a minute to work." She quirked a smile as she circled the apartment to find a top floor balcony, and Jake understood.

"I can't believe I'm allowing this." Jake checked to make sure they were alone as he felt the sun complete its downward trek. A woman and child rounded the corner, and Jake held his breath, but they passed out of sight before the sun had fully set.

Before leaving for China, Alvara had retrofitted most of Jake's and her shirts to create wing slits, and Jake was interested to try them out. As his wings burst forth, they emerged through the slits, leaving his shirt intact. Both Jake and Alvara grew wings as long as their arms were wide; long enough to allow powerful lift and control, but small enough they could be folded behind their backs. The feel of wings on his back helped dispel some of his anxiety, and Jake felt a growing optimism that this plan might just work.

"Finally," Laerik muttered, coming to rest on a trash can next to the apartment. "I kept feeling like I was talking to myself over here." Jake winked at her and she ruffled her feathers.

They leapt from the street, Jake following Alvara partway around the building to a thin balcony nearly covered by small potted plants. Jake picked a spot on the railing and managed to stall at the right moment to stick his landing. Alvara decided on the less orthodox method of grabbing the edge of the balcony above to slow her descent, swinging for a second on the rim before dropping to the plant-less floor of the balcony.

"Ouch," she hissed, lowering her hands. Jake could see they had a few deep gouges that began to ooze blood.

"Jeez, Alvara! Those look deep. You might want to watch swinging from stucco in future," Jake said as he handed over his handkerchief, which she wrapped around her injured hand and held in place. Laerik swooped up to join them, but Jake shooed her away; this interaction would be difficult enough without explaining her presence. Laerik let out a frustrated squawk, but she left to wait for them on the tree where their bikes leaned.

As much as they had invaded this family's privacy already, Jake would have felt strange not to knock before entering. So he knocked upon the glass balcony door. Alvara then handed back the handkerchief, spotted with blood. "Thanks, Jake."

"You should probably leave that on a bit longer, Alvara."

"What? It's fine," she said, and she lifted her hand to show him. The skin was unbroken and smooth. No hint, no sign could he see that she had hurt it in the first place.

Before he could ask her about it, Mr. Zhu came to the door. He was tall and severe and livid. He opened the glass door a few inches. "You are not welcome here. Get out of my place! Get out!" Still yelling, the man came through the door, picked up a potted plant, and threw it at Alvara's head.

She yelped and fell backwards off the balcony, and the man turned to take a swing at Jake. Jake threw himself backward against the edge of the balcony to dodge the man's blow, and felt a sharp pain as his wing was twisted between his body and the concrete wall. Before the man could strike another blow, Jake shoved hard on the man's chest, sending him sprawling back through the open glass door and into the apartment with a loud crash.

Hoping his wing wasn't seriously damaged, Jake braced himself and vaulted over the edge of the balcony. After a twinge of pain his wings held, and he angled for where Alvara stood, wings folded, face a mask of worry. Adrenaline coursed through his body in response to the intensity of Mr. Zhu's anger. Jake tried to catch his breath as he came to rest next to Alvara.

"Are you all right?" Alvara asked, eyes darting over him and looking for injuries.

"Fine," Jake said, grabbing Alvara in a quick hug. "But let's not hang around here."

Laerik glided down and landed on Jake's shoulder. "What happened, did you meet her? I didn't even see you leave. That was fast," she said.

"No, her husband wasn't pleased to see us. He attacked us," Jake said.

"Oh no!" Laerik said, nuzzling Jake's cheek. Her feathers were scratchy and cool.

"Ultimate fail," Alvara muttered, "I can't believe he chased us off like that." She was shaking, and blinking away tears. Jake knew how she felt; he was feeling unsteady himself. He had never been treated like that before.

Laerik clacked her beak. "You guys just need to think smaller. Back in a bit." She flew off toward the building.

Alvara watched Laerik ascend. "No way will that guy let a bird in when he screamed at us like that. I wonder what she's up to."

"No idea, but she's surprised us before." He closed his wings and sat against a building, leaning against his wings for support. The downy feathers were better than an easy chair. Alvara joined him, mirroring his pose. Jake kept one eye out for Mr. Zhu or any other pursuers, but he only saw scattered individuals returning from work to apartments scattered along the street. None paid he or Alvara much attention.

The sky darkened, and beams of color bled across the tops of the buildings across the street. Lights filled the apartments. He felt strangely peaceful, sitting there with Alvara letting the night fall. He was almost sad to see Laerik fly back and swoop down to land next to them on the sidewalk. She puffed up her chest with pride and spat out a roll of paper.

"Thank me later," she said, "you've got a meeting to make. Or, you know, thank me now, and again later, whatever you like."

Jake took the paper and unrolled it, and Alvara leaned over to read with him. Jake blinked a few times, because what he saw were Chinese characters scrawled across the paper. Yet he could understand their meaning as a whole, without knowing any Chinese himself. After staring at the symbols for a moment, the knowledge entered his mind: she would like to meet them. If they walked two blocks north and three blocks west, they would reach a small park, where she would join them in a half hour. She had signed it with the two characters that spelled "Biyu."

"You rock, Laerik," said Alvara, and Jake knew she had understood the Chinese as well. Laerik straightened the feathers on one wing with her beak, glancing up to nod before finishing her grooming. "Do you ever stop preening?" Alvara asked, exasperated.

Laerik shrugged. "A lady has to keep clean. Let's go," she said.

They stood and leapt from the empty street into the sky, and their wing beats echoed off the nearby buildings in the quiet night air. Two up and three over, Jake thought. He could see the trees already. He rubbed his hands over his arms as he flew, as the night had grown chilly, and checked for witnesses to their flight. Though scattered cars rumbled down the streets below, no faces turned up to watch.

Jake found a place to touch down, and used powerful wing strokes for a gentle landing. The park, though no more than half a residential block, was landscaped with an eye to serenity. A geometric convergence and divergence of pathways disappeared into the gloom. Isolated street lamps reminded Jake of lighthouses amid a sea of black. Crickets made a harsh intrusion to the silence, even in comparison to the loud rush of the wind during flight. They waited for a few minutes, before hearing a sound down a path to their left.

A woman walked towards them, her steps tentative. She was in her mid-forties, and beautiful, with high cheek bones and dark hair in a braid almost to her waist. She gasped when she noticed their wings, and put a hand to her mouth.

"A bird came to speak to me," she said. Her voice was musical. "I often speak with birds, and so I listened. Though she told me of them, your wings surprise me." Yet that wasn't what she had said. It was a bit disorienting to hear her speak in Mandarin, but still have the understanding enter his mind in English. He found if he didn't think so hard about it, the meaning came easier.

"Thank you for coming to meet with us, I'm sorry we scared you," said Jake.

"I am also sorry for how my husband greeted you, you must forgive him. Please, welcome to Shanghai. It is a blessing that we can understand one another. My name is Zhu Biyu, but you may address me as Biyu."

"My name is Jake, and this is Alvara," Jake said.

"What lovely names, this Alvara and Jake."

"That's very kind. We've traveled a long way to meet you, Biyu. We wanted to show you that you do not have to be alone," and Jake spread his wings, careful not to hit anything. Alvara gave tribute to his words with a less dramatic wing flick of her own.

Biyu's response was tears, though Jake at first thought it was a trick of the low light. She bent her head, but did not lift a hand to wipe them away as they dripped onto her blouse.

"Biyu, please don't cry," Alvara said. "Having wings is a blessing, and a great one. It can bring joy to so many people, sometimes people with no hope at all before you show up. I know it can get lonely, but now you have us to share it with." She walked toward Biyu, but Biyu held up a hand to stop her.

"Wings have never been a blessing to me, but only a curse," she stated, though the tension in her posture bespoke some strong emotion.

Biyu did not look at them as she spoke. "I kept my wings a secret from my husband, all these years. He did not seem to see them, but I took care to make them small and discreet, just in case. Two nights ago, I decided to show him my secret, to be fully married with my husband." She finally met Jake's eyes. "My husband Huaide is a good man, though he often screams at me. Yet on that night he did not yell, he just stared at me and said, 'You dishonor yourself, and you dishonor me. This shame is not tolerable.' He could not allow the possibility of my secret to be discovered, because it would ruin his belief in a balanced and successful home, and so that night he tore the wings from my back." Alvara gasped, but Biyu ignored her and continued.

"When they came, these wings brought nothing but sorrow, and now they bring a fading pain. The broken edges have grown back these past two nights, but each time they bring less pain and are harder to see. I think they will disappear and never come back. I pray for this."

Jake didn't know what to say. "Please, you can look," Biyu said. She lowered the back of her blouse and turned to expose her shoulder blades. One wing bone fragment stuck out farther than the other; both contained bits of gristle, caked blood, and some down feathers, but nothing more.

"Ouch," Laerik muttered and flew over to Biyu's shoulder. She nuzzled her cheek, and Biyu let her, before Laerik returned to a nearby branch.

Jake was afraid to get closer, afraid almost that her tragedy would somehow reach out to affect his life. Alvara stepped forward.

"I am so sorry, Biyu. You didn't deserve this, and your husband doesn't deserve you if he treats you like this. If there's anything either of us can do, then we'll do it, just ask," she said, and attempted a smile.

"Oh, Alvara, Jake, now that we are friends, we must exchange a feather. It seems right, I think, that we do this. I have few feathers left, but I can manage two." She glanced toward Laerik, but the raven shook her head and bowed. So Biyu reached behind her back, wincing in pain, and came back with two soft downy feathers, one yellow, the other a red so deep it was almost black, before covering her shoulders again.

Jake reached behind him to grab a mottled brown feather from the underside of one wing, and exchanged it for the red down feather, which he put in a pocket of his wallet. Alvara passed over a snowy white feather for the yellow one. She was right, Jake thought; it did feel somehow fitting. He couldn't imagine what Biyu had gone through, and yet she was still offering them friendship.

"Biyu, you are an extraordinary woman, and it has been a pleasure to meet you. We also came to warn you; a man wrote me an angry letter about using my wings, and we wondered if he had managed to contact you as well."

"No," she said, "no one has contacted me about my wings. And if they are worried about use . . ." she shrugged. "I will not be using any wings ever again, if these disappear as they seem to be doing." She saw their faces. "But please, do not feel bad for me; my husband loves me very much, and these wings no longer bring me any joy; I feel freer now that I am liberated of them."

Alvara bit her lip but didn't reply; Jake too wondered how Biyu could stay married to such a man. "Thank you for speaking with us, Biyu," Jake said. "But we have so many questions, I'd love it if we can meet sometime again."

She stopped smiling. "No," she said, "I do not think that would be wise. I am already late to return home." She gathered her shawl around herself and turned to walk away, not even saying goodbye. He tried not to blame her, but her rapid departure still stung. She had as good as said she hoped they never met again. It was such a waste. Jake searched the trees for Laerik, but before he could find her, he heard his name and turned around.

It was Biyu. She looked anywhere but directly at him as she spoke. "Please, take this card," she said. "It has the name and address of a man who was very helpful to me. Very helpful. He knows a lot about us, and may be able to help you too." She handed Jake the card, and as he reached to take it, his hand brushed hers for the first time—

Unseen hands grabbed his shoulders and threw him backwards, and his vision clouded for a moment as his eyes went dark. He opened them and blinked a few times, but colors stayed fuzzy around the edges. Jake could see that he was nowhere near the park of a moment ago, but was standing against a wall in the living room of an apartment.

It was old-fashioned and austere, with only two couches facing a small plastic table. There was a picture of Mao framed on the wall, a few books on a shelf and a small table with a TV. Jake could see out to a balcony covered in plants, and realized he must be standing in Biyu's apartment. The sun had not yet set; its fading light streamed horizontally through the tops of the windows.

Jake saw Biyu with her husband, Huaide. He was pacing between the couches, and she stood behind a couch, pleading and asking for forgiveness. Neither of them glanced at him, even when he waved his hands over his head and shouted "Hey!" at the top of his lungs. When the sun set and Biyu grew magnificent, multi-faceted and colorful wings, Jake realized what he was witnessing; a memory. And he knew what came next.

"Huaide, please, we needed the money!" Biyu pleaded, and Huaide waved a pile of bills and slammed them down on the table, yelling in Mandarin. That didn't sound like part of the story Biyu had told to them.

"No, that's not true, I would never do that. I can still help—" Huaide cut her off by slapping her, but she barely registered it. He pointed at her and moved until he was right in her face, and spoke some harsh words. Jake wished he could understand what Huaide was saying; half of the conversation wasn't enough. Biyu's eyes got wide, and she turned to run, but her husband grabbed her by the wing and pulled her back. She didn't turn to fight, just tried to escape, but he held her fast.

He then spoke with a grave solemnity. Jake could tell it wasn't directed at Biyu, but at someone or something unseen; he glanced heavenward and then closed his eyes as he spoke, pulling from the sheath on the table a ceremonial-looking dagger. It glinted dully in the evening light. "Stop!" Jake cried out involuntarily, though he knew these scenes had already occurred. The dagger came down upon her wing, splitting the bone with the first blow.

Biyu screamed, but Huaide held her still while he hit the wing again, causing the bone to fully sever and the wing to come off in his hand.

"Please," Biyu sobbed through gritted teeth. "I did it for us. The wings of Feng Huang are too precious to squander. At least let me finish what I've started; I can be honest, just believe in me again." She turned to reach out a hand to rest on his arm.

He held her arm close, but then he pushed it away, and barked a short phrase in Mandarin. She trembled, and Jake watched in horror as Huaide broke off her other wing. It was terrible to see Biyu lying on the floor, and be unable to help her.

He hadn't noticed before, but Jake didn't see Biyu's first wing anywhere. As he watched, the second wing dissolved in Huaide's hand. Huaide grunted in satisfaction, and caressed Biyu's hair with surprising tenderness. Then he walked out of the room, leaving his wife on the floor.

She lay there, breathing in short gasps and bleeding into the rug, as the moon rose into the sky. The moonlight was too harsh, Jake thought, almost like the sun in daylight. He reached up to shield his eyes as the room got too bright to bear.

When he could see again, a woman sat cross-legged on the rug with a sleeping Biyu cradled on her lap. She had dark hair one moment and a silvery blonde the next, which flowed over and around a circlet on her head and down to her waist. She was wearing a gown of some sort, though Jake couldn't tell the color in the light. Jake couldn't see her face, because her silhouette was dark in the brightness of the moon.

She spoke, with a voice both warm and so very cold. "Hush, hush, my child. Curse you, daughter! Bless you, always. Sleep with the sweetest dreams, hope with the blackest feathers; you've lost your wings and found your freedom at last. Such pain, such pain, little toy phoenix, is your reward and your price for both our sorrows. Rest, and never rise to start wildfires again. May your new brother or sister appreciate the gift you forsook." Her eyes unfocused, and she sighed. She kissed Biyu on the forehead and lay her to rest on the rug with tenderness. Biyu's wing fragments had stopped bleeding, and she relaxed into peaceful slumber.

The woman stood and turned to look directly at Jake. Before he had a moment to wonder how, she spoke to him. "Jake, find me where the sun may stay long after it sets." And she was gone, in a sudden swell of soft light.

"—Now I must go," and Biyu disappeared into the night before Jake could say anything. Though shaken from the sudden displacement of the vision, he examined the card in his hand. Its worn edges were soft with use, and he saw Chinese characters and a picture of a window; it was some kind of advertisement. He turned the card over and saw a man's name and address scrawled in an untidy hand, with a few characters of Chinese beneath those. There was an English translation, and he squinted to read it in the dim light: "For help taking flight."

Chapter 10

"Jake, is it necessary to be this scientific?" Alvara asked. They sat across from each other at a restaurant Jake had sworn served breakfast. However, breakfast in China meant dumplings. Alvara had her cell phone timer up, and her finger hovered over the start button. She would have greatly preferred to continue injecting coffee directly into her bloodstream.

"Alvara," Jake said, holding his pocket knife to his forearm. "We have to figure out if the speed at which your cut healed yesterday is general to all people who grow wings, or specific to you. Because it's not normal."

"But do you have to . . . oh that is just wrong," Alvara said as Jake dragged the knife through layers of skin. Blood welled up in the injury and dripped down his arm towards his hand. Jake pressed a towel to the cut as Alvara started the timer. She glanced around the dimly-lit restaurant, but their booth was moderately private.

As they waited, Jake checking the cut every few seconds for signs of closure, Alvara's mind came awake and whirred with the complex events of the day before. Jake's explanation of his vision had only left Alvara with more questions. Biyu had clearly withheld some facts about her husband and the loss of her wings. Yet Alvara still felt sorry for her. The image of Biyu's brutalized wings flashed in Alvara's mind, and she felt a pang of nausea. She was definitely done with the dumplings.

"Healed," Jake said, awe in his voice.

Glancing down at her timer, Alvara said, "One minute. That's unreal." They both looked at the bloody towel and Jake wadded it up and shoved it in his pocket.

"I wonder what the limit is," Jake mused.

"Um, let's not test that right now, okay?" Alvara said with some alarm. "I haven't finished my coffee yet."

Jake chuckled. "You're right, we'll just keep tabs on it." It was cool, and a little strange, how comfortable Alvara was around him. Most adults, foremost her aunt, always made demands on her, be it time or attention or work. Jake asked very little of her beyond her company in this strange adventure, and she was glad to give it.

"You're thinking about that vision," Alvara accused, sipping her lukewarm cup.

"Sure," Jake said, attempting to use the chopsticks to pick up another dumpling, then giving up and spearing them one at a time.

"That whole evening was crazy," Alvara said definitively.

Jake rubbed his chin, his face curving into a frown. "I think the vision means we're on the right track. And the woman in the vision . . . she was something else." Jake said. "I know you aren't sure about this Goddess idea, but I swear to you, Alvara, she did not feel like a normal human being."

Alvara let out a breath. "I understand," she said, though inside her mind was in turmoil.

"How do you feel about checking out that card Biyu gave us?"

"I don't trust her. She wasn't honest with us, and she's staying with a husband who ripped her wings off," Alvara shuddered.

"I know. She's got her own agenda, and we haven't figured it out yet. But maybe this man will have information we can use; maybe he'll know how to get in contact with that woman I saw." A frowning waitress interrupted their conversation as she took their bun steamers, side plates, and credit card. She muttered to herself in Chinese as she walked away, and Alvara was reminded of the odd sensation of hearing Biyu speak and simply understanding. Clearly it didn't transfer.

Jake stared off into space again, deep in the memory of his special vision, and Alvara felt suddenly annoyed. "Jake, I know you're, like, dying to meet her now. Especially after she gave you that deliciously cryptic message, 'Jake, find me where the sun may stay long after it sets,' without ever saying what she meant." Alvara took a deep breath, trying to calm her tone. "But don't just assume that she will help us. We need to be careful."

"Of course we'll be careful," Jake said cheerfully. The check arrived and he signed it without looking at it. "But let's go meet this man, keep our inquiries general, and see what turns up. Fair?"

"Sure, you're the boss," Alvara replied, and her phone buzzed. An email from Max had arrived; score one for the restaurant Wi-Fi.

"Anything interesting?" Jake asked.

"Just an email from Max," Alvara said, and blushed, thinking of her goodbye at the airport.

Thankfully, the email didn't mention the airport at all. Their cover story remained intact, as Max had slept over at his friend's house in another city. They had eaten so many malted milk balls the other night they had nearly passed out, and he hoped she was learning 'de-flight-ful' information about stuff. She winced at the terrible pun. And he missed her.

She ignored the warmth spreading into her chest and lifting the edges of her eyes, and emailed him back, saying he was a dork and that she missed him too. Alvara also mentioned meeting Biyu, though she wasn't ready to explain what had happened to Biyu's wings yet. Alvara watched Jake scroll through news stories on his phone. He noticed her attention.

"When the biggest news is that the moon is a hundred meters closer to the Earth than normal, I call that a good day for the human race," Jake said, stretching.

The taxi halted in front of a four-story dilapidated office building, one of the many uninspired tan concrete bunkers squashed into the narrow industrial street. Chinese characters on a sign near the entryway were followed by the English words 'Zhong Offices'.

Alvara squinted at the structure through the harsh afternoon light. "If they cleaned off the pigeon droppings and gave it a new coat of paint, it would at least reach the level of boring," she said. Jake grimaced and handed the cab driver a few yuan.

As the door was unlocked, Alvara let herself in to a small lobby, which was decorated with a side table containing a vase of fake flowers and a framed page of calligraphy. Stairs led up and to the left, while a display board on the right listed business room numbers in white lettering. Xiu Li was the only business listed on the third floor, confirming the listing on Jake's card. The smell was a battle between Pine Sol and mildew.

Jake had already started up the stairs, and Alvara jogged to catch up. At the top of the stairs, Jake was waiting for her, holding the door. They walked out together into another hallway, which angled left to a single door at the end.

Alvara pushed it open, revealing a cheery little office. The light green of the walls complemented the small potted plant on the counter, and three chairs rested against the wall, facing a huge desk covered in papers. Other than the door they entered, two doors led off the room, both on the back wall. A young man, not more than 30, sat at the desk, writing and mumbling to himself. As he heard them come in, he glanced up and smiled, saying, "Hello, please sit down and we can talk in a moment. Do you have a card?" Jake handed him the card from Biyu and the man nodded and smiled again, gesturing for them to have a seat. Alvara noticed that he was one of the handsomest men she had ever seen, with dark hair that fell into his eyes and a confident smile.

She and Jake situated themselves in the chairs, which, in addition to the sterile feel of the place, heightened the impression of being at the doctor's office. The walls were bare except for a large threaded canvas on the wall across from the doorway, which portrayed an ocean sunset in an ecstasy of woven, colored threads. Jake made a sound between a sigh and a grunt, and she found herself looking at Jake, really *looking* at him for perhaps the first time.

He was old, but not ancient; certainly not as old as their running jokes implied. His hair was tending to grey, with some pieces of the deep brown she was sure it used to be, and his wrinkles, which had begun to soften his features, distracted from his discerning blue eyes. Sitting in that chair, leaning back with his hands resting on his thighs, he looked his age.

But Alvara could also see vitality, and strength, in his posture. He was above all reliable, and despite her experience with most of the adults in her life she trusted him instinctively. She had been happy to discover it wasn't just their shared wings that kept them together; Alvara had never met anyone like Jake, and if anyone could unravel the pieces of their purpose, it would be him. That is, if he didn't drive her crazy with the frustratingly paternal way he treated her. She needed a friend, not another father.

The man behind the desk finally raised his head, setting aside his papers. "What can I do for you?" he asked.

"What is it you do here, exactly? Your business card was not very specific," Jake replied.

The man laughed, and Alvara felt like laughing too; his laugh was full of joy, and infectious. "Oh, sir, you have missed my joke. I wrote on the card 'for help taking flight', but, you see, I am a financier! My business is in helping others to finance their dreams, so I help them to 'take flight'. Biyu gave this card to you, yes? She and I have laughed at that joke many times. But I have not introduced myself."

He pushed his chair back and stood to walk over to them. "My name is Xiu Li." Alvara had trouble not beaming as he bowed first to her, and then to Jake, before pulling up the third chair to join them. He leapt forward, until he was just a few feet away. "Would you like some tea?"

"Yes, please," Alvara chimed in just as Jake answered "No, thank you." Xiu Li smiled and went to turn on the electric kettle before sitting once more.

"So how do you know Biyu? And what type of financing?" asked Alvara.

"I love this custom!" Xiu Li held up the tea cup to demonstrate. "It is like we are already friends. Biyu and I have been friends for a long time. Sometimes she comes to me for financial services, and sometimes for advice. You see, financier is my main business, but I do whatever I can to help others reach their full potential. Individuals like Biyu fascinated my father, and he performed extensive research concerning her condition."

"Her condition?" Jake asked.

"It is such an exciting secret. But I am afraid that if she did not tell you, it is not my place to reveal it." Xiu Li shook his head with remorse, and his hair framed his earnest eyes as they stared into Alvara's own.

The kettle hissed, and Xiu Li turned to pour cups for each of them. Alvara realized it was all a charade. Biyu had told this man what they were, but he wanted them to tell him themselves, rather than revealing what he knew in a rude manner.

"It's no secret to us," she said. "We also grow wings."

Jake followed her lead, his voice tight. "That's how we met Biyu in the first place."

"That is such exciting news! It is such an honor to meet the two of you." He wouldn't say more until he had bowed again and handed them both steaming cups of green tea. "Then it would be my pleasure to talk more about Biyu's condition. You see, she is the guardian of Feng Huang!"

"Feng Huang?" Alvara asked.

"It is the phoenix. You know this bird?" Alvara nodded. "Each night Biyu grows the wings of Feng Huang, which represents honesty and loyalty, and is considered to be very good luck."

"That's fascinating," Jake cut in, "but we were wondering what kind of research your father did about people like us."

"Jake, may I call you Jake?"

"I didn't give my name," Jake enunciated.

Xiu Li smiled warmly. "Of course, Biyu spoke about the both of you, I am so pleased to meet you. I have so much to share with you, as I shared with Biyu. Please come with me." And he pushed his chair back and walked over to his desk. He held open the door on the right, and they walked through into a room not much bigger than a sizeable closet.

The walls of the room were plastered with photos and news articles. One was about a search for a white tiger sighted in rural India. Another appeared to do with a mermaid sighting, and looked like the Chinese version of a tabloid, with big, blocky letters for emphasis. Everywhere photocopies from textbooks were intermingled with handwritten notes and arrows connecting distant ideas. It was hard to get a coherent picture of what its purpose was, though Xiu Li stood back and allowed them time to peruse the display. Alvara's eyes drifted over the clippings and copies and came to rest on one in English. It was an excerpt from a textbook on Greek Mythology.

"One of the most compelling myths to endure into our time is that of Daedalus and his son Icarus. Entrapped on the Isle of the Minotaur, Daedalus, a genius inventor and brilliant craftsman, fashioned two sets of wings out of wax and feathers that he found scattered along the shore of the isle. Taking a pair for himself, strapping the other pair to his son's back, he planned their escape. He issued this warning to his son, "Icarus, though we may fly, these wings are made of wax. If you fly . . ." *Too close to the sun*, Alvara thought, and turned back to Xiu Li.

"So . . . you're interested in myths, then?" she asked, unsure as yet how the clippings fit together. It was similar to her own sporadic research, but these documents didn't seem very scientific.

Xiu Li smiled. "Very good, Alvara. But I would not call them myths; they are accounts of truth." Before she could reply, he added, "Not all of them. But my father had a passion for strange and fantastic creatures, and, alas, he passed it on to his son." He turned to Alvara. "I saw you looking at the story of Icarus; a sad one, yes? But," and he smiled, "there exists in it a mistranslation. Can you guess what it was?" He spread his hands, but Alvara wasn't sure what he meant. Jake didn't offer a guess, so Xiu Li continued.

"Daedalus warned Icarus not to fly too close to the sun, but it was not because they had crafted their wings from wax. Their wings were flesh and blood, but could not exist after sunrise. Icarus, in his youth and folly, flew too close to sun*rise* and lost his wings, plummeting to his death in the ocean below."

It was a dramatic restructuring of the myth Alvara remembered, but it fit with the facts she knew; Icarus and his father had been like them! They were part of a history that was very, very old. "Wow," she said.

"We can't jump to any conclusions," Jake said. "Where did you learn this account of the story?"

"I understand it is a lot to take in. I can show you the documentation another time; it is from a Greek manuscript from the 4th century BCE. But here, this is one that I discovered only recently. It is from the 1560's, England."

He handed them a high-definition photograph of the original orange vellum, as well as a translation from Middle English made during the late 18th century. Jake and Alvara leaned over to read the translation.

The page began mid-sentence.

" . . . *the benevolent hand of Our Father that showed me his whereabouts, though the man had attempted to waylay me. The sun was nearing the horizon when I came upon him, and the hovel in the wood where he had taken some shelter from the winds. Though I asked for him to return with me, and offered him shelter and what food we had to share, he would not agree. He had about him a haggard look, and begged me to leave him to die. I approached him, but he cowered like a beaten hound, and so I stopped. He gave a shriek, and I covered my ears at the sound. When I next glanced at him, he had performed some foul spell, sprouting wings like a demon. He shrank back from the sign of the Lord, and flew off into the night. It is with renewed vigor that I do His work, in this . . .*"

Jake had finished reading first, and when Alvara glanced over at him, he was staring into space, rubbing his chin with one hand, features gaunt in the dim light. She hadn't missed the importance of the monk mentioning that he went to find the man nearing sunset; she wasn't one to believe in coincidences. Alvara thought about the poor man he had found. What could his life have been like, growing wings every night with no idea why? He may have thought he was a demon, cursed to roam the nights without anywhere to call home. Her heart went out to this man she had never met, and she offered a silent prayer that now he rested in peace.

Jake had wonder in his eyes as he took in the rest of the room. "But it's not just wings," he said. "Are you trying to tell me that all the stories on these walls are true?"

"Oh no," said Xiu Li. "Wings are a special hobby of mine; these others are just present as a collection. I do not have the time to indulge myself and discover if they are all true, and Biyu is proof enough of the stories of winged individuals. But please, continue to study the information available here. Would you like to share in dinner?"

Alvara noticed that she was starving. She checked with Jake, and he nodded. "That would be very kind," he muttered, his attention on the book he'd just retrieved from the bookcase.

"I will bring you food even Americans can enjoy." Xiu Li smiled at Alvara as he walked out, and she found herself smiling back. He seemed to be a genuine friend to them, someone they could trust. After he passed by, she got up to begin examining the articles again.

"Alvara, we have to get out of here."

"Jake, what? What's wrong?"

"I don't trust that man, Alvara. He wants something from us."

"Are you kidding? He's one of the nicest guys I've ever met."

"The way he looked at us when he thought we were just reading the entry. It was hungry, Alvara. He needs us, and he's just letting us into his little den to gain his trust." Jake was completely serious.

"Jake, you're full of it. I know you want to be careful," she started.

"Well, I—"

"But we need to trust someone! He just wants to help."

"I have to disagree. We should leave now." He stood up, opened the door to their small room, and strode into the main office. Jake tried the door next to theirs, and leaned his head out again. "Bathroom," he said.

"This isn't some investigation, Jake! Will you sit down?" He ignored her, and walked to the door they had entered. He tried the door.

It was locked.

He came back to the small room behind the desk. "You still think this is just a friendly visit?" he asked.

Her heart started to beat faster. "Maybe he locked it accidentally."

"Maybe he did. But do you want to trust that?"

"No."

"Okay, then we should bide our time and try to find a way out of here. The only window is in the restroom, but it's too small for me to fit through. We could try to break down the front door, but I would rather wait until he comes back and then see what he wants." Jake sat down again next to her.

"Me too—it may not be anything. I hope it's not. Maybe we should pretend we didn't notice and keep reading?" It was strange how the simple fact of a locked door could make the cozy office into a prison.

"It seems like the best plan for now. Let's see if we can learn anything. But be ready to act if he returns." He went back to the book he had grabbed and turned pages with such force that some tore.

She turned back to the wall clippings, her eyes darting across headlines with a heightened sense of urgency. There were a few promising options, and she pulled them off the wall and took them back to her seat. One was an excerpt from a Wiccan worship book, all about the moon and its properties. In it, she learned that moonlight was an essential ingredient to make scrying glasses that could be used to see the future, that moonlight would help improve intuition, and that certain spells requiring moonlight would work best on the night of the full moon. It was crap, so Alvara tossed it aside in favor of the next document.

This one was an email entitled, "Re: crazy stuff I seen." Xiu Li had dated it three years before, and it took Alvara a moment to realize the email was about her.

dude i know u think ima crazy stoner. and, you know its not far from the truth, but i swear on my moms grave i was virtually sober. i was coming home from zachs place but had work 2day so didnt light up so driving was cool. i saw this chick in the sky – she was wearing all white, and i was like whoa and stopped the car and saw her fly over the street, she had freaking wings man then she was gone but i never thought i dreamed it. ill paint her tomorrow and ull c. robbie

A chill passed through her. Though no one would have a reason to believe anything this guy ever said, somehow Xiu Li had gotten this email. She tried to stay calm, slowing her breathing deliberately. But she didn't want to read any more.

"Jake," she whispered. "This email is about me. This guy must have some serious resources." Jake walked over to read it and frowned.

"Not good," he muttered, and went back to the articles.

She spotted a Bible on the shelf, and smoothed its weathered binding. There was a post-it note, and she opened to that verse from Isaiah she knew by heart. Xiu Li had found it too, so it wasn't hers anymore. She shut the book with a thump.

"I can't take this anymore," she blurted. "Where is he? It's been over an hour."

"I'm worried I know the answer." Jake replied.

"Tell me."

"He might be waiting for sunset. After that, I'm not sure."

"But sunset is in fifteen minutes! He should—" But the sound of the door to the office creaking open halted her words. She tried to take a breath to steady herself, and smiled her best smile as Xiu Li walked back in, carrying two blue bowls of rice with some sort of meat on top.

"Apologies for my late arrival. I took the liberty of bringing chopsticks. You want the full experience, yes?"

"Thanks," said Jake, and they both accepted the food. It wasn't lost on Alvara that he hadn't locked the door behind him. She considered making a run for it, but Jake didn't meet her eye. Neither of them touched their food. "So," Jake said, "you seem to have found a lot about these wings. What kind of thing did you help Biyu with?"

"Yes, well you see, she and her husband had some financial troubles, but I have helped them." That must be what Biyu meant when she had said they needed the money, Alvara thought. "I help people realize their dreams, as I have said. You and your friend needed information, and so I have given this to you freely. If you have read, you now know that you are not anomalies, that there have been Children of the Moon throughout human history. In return, I ask a simple gift."

"What gift?" Jake asked. His voice had grown cold.

"All the feathers you grow for the next month or two," he replied. "We'll see how I feel about our debt at that later date." His smile looked as real as before, but Alvara was no longer adrift within it. Now it just gave her the creeps.

"What do you want our feathers for?" Jake asked.

"It is not a use you would understand. Unless you know of Chinese medicine, and that rare parts of animals are very potent."

"I know that this trade you're talking about is the reason most beautiful animals in this part of the world are going extinct," Jake snapped. "So our feathers are just the newest fad, is that it?"

"I am not here to argue with you, Jake. It is not important that you believe in what I sell, but that my customers do. Biyu understood this, and you will too."

"So you stealing her feathers was what she meant by help?" Alvara asked.

"What about if we each give you a feather?" Jake asked. "Will you allow us to leave?"

"This is not a negotiation, Jake, my friend," Xiu Li stated. "This is the price for my information and assistance. And it is a good thought, my dear Alvara," he mentioned, seeing her glance at the door, "but the door locks automatically, and even if it did not, running would be ultimately futile. I have men surrounding the building, in case you should attempt to escape. It is quite unfortunate that Biyu is no longer capable of selling her feathers to anyone, but by sending you to me, Biyu is free to continue in her nice apartment and I can more than make up my losses. And I may reconsider how many feathers I require to let you go, should you prove to be difficult. But I do wish we could all be civil," he said, sitting down and smoothing his suit. "It is something I hear Americans do very well. It will not be long now, no? I look forward to making this as painless, or as painful, as you desire." He smiled and leaned back, glancing at his wristwatch.

Alvara couldn't seem to think clearly. Should they try to make a run for it? Before she could come up with a coherent plan, Jake grabbed her arm and pulled her into the restroom, locking the door behind them.

"Jake," Xiu Li said through the door, "I have the key to that lock; you cannot stay in there forever." Jake glanced around the restroom. It was old, in disrepair, with exposed pipes everywhere. Jake glanced out the one small window, and ducked out of sight of the street below.

"Alvara, listen to me. You have to get out of here," he whispered. "I think you can squeeze through—"

"Are you kidding?"

"You need to get away, and get help, and—"

"Jake, I can't just leave you here! What if he hurts you?"

"Not something we can argue at this point, honey. Do you think you can fit through the window?"

"Maybe, but aren't there guys below?"

"Yes, and armed. You can reach some cover before they can get a clean shot."

"Jake, I'm scared!" Tears of frustration filled her eyes.

Jake leaned his back against the door, bracing himself against the opposite wall. "Alvara, it's okay, time to focus. Go find help." A force slammed into the door, and Jake fell forward a bit, but the door held. "He'll get the door down soon," he said, breathing hard. Their eyes met. "Alvara, you can do this."

She blinked a few times and swallowed hard. "It 'works' for me," she whispered, making quotation marks with her fingers. Jake smiled.

"Atta girl. Don't worry about me, come back soon."

"I will, of course I will," she said. "But, your feathers!"

He smiled wickedly, and it gave her strength. "We'll see how many feathers he can get out of bat wings. Sunset's coming, get gone. Good luck." Jake held the door again as another pound shook the tiny bathroom. Alvara shed her outer jacket. She peeked out the window, and could see a man on the ground, but he wasn't facing up; his eyes were on the rear exit of the building.

Alvara stood on the sink, which creaked under her weight, and got ready to lean out of the window. It would be difficult to time; there was no way she would fit through with wings, and no way she would survive the fall if she didn't have them. She took a deep breath, and felt sunset coming.

Bracing her hands on the edge, she counted down the moments. Then she leaned sideways out through the window, head first. Her hips caught on the window, but her shoulders were through, so her wings grew in, large and powerful. But she was stuck; unable to get out, and prevented from slipping back inside.

The men below would notice any minute, though she tried to make no noise. She heard a shout, and cranked her neck around to see a man gesturing at her furiously. She gasped and strained to pull herself through the window, but only a strong force on her legs allowed her to move. As she scraped free of the window, she heard a concussion behind her. She glanced back to see Jake struggling, men grabbing him through a cloud of dust from the broken door, before she tumbled past the open window.

With a few beats of her wings she righted herself. A man shouted up to her, "We don't want to have to hurt you. Please come down." *Your idea sucks*, she thought. Out of the corner of her eye, she could see the man taking aim with a gun.

She flew at top speed as he tracked her trajectory. She waited for the shot, but felt the air of its passing on her shoulder. She turned to see a pigeon diving at her assailant's head.

Alvara flew, holding her arms close to her body to present a smaller target, every moment expecting the impact of a bullet. Wings and lungs burning, Alvara collapsed behind a ventilation system on an industrial building five or six streets away. Trying to keep it together, she succeeded in steadying her breathing. She listened for pursuit, but heard nothing above the distant hum of traffic. She was alone.

And she had left Jake behind.

Chapter 11

The sun's absence chilled her as Alvara tried to figure out what to do next. She could file a report with the local police that Jake had been kidnapped. But her wings made that risky, and tomorrow morning might be too late. She could try to sneak back to the office, but just the thought of coming within range of those men with guns again made her shake with fear. Alvara jumped as a crow swooped down to land on an exposed pipe nearby, but then she recognized Laerik. Alvara swallowed to keep from crying.

"Laerik, man am I glad to see you," she said, reaching out to stroke the glossy feathers.

Laerik leaned in to her touch. "Sure, me too," she said, "but I thought Jake was with you. What happened?"

"It was a trap," Alvara said. "Xiu Li came across as this researcher of wings, totally friendly, but then he just wanted to take our feathers to sell on some black market, when we wouldn't agree. Jake helped me get away." She swallowed, and bit out the next words, "Jake couldn't fit through the window." It was such a pathetic reason to leave a friend behind.

"Aw, Goddess that's rough. Well, what are we waiting for? Let's go get him," Laerik said.

Alvara's heart sped, but she forced herself to speak normally. "I don't know if I can get close enough without them seeing me. They are probably still looking for me. But you could," Alvara realized suddenly.

"Having a hard time tracking him," Laerik said, "So you show me the building and I'll scope it out."

"Great," Alvara breathed, and allowed herself a brief moment of hope as they leapt into the air.

"Empty?" Alvara repeated, disbelieving. "Are you sure?" She and Laerik hovered above the cloud layer, nearly atop the building, but out of sight of anyone below.

"Fluff, I peered in the windows. Lights off, no one home. And I still can't sense him."

"Has that ever happened to you? Not sensing him?" she asked.

"Sure, sure," Laerik said. "It means he's asleep."

Or something worse. Alvara beat her wings to stay level and felt a rising panic. "So Jake could be anywhere. We don't have evidence, and there's no time to wait for the cops. All we have left is Biyu."

"Didn't she send you to this guy in the first place?" Laerik asked.

"She did. I don't trust her as far as I can throw her. But she might know where Jake is. Which means she's our best bet." Alvara took a deep breath. "So let's go," she said.

They didn't talk much en route. Laerik had a bit of trouble keeping up, so Alvara slowed the pace. The temperature was dropping, and Alvara regretted the loss of her jacket as she hugged her arms.

The apartment wasn't more than a few miles from the industrial district. Alvara flew directly up to the balcony, hoping Biyu would be there and would be willing to talk with them.

She tapped on the glass, and saw a light go on behind the curtain. Huaide pulled the curtain back, and she tensed for another confrontation. When he saw her, his face darkened, and he covered the door with the curtain again. She tapped again, but there was no reply this time.

All the frustration Alvara felt came bubbling to the surface at once, and she smacked her hand on the window until he threw back the curtains again. When he cracked the door, she spoke first.

"Don't you dare yell at me, Zhu Huaide! My friend is in trouble and it's your wife's fault. He needs your help. I need your help. I don't know what else to do," Alvara felt her eyes fill with tears, the anxiety for Jake finally hitting her hard.

Huaide stepped back, as if to shut the door, but instead he muttered, "Come in, my wife is not at home. But no bird." Alvara followed him inside, wiping her eyes with the back of her hand.

He poured two cups of tea and sat down across from her. She didn't dare relax; she had seated herself in the nearest spot to the sliding door exit. She took the tea he poured for her, and sipped it only after he did.

He sipped and set his cup aside. "I do not know you, young woman."

"My name is Alvara," she said.

"You are obviously American, and not someone I would expect to see at my home. But with every rustle of feathers you remind me of my wife, which I will not tolerate." His voice was smooth.

"Why would you destroy your wife's wings like that? How can pride be that important?" Alvara said, frustrated.

"I do not expect that you understand. Those wings brought only harm to our family; her actions shamed me greatly."

"Shamed you? By growing wings?"

She could finally see emotion on his face. It was surprise. "Is that what she said, that I was ashamed?"

Alvara nodded. He put one hand over the other in his lap. "Then she did not even tell the truth to herself." He frowned. "She saw her wings, the wings of Feng Huang, the phoenix, as a great honor. They were beautiful, but I worried that her belief in the supernatural would bring her away from real life." His eyes were taut with sorrow.

"But three days ago, I followed her and found out she had been selling her feathers on the black market for years. She was using them to settle our debts, without my knowledge! Furthermore, she had settled our debt long ago, and had begun to gamble with the feathers, increasing the debt again. I confronted her with the money from her last win, and she told me everything. The magic in the feathers was what drew her away from me, and made her the instrument of her own suffering. So I learned how to give back the gift, to remove them so they wouldn't grow back."

"How could you, Huaide?" asked Alvara, her mind spinning with the new information.

He sipped his tea. "I made the right choice," he said.

Alvara felt that, just maybe, she could trust him. She was willing to take a gamble on it, and hoped she'd win this one. She had been dead wrong about Xiu Li. "I need your help," she admitted. "Biyu sent us to the man who she used to sell to, and he tried to imprison us to harvest our feathers. I got away, but they took Jake. Will you help me find him?"

Huaide sized her up, considering. He swirled his cup and sipped his tea, pausing between each sip. Alvara felt that this deliberation might be necessary in some way, so she held her tongue and stayed still through a sheer force of will. When Huaide finished his tea a couple of minutes later, he said, "I know of two locations that this man did business with my wife. I will come with you to see."

"Thank you," Alvara exclaimed. "Let's go," she stood, her wings billowing out behind her.

"One moment," Huaide said, and cleared the tea. He returned, slipping a small handgun into a holster as he walked.

"You have a gun?" Alvara breathed, disconcerted.

"I have a friend who is Jingcha, a cop. He got me the hunting permit. I was afraid for my wife," Huaide added, "with good sense, it now seems."

"Great," she said in a small voice, and followed him out the front door and down the stairs to the garage. Alvara hoped she was correct in trusting Huaide as she got into his car, adjusting her seat to accommodate her wings. She waved out the window to Laerik as they sped into the night.

Huaide didn't speak as he made one turn after another, taking them from a residential district to a forgotten freeway underpass littered with trash. They passed tarp-covered homeless, wrapped in scarves and jackets, huddled around fires or sleeping on the dirt. Alvara closed her eyes and prayed for their mission, and for Jake, and she felt a peace settle around her despite her worry.

Huaide turned off the headlights before making a final turn, coasting to a stop before a rectangular warehouse with no visible markings. Alvara could see light coming through evenly spaced windows, but no one was visible outside the building.

"This is it?" Alvara whispered.

Huaide nodded curtly. "We will see if your friend is inside. Then we will get him out."

Alvara almost asked for more details, but Huaide had already stepped out of the car. She took a deep breath and followed him across the street, her eyes scanning for any sign of movement.

As they picked their way closer to one of the windows, Alvara heard a voice grumbling in Chinese. Another man's voice replied. So at least two people waited inside. She crouched down below the window, making sure to keep her wings pressed to her back. Huaide joined her and gestured from her to the window.

Alvara, heart racing, slowly peeked over the window ledge. She blinked to adjust to the bright lights, squinting until she could make out the scene inside. Three men lounged in folding chairs, each carrying a gun. None was Xiu Li. A fourth man sat facing Alvara, slumped forward, unmoving, hands tied behind his back. Though she couldn't see his face or his wings, Alvara recognized Jake.

She crouched down again, trying to get her breathing under control. "Jake's here," she whispered to Huaide. "We have to help him." After the bright interior, she couldn't make out Huaide's expression.

"Stay down," Huaide whispered. Then he projected harsh, authoritative words in Chinese. A loud voice responded, and bullets ricocheted through the window above their heads.

Alvara screamed and flattened herself to the dirt. Huaide shouted, "They did not believe that I am Jingcha. I am sorry." He pulled out his gun, but Alvara could see his hands tremble.

"Please," she whispered, praying aloud into the night. "Please God, please help us. We need you."

Alvara's gasped as a strange sensation shuddered through her. Her gut clenched, her back arched, and goosebumps rose across her flesh. The sensation left her, and she slumped over, exhausted.

The bullets stopped, and she heard voices begin to shout in Chinese, but she could hear the terror in their cries. The voices receded until silence returned. Alvara felt a hand on her shoulder, and she flinched.

"Are you hurt?" Huaide asked, eyes scanning her for bullet holes.

"Fine," Alvara breathed, still processing her body's response to the conflict.

Huaide glanced through the window and crouched again. "They are gone," he said.

"What happened? Why did they leave?" Alvara asked, pushing herself up into a standing position on unsteady feet.

"They yelled about demons," Huaide said, giving her a long look. "Then they ran."

Alvara could worry about that later. "They might come back, we have to get Jake," she said, stumbling toward the nearest door and hauling it open.

"Jake!" she yelled, and ran over to him. The small bat wings on his back looked broken, but at least they were still attached. When she laid a hand on his shoulder, he groaned and opened one black eye.

"Late for the party," he mumbled, though his mouth was so swollen he garbled the words. He peered at her, squinting. "Glad you're okay."

"I'm not the one who got left behind! Oh, Jake, I'm so sorry. Let me help you." She tried to untie his hands, but the knots were caked in blood. That was the moment Laerik swooped in, cawing in dismay. Huaide followed, pulling out a pocket knife to cut the bonds.

Once free, Jake flexed his fingers and wiggled his wrist a bit and winced, but his injuries began to heal as she watched.

"Huaide," said Jake after Alvara had helped him to his feet.

"Do you need hospital?" Huaide said.

"I should be okay," Jake responded, flexing his wrists.

"I have to leave," said Huaide, and turned to go.

"Thank you for helping us. You didn't need to do that," said Jake. His injuries were healing quickly, and he rolled his shoulders and brushed some dried blood off his temple.

Huaide stared at him, considering. "The girl needed help and I could not refuse her," he said softly.

"How did you know how to cut off Biyu's wings?" Jake asked. "The words you said, using the dagger, even the solemnity of it? It sounded like a ritual. Because normally her wings would grow back, isn't that right?"

"Why are you asking me this?" Huaide retorted, glancing away.

"Because we want to know where you got the information," Alvara said. "Whoever told you might be able to tell us more about who we are."

"Stop trying to find your destiny," Huaide said, gesturing at Jake, "those you care about will get hurt. Go back to your life in America, and just live. You have a long time to go." He walked away, but Alvara called out again.

"Please, Huaide! At least allow us to talk with this person! We'll be leaving soon and will be out of your way. But there may be some actual good we can do in this world! Please help us."

Huaide sighed. "So stubborn, you cannot see when I am trying to help you. But I will send your information to the man you spoke of. He can decide whether to contact you or not. I'll just need your phone number."

"Mine has service here," Jake replied.

It was a strange exchange, Alvara thought, as she watched an older man covered in dried blood and with bat wings give his phone number to a well-dressed Chinese man with a holstered sidearm. A very strange exchange.

"Thanks, Huaide. I don't know what I would have done without you tonight," said Alvara.

Huaide nodded, but his brow furrowed as he looked at Alvara. The men had run off screaming about demons, and Alvara felt a chill pass over her as she wondered why. Huaide turned and walked to his car, driving away into the night. Laerik flew down to perch on Alvara's shoulder.

"So are you really all right?" Alvara asked, examining Jake for any obvious injuries and finding none.

"Yeah, I'm all right. Though a bit worried about the fact that Xiu Li cut off a piece of my wing and took off with it. The man is batty, I tell you."

After a short delay, she chuckled half-heartedly. "If you can talk in puns, you must be feeling better." Laerik groaned.

"All I need is some sleep," Jake said with a yawn.

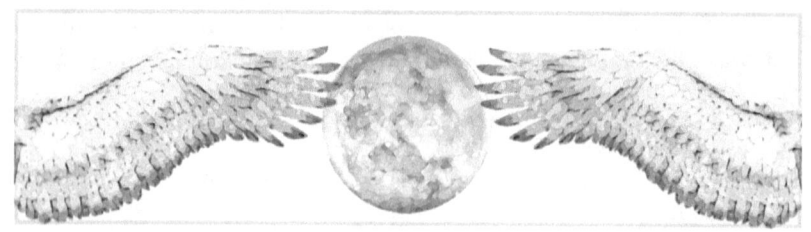

Chapter 12

Jake stretched, the bones in his arms and shoulders popping. The bed had been comfortable enough, but his chair in the lobby could use an extra pillow. He craved a hot shower, though the one the night before had gotten off all the blood.

He didn't think he'd ever be rid of that man's filth, of the sickly sweet of his smile as he broke the bones in Jake's wings one at a time. Jake deliberately picked up his cup of tea and pushed away the memory.

When Alvara finally wandered down to meet him in the lobby, he passed her a cup of now lukewarm coffee. She blinked slowly and nodded in thanks, and they sipped their drinks in silence.

"You feeling any better?" Alvara asked.

"Physically, all back to normal," Jake forced a smile.

"Good," Alvara said, frowning.

"The man at the front desk handed this to me this morning," Jake said, keeping his voice neutral. "Said someone had left it for us earlier last night." He waited while she read.

Jake Coughlin:

Perhaps I was not clear in my previous letter. Or perhaps you are distracted, wondering if that flight attendant from the flight to Shanghai will decide to turn you in; she was very helpful in locating you. Whatever the excuse, my patience is running thin. It is imperative that you discontinue use of your ability in the next twenty-four hours, or I will be forced to use any means necessary to guarantee it, including the removal of your friend from your amiable company forever. Contact me, Jake, so that we might know each other better, or I will do more than contact you. This is your last warning. You have until sunset tomorrow.

Regards,
Mr. Robert Noon
Legion of the Light

When the front door of the hotel clanged open, both Jake and Alvara jumped, but it was just a middle-aged man in khakis. She tried to cover her nerves. "Who does this creep think he is? Some kind of magic cop?"

"Alvara, this man is powerful. Maybe the flight attendant did work for him, or maybe he just convinced her to talk, but he's closing in on us." Jake shook his head, wondering for the third or fourth time this morning why Robert hadn't just waited around at the hotel for them to return last night. Alvara looked like she was trying hard not to think about it. "In all of Shanghai, he found us at our hotel; he has resources we don't know about, and keeping up with us is no challenge." He took a deep breath. "I hate to say it, but if we don't get any info from Huaide's friend today, we may have to contact this man. I don't want you to get hurt."

"I don't want to get hurt either. But I still hate how cold he sounds. There's no way I'd want to give in to him; we don't know what he would do with us. I am so sick of everyone trying to take advantage of us," she said bitterly.

"For now let's just hope we have a backup plan before sunset." With nothing more to decide in the moment, Jake figured it was time to change the subject.

"So, plan for the day," Jake said. "How about some sightseeing?"

"Jake, is this a joke to you?" Alvara asked. She wasn't smiling.

"I just thought after everything, we could use a bit of down time," he explained.

At a glance to a young couple who were walking past them, Alvara lowered her voice. "You could have died last night, Jake. I almost didn't find you," she said, her voice growing hoarse with emotion. She closed her eyes for a moment.

Jake sighed. "I know," he said. "But you did. Somehow, I knew you would. I guess you could say I had faith."

Alvara managed a smile. "Me too. It's nice to be right."

Jake laughed. "Sorry I made light of it. What would you like to do today?"

"I think it's called keeping a low profile," Alvara said. "Xiu Li's men might still be looking for us, and Robert Noon knows about this hotel. I think we should check out and get a new one."

"Good idea," Jake agreed. "And hope Huaide's friend gets back to us before sunset."

"Exactly," Alvara said. "I think that's my cue to find some non-dumpling breakfast from that café next door. And yes, I'll be careful," she added before Jake could argue.

"I could use a muffin," he said instead, and she rolled her eyes and clanged through the front door. He watched her through the lobby windows until she disappeared into a building that looked like a strange mashup of a Chinese food restaurant and a Denny's, with a diner structure covered in bright red lettering.

Thinking Alvara could use some time alone, Jake dug through the bin in the lobby for an English newspaper. No article in particular caught his eye, and so he settled in to read an editorial on children's belief structures in the modern world.

The article spoke about the recent outcry against Disney movies and fairy tales, and the increase in popularity of motivated, life-oriented literature. Jake kept reading about how children were more balanced as they grew up if they were 'able to ground themselves more firmly in reality' with childish tales on how to work hard at chores and balance a budget.

He couldn't believe this crap, but found to his surprise that the article quoted a member of the Legion of the Light. According to the article, the Legion was a conservative organization with a young woman as their spokesperson. Fresh out of law school at 24, she was considered a prodigy. Her name was Isabella Dusk. Could she be the "I" who had threatened them in the first letter?

The article quoted her as saying, "It is the responsibility of those who have been through the system to reveal the system's faults, and as such, the privilege and duty of every responsible adult to enable his or her child to grow up free of the fetters of unrealistic fantasy. Only with these educational improvements can we build a better future, with more adults who are suited to the realities of a modern world, and equipped with the skills and perspective needed to improve that world."

At the sound of the door, Jake looked up to see Alvara. She handed him a bag that smelled of fresh blueberries, but she looked concerned.

"Jake, look at this text from my aunt," she said.

"That's one text?" he asked, seeing the paragraphs.

"She always does it like that. Just read," Alvara insisted.

> *Alvara,*
>
> *I hope you are having a good time with Max, and that you are enjoying all the hikes you two are having planned. You need to keep up the exercise or you will be having to be careful with your figure. How has it been spending time with Jake and his family? He seems like a nice man, I hope you have not been making for him too much trouble.*
>
> *Pues, I got a very strange phone call last night, which is why I am emailing. The children's hospital from downtown called. Many children there have been talking about you. They said, and I am not making this up, that you had wings and were their 'guardian angel' and that you have helped to make them better. What have you been doing to them, Alvara? The hospital people are wanting to talk to you, Alvara, so make sure you talk with them when you are done with the camping and tell them you will not be visiting with them again. It is strange, with these dying kids who are now doing fine, that they had a vision of you. It seems you are the good influence, this time, but you will need to work harder after this trip so that you can make your own way in the world.*
>
> *Tía Alicia*

"Jake, it could be a big problem if someone believes these kids," Alvara said when he looked up.

"You're not kidding. You should be careful; if those kids are talking about your wings that man will have found out about it by now."

"Yes, but read it again."

Jake did, and felt a chill spread down his spine. "Oh. Dying kids," he said. "Curing a terminal illness is a whole different ball game than cuts and scrapes. This is huge, this . . ." Jake had a sudden thought. "Alvara, you didn't happen to give any of the kids one of your feathers, did you?"

"It seemed nice, finishing a visit with giving them something to hold on to . . . wait, wait. You don't think . . ."

"The feather is responsible? I think it must be."

"But that means that Xiu Li is not just a crazy drug dealer. These feathers really are worth a fortune! Jake, we need to be even more careful."

"Think of what we could do with these feathers, Alvara. We could give them away to those who need them, not saying where they are from."

"Whoa, remember Tess, who met us on the beach? I gave her a feather, and she had barely a scratch from a massive knee surgery and virtually no physical therapy! And the surgery was only a couple weeks before we saw her that day, fully healed. Heck, I'll just walk through the hospital next time I'm there, passing them out. Finally, a real sign that these wings have some higher purpose," she smiled.

"No, Alvara. You couldn't do that."

"Why not?"

"We have stumbled into incredible power; it's hard to even see all the implications. If these feathers can cure terminal illness, then they would change the face of the planet. Not just people who are dying would want them. Don't you see? Everyone would want one. Where's the limit?"

"Whoa. I didn't think . . . I mean, we don't grow that many feathers. How could we choose who gets them?"

"And would they even let us choose? If word got out . . . it's a whole lot bigger than just helping children in one hospital. It's too much, thinking through all the implications. We'll talk about this later; remind me, okay? For now, restrain yourself from hawking feathers in the city streets."

Jake heard Alvara groan as he glanced down at his phone. "I'm starting to worry that this guy hasn't contacted us yet," he said.

"Can I see your phone?" Alvara asked. Jake passed it to her, and she smirked at it.

"Jake? You do realize that you have to add the hotel wifi in order to get messages, right?"

It was Jake's turn to groan. Alvara passed him the phone and picked up the newspaper he had been reading. As soon as Jake agreed to the terms, a reply to his email appeared. It consisted of four lines.

Whose is the face that's always facing?
Whose is the dark road ever tracing?
Whose is the lonely white wolf's ode?
Whose is the light that's always borrowed?

What the hell, Jake thought. Was this man playing some sort of game with him? He read the lines again, and felt a riddle. The first line didn't really tell him much, and the second didn't speak to him either. Wolves usually travel in packs, so what did the lonely wolf part indicate? He moved on to the last line. A light that's always borrowed . . . a mirror always borrowed light, but he couldn't make that fit the other three lines. A candle borrowed light from a match, and a lake, the ocean, and a lover's eyes borrowed light as well, but none of them got him anywhere. He went back to the wolf, the lonely wolf. An ode, what was an ode again? It was a song. He knew the answer. The moon.

It all fit; the moon's face was always facing the Earth, it traced a dark path through space, a wolf sang to it, and its light all came from the sun. Jake was happy to have solved it, but to what purpose? Had it been some kind of test? He sent his response and went back to browsing the internet. But almost immediately, he received a response:

3 p.m. today, Chengxu Temple, Zhouzhuang, Jiangsu Province.

Jake couldn't believe their luck; the guy wanted to meet with them! He looked up the address on Google Maps and saw that it would take them a couple hours to get to Zhouzhuang by car. He would hire one; so that might be another hour. He also discovered that the town was a popular tourist destination, the "Venice of the East". They should probably leave soon in order to drop their stuff at a new hotel before making their appointment.

Jake walked over to where Alvara was sitting. "Saw the article you had open," she said. "I'm just trying to decide whether I liked the Legion of the Light less before or after reading it. It's like they are out to destroy any kind of magic."

"Well if they are destroying magic, we're first in line," Jake replied. "That's the bad news. But the good news; I got a reply from Huaide's friend, and we're heading to the countryside to meet him at 3 p.m. today."

"That was fast. Did he mention his name?"

"Nope, but he did send us this strange riddle. It took me a while to crack it." He showed her a copy.

She read it through once. "The moon," she said. "Neat riddle."

Jake tried not to feel outdone. "I thought so too," he grumbled.

"So we'll drop our stuff off at a new hotel on the way?" she asked.

"My thought exactly."

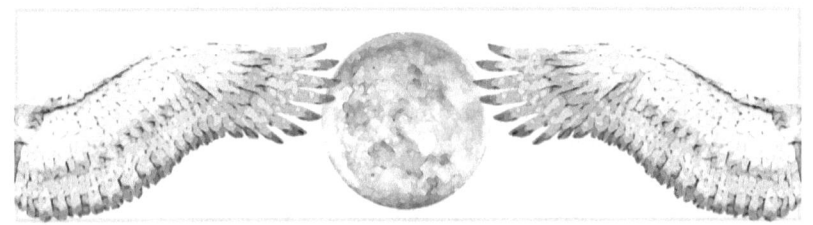

Chapter 13

The sun was past its zenith by the time they left the suburbs of Shanghai and entered the A9 Expressway, car windows lowered to take advantage of the breeze. A man outside their hotel had been willing to drive them first to another hotel, and then all the way to Zhouzhuang. At least, he was willing after Jake had shown him the Chinese characters, as the man spoke only a few words of English. The radio's muttered Chinese commentary provided a pleasant white noise soundtrack as they drove.

The sprawl of the surrounding cities reminded Jake a bit of the areas around Los Angeles, but here, greenery sprouted from every available concrete crevice. They passed through residential areas, one after another, each one with apartment complexes or squat, walled houses crammed into the available space. He could see columns of smoke coming from some of the windows, which he now knew was due to the burning of charcoal briquettes for cooking meals. Clouds chased each other across the deep blue vault of the sky, and grass carpeted both freeway embankments. The peaceful scenery finally helped Jake begin to shake off the events of the night before.

He glanced over to see Alvara buried in a book. "What are you reading?" he asked.

"A book for school," she replied, and he smiled in wonder. She had spent last night freeing a hostage, and today she had returned to schoolwork. He shouldn't be worried about her home life. The girl could handle anything life threw at her.

"Alvara, I just want to share an aspect of my life I haven't really felt comfortable talking about before."

She closed her book with a finger to mark her page. "Sure Jake, go ahead."

"So, you asked me the other day about why I didn't fly any more, and I wouldn't talk about it." She nodded once. "Well, I was married, many years ago, to a woman named Aurora. I loved her very much." Jake waited for the emotional onslaught, but to his surprise, he held himself together.

He pressed on, staring out the window as he spoke. "One night we were sitting on a cliff near our old house, and part of the cliff collapsed. She managed to grab my hand, and then a root, but I couldn't pull her back up. I could have run to the car for the rope," he said. His voice turned rough. "But it was less than a minute before sunset, and I waited for my wings to grow so I could fly down to save her."

"What happened?" Alvara breathed.

"She fell," Jake said simply. "Before the sun had fully set. I was too late. I never found her body."

"Jake, I am so sorry," Alvara said. "That must have been terrible." She put a hand on his shoulder. "I know as well as anyone what it's like to wish you had done something differently, but your wife's death wasn't your fault."

"That's sweet of you to say, Alvara, but it was."

"Begging your *pardon*, Jake, but it wasn't. You can't blame yourself."

"Alvara, you don't understand—"

"Like hell I don't understand about blame! My mom died giving birth to me, and do you even know why my Dad went to that Party City in the first place?" she said sharply.

Her tone derailed his annoyance. "What? Why?"

"I begged for green balloons for my birthday, and wouldn't accept that he just bought me blue and red." Alvara's voice was cool. "So he went back out again to get some balloons for my party the next day. It was late at night, and not the best neighborhood. You know the rest."

She continued. "I'm sorry for your wife Jake, but don't you dare talk with me like I don't know what it means to blame myself for the death of someone else. I learned that it wasn't my fault; *you* just haven't figured it out yet." She turned to stare out the window.

Jake stared, at a loss for words. How could Alvara know that it wasn't his fault? Without his damn wings and his foolish pride, Rory would still be alive.

The road narrowed as the houses grew into farmhouses, separated by disorganized clumps of wheat and sorghum, with goats and sheep free to roam between grass patches. *But what if he had run to get the rope initially,* he thought. How much worse would it have been to come back to find her gone? It would have meant abandoning her. He did the only thing he could have done; try to stay with her and hope she could hang on until he could help her.

He found himself scratching his fingertips compulsively and stopped. He felt as if he physically couldn't let go of that guilt.

These past decades without Rory, he had selfishly clung to the belief that chance and circumstance did not have a role in what happened, because it would let him keep his grief forever. If he admitted that it had been out of his control, would it be like losing her again? Or would he finally begin to heal?

"Alvara, I'm sorry," he said after a while. "I don't know what that could have been like for you, learning to let go of that guilt by yourself. I've had this guilt wrapped up for so long that I need to untangle it to fully let it go. I'm . . . still learning. But thank you for helping me to realize that fact." He half-smiled in her direction.

She shook her head, the ghost of a smile on her face. "Jeez, Jake, you're a stubborn old man. I've got to be able to teach you something for once."

He forced a chuckle and returned to his thoughts. Alvara resumed reading, shaking her head.

They skirted a huge lake, and Jake got the impression they had left the city and outlying districts behind. Alvara stopped reading to join him in peering out the window.

They made their way along winding, hilly roads. In one of the waterways they passed, Jake saw a man standing in some sort of canoe, poling along, headed for a cluster of low wooden buildings on the other side. They drove through wide terraced fields, some of which were host to scattered workers, bent horizontally to tend crops in the afternoon sun. The crops were almost painfully green.

Taking another bridge across an expansive lake, they approached the city of Zhouzhuang. At the entrance to the city, they thanked the man and paid for their trip, as well as for admission to the city. An old lady in the parking lot thrust a map into their hands and then held out her hand until Jake gave in and paid her. Once they had completed the formalities and dodged the other hands waving brochures, they walked into the old section of the city.

A walkway ran along a deep green canal to their side, and they strolled along the cobblestone path amid a group of Chinese tourists talking amongst themselves and taking pictures. Most of the buildings Jake could see had been restored. Many had exquisitely carved wooden roofs that sloped up at the edges, painted in browns, whites, and deep reds. At intervals along the waterway, strings of five spherical red lanterns hung out over the water, bucking and twisting in the breeze. They emerged into a central square of sorts, and Jake could see why it was a tourist town.

Smooth stone walkways crisscrossed the maze of canals, as ancient as the surrounding architecture. Gondoliers pushed aside graceful willows like curtains as they piloted their boats through the waterways with a massive paddle at the rear of the boat. The tourists pointed and snapped pictures as they floated past. The swaying of the gondoliers as they paddled their boats was hypnotic. He could hear them singing as they passed, strange shrieking chants that were at home in the medieval town. The square was a standoff; one side held hawkers, yelling about their wares in Mandarin and English as they held up woven hats, painted shoes, and all manner of pottery and foodstuffs. The other side hosted two restaurants, both with excellent views of the canals, housed in the Chinese equivalent of stately family mansions. In all, it was an idyllic place.

Jake glanced at his watch. They had about an hour to meet the man, and Jake was starving. "Alvara, you getting hungry?"

"This place is incredible. Yes! I could do with some food. One of these restaurants?"

"Let's walk a bit, and stop at one farther in." She shrugged, so they kept walking, skirting the square and attempting to dissuade the yelling vendors with marginal success. By the time they ended up at the other end of the square, Alvara was holding a small, foldable red lantern with a bemused expression on her face.

"A small price to pay for making it across the square in one piece," she chuckled, folding it and placing it in her satchel. They continued around the curve of narrow streets, past walls laced with different colors of moss, and one covered with ivy. Green appeared in this town when you least expected it, Jake thought.

As they crossed their third or fourth bridge, Jake noticed that the granite walls next to the lapping water had begun to crumble and decay. It reminded him of Venice, whose waterfront buildings had uninhabitable first floors. He wondered how long this town had already withstood the constant wearing away of the water, and how much longer it would last.

Their narrow walkway opened into a much smaller square, three walls of which made up a single restaurant. Tall, movable shutters instead of doorways beckoned, each topped with three of the hanging red lanterns. A few patrons sat at scattered tables, but it exuded peace, unlike the raucous first square they had entered. As one, they agreed this was the place.

Lunch amazed with every bite. Jake forced Alvara to try a bit of his dish, which was a specialty of the town; pig leg. It was bursting with flavor.

"Wow, I know my new retirement plan," Jake joked.

"Good idea. With all the fat on that leg, retirement will be short and sweet," Alvara retorted. Jake made contented noises after trying her fish, but maintained that it had nothing on the pig.

As they left the restaurant they were both in better moods, and began their walk toward the Temple. According to the map, it wasn't far from the square where they had eaten; just a few streets East and a couple North. After a pleasant stroll, they crossed a graceful stone bridge and came to Chengxu Temple, which overlooked a broad stretch of water.

It was a languorous structure, painted in oranges, reds, and browns, with three layers of curved grey roofs and red wooden pillars. It exuded peace with its very construction, but with their meeting fast arriving, Jake's nerves flared into life. Until Xiu Li had made his move, his office had been peaceful too.

At least this was a public venue. Jake counted at least three police officers observing the bustling square. It shared few characteristics with the isolated warehouse where he had been unceremoniously dumped, screamed at, tormented . . . Jake had stopped amid the flow of traffic, and Alvara turned back some distance ahead, scanning the crowd until she saw him.

She offered him a thumbs up. He returned it, his hands clenching into fists after she turned away. Jake would do whatever it took to ensure that Alvara stayed safe.

It was five minutes to three when Jake caught up to Alvara and paid their entry fee at the small stand to one side of the door. As there was no pile of shoes by the door, Jake led Alvara inside without removing his shoes, his every sense attuned to possible threats.

The steps were slippery with age as they descended into a lower courtyard. Turning a corner, they were greeted by a pavilion bedecked in red Chinese letters, providing the backdrop for an elaborate red and gold shrine. Three male figures coated in gold were faced by Chinese men and women, who prayed to the figures. Lit candles covered most available surfaces, and more were available to one side of the shrine next to a donation basket. Jake tried not to disturb the worshippers as he and Alvara passed through the pavilion and into a garden, which held an old man napping on a bench.

The man had a full, grey head of hair, and a short beard that coated his chin. His skin hung in loose folds off his prominent cheekbones, and he wore a necklace with an opaque, luminous stone as the centerpiece. If it weren't for the necklace, his grey sweater and faded greenish pants would have been perfect camouflage for the stone bench and greenery surrounding him.

"Hello, sir?" said Alvara, tapping him on the shoulder. "Excuse me. Are you here to meet us?"

The man blinked a few times and sat up. He didn't look at them at first, just stretched his arms and leaned his head in the cardinal directions to stretch his neck. He promptly stuck out his hand, still not so much as glancing in their direction.

"Come on," said Jake, exasperated, "we've already come a long way to meet you. You want money? Is this just some sort of scam?" In reply, the man nodded vigorously and beckoned for money with his fingers.

"Alvara, this isn't the guy, let's keep looking." Jake walked away, leaving the man with his hand outstretched, staring at nothing.

But Alvara didn't follow. Jake saw her reach into her satchel and pull out her wallet, emptying it into the man's hand. Over a thousand yuans barely hit his palms before they disappeared into a pocket in his pants. The man clapped twice, and said, "Life is scam! Life is scam! You see? Come, follow." He reached out his hands for Alvara's, but she jerked away.

"Back off," she said. "You want us to follow you, fine. But keep your hands to yourself."

Jake noticed the way he had reached for her hands, and stared at the man's eyes. The man seemed to be watching the garden, but then Jake realized the truth. Reaching behind the stone bench, the man lifted a white cane.

Alvara flushed as she realized her mistake. "Sir, I can help –" she began.

"Follow," he repeated, striding from the garden, his cane skittering across the paving stones as he checked his path.

"You never said your name," Jake said. The man stopped.

"Name not for me," the man said, as if tasting the words. "I am without name. You may say 'Wu Ming'."

"What does that mean?" Alvara asked.

"Name-less," the man grunted, and resumed his path through the temple.

Wu Ming led them through small stone rooms, with thin mats as their only ornamentation. They walked through larger halls with intricate wooden shutters over the many windows.

"The Daoshi," Wu Ming said suddenly, as three monks came into view around a corner. "Do not touch," he added.

Jake realized they had left the tourist section behind as the monks shuffled past at the far edge of the hallway. The men wore black pants, white shirts with cloth clasps, and black headbands, with their long hair tied in topknots and secured with a wooden stick. As Wu Ming led them through the interior of the temple, one group watered courtyard plants out of a large metal can, while a solitary monk practiced calligraphy in water on the paving stones. As they passed, Jake noticed that while the recent letters were visible, the earlier letters had faded and evaporated.

Jake had noted the twists and turns they had taken to reach this point, but was not confident of his ability to find his way out. However, he also doubted that anyone else could find them here, deep within the temple.

A sliding screen revealed a dark stairwell. Wu Ming gripped a modern bannister and quickly ascended; Jake and Alvara were left to feel their way up behind him. The thud of their steps sounded louder in the absence of light. Jake bumped into Alvara when she stopped in the darkness, and he mumbled an apology.

He heard Wu Ming grumbling in front of him, and the clank and clatter of keys turning on a key ring. He finally inserted the correct key and turned it with a click, flooding the stairwell with light as the door swung upward. The man crawled into the light, and Jake followed cautiously.

Jake blinked at the brightness surrounding them. They were alone on the roof of the temple, on a small yellow platform that stretched only three strides by two, before the lip of the roof curved down and out into elaborate peaked edges. As long as they didn't stand, they would be hidden from the ground below by the steep curves of the roof's edge. Across the canal, they were at the level of the treetops, which whispered and swayed, obscuring most of the town's buildings.

The man sat on one of three tan mats that were laid in a triangle, and made shooing motions until Alvara scooted over to sit on another. Jake sat stiffly, bracing himself with one hand.

"Are you the one who gave Huaide the dagger?" Jake asked. The man nodded.

"I gave dagger. I gave words. No more wings."

"Why would you do that? Help him to hurt her?"

"Wings curse for her. Wings curse for him. You see? I help," Wu Ming said, his tone sharp.

"Who are you, that you have that kind of power?" Jake asked, tired of this game.

"I am no one." The man replied, his sightless eyes fixed in the middle distance.

"Perfect," Jake fumed.

"You both are someone, if you choose being," Wu Ming added. "Yueh is sad; she miss lover, she miss Children. She is alone."

"Who is Yueh?" Alvara asked.

"She is Moon," he replied. "Yueh is not only name, it is one of many name. You are Yueh-Children, yes?"

"We think so," said Jake. "But how do you know this?"

"I listen," Wu Ming explained. "I listen close. May I listen to you?"

"Like a meditation or something? Sure, why not," Alvara said, though Jake could see she was mostly humoring the man. "What do I have to do?"

Wu Ming touched the mat next to him. "Be still," he said. "And give hand." Alvara uncertainly placed her hand into the man's open palm, took a deep breath, and closed her eyes. When Jake looked at Wu Ming, he was startled to see the man's gaze fixed on his own. When the man neither blinked nor moved, Jake figured it must be a coincidence. But he still shifted on his mat until he no longer met the man's eyes.

A cool breeze tickled her skin, and Alvara opened her eyes. She stood in an alpine meadow, crisp and fresh with the smell of melting snow in spring, surrounded by tiny wildflowers of a hundred colors and varieties. She was not alone.

Hello, said a young Chinese man. *I will help you to navigate and find your answers.*

You're the man from the roof, said Alvara. *What is this place?*

It's not a place, Alvara, but is the calm inside yourself where we can seek answers to your questions.

Okay, Alvara thought dreamily. She had never felt such perfect peace. A small brook tumbled in and among flowers and moss and lichen before it disappeared from view. Alvara reached down to touch the water, and gasped with pleasure as the cold numbed her hand.

Alvara, it is very easy to get distracted here. Your questions? The man asked her patiently.

What's going to happen to us if we can get away from the Legion? She wanted to know. The man stared at her as he considered, and she didn't know why his gaze was so unsettling.

We shall see, the man said. *This place is dangerous, and you must never come here on your own. Where we are about to go is much more so. Please take my hand and do not let go, but let your eyes remain open so that you might understand.* He gripped her hand and strolled across the meadow until they came to a series of three caves. *Your past, present, and future*, he said. The first on the left was worn almost smooth with time, and beckoned her with a sandy bottom and flickering lights in its depths. The central cave was in constant motion, with stalactites and stalagmites growing and shrinking as she watched. They stopped in front of the third cave on the right.

This cave was a perfect hemisphere, but only a single step past the entrance, darkness fell. The sound of voices could be heard echoing off the unseen walls, but she couldn't understand the words, and felt herself drawn forward. The strong hand and serious face of the Chinese man halted her in her steps. *Whatever you do, whatever you may see, do not let go of my hand or I may not be able to find you,* he said. *We go to experience your future.* As peaceful as she felt, a chill passed over her at those words. Together they stepped inside and a fierce wind swept them away.

Alvara feared the man's hand would be ripped from hers, such was the force of the wind that swept them through images almost too quick to be seen. She saw herself graduating from college, strange how old she looked, then she experienced image after image of herself; flying with wings, crying, kissing someone (what?), laughing with Jake, flying again (in daylight?), talking with an older woman with dark hair, emaciated in a cage with a man staring down at her and laughing, Max dead under an empty sky (No!), surrounded by children, at a funeral (whose?), faster and faster with image after image until she wanted to scream, to do anything to make the visions stop, not being able to feel her hands or feet or body but desperately trying to hold on.

The man held Alvara's hand for a long time. Jake grew impatient, though he tried not to show it. Cross-legged was not his favorite position, and the hot sun on the back of his neck became uncomfortable. The minutes ticked by, and Jake counted the metal whorls that edged the upper tier of the roof behind him. After wiping some sweat from his forehead, he glanced at Alvara and the older man. Their eyes were closed. Alvara scrunched her forehead as if concentrating, but gave no other impression of being awake.

"Alvara?" Jake called. "Everything okay?" She didn't answer, which he took as confirmation that the man had her in some sort of trance. He stretched his legs out in front of him, settling on folding his arms across them to brace his back. It was uncomfortable.

"Max . . ." Alvara moaned, eyes screwed shut, tears trailing down her cheeks.

"I'm here, Alvara. It's Jake. Don't cry. It's just a dream." He reached over and shook her shoulder, but she didn't wake up. He tried again. "Wu Ming, whatever you're doing, stop now. She's done." Jake wondered if he should try to find help, but didn't want to leave Alvara.

"Please . . ." Alvara whimpered, and then awoke with a start, her features perfectly calm. She wiped tears away in confusion, pulling her hand free from Wu Ming's grip as he, too, opened his eyes. Jake left his hand on Alvara's shoulder. She looked unsettled.

"Alvara, are you all right?"

"I'm okay. It was so strange, but it's slipping away, like a dream. We were in a field, at first, but then I sort of fell into a whirlpool that felt dangerous. Everything was light and sound, sort of swirling around, and I worried I would lose . . . people I cared about in there. It was really weird. Was it real?" she asked Wu Ming.

"What kind of stunt was that, anyway?" Jake added. "What did you do, some sort of mystical trance?"

"We listen together. We see possibilities, some real, some not real, but all possibilities. That is all," the blind man said, cracking his neck and rolling his shoulders. He nodded toward Jake. "Will you listen with me?"

"Why would I?" Jake said, suddenly angry. "Alvara and I have been up front with you, asked for your help, and you drag Alvara into a bad dream that told us nothing. You seem to know an awful lot about the Moon that you're not telling. Why not just answer our questions instead of cloaking everything in mysticism?"

Wu Ming shook his head and smiled sadly. "I know no answer. You know answer. We listen, maybe hear answer. Yes?"

Jake saw that the man's blind eyes drooped with exhaustion, and realized how much this 'listening' took out of him. The situation was absurd, but Jake's life had bent that way ever since Laerik showed up on his windowsill. Wu Ming was trying his best, Jake realized, but didn't have the answers he and Alvara sought. They needed to get the Legion off their backs, and this man had an idea that could help.

"All right," Jake agreed. "But Alvara, try to wake me before sunset."

"Sure, Jake," she said, concerned. "Were you trying to wake me up before?"

"Yeah, but you didn't stir."

"I thought I felt something, but I couldn't be sure where it came from. Just try to pay attention and wait for the wake-up call," she said.

"Will do," said Jake. He took a deep breath, placed his hand in the older man's hand, and closed his eyes. Nothing happened for a few moments. He felt the heat of the sun, oppressive on the back of his neck, and listened to his breathing. He felt himself sink into the breaths. Like descending a long, cool slide, Jake slid into an awareness of himself. And he was not alone.

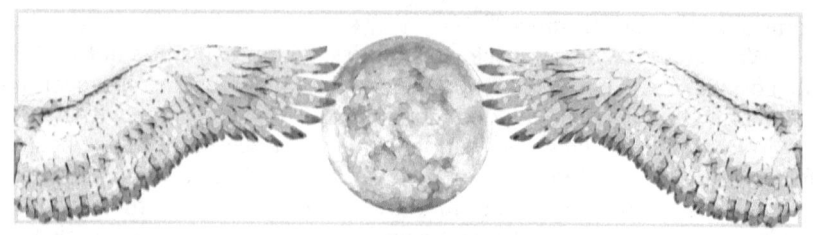

Chapter 14

Hello, said a young Chinese man. *I will help you find your answers.*

You are so young, said Jake. *Are you still the same man?*

Look at yourself, said the man. *You are also young.* Jake saw that they sat in a merry little one-room cabin. The only light came from a fire in the hearth. He and the man sprawled on a suede couch with their feet resting upon a wide footstool below. On the walls were pictures of Jake's mother and father, Alvara, the little girl Jenny, and his wife Rory, and his heart warmed to see them all there. Jake peered at his hands and felt his features. They were the strong arms and unlined face of a man in his late thirties.

What is this place? Jake asked.

Think of it as your soul's antechamber, said the man wistfully. *We rest here until we are ready to seek your answers.*

Fine by me, Jake said with a grin. His back no longer hurt, his vision was clearer, and he felt more alive than he had in a long time. If that meant they had to rest for a bit, so be it; he was ready and raring to go as soon as his guide gave the word. He stretched his arms and leaned back to relax, but as suddenly leapt to his feet. *Okay, I'm ready to go!* He laughed. *What's next?*

The books on the table over there are all about you, Jake. The Jake of before, the Jake of today, and the Jake yet to come. First rule: don't come here alone, or you may never leave. Second rule: only quick peeks into the third book. It is easy to get lost. Understand?

Yes, Jake said. He did understand. This was like a game.

Repeat the rules back, Jake. They are important. Jake repeated them, like a good boy. He felt as if some part of himself were missing, something *more,* but dismissed it out of hand. He needed to be careful, he remembered, but of what he couldn't say. At least there was a game.

Which book do you pick? The man gave him the choice! Jake leaped over the couch to stand in front of the books. The blue one on the left was large and musty, and made Jake want to sneeze. He opened the cover . . .

and stood on a cliff overlooking the ocean. He loved the smell of the breeze, and skipped along the ledge, kicking rocks off the side and watching them make little splashes in the water below. Ahead of him a couple sat on a blanket staring out to sea. Jake was terrified, but he didn't know why. He spotted a girl hiding behind a bush, not far from where the man and woman sat. He ran over to her.

She had a heart-shaped face and fine white hair. He followed his instinct and put his arms around her, and they both flinched as a rumble shook the cliff. The little girl was crying, and he asked her why. She said she couldn't help the woman, though she tried. Jake thought that was sad and cried too. He peered over the girl's shoulder and saw a young man running toward him. He let her go and walked over to the man, and he took Jake's hand in his own. *Don't run off here, Jake. This is not a safe place.* Jake said he wouldn't, and the man pushed the edge of the sky aside and they walked back to the room with the fireplace.

The man sat down again with Jake. *I know it's hard to be here. It took me many years of traveling within to be comfortable bringing my whole self in here. You're just a kid, so this is hard, but you need to remember what it's like outside. Why are we here, Jake?*

A tough one, Jake thought. *You said there were rules?*

Good, but before that. Look at the pictures on the wall, they are there for remembering. Who is the girl with dark hair?

She's my friend, Jake replied. *Her name is . . . Alvara.* Jake had a sudden rush of information that sent him reeling. *We are here for answers! I'm not a kid at all, I'm a man!* He felt shaken. *How could I forget?*

When you are listening inside like we are, all the Jake's from every age are here together. It is hard to stay focused. The man sighed. *I had hoped you would pick future, as there was much Alvara did not see, but you did learn of your past. The young girl with you was the Moon.*

Yes, Jake recalled the little girl on the swing. *Then, she must have been the girl Alvara and I dreamed of on the plane?*

She is often a young girl, but is also a woman, and is also something old and difficult to understand. Even here, I do not think I can put it into words. What did you want to know about her?

How we can get to her, Jake answered. *She told me to find her where the sun may stay long after it sets, but I didn't know what that meant.*

But that is no instruction at all, Jake, the man replied impatiently. *She means the moon. The sun may stay on the moon long after it sets on the Earth. Let me see.* The man pulled his short goatee for a moment, while the fire crackled. *We have until the fire burns down.* They both examined the fire, and saw it was about halfway burned down to coals. *If you stay here,* the man decided, *I can go journey into your present to see how you can meet the Moon.*

I could come with you, maybe see something you miss. Jake said.

We don't have much time, and I'll be faster alone, the man said with a smile. *Stay here.* He opened the second book, a brand new red hardcover smelling of binding glue, and disappeared into it. Jake walked over to peer into the open book, and could read words spreading themselves across the page. As long as he didn't get too close, he could feel that he wouldn't fall into it. From the writing sprawling across the page, the man appeared to be jumping around their recent events searching for clues. Jake turned his attention to the book to his right.

It was a dark green book, yet it also was not yet a book. The cover had a hazy edge, lacking in definition, and though Jake could see writing on it, none of the words stayed solid long enough to read. He ran his hand over the embossing, and felt the book become hot, and then cold, and then hot again beneath his hands. It also tingled a warning, and he removed his hands with a gasp. Jake thought he knew what Alvara had meant when she had said that she had fallen into something dangerous; there was nothing comforting about this book's presence in his antechamber.

Jake had a sudden impulse to open the book to see what was inside. The part of him that believed his wings had been meant for more, that hoped that someday he would be happy again; those parts were difficult to silence. His hand returned to the cover, feeling the fluidly-shifting energies beneath. He took a deep breath, and withdrew his hand.

Jake, don't! The man yelled, appearing from the central book. In his surprise, Jake's hand brushed the edge of the cover upwards. With the force of a crashing wave, Jake was sucked into the swirling maelstrom of the book. Jake reached out for the man's hand, but missed, and he disappeared into chaos.

Jake felt like he was treading water, but with every kick and every pull downward of his arms, the scene changed. His legs beat and he flashed through a summer day, a freezing night, a slap from one direction followed by a caress from another. He couldn't get his bearings, didn't know which way was up, but kept trying. Far below him, Jake saw a man with dusky skin and eyes the bright yellow of a midday sun, and felt drawn to him, like they were kin in a way he couldn't explain. The man raised a gun, and Jake spun, the man disappearing in a swell of light and color. Jake flew over a frozen world, the last of humanity huddled together for warmth with no end to the bitter cold in sight. He beat his wings, and saw huge waves crashing over the cities, the Moon filling half the sky and drawing closer. Another beat of his wings, and he saw Alvara flying away from him; he tried to reach her but the vision spun away. On the next downbeat he flew through a spring day with nothing amiss; hundreds of thousands of humans going about their business in the city below. He felt as if he would go mad, and folded his wings around himself, going into a dive.

He curled in a ball with his eyes closed, and the world was silent again. He heard water, from nearby, a stream of some sort. He didn't want to move, for fear that the horrible visions would come rushing back, but no such thing occurred.

Someone ran a hand through his hair. His head rested in a woman's lap, and he relaxed into the touch, slowly unwinding his body. "I always knew you were just a big baby," a voice above him teased, and he finally opened his eyes, blinking to focus.

A face came into view, one he knew well, even in the dim light of a pine forest at sunset, even upside down. Her nose was still crooked from where she had broken it. Her mouth turned up in that half-grin he could never forget. Even her eyes sparkled. "Rory," he cried, and sat up. He fell into her arms.

It was an infinity and no time at all, holding her. Time ceased to exist for him here, in this strange place inside himself where he could see and feel her again. He held her to him, smelling her hair and feeling her heartbeat, until she gently pulled away.

"God, it's good to see you," she said, grinning.

"You're telling me," he managed, then frowned. "How can this be the future? You aren't here anymore, Rory." It hurt to say it, but it was true.

"It's not the future," she said, and looked like she wanted to say more but stopped herself. "I just wanted to see you. I've missed you, Jake, every moment. But you have to go now."

"What? I can't!" Jake protested.

"Yes you can. Your hearth is almost out, and you need return before that happens. I'm out of time too; I just came to help you find your way out."

"Rory, don't leave. I don't care if this isn't real, I don't want to lose you again." Jake held her hand against his cheek. Hers was the same face he had lost, long ago; she hadn't aged a day, here in his mind.

"Oh, Jake. I didn't say it wasn't real, I just said it wasn't the future. Now go," she said, pushing him away. Nothing happened. "Go!" she yelled, shoving him hard with both hands.

He fell, his eyes flying open. Alvara peered over from where she crouched on the roof, her wings framing her face.

"Jake," she whispered. "Thank God you're awake. You missed sunset; I've been trying to wake you for the past few minutes. They're here!"

He shook his head a bit to clear it, getting reacquainted with his older body again, and the weight of wings on his back. He blinked in the dim light. "Who?" he asked.

"The Legion! They surrounded the place a few minutes ago, and I think they're searching for us. It's only a matter of time before they try the roof. We have to go."

"You go," said a voice from the other mat. They glanced up and saw the man pointing to where the moon had begun to rise over the stone roofs of the town.

"To the moon?" Alvara asked. "That makes no sense. The moon is hundreds of thousands of miles away, across a vacuum of empty space. How are we supposed to go there?"

In response, the man flapped his arms goofily and pointed to the moon again. "It is answer," he finished in triumph, crossing his arms in front of him. "You pay for good question." When neither of them moved to go, he turned his head to the side as if listening. He stopped smiling. "No time, Jake, Alveera. You must go now. Believe you get to Moon, you get to Moon. See?"

"This is crazy. There's no way back, no way out," Alvara said, looking at Jake.

Jake felt calmer, more resolute. He reached to pull Alvara into a hug. "Nowhere to go but up," he said. He spread his wings.

Alvara smiled, her eyes wide. "All right," she said, "This is insane. Let's fly." They took off from the roof almost straight up, their wings thudding harshly in the cooling air. They heard shouts from below and an explosion as the door to the roof burst open. Though Jake didn't crane his neck to look, he felt the presence of the man from the vision, the one with yellow eyes. Jake spun into a dive, and heard gunfire from below. There was no thud of impact. Jake strained to regain the altitude, breathing hard, and caught up to Alvara. They continued onward and upward, and quickly moved out of range.

It was tiring work, flying for altitude. They took some breaks to circle and catch their breaths, but climbed higher and higher. The town spread out below them in a network of waterways, and became patches of color that blended together as they ascended. They burst through the highest layer of clouds. The emptiness above them sprawled in an infinite void. They flew farther and farther, and the air became scarce. The clouds were a mottled carpet of grey far below, and the air was so cold that Jake shook. Jake breathed fast and deeply, but he couldn't get enough air. "Try . . . to think of . . . the Moon," he gasped between breaths.

"Jake . . . I can't breathe . . ."

"Try . . . I know we're . . . almost . . . there." Jake tried to think of the Moon, the woman he saw that night in his room, but images of Rory in the forest kept eclipsing her image. Jake realized he was about to pass out, but kept flying. Alvara, who flew above him, stopped beating her wings, and tipped back toward Earth. Before she could fall far, Jake thought he saw her shimmer and disappear. His consciousness was fading, but he saw a woman smile down at him with hair that danced. She reached out a hand, and he knew no more.

Chapter 15

Alvara's eyes snapped open, and she was filled with an intense panic. She floated underwater, and every direction was the same formless black depth. Stifling her terror, she held a deep breath she must have gotten somewhere and tried to focus, floating in the cold water. The silence and the darkness were oppressive.

She searched around herself in every direction and finally saw a dim light below her. She struck out toward it, not having breath left to evaluate other options, her satchel and waterlogged shoes slowing her. Her swimming became more frantic, but the dim light grew closer. Her chest ached and her vision flickered.

She broke the surface, gasping for air, coughing as she tried to calm down. She treaded water for a moment before attempting to get her bearings.

Her eyes adjusted to the dim light. She had ample opportunity to discover that the water was fresh, having swallowed no small amount in her struggles to be free of it. Treading water in the cool semi-darkness, her eyes tracked the water horizontally in hopes of finding the horizon. But instead of reaching sky, the surface of the water curved up and away from her. She squinted to see better, but she lost its edge in the murk above. Far, far away upward she could see a hazy moon, but that couldn't have been the light she saw before.

It resembled a cave of some sort, with some kind of opening in the roof, or was it more like a huge bowl? And how did the water travel up the sides like that? She couldn't quite remember how she had gotten here; she had been flying with Jake.

"Jake," she called out, surprised at the soft croak of her voice. The only reply was the soft lapping of the water. Where was he? She couldn't remember.

In the distance, she saw what must be the source of the light. The small point wavered; maybe a fire, she thought. The desire to be warm and dry overwhelmed her, when it seemed that all she had ever known was the cold and wet. Jake might already be there. She swam, clumsily, toward the shore that hosted the small campfire light. She stopped once in a while to clench and unclench her hands, which were going numb. Through her weariness, she swam on.

A hand reached out and grabbed hers. Alvara held on and was lifted out of the water, up into the cool air. Two arms wrapped around her, pulling her into a warm hug. Alvara couldn't have resisted even if she had wanted to. She relaxed into the hug as she felt the damp leave her clothes, turning them fresh-from-the-dryer warm, with the slightest hint of jasmine.

"There, now, all is well, Mother is here. Come, walk with me." It was a woman's voice, low and comforting. Alvara glanced up to see eyes the grey-white of the moon and waves of silver hair pulled back to frame a heart-shaped face, which smiled down at her.

"Are you . . ." Alvara began. *It couldn't be.*

"Please, daughter, let us walk together back to the fire."

"You're not my mother. Who are you?" Alvara asked.

"We will speak of these things soon." She put out a hand, and Alvara took it after a moment of consideration. Only then did she realize that they were standing on top of the water. It made her dizzy, and she felt as if she would fall, but the woman's hand held hers, and she steadied herself.

"If you walk normally, you will get used to it. Unless you would rather swim?" the woman smiled.

"No, I'll walk," said Alvara, and moved toward the shore. The woman danced lightly across the water, while Alvara's steps were more careful. Her feet were wet, and if she didn't lift them high enough, she splashed water around her shoes and ankles. She began to get the hang of it, and managed a small smile. She was walking on water!

The touch of dry land jolted her back to the present, and she trudged up a sandy slope toward a campfire that popped and shed light. A silhouette in front of the campfire stood and came toward them.

"Alvara? Are you there?"

"Jake!" Alvara replied, happy that her voice had returned. She let go of the woman's hand and ran up the beach to where Jake stood. Jake swept her into a massive bear hug. Jake was fine. They were both fine. Relief washed over her. "Did we make it?" she whispered.

"I don't know yet. She wouldn't say much. But I think we may have," he said. He sounded tired, and she wondered if he had had to swim his way here like she had. "I'm so glad you're safe; I was worried. Let's go sit by the fire."

They turned to walk together across the sand and toward the flickering light, and saw that the woman was already there, with her back to their approach. As they grew closer, Alvara caught a whiff of meat roasting on sticks over the fire, and realized she was starving. They quickened their pace, and took a seat next to the woman. She rotated the spits, staring into the flames.

"Excuse me," Alvara asked, "but are you the Goddess of the Moon?"

"Mmmm," sighed the woman, sampling a piece of the meat. "Would you like some?"

"Um, sure," said Alvara, and Jake nodded.

"Sorry, but you didn't answer my question." Alvara didn't want to be rude, but needed to know.

"I did not answer because it was a silly question," the woman proclaimed. "Though you could not have known that, child," she added.

"Names are strange creatures. I have hundreds of them," she said as she passed out the meat on wooden plates. "Shall I list a portion for you? Yueh, Coniraya, Chup Kamui, Tsukuyomi, Metztli, Yin, Wadd, Napir, Sin, Fati, Nanna, the Lady, Ilazki, Hubal, Leukothea, Selene, Máni, Anumati, Chandra, Dewi Sri, Luna, Silawe Nazarate, Losna, Mayari, Lona, Meness, Ngalindi, Gleti, Thoth-Seshat, Igaluk . . ." As she spoke, Alvara noticed that she clenched her jaw and the muscles in her neck, and her hair kept changing color and length and consistency. *Weird*, Alvara thought.

". . . As well as Goddess, Queen, or Moon in almost every language that has ever been." She kept trying to push her now shoulder-length brown hair over her ears, but it was too short, and kept falling into her eyes.

"So, which one are you?" Alvara asked.

"All of them," she answered softly, finally letting her hair rest, though it was now blonde and in ringlets. "Even the silly names, like Mr. Moony Pants. I am all that people see when they see me. I am Mother, to you two," she added.

"Lady," Alvara said, "I have a mother." *Had*, she thought. "What name do you want me to use?"

The woman sighed. "You can call me Selene, if you would like a name that is pretty and safe to call me."

"Why did your hair just change color?" Alvara asked. When Selene didn't answer at first, she explained, "That's not normal, where we're from."

Selene shifted her weight, and waved her hand to dismiss the question. Then she beamed at them. "After all this time, my Children have come home. I cannot believe how you have both grown." Her eyes glistened, and she dabbed at them with the edge of her sleeve. "I am sorry. But it has been so long since one of my Children has come to visit, and now I am blessed with two of you."

"Thank you, Selene, for helping us to find this place. Where is here, exactly?" asked Jake.

"This is my home. It is the valley of the Moon," Selene replied. "I am surprised you did not notice that the moon is out and you are both missing your wings."

Alvara hadn't noticed. But Jake was way ahead of her.

"The sun may stay long after it sets," he said.

"Yes, Jake! Good," she said, clapping her hands together with delight. "It is often a kind of day time for me, as is the case now, so it will be for you as well. But please, eat, and we will talk more when you finish." They didn't need to be told twice. Alvara bit into the meat, and it tasted like nothing on Earth. It was hearty like beef, but tender as rotisserie chicken, and exploded with a smoky, fruity flavor Alvara had never experienced.

"Wow," said Alvara, but didn't want to waste any more time talking. She could ask her questions after she ate.

They both devoured their food, and Selene passed them each a goblet of wine to wash down the meat. Alvara had never had wine before, but enjoyed the flavor well enough, which was a spicy mixture of apple and honeysuckle.

As they sipped the wine, Alvara watched Selene. She reached into the fire and cupped some of the flames in her hand, rotating her hand and allowing the flames to lick around the edges before going out. Alvara wasn't sure how she did it, but she had already seen Selene walk on water, so decided not to comment. She polished off the rest of her meal and most of the wine in silence.

"That food was fantastic!" Alvara exclaimed when she finished. She actually felt a bit giddy. "And walking on water! It's so nice to be able to relax. It feels like we've been on the run forever!" Jake smiled and poured the rest of the wine in her goblet into his own. She pouted, her head fuzzy.

"We have so many questions," Jake said, "so much we couldn't discover on our own. Do you mind if we ask you about them?"

Selene smiled and shook her head. "I will answer what I can," she said.

"Who was the man who met us in China?" asked Alvara. It was the first question that popped into her head. "He seemed to know you, and us, very well, though we had never met him before. He went out of his way to help us."

"That is his job, my darling. His title is Caretaker. He is reborn each life, and chooses to give up his vision for the knowledge and meditative abilities to watch over all my Children, including you both."

"He didn't seem to help Biyu; quite the contrary, actually," Jake argued.

"Biyu," Selene began, and her face fell. "Biyu was a special case. Her gift was a mistake. My mistake. I did not see how it would tempt her into dangerous dealings. Though it hurt me, it was the right decision for her husband to make," Selene replied. "The wings will soon pass to a newborn, who will grow them in time."

"Wait, so now there'll be another kid somewhere who will grow wings?" Alvara asked. Selene nodded. Alvara felt more alone, knowing it was down to just Jake and her now. And a baby somewhere who wouldn't have wings for years yet.

"So our wings come from you," Jake stated. "Why wings? I mean, if you have power like this, you could cure disease, or give gifts to help alleviate poverty." Alvara knew it had bothered him since they had discovered the healing abilities of the feathers.

"If I were to make everyone just a little bit healthier, no one would notice, Jake," she smiled sadly. "A gift has to be to an individual to really matter. And honestly, what can surpass wings for freedom? It is the one thing I could give that I did not have for myself."

"What do you mean, you don't have freedom?" Alvara asked. "You can do whatever you want. Jake saw you in that vision at Biyu's house, consoling her when she lost her wings."

"That was not me," Selene snapped. "It was just a projection, like a dream for me. I can never leave here. Never, never." She wrapped her arms around herself. She muttered something.

"What?" asked Alvara.

"It is his fault," she snapped, and her face contorted into rage.

"Who?" Alvara repeated.

"Him!" Selene closed her eyes and pointed, but it was just an arbitrary direction out to sea. "My opposite, my balance, my former lover, my former friend, and those are just *my* names for him!" She leapt from the sand and flew off into the night sky with a shriek. Alvara reached out her hand to Jake's, and he squeezed it. They both searched the sky. But Selene floated like a falling leaf down to her spot by the fire, calm once more.

"I am sorry," she said, and took a deep breath. "You would probably call him Sol. We are the last ones left." Alvara let go of Jake's hand, discomfited by Selene's outburst. She hoped Selene would explain what she and Sol were. She didn't. "He seems poised to destroy the world, the fair Earth, and there is nothing I can do about it."

"He's like you? How would he destroy the world?" Jake asked. "And why?"

"He has always been petty and power-hungry," she sniffed. "I do not think he needs another reason. Now that we are the last ones . . . only I am left to bar his way."

"What do you mean, exactly? And the last what's?" Alvara asked.

"He has been increasing the power he gives to his Children," Selene said. "Over time so that most people cannot notice, but it has tipped the balance between us. I do not know where he is getting the power from, but his Children could end up destroying the world, or ruling it, whatever he desires." And she met their eyes with a hopeful expression. "Unless you stop them."

"Who are these Children?" Jake asked. Alvara realized the answer just as Selene spoke.

"You might know them as the Legion of the Light, curse them," she sneered.

"So they're like us," Jake whispered.

That explained why the Legion had been after them, but Alvara was having trouble taking it all in. "Wait, hold on. Please just tell us what you are, and where we are." Alvara's head throbbed, but at least her brain felt less fuzzy and she could think clearly again. "We want to hear about the problems we've encountered, we honestly do, but at least help us to shed some light on our current situation first."

"Yes, fine. Oh, delightful. You have a lantern." said Selene, gesturing to Alvara. It wasn't a question. Alvara reached into her bag and removed the red lantern she had purchased when crossing the town square. It felt so long ago.

Alvara handed the lantern to Selene, who stretched the delicate paper and wooden construct into its full ovular shape. Selene reached into the fire and gathered a handful of flame, which she used to light the wick inside the lantern. Selene held the lantern behind her and proceeded to throw it in a perfect fastball, straight out over the sea.

Instead of continuing in a straight line, however, the lantern's path curved upwards, though it continued to track the surface of the water. Alvara craned her neck backwards. The lantern shed a brilliant red light over other land formations, as well as lakes and streams, up and over their heads and back around the other side, coming across the land from the other direction. When it reached them, it dove into the fire amid a shower of sparks.

"This place is my prison," Selene said, "and a perfect sphere. Think of yourselves as being inside the Moon, though it is a poor analogy. As for what I and Sol are, it is impossible to describe. He and I are similar. We have power, but we also have limitations. I am tired of this campfire, let us be somewhere different."

"Stop this," said Jake, before Alvara lost consciousness.

Alvara awoke reclining in a lawn chair, wearing sunglasses and a swimsuit, the plastic chair straps digging into her exposed skin. She felt a bit groggy, but managed to sit up. Behind her grew a tremendous garden, filled with too many flowers to count; the heat and heady aroma was overpowering. Jake slept in the garish plastic chair beside her, dressed in board shorts and T-shirt, and on her other side lounged Selene, with long red curls, a relaxed expression, and a yellow sundress. The light was pretty dim for sunbathing, and Alvara noticed a full harvest moon in the sky.

"Much better!" Selene said with gusto, and clapped her hands.

A servant came out from the garden path, and Alvara suppressed a scream; the man had no face; just a grey clay facsimile of one, as if a toddler had fashioned it with pudgy fingers. The servant creature handed her a piña colada, and Alvara managed to take the glass and set it on the table without touching its misshapen hand. She leaned over and squeezed Jake's shoulder, and he awoke with a grunt. He noticed his outfit.

"This is ridiculous. Give us our clothes back!" he demanded.

"But I thought you two might want to relax," Selene replied. "You said you were tired." She formed her bright red lips into a pout, but waved her hands over them in a dismissive gesture. They were wearing their own clothes again.

Jake sat up and rubbed his temple. "Don't change this world without our permission, Selene. It's hard enough getting our minds around where we are. If you decide to change something, ask us first." The servant creature waited near the mansion on the other side of the pool, still watching them. Alvara no longer felt like running away, but his stare was unsettling.

"Do you require anything? Are you too cold, too warm, uncomfortable? I want you to be comfortable here," Selene said earnestly.

"We're all right," said Alvara. "I'd appreciate it if you'd ask him to leave though." She pointed. "He kind of gives me the creeps, no offense."

Selene waved a general hand in his direction, and the creature crumbled. He tried to run, but his legs broke and he fell to the ground. He wrapped his arms around himself. His beach clothes became the indistinct clay-like grey of his skin as he dissolved into a pile of powder.

"Hey, you didn't need to destroy him!" Alvara said in horror. "He didn't do anything wrong."

"It is no matter, dear, to fashion another golem out of the surface of the moon, if you need anything else. Do not worry," she said, and smiled. Alvara couldn't get the golem's empty face out of her head, nor his attempts to run from his fate. Fashioned from belief and circumstance, she and Jake were drifting deeper into currents of power they couldn't begin to fathom, much less control. Was Alvara as easy to destroy and make again?

Selene rubbed one arm with her other hand, appearing uncomfortable. Alvara wondered how it would be to live alone for so long, and found that she felt sorry for the strange, lonely lady. "Selene," she said, "Even if it's easy to make those servants whenever you want, you shouldn't harm them without a good reason. It seemed to me that he was sorry to be . . . killed."

Alvara waited while Selene considered, her fingers braiding her wiry black hair until she held a pale braid in her hands. "I have never thought about it like that," she mused, letting her hair drop. "Thank you for your suggestion. I shall try to be more considerate of their simple lives in the future."

Alvara nodded, glad she had spoken up.

"But please," Selene smiled, and Alvara could see that it was genuine. "Might I ask about you two, and your lives? I very much want to know how you have been. Are you happy?" She drew up her knees and wrapped her arms around them in a childlike pose, friendly and interested.

Jake deferred to Alvara, and so she told the story of her life so far. Though Alvara hesitated at first, Selene was an excellent listener. Alvara spoke of her relationship with her father, and Selene cried as Alvara told her how he died. She spoke of her belief in God and her friendship with Max, her time at school as well as her complex relationship with her aunt. She even spoke about her adventures with wings, and Selene lit up with joy as she spoke. Selene was somehow like a close friend; a bit odd, of course, but also trustworthy.

When Alvara finished, Selene got up and came over to give her a hug. Alvara relaxed into her jasmine-scented security. "I am so proud of you, daughter," she said, and Alvara tensed.

"Stop calling me that," she demanded. "I don't like it. I have a mother already. I talked a lot about myself, but I barely know you."

"I hope we are getting to know each other better," Selene replied, relaxing her hold to smile at Alvara. "And I am proud. You are using your wings to help others instead of just keeping them for yourself. That is difficult, you know, that does not happen very often. It makes me so very happy. Thank you for honoring my gift." She squeezed Alvara's shoulder, and then went to sit down again, turning to Jake. "I would love to hear your story as well, Jake," she continued. "It would be an honor."

To Alvara's surprise, Jake spoke. Alvara listened as Jake started from the very beginning, growing up with his sister and his single mother in a small town in Vermont, and growing wings one evening when he was a boy. He spoke of his love of flying, of going to University to study ornithology, and then of his advanced degree in the field. He told of hiking in the woods by his house in Northern California and hearing beautiful music, and how he learned that the voice belonged to Aurora, who became his wife. Jake's account of how he couldn't have children, despite how much they both wanted to, brought tears to Alvara's eyes.

Both Alvara and Selene cried when he spoke of losing Aurora over the cliff that night. He haltingly spoke about how he ended his studies with birds, discontinued his nightly flights and began his photographs, and moved to Venice Beach, where he opened the shop. He stopped talking, and the silence around them was complete. Selene got up to approach Jake, but he held up his hand, and Alvara noticed the sharpness of the gesture. Selene stopped.

"I told you this so you would understand. I know you are anxious to tell me how much I have honored your *gift*, but please spare me the need to reply. The one moment in my life where my wings could have made a difference, where you could have made a difference for me, you let me down. I saw you crying in that vision on the cliff; you were there! You wasted your gift on me, do you hear? Wasted! For a long time, I believed it was my fault, but it was yours! Why didn't you help me save her? Why?" Jake yelled, and Alvara could see tears in his eyes. She wiped her own away.

Selene stood there with a lost expression, and her eyes fell. Her vibrant red bangs seemed to dim. "I tried, Jake," she said, her voice breaking. "But I was not really there, do you see? Had I been in the sky, I might have, could have . . ." She stared at Jake, and Alvara could see that her eyes glistened with restrained tears. "By the time I rose, she was gone," she whispered.

"I never found her," Jake said, and his anger faded. "Could never even lay her to rest."

"How could you have?" Selene asked, frowning.

"That's what humans do; we have a ceremony to bury those we love. I could have at least found her body," he said scathingly, but she shook her head.

"No, no, she is not dead, Jake. She is gone."

"It's the same thing," he spat.

"No, Jake. Listen," and she came over to kneel next to him. "Rory is not dead. She was taken, but not by me. He has her."

"Stop playing games, Selene. I know you're not used to visitors, but this is crossing the line. I don't want to hear your fantasies. I know what happened."

"But Jake! He was there too! And he was truly there, just passing through, but able to reach out and snatch her away and save her forever. She is—"

"Stop," Jake said, and his voice was dead, like driftwood. "Just stop." Alvara could hardly recognize him as the easygoing man she knew. He stood up with glacial slowness, his back straight and unyielding, and walked toward the campfire, which was just visible in the distance. Selene looked like she might try to go after him.

"Don't," said Alvara. "Don't follow him."

"I just wanted to tell him that—"

"I don't want to hear it," Alvara interrupted. "Either you're full of lies, or Jake needs to hear this one first."

"Yes," Selene agreed, and sat back on her beach chair. They both leaned back and watched the 'sky', but there were no stars to admire here. Just the strange full-moon-within-the-moon. Alvara hoped Jake was all right, and resolved to search for him soon. But another thought crossed her mind.

"Selene?" Alvara asked.

"Yes?"

"How does this all work, with you and Sol? What are you, really? I don't understand. I'd appreciate you trying to explain, at least." Selene was silent for a while. Alvara wasn't sure she'd answer, but she finally spoke.

"I guess you could say we are made of belief," she said. "There is only so much left on Earth, and it is split pretty evenly between us. We are the last cosmic shapes in the sky that hold any real mystery, and so people pin their beliefs on us. And that is why we are still here."

"That doesn't make sense," Alvara answered, "there are still all kinds of religions left on Earth, with people believing in Buddha and Mohammed and Jesus and God and the Devil. If you're made of belief, then so are they, right? What happened to them?" She wondered if she wanted to hear Selene's answer, or if it would even make a difference, but the words had already left her lips.

"Long gone," Selene said with an unkind chuckle. "As I recall, the 'good' ones are busy keeping the 'bad' ones chained," she made quotation marks in the air and shook her head. "A full-time occupation, as you might imagine. They will not be back. No," she yawned, "just the two of us, who never picked sides." She noticed Alvara's expression. "Do not worry, daughter, you do not need some silly omnipotent creator; he did not have time for anyone even when he was around."

"Don't say that about God!" Alvara shouted. "That's not true, I don't believe you!" She stomped off toward Jake, hoping Selene wouldn't follow. Hot tears crinkled the edges of her eyes. As if she hadn't cried enough already today.

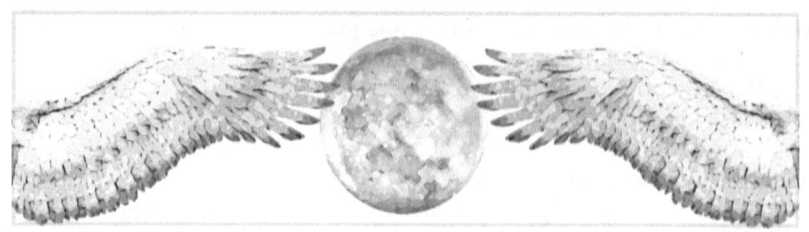

Chapter 16

Alone at last, Jake could finally think. But he didn't want to. Couldn't. He let his mind wander from the false sand dune to the swells of the false sea, curving away into the darkness. His heart felt hard in his chest, and Selene's words beat themselves against the door to his conscious thoughts, but he refused to allow them entry. He felt the absence of Rory, instead. The breeze was chilly, but Jake enjoyed the cold, as it matched his feelings. Rather than unlock that door in himself, he preferred to stare at the waves and just be alone.

As he stared into the darkness, he heard someone settle into the sand beside him. He relaxed when he realized it was just Alvara; he didn't want to have to deal with Selene right now.

The only sound came from the water sliding over the sandy shore. No insects or birds called here; the silence was absolute. Its heavy omnipresence was familiar. It reminded him of the dream Alvara and he had shared on the plane to China.

It was hard to believe that Selene was that lost and lonely child. What can you do for millennia when your only companionship is thousands of miles away, Jake thought, and felt such sorrow for her that his lingering anger dissipated. He noticed that Alvara was crying silent tears.

"Alvara, what's wrong?" he asked.

"I . . . I asked . . . Selene is such a jerk!" she sobbed, but couldn't continue. Jake put an arm around her shoulder.

Alvara sniffed, and wiped her eyes. "I almost drowned, and then . . . and then she told me that God was gone for good and didn't care about people, which I know isn't true!" She shook her head, and Jake didn't say anything, but just continued listening. "I mean, He wouldn't do that. I hate that she made me doubt Him, even for a second."

"It'll be okay, honey," Jake replied. "What does she know, cooped up in here? She's just trying to rile you up, and I wouldn't worry too much about it." Jake squeezed her shoulder.

Alvara sighed and took a few deep breaths. "I'm okay," she said. "Oh, I was glad I got to hear your story. I'm so sorry about your wife. I'm just, really sorry."

"Thanks. It was hard, but it felt like the time to tell the whole thing without feeling ashamed." They were silent for a minute or two.

"This place is so strange, and Selene . . . I don't know what to make of her. One minute she seems to care, the next she's insulting me. What does she want?" asked Alvara.

"I honestly don't know. But it seems like she wants to help, rather than harm; I feel a bit sorry for her, alone in here with only her golems. It's got to be pretty painful to feel betrayed by the only one you thought you could trust."

"Yeah, but Jake, what about what she said about the problems on Earth? And about your wife?"

"I've been trying not to think about that; it's the one thing keeping me from trusting Selene. I feel like she's trying to grasp at straws to control us, to get us to do what she wants."

"But what if what she said is true? What if . . ." She didn't finish, but Jake finished it in his head, *what if Rory is alive.* There had been that time when he heard her speak to him at her grave. And when he was lost in his own dreams of the future, Rory had saved him. But that proved nothing; of course Rory would be a part of his subconscious, as he had never stopped carrying her with him. Jake couldn't even conceive of what Selene had told him as being true. He felt as if doing so would break the brittle peace he had made with himself, and nothing but darkness lay beneath.

"I'll think about it," Jake lied.

"Good," said Alvara. "Also, she finally answered my question about what she and Sol are."

"In a useful way?"

"Somewhat. She said that they were creatures of belief; that they are made out of it, somehow, and that that's where their powers come from. She also told me what happened to the other deities, but I don't believe it. I think you're right, she was just trying to get under my skin."

"What did she say happened?" asked Jake.

"Well, she said that most died out or left when people stopped believing in them. The main ones people still worship today became guards on a prison of evil entities still around." She took a breath. "The guards included, according to Selene, God. But He wouldn't just abandon us like that. I think she's just making stuff up because she doesn't know."

"It would make sense that she wouldn't know; she said she was a prisoner here. So you're saying that according to her, the other entities besides the sun and moon just up and left Earth? Why did she and Sol stick around?"

"Something about they decided not to pick sides, and just picked up all the diluted worship that was left on the world to survive."

"Well that narrows the issues, then. Just two powerful beings to worry about."

"You forgot us," corrected Alvara, and pretended to flex her arm. Jake laughed.

"You've got to stop and wonder, sometimes," he said, leaning back in the sand. "To all appearances, we're inside the moon with a woman who is one of the last of her kind, attempting to discover why people care so much that we use or don't use our gift and whether the Earth itself is truly in danger." He smiled. "We could assume we're just locked in a padded cell somewhere, though I'm not sure it would improve our situation."

"Are you kidding? A padded cell sounds downright charming right about now," Alvara said. "How about we go back and talk some more with Selene, and try to figure out what's going on and how to get back home?"

"And then the padded cell? I could use some soft cushions to rest my aching back."

"Move it along, Gramps," Alvara said with a chuckle.

"What are these Children of Sol like?" Jake asked Selene, who looked up from where she had been pacing near the fire. Jake wondered about his vision of the man with the yellow eyes.

"Jake, my son, I am sorry I upset–" Selene began.

"Just answer the question. Please," Jake added, his jovial mood gone.

"I do not know his current brood," Selene answered. "They have sometimes existed in harmony with my own Children, and sometimes in opposition, but his Children seem to be antagonistic to humanity this time around." Jake leaned over to warm his hands at the campfire.

"You have heard of the warming of Earth?" Selene said. "The levels of the gas the creatures of the Earth exhale are only part of the problem. Over the past century or so, Sol has given his Children more and more power, but to what end I cannot really see, and it is causing the temperature to rise. All I know is that there is now an imbalance between us, which must be remedied. I think I can fix it, but I will need you to help on the Earth."

"What do you mean?" asked Alvara.

"You must kill the Children of the Sun," Selene answered. "The birds will help you find them. They threatened you and tried to kill Jake, yes?"

"Wait, don't be ridiculous. Kill somebody?" Alvara protested.

"No one is going to kill anyone," said Jake, his voice firm. "We can go talk to these children, and see if they know what they are doing. Have you tried that yet?"

"Jake, talking will do nothing. The Children of Sol do not see reason; what they all have in common is self-righteousness. They will obey their father before they listen to you. Do you want to watch Alvara's aunt waste away from skin cancer? Or how about your sister, living in Florida? I am not threatening you, either of you," Selene said, raising both hands as if to reassure them. "I care very deeply about you, and do not want to see you suffer. Sol has the power to make these threats come to pass. Please just be careful. If you go to speak to them, you will not be able to leave again."

"How can you know that? You said you don't even know them," Alvara accused.

"I helped once," Selene begged, "I simply could not bear the thought of losing both of you. And then Alvara reached out, enabling me to intervene. But against his Children, I cannot."

"What do you mean?" Alvara asked.

Selene turned to her. "You asked, and I gave another of my gifts to the men who were holding Jake. So that you could set him free."

"A gift?" Jake said.

"Lunacy, of course," Selene said, smiling. Jake felt a chill pass down his spine. Though he had been in bad shape, he could remember the men's screams as they fled.

"I asked for help," Alvara whispered. "But not from you. And not that," she added. "Are the men still . . . crazy?"

Selene waved a hand and changed the subject. "I cannot help you against his Children, not directly. You two must take this burden upon yourselves."

Selene stared at Jake, her voice passionate. "I know this is hard to hear, Jake, but Sol has Aurora captive, and has kept her there for many years. If we manage to prevent his plot, you may be able to set her free. And I can assist in that respect."

"How do I know you aren't holding this over me to get us to do as you ask?"

"Jake, I would never do that; I can prove Sol has her, if you are willing. I can show Aurora to you."

"Will I be able to speak with her?" Jake asked. His heart twisted at the possibility.

"Perhaps. I will need to get inside your head to find the link you still have with her, and follow it to its other end. As long as that is still intact, I will be able to locate her and you may speak with her for a short span."

"How short?"

"Time," Selene waved a hand, "is time. A few moments."

"Jake, are you sure you want to do this?" Alvara asked.

Jake whirled to face her. "Alvara, how can you even say that? If we were talking about your Dad, what would you choose?"

Alvara bit her lip, but nodded once, clearly worried.

Selene sat next to Jake and reached out her pale hand. For a moment, Jake stared at it. "Where do you think the Caretaker got his abilities?" Selene asked with a smile. "Do not worry, with *me* you will not get lost."

Jake put his hand in Selene's, closed his eyes, and thought of Rory.

Light and heat flashed behind his lids, and he squinted into the glare. Jake heard singing, and it was a song he did not recognize. But the voice belonged to his wife.

She stood, silhouetted in the sunlight, facing away from him. He could listen to her forever, but he had to see her. Moments, Selene had said.

"Rory," Jake called, and she turned.

His wife, his beautiful wife, had aged. Her lovely hair had thinned, and was more than half grey. Lines crisscrossed her face, and she seemed smaller. But her eyes were the same. It was really her. She was alive.

"Jake, you're here!" she exclaimed, and ran to him.

And passed through him, like he wasn't there. She stumbled, and nearly fell. He reached out to her, but one arm remained at his side. Despite pulling with his full strength, he remained shackled in a grip he could not see.

She approached, hovering inches away, eyes taking in the changes in him as well. "Oh my love," she said, her hand passing through his shoulder again. "Not here yet, clearly."

"Rory, I don't have a lot of time. I needed to be sure . . . I needed to see you." He cupped her face, just above the skin, dying to touch her.

A pressure built in his imprisoned hand, a heat that quickly became unbearable. "Rory, I love you!" he said desperately.

"Find me," she said, tears in her eyes, as she disappeared and his hand exploded in pain.

Jake lay on the sand, gasping, as his flesh burned. Selene whimpered, and then was silent. He felt Selene grip his wrist, and coolness spread down his arm, the pain fading to an echo. Jake lifted his hand, and saw on his palm a fresh puckered scar in the shape of a sunburst.

"What happened?" Alvara asked. "Are you guys all right?"

"She was really there," Jake said in a whisper.

"Sol did not take kindly to us intruding upon his domain," Selene explained, brushing one loose brown curl back out of her eyes. "Seemed to think we were spying, and gave us a warning," she said, waggling her burned hand as evidence. "He is impossible."

"He wasn't there," Jake said. "It was just me and Aurora," he paused for a second with a half-smile on his face. "And then I guess he kicked us out. That must have taken a lot of power."

"Of course, and that is the danger!" Selene said, exasperated. "He is very dangerous, and his Children are no better. You must destroy them."

"Why do you keep coming back to that?" Alvara asked. "There has to be another way."

"You could try asking them nicely not to destroy the world." Selene said sarcastically. "Also, every time you use your wings, and especially their healing powers, you increase the belief I have to draw on, just as they do for Sol when they use their abilities. They can't allow it, that imbalance; you cannot just coexist."

"That's great, maybe no one has to die then," Alvara said, "we can just fly around and heal people or something."

Selene's tone had changed to a pleading one. "It would not be enough. I want you to live, and . . . I want you to protect the Earth. All my long life, She has never turned her back on me. Mother Earth. She is my only constant, my grounding force. I love the Earth more than anything," she shuddered, and broke into harsh sobs. "You have to save Her."

Jake felt sorry for the woman, or Goddess, or whatever she was, but he had gotten to see his wife. She was alive. At the moment, it was difficult to care about the potential plight of the rest of the world.

Alvara stood and walked to where Selene was crying into her hands. "We'll do our best," she said, patting her shoulder.

Selene wrapped her arms around Alvara and wept into her shoulder. "Thank you," she wailed.

As Selene cried, her body changed and shrank as her middle age fell away. Her short brown hair lightened to almost white, and grew down to her waist. Her gown changed to a child's dress, and her features morphed until she was the little girl from the swing.

"I want my mommy," the child said, and her voice tinkled like little bells. She continued to cry, and a very confused Alvara didn't quite pull out of her grip. Jake did not understand what this change meant, but it felt different than the rapid alterations to hair color. Jake heard a sound in the distance.

"What was that?" he asked. The sound came again, and it was unmistakable this time; it was the combined blood-curdling call of a pack of wolves. The little girl raised her head, and her tearful expression was terrified. She wiped her eyes with one small hand, and said, "You have to run, go now; I cannot protect you!"

"We can't just leave you," Jake replied. "What are wolves doing here?"

"Not wolves, worse, worse," the little girl said. "I am sorry. You are in my prison and so are they. I thought we had more time. Please run; if you swim in the ocean you will find your way back to your bodies."

"Our bodies? You're not making sense. We're right here," Alvara said. The cries of the wolves had increased in pitch.

"Just a dream, just a dream, just a dream," the girl repeated as she shook her head with her hands on her temples and rocked back and forth. Jake didn't know whether Selene was saying that this trip had all been a dream or that the wolves weren't real. If it was a dream, what was she afraid of?

"You heard her. Let's go, Jake," Alvara said, gripping his hand.

"But what about Selene?" Jake asked. "What will the wolves do to you?"

Selene continued her rocking, and did not answer.

"This is her prison, Jake. She can't leave. But we can," Alvara said, tugging Jake's hand. The sound of paws striking sand was audible over the frenzied howls. "We need to go now!" Alvara shouted.

Jake nodded, and they took off at a run toward the water. Instead of running out on top, both Alvara and he splashed their way in and swam out to sea.

When he was a ways out, he tread water and looked back toward the shore. There was no sign of the wolves. Selene, an adult once more, stood at the edge of the water and stared toward them. Jake raised a hand to acknowledge her. But Selene stayed motionless. Jake and Alvara swam farther into the sea.

The water was cold, but Jake set a moderate pace, and they stopped periodically to rest. During one of his periods of swimming, Jake put one arm in front of him, but when he tried to pull back the water, he noticed he held only air. He wasn't swimming; he was falling.

He shouted as he fell. It was full night, and his body was freezing as the sharp wind whipped past. He noticed his wings furled around him. He let his wings snap open, seeing spots in front of his eyes from the force of the brake. Blinking to clear his head, he turned most of his speed into a forward glide, and circled around to search for Alvara. She was below him, but also circling, so he tipped his wings to glide downward to meet her. He could see lights spread out in a carpet beneath them, and, shivering from the after-effects of adrenaline and exhaustion, wondered where they had ended up.

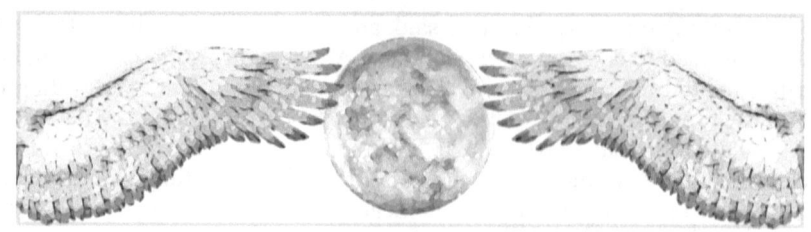

Chapter 17

Soon.

Hours, days, years, have very little meaning.

It is laughable to think in days when her dance grants those days their endings and beginnings. She cannot await sunrise or sunset; bound by night break and night's end, she lives all moments of the night at once. A star-pitted emptiness is her only home. She does not know if he will visit in an hour or a year, but can feel that it will be soon.

It makes it difficult for her to relate to humans, those creatures of the moment. They are always in such a rush; it is their defining characteristic. Their impatience; impatient to grow up, impatient to get a job, impatient to find their true purpose for being, until they reach old age when their impatience wears out, and they wish for more time before expiring. It makes them fascinating, that they can feel time so acutely, like the moment matters, that the present is superior to the past or the future.

She feels the universe turning; how can one moment compare to that?

In her delight and her wonder at their short but bright lives, she and he both bestowed gifts upon them, creating a Child of each but formed by both. It was the best decision they made together, as those Children fulfill them in ways they had not dreamt of before.

The present is different than much of her past, allowing her to focus upon it. Against his judgment, she has succeeded in her goal. She is no longer bound by the fluctuations of form that had plagued them both; she has sealed her shifting image into what she sees as her real self, despite the profusion of her names and profusion of selves those names came to represent.

In a clear pool near where she sits, if it can be called sitting, she gazes upon her image again. A beautiful human face beams back at her. Her eyes are the light grey color of a shadow on the moon, her skin the pale white of the moon's fine powder, and a sheet of dark hair frames high cheekbones, black like the night she inhabits.

And it feels so wonderful, this escape from her volatile self. She inhales the night and looks through the sky to the Earth below, and feels joy. She reaches to delicately push back her hair from her face, and it is still her hair and her face when she completes the gesture.

She laughs and springs to her feet. The night of her home is still, the forest she creates within her mind a pleasant place to reside. The dew on the grass is cool beneath her bare feet, and through its whisper she feels connected to the Earth she loves, rotating through the void below. As she has for millennia, she begins to dance.

No one had ever taught her how. No one needed to. The freedom inherent in dancing is strong in the minds of her life-givers on the Earth below, within those humans who stare up at the moon and see something more. And if she believes in anything, she believes in freedom. Her feet and hands move as she twirls and leaps, and gravity is in her mind alone; she soars to the music she alone can hear.

And he comes. Sometimes she passes in front of him, other times he passes in front of her, in an endless spiraling dance around their Earth. She knows the truth about time, that human folly, in those moments; time is not a line, but endless loops, the paths taken before and to be taken again wearing grooves into the fabric of the universe.

He greets her as he approaches. She feels his heat.

"You," he says, and she hears his name for her like a secret tattoo upon her flesh.

"You," she replies, and knows he hears his name within the simple word. They did not create their many names, and it feels wrong to use ones others had given them for each other. He comes nearer, and she can see him at last.

How to describe him, when none like him had ever existed? She can say that his hair is red, and then brown, and then a tightly curled black. His features are strong and young, and then old and powerful and bearded, and then round and jovial, but she knows him. She knows his heat, and his constancy, and his love for her, and looks deep into his eyes.

And finds nothing.

The absence confuses her for a moment, as he sweeps her into an embrace. He seems distant, though he holds her with his characteristic fervor. She wants to ask what is wrong, but hesitates.

As he pulls back, he half-smiles as he runs his hand through her long dark hair. "So it is true," he says, shaken. "You did it."

"Yes," she declares, but continues in earnest, "It feels good, really good. To be stable, to be wholly myself. I know it worries you . . ." she trails off, because his brow wrinkles.

"He said you would not notice a difference, not at first," he begins. "But He worried, and I continue to worry, how much of yourself you will lose by preventing the changes. Even He allows them—"

"Look, I am fine, just finally in the body that truly belongs to me. And why do you trust Him over me, anyway? He said He had never done it. Wait," she ends in a whisper. "I understand. He spoke of me, did he not? What did he say? What?" The last is a roar. Gone is her composure, gone her quiet joy that had sustained her until he arrived. It frightens her that she is so angry, but she feels vindicated when he will not meet her eyes. She is right; he is deceiving her.

How could she be anything but first in his eyes? And why is she so confused? A part of her is slipping away, but she doesn't know what it is.

What if . . . she has a thought, and it meanders into the forefront of her mind, filling her with rage and breaking her heart. What if He has turned her other half against her? She must not let on, not at first, not until she can determine how deep the betrayal runs.

The trees around the clearing lose their leaves, not one by one as on Earth, but in a brilliant rush of red and gold and a sudden universal collapse of every leaf to the ground, and there is a sound like breaking glass. It is beautiful, and sad, and she feels the urge to cry, but no tears will come.

"Are you all right?" he asks.

"Fine, Sol," she replies sweetly.

Chapter 18

"Please, sir, we're exhausted. Your sign said that you have rooms," Jake was trying be civil, but his composure was starting to crack.

"Oh sure, we have rooms, but ah, I can't say I like the looks of you both. You don't have no bags or nothing." The man exhaled, and Jake could smell a sour tobacco scent that fit in with the drab surroundings.

"Yes, but we already spoke to you of how someone robbed us," Jake explained with patience. He was quickly running out of it.

"Ya, but, that don't explain how you have a credit card left to pay for the room, you know what I'm saying? I don't want to get involved with nothing, you hear?" The man appeared to very much want to get involved. He feigned disinterest, peering into a dank corner and chewing on the end of a toothpick, but he was on the edge of his seat. The small motel appeared on the verge of financial ruin. The edges of the ceiling sagged down to give the room an oval appearance.

A pamphlet in the lobby had let on that Jake and Alvara had glided, exhausted, into rural New Hampshire a few hours after sunset. It made a strange sort of sense that the Earth would rotate while they were visiting with the Moon; it was no less believable than anything else. At least they didn't need to buy a return ticket from China, Jake thought, but couldn't even feel relief. He felt like he hadn't slept in days.

The man leaned forward even more, and Jake waited for his potbelly to pull him right off the chair. He beckoned Jake forward, whispering, "And you know gramps, between us gents, this situation ain't sittin' right with me. I run a respectable establishment here, and that girl, she looks underage. Now I know there ain't no hanky-panky between you two—"

Jake felt revolted, almost as if this man's oily mind had soiled them both. "We don't need any of this crap," Jake said, and beckoned to Alvara. "Let's try somewhere else."

"Now, calm down sir, I didn't mean no disrespect to you and your *granddaughter.*" Jake gave him a steely glare. "I'm just saying somebody with a dirty mind could wonder, but maybe a bit extra could prevent anyone knowing you was staying with an underage doll." He winked, and Jake resisted the urge to slug him.

Jake wanted nothing more than to walk away and leave this man with his tobacco-stained wallpaper, but Alvara was nodding off where she leaned against the counter. "You treat us with a minimum of respect, and we'll add an extra thirty dollars for your non-smoking room with two *single* beds."

The man smiled, or at least the creases of his mouth climbed a short way up his pudgy cheeks. "Of course, sir and miss. Right this way." He swatted the wall behind the counter as he climbed down from his chair to remove a room key from one of the pegs, leaving the majority of the pegs still in possession of unused keys. Jake and Alvara followed him around the side of the building to a turquoise door identical to the nineteen others flanking it.

"Have a good night," the man said, handing Jake the key and whistling as he left them alone.

Jake was just relieved to see him waddle away. They got into the room, and Jake planned to talk a bit with Alvara before they headed to bed. But as if he was on autopilot, he slipped under the covers with his wings tucked along his shoulder blades, and he was asleep almost as soon as his head made contact with the pillow.

Jake awoke to a single beam of light centered on his left eye, and rolled out of the way to try to get back to sleep. But he caught a glimpse of the late hour on the bedside table and reconsidered, yawning and stretching his way into alertness. He recalled the dream from which he had awoken; it was of flying, which was unusual for him. He had glided over a city with Rory and Alvara, who both had wings. Suddenly, Rory and Alvara's wings had disappeared, and they had begun to fall. In the dream, he knew that he only had time to save one. He had dived after Rory, and reached out his hand to grab her when she was swallowed in a yellow flame and disappeared. He then turned and stared into Alvara's eyes as she fell, sure that he couldn't reach her in time.

Well, at least the dream made sense, Jake thought. He worried about the people he cared about, and wanted to protect them. Of course Alvara topped the list. And Rory, well . . . perhaps he could worry about her again. It was still difficult for him to grasp, but the smallest hope had wedged itself into his mind that he might be with her again. Jake knew that if his time with her had been an illusion, he would never be able to return to his former modicum of contentment. He couldn't relinquish grief twice.

Jake tried to shake off these sinister thoughts, and set his mind to planning their next move. Maybe some coffee would help, but he'd never trust a cup brewed in this establishment. Jake's nose wrinkled as he took a cautious whiff of the armpit of his shirt. They'd have to buy some clothes, as a first order of business. Next, they'd figure out what the hell to do about the Legion.

But first, a day of recuperation.

Alvara yawned and blinked a few times. "Good morning, sunshine," Jake said.

"Can we not talk about the sun right now?" she replied sleepily, yawning again and rubbing the edges of her eyes. "I'm glad we made it to these nice beds last night."

"Yeah," said Jake. "I was frozen and about ready to fall asleep flying."

"Uh huh." She sat up. "What the hell was that all about, Jake?"

"What do you mean?" he asked.

"All of it," Alvara sighed. "Freaking trip to the moon and walking servants and strange woman and pack of wolves, that's what I'm talking about."

"I don't know. My brain's turned to mush this morning, and I can't seem to figure anything out."

"Mine is just gone," she rubbed her eyes again. "It was so weird. I mean, she treated us like superheroes. 'It is your destiny to save the world,' and all that," Alvara continued. "What makes her think we would buy that? We grow wings and heal people; we're not killers."

"If the world is really in trouble, we may have to consider going up against the Legion in some way," Jake replied, though Alvara snorted as if she didn't believe it. "For now, we need more info. I thought we could head to the library and read up on the Legion." She fell back onto the bed in mock exhaustion.

"I hope Laerik is all right," Alvara said. "She must be so worried. I wonder how long we've been gone. It felt like maybe a day up there, but who knows, right?"

"Laerik got herself to China, she can get herself home," Jake said. "That bird never ceases to amaze." Alvara smiled.

A harsh pounding began. A muffled shout of, "Open up, this is the police!" followed. Stunned, Alvara stared at the door, but Jake tried to dismiss the situation with a sweep of his hand as he walked to open it. He was more perplexed than concerned. A fit young cop, flanked by a tall cop and a female cop, confronted him. The man who owned the motel stood behind them, rocking back and forth from his toes to heels.

"Are you Jake Coughlin? Is there a young girl here with you?"

Jake nodded. "What's this about?"

"Sir, I'm here to investigate an alleged kidnapping."

"Kidnapping?" Jake asked in disbelief.

"Just doing my civic duty, sirs; the situation didn't seem right, I told you," the man crooned, but the first cop glared at him and he returned to silence.

"Alvara and I are traveling together; I didn't kidnap her."

"Then you can explain why Max's mother thought that Alvara and her friend Max were on a camping trip in the Santa Monica Mountains in California, and why the two of you are in a motel outside of Durham, New Hampshire."

Jake was at a loss. "Well, it's a bit complicated to explain—"

"That's what we thought. You have the right to remain silent—"

"Jake! What's going on?" Alvara peered around the edge of the door.

"Don't worry, Alvara, we'll sort it out," Jake said as they placed his hands in cuffs and led him to the car that waited in the motel parking lot.

Jake watched the female cop take Alvara aside, probably to make sure that she was all right. He trudged to the car, shoes scraping the pavement, his mind spinning to try to come up with a way to explain their presence here without using the crazy and convoluted truth.

Jake felt that sensation of being watched again, just like in his vision and on the temple rooftop, but couldn't tell where it originated. It made his hair stand on end.

A blur darted across Jake's peripheral vision, and the tall cop let out a soft cry and fell to the ground. Jake glanced around, but couldn't see anything out of the ordinary. All he could see was the relatively empty motel, surrounded by deciduous forest, with a small stretch of highway visible through the trees. Nothing moved other than the remaining cops.

The fit cop drew his weapon. Instead of bending over his unconscious partner, he scanned the area. Jake watched the cop near Alvara, and saw the whirlwind as a flash of blonde hair sped into her, punching her maybe ten times in the course of a second, and speeding away again before she hit the ground. Alvara stood alone now, but froze, her eyes wide with fear. They reflected Jake's burning question; who was doing this, and how?

The fit cop next to Jake ran to the car to call for backup, but before he could reach it the whirlwind intercepted him. The man tripped, but recovered and turned to face his attacker, who Jake guessed was female. The fit man took a few hits, but returned one with a smack of his gun. His attacker grunted in pain. A few more unseen hits, however, and he too lay unconscious on the floor. The blur darted after the fleeing motel owner. As she reached him, she delivered a blow to the back of his head and he dropped with a squeal. When all fell silent, the woman came to a stop, and Jake got his first good look at her.

She was young, in her early twenties, with her blonde hair tied back in a low ponytail at the base of her neck. Her eyes were golden, a few shades darker than her hair. She was breathing hard, and collapsed into a kneeling position. Sweat drenched her black workout pants and tank top. She straightened to brush a stray lock out of her face and behind her ears. Jake walked toward Alvara, not turning his back to the woman.

The woman muttered, "God that sucked." She breathed hard for a few moments, grumbling in a vaguely British accent, "Bloody sun and his bloody . . ." and staggered over to the fit cop. On the way, she reached into her pocket and removed a syringe, which she slammed into her leg, wincing a bit.

When she reached the cop, she rummaged along his belt until she got another set of handcuffs, and before either he or Alvara could complain, she stood next to them again with Alvara already cuffed as well. She glanced down at one of her nails and scoffed. "Damn it, I just had these painted." The whole encounter had taken less than a minute.

"Who the hell are you?" Jake asked.

"Oh right, you might still think this is some sort of rescue mission. Not exactly, Mr. Coughlin." She flashed them a grin. "My name is Isabella, pleased to meet you. Isabella Dusk, you might know me as 'I'."

"You're one of the Children of the Sun," Jake said. They clearly had a different gift.

"Clever, this one. Did you think Robert and I had just forgotten about all those warning notes? Just had to defy our reasonable request? Of course, I've heard that you already know my new friend here." She gestured to the car driving up to the motel, and Jake watched as none other than Xiu Li stepped out of the passenger seat, sharply dressed in a dark grey suit and blue tie.

He walked toward them, all smiles, and Jake fought to contain his horror. He struggled and failed to escape from Isabella's hold. Though she held him with only one hand, he couldn't budge an inch. When Xiu Li laughed, Jake's whole body shuddered with fear.

"Ah Jake, Alvara, it is so nice to see you again. It was kind of you to leave me this little souvenir to remember you by." To Jake's disgust, Xiu Li reached into his pocket and brought out a plastic sample bag containing the piece of Jake's bat wing. "It made tracking you both so much easier. Though you did drop off the radar for about a week, which was indeed curious. No matter, we are together again, as planned."

"Your attitude, Li, is not to my liking," Isabella said. "And we will be on our way."

Isabella dragged Jake and Alvara together to the waiting car. Alvara resisted, but didn't make headway, until a murder of crows distracted Isabella, diving and clawing at her face and eyes.

Alvara broke free and ran. Gripping Jake with one hand, Isabella swatted at a crow with her free hand. She struck it so hard it hit the ground and stayed there. The rest of the birds dispersed amid loud screeches. Jake muttered under his breath for Alvara to run faster. *Damn their lack of wings!* Before Alvara had gotten out of the lot, Xiu Li grabbed her by the wrist, and she screamed and tried to wrench her hand away. "Get off of me!"

Xiu Li drew his ring across her skin, cutting her cheek in a smooth gesture that imitated a caress. Alvara's lip quivered. She raised her head defiantly, though it must have hurt. As they watched, the cut closed as if it had never existed.

"Such a prize you are, little Moon-child," Xiu Li said.

"Let go of her!" Jake yelled, thrashing in earnest, but he couldn't break out of Isabella's supernaturally strong grip.

"This can be gentle or rough," Isabella said curtly, giving Jake's wrist a sharp tug and taking Alvara from Xiu Li with her other hand. "Hurting you is optional, and I would prefer not, regardless of the damage you have done." She dragged them across the parking lot of the motel.

"Help, someone! Help!" Alvara screamed to the empty lot and the empty stretch of highway. No one came.

Despite their struggles, Isabella shoved both of them into the back of the car. A metal grate divided the rear seating from the middle row, where Isabella and Xiu Li rode behind the driver. Alvara shook with fear, and Jake wanted to comfort her, but was so frightened he couldn't think. After a minute or two of the car's progress, he kept his terror under imperfect control, allowing him to at least consider their situation.

"So how did a powerful person like yourself end up with the slimy likes of Xiu Li? It can't have been by choice," Jake said to Isabella. Alvara glanced toward him, but he stared ahead.

"We have similar interests," Isabella replied. "When we saw him near the temple last week, we discovered that he would be willing to blood-track you, which he said was very accurate, in exchange for a few feathers from each of you. It was a bargain."

Jake had a sudden thought. "What have you done with Laerik?"

"Oh, your pet raven is safe enough; we will be meeting her soon," Isabella replied. Jake hoped Laerik was all right.

"What do you even want with us? We are no threat to you or your organization, just leave us alone," Alvara said.

"Oh please, do not play innocent." Isabella craned her neck to frown at them. "Unfortunately, every time you go flying around at night, you bring this world closer to destruction."

"What are you talking about?" Alvara said.

"I went along as we tried simpler methods, but Mr. Noon and his little warning notes were not enough, so now I'm in charge of your case. No more questions."

Isabella pushed a button and a dark glass partition rose, cutting off the sound completely. It also cut off most of the light, as the back compartment lacked windows. A dim bulb glowed overhead.

"Hey!" Jake yelled a few times, but the block stayed up. "Dammit," Jake said. He wondered what to do. His mind was blank. "We'll figure some way out of this," he said.

"That's a laugh," said Alvara, her eyes sharp. "I gave it my best shot, and you saw what happened. Did you see the way Isabella could move? We wouldn't get ten steps or two wing beats in before she would catch up with us!" She paused, and whispered. "And Jake, Xiu Li is here. I barely escaped from him last time, and the way he looked at me . . . there's no one left to get us out of this. There's no way to escape, and my brain is just racing in circles and making me more and more afraid."

"There may be some way out of this," Jake repeated.

"What do they want us for?! We don't even know!" she was all but shouting. "They could be . . . taking us somewhere to do experiments on us or something! I mean, they could just want to see how much pain we can take with our stupid healing abilities!" She was breathing faster now.

"Alvara, just calm down, we'll figure this—"

"God, I can't believe I was stupid enough to listen to Selene! Or you, for that matter." She gave a sarcastic chuckle amid her tears, "we're not superheroes, Jake. Big surprise. I wish I had never come." She leaned over to wipe her eyes on her T-shirt and turned away from Jake toward the imaginary window. He thought she kept crying, but he couldn't be sure.

"Alvara—"

"Shut up."

He did. Her words had found their mark. Alvara looked up to him; he was the one with the crazy ideas and plans. He had gotten her out of danger last time, and if he could have one wish she would be free of it again.

But this time he couldn't protect her. The thought fueled his anger. They were overpowered, sure, but that just meant they had to be smarter than the opposition. He would find a way out of this.

He expected that the Legion of the Light would be reveling in their victory, but he was dumbfounded by Isabella's holier-than-thou attitude. She had said that he and Alvara were 'bringing this world closer to destruction'. It was more than odd for her to turn the blame back on them.

It could be that Isabella and Robert didn't know that their actions harmed the world, and that Sol was the only guilty one. Jake wondered about that for a while, shifting his wrists to try to relieve some of the discomfort of the handcuffs jamming into his back. He tried to intuit the purpose of their organization, but came up empty. Maybe they didn't even know.

Jake thought back to the conversation with Selene. She had seemed strange, lonely, and awkward, but also genuine. He didn't think she had lied through her teeth. She had believed what she told them, but Jake hated the lack of solid information.

He and Alvara's lives were in danger. Xiu Li was more than capable. There had to be some way to get answers before this situation erupted, but Jake had little faith that talking would get him or Alvara away from Xiu Li.

After driving awhile in semi-darkness, the car came to a stop. Bodyguards ushered them out onto the tarmac of a runway, where they entered a private plane awaiting them. Isabella walked alongside her captives as they went to the back of the plane, where cages lined the walls. Each was big enough to hold a crouching human being, but the only occupied one was on the far wall. Jake couldn't make out the details.

"Don't put us in here!" Alvara yelled, struggling. "We're on a plane, we're not going anywhere."

Isabella frowned, and replied, "I'm sorry about the cages. It's protocol until we know more about you and your abilities. Don't give us any reason to use harsher measures." While one guard unlocked Alvara's wrists, Jake's guard pushed him into one of the metal cages. He grunted as his knees smacked painfully on the cage floor.

"Isabella, let us out!" Jake shouted. The guards held the door for Isabella and then exited, leaving Jake and Alvara in silence. Jake shifted his weight to a sitting position and massaged his sore knees. The cage was clean, with wire mesh reinforced with bars the size of this thumb. There would be no busting out of these.

"Hey," Jake said to Alvara, but she leaned against the side of her cage with her back to him and didn't answer. He couldn't blame her. He considered speaking to her again when Jake heard a cough from the cage on the far wall, and turned his attention to the third prisoner.

Upon closer inspection, the cough came from a kid who was barely 18.

He wore a dirty T-shirt and ratty jeans, and crouched behind a small cot. His face, or what Jake could see of it, was tight and gaunt, as if the skin was too small for the angularity of his cheekbones. The kid coughed again, and turned to peer at Jake with narrowed eyes.

"Hi," Jake said. "Don't worry, I'm not going to hurt you."

The kid laughed at that, causing another coughing fit. "Like I wouldn't see you coming. I'm just trying to figure out if you're going to flip or what."

"Flip?" Jake asked.

"Freak out, buddy. It's pretty standard. The moon ain't full, but tonight will still be a mite interesting for you and your friend there." Alvara lifted her head.

"What are you talking about?" she asked. Her cage was on the other side of Jake's, and she stared past him to the guy in the far cage.

"You'll see, sweet cheeks," the kid promised and shivered, as if with a fever. They all felt the plane begin to move, and tried to hold on to the bars of the cage during takeoff. Soon the plane stabilized again.

"Kid, what's your name? Mine's Jake, and this is Alvara."

"I'm not a kid, buddy, but whatever. The name's Ridge, on account of my ridge, see?" And he leaned down to show the scraggly overgrown Mohawk in the center of his head. It was easy to see that he had been in captivity for a long while; the rest of his hair had grown long enough that it covered his scalp. "Ouch," he muttered, and proceeded to scratch his neck. Jake saw him find the offending flea, pinch it, and toss it to the floor of his cage.

"Why are you here? Do you know where we're going?" Jake asked. He hoped the kid had some idea at this point.

"Hah," he replied, sitting cross-legged on his cot. "I'm just in for being me," and he flashed a smile. "Special treatment, you could say. Isabella calls me her pet project. I've been in the back of this here airplane for maybe a month now. They let me out for bathroom runs and whatnot. I'm just waiting for the right opportunity." He gave an unhappy smile. "It's been a while since I've seen the moon, and I can't say it's very good for me."

"Do they, um . . . do anything to you?" Alvara asked quietly.

"Nah, they don't beat me or anything, and I get enough food. Just keeping me here seems like what they want to do. Robert and she keep muttering that the treatment will work, but I think it's a load of crap."

"So you've met Robert," Jake said. "What's he like?"

Ridge shrugged. "One strange dude. Indian, middle-aged, creepy yellow eyes, reminds me of a scientist. No lab coat though. I think he just sees me as an experiment. Not a person," he added, anger coloring his voice.

"Have you tried to escape?" Jake asked.

"When exactly would I do that? The only time they let me out of the cage is during the day when the plane is in the air." He took a deep breath and closed his eyes. "How about you two? Why are you guys here?"

"Similar, I'd guess," said Jake, "though we haven't figured it all out yet. Isabella kidnapped us this morning."

"You'll get used to the bitch. Swell."

They stopped talking as the door opened, and Isabella entered alone. "Sorry to interrupt this little party," she joked, and walked over to Ridge's cage. He braced himself for some sort of confrontation, though she didn't seem threatening. The hate in his eyes was palpable. "Come on, it was just a joke," she said, discomfited by his glare.

She turned to the others. "And my two new guests? I had a couple questions I know you would love to answer." She gestured to the door, and a guard brought in a red hot brand and handed it to her. There was a sunburst pattern on the glowing end. Sweat trickled down Jake's forehead, though the brand glowed several feet away.

"Now Jake," she said. "I am going to ask you if we have discovered all that you two can do. We know about your ability to fly and to heal yourselves. Is there anything else we're missing? It's important for your correct registration, you see." Jake didn't respond. "Really, Jake? I don't want to hurt Alvara." She reached the brand through the bars of the cage, forcing Alvara up against the far end as the brand got closer and closer to her. As it approached the skin of her arm, Alvara whimpered with fear.

"Isabella, that's all we can do!" Jake shouted. The brand touched Alvara's skin. She screamed in pain, and Isabella withdrew it. Alvara kept her lips pursed together as she cried, holding her arm and shaking.

"Are you sure?" Isabella asked. She seemed uncomfortable and earnest.

"Wait, wait! The healing isn't just for us; the feathers work on others too!" Jake yelled in a rush. He had forgotten the blasted feathers.

"Ah," Isabella said. "Exactly the type of thing that I thought Xiu Li was holding back! Thank you for the tip. Sorry, but I know you can heal, Alvara. You should not even have a scar."

She considered Jake. "I don't like to cause pain. I wish you both had not forced me to these methods. You may not fully understand now, but that does not excuse your actions." She appeared sincere, which made Jake wonder if she was insane.

"Go to hell," Jake spat.

"Well, perhaps Robert will have more success. Enjoy your lunch." She sighed and left the room, and a female guard entered with a plate of food for each of them, closing the door behind her.

Jake asked, "Alvara, are you all right?"

"Damn it," Alvara muttered, blinking back tears. "It'll be fine in a minute."

"I'm so sorry, Alvara," Jake said. He was shaking. "I shouldn't have dragged you into this. I was a fool to assume it would all just work out." What had he been thinking? It was one thing to decide to go gallivanting off on a harebrained quest for his own satisfaction, but quite another to drag a young girl into it with him. Neither of them was prepared for what they encountered. And now Alvara had been tortured, and he didn't prevent it.

"Thanks Jake, but I'm not sorry I agreed to join you," Alvara replied. "There's still more time, though; just be patient," and she offered a half-smile. Her strength made him so proud, and he set aside his guilt for another time.

"That means the world to me, Alvara," he said.

They ate their meals, which consisted of peanut butter and jelly sandwiches and water, in silence. The minutes and hours passed, though it was difficult to tell how many. They agreed in hushed tones that it would be safest to grow bat wings that night. The plane landed and took off again. Jake thought he had snoozed, but woke with a start a minute or so before sunset. "Good timing," Ridge said, and Jake turned to stare at him. He was on edge, and kind of twitchy.

"Does something happen to you at sunset?" Jake asked.

"You could say that. It may look a bit freaky, but I'm sure you'll deal with it."

"Well, both Alvara and I change during the moon too—"

"Fascinating," Ridge said, and then doubled over. As Jake and Alvara grew bat wings, Jake kept staring at Ridge. Ridge was shaking, curled into a ball and letting out little cries of pain. Finally, his body relaxed, though his eyes remained tightly shut, and he mumbled softly to himself.

"Ridge?" Alvara asked. "Are you okay?"

"Yeah," he breathed. His eyes opened. His left eye was his normal deep brown. The entirety of the other was a milky blue.

"Wait, you grow wings?" he said in disgust. "Not fair."

Chapter 19

Ridge appeared unchanged, minus the blue eye. Alvara couldn't help but giggle as the tension broke. It was just so ridiculous. He had built up his change so much, and it had been a long day.

"It's not funny." Ridge sulked in his cage.

"No, it really is," Alvara said between gulps of air. "I thought, I thought you were like a werewolf or something," she said, and collapsed into snorts of laughter.

"So you're saying I'm sexy?" Ridge asked hopefully, the hair flopping into his eyes not helping her giggles in the slightest. "What are you, vampires?" he retorted.

"Ew, no," Alvara replied, trying to bring her laughter under control.

"I'm not sure there is a name for us; we just grow wings at night," Jake said, and turned so Ridge could see his bat wings better through the holes he had ripped in his shirt.

"Like creepy angels?" Ridge asked.

"No," Alvara said firmly. "We're Children of the Moon Goddess."

"Get out," Ridge said. "My Mum told me about you." He chuckled.

"Really? What did she say?" Jake asked.

"She said that you guys were rare, even rarer than we are, but that you helped to balance excess energies." Ridge waved his hands in a vague way.

"Energies?" Jake asked.

"Yeah, you know; the extra belief stuff that floats down and changes people. There's a lot more now than there used to be, which is starting to freak my family out."

"Strange," Jake said.

"Wait, so there are others like you? And what are you, really?" asked Alvara.

"I'm a Seer," he answered proudly. "Well, you know, not a full one, but I can See glimpses of the future from time to time. Only in my right eye. And that eye is blind at night. And nothing big, just snippets."

"That's got to be cool," Alvara encouraged.

"It's all right," he said, and focused hard on his fingernails as his ears turned red with the compliment. She hid a smile.

"You should see my little sister Sheila, though," Ridge said. "That girl has some crazy abilities. Though she was having a bit of a rough patch before I ... ended up here."

"Wow, so she can see the future?" Alvara asked. "That would have come in handy like a thousand times lately." Her face darkened.

"You would think," Ridge said. "But it ain't perfect. I'm here, aren't I?"

They were silent for a while.

"Alvara, what we need most is information. It might be really useful to meet your family, Ridge. And especially Sheila," Jake added.

"We're not known for being friendly to those outside the family," Ridge said, eyes narrowed. "And I imagine after I get out of here, that's gonna be cranked up to eleven. Don't count on it." He wrapped his arms around his legs and stared into the distance with his one clear eye.

Before Alvara could respond, they felt the plane land on a second runway. Four guards entered the room. They stopped short when they saw her and Jake with wings, hesitant to approach. Instead, they tossed wrapped peanut butter and jelly sandwiches into the cages. Ridge glared at his with mild disgust.

"Isabella will be here to fetch you shortly," one said before they retreated, closing the door behind them. Alvara tried to eat, but the sandwich was too sickly sweet to choke much of it down.

"Hey," Ridge said. Alvara looked up from her unfinished sandwich.

"Alvara, I'll make you a deal," he said. "I know you're prisoners too, but at least you're getting off the plane. If you somehow get away, please don't let them keep me here," he said, desperation creeping into his cocky tone. "Get me out of here, and I'll do whatever I can to help you guys. Take you to my family, whatever. Just please, help me," he said.

"Ridge, I don't know what I can do," Alvara said. "But if we can, we'll get you out of here. I promise," she repeated.

"What's the hold-up?" Isabella called from the hallway. She entered the room and saw them, coming to an abrupt halt. "Oh," she said, wrinkling her nose. "Bat wings! How interesting . . ."

She waved to the guards to bring Jake and Alvara with them, securing their wrists with handcuffs and their wings with a specially-designed cuff that pinned the pinions together. They had to try two cuffs to get some that were small enough that they could fit the bat wings. Alvara wondered if Isabella's super strength lasted into night. She doubted it. But neither Jake nor she would be flying anywhere.

Alvara glanced back at Ridge, whose eyes fell as guards ushered them out. She would never have left him here regardless of her promise. He seemed smaller now and very alone in the long corridor of empty cages.

Alvara bent her knees to fit through the small door of the plane, but still managed to bang one bat wing on its metal edge. She saw a world of oranges and pinks, the aftermath of sunset. Alvara saw the gibbous moon rising in the sky, and wondered if Selene could see what had happened to them, and whether she cared. Meeting the goddess, speaking with her, made God seem so much farther away.

She followed Jake across a much shorter and squatter runway to a waiting black car identical to the first, and managed to wedge herself and her wings into the back seat again. At least this car had windows.

Alvara watched through the tinted glass as they drove off the runway and into a dense forest. There were no signs or landmarks to provide a hint to where they were. They had flown for hours, so perhaps they were in Europe. The bit of sky Alvara could see went from russet to gray. They passed a green highway sign, and Alvara read a blurred 'Seattle' near the top, but couldn't read the mile number next to it in time. So they were in Washington, the Pacific Northwest. Sometimes lights flashed through the trees, but their speed was such that Alvara couldn't identify them.

So much of her life, she had moved of her own volition, choosing her secret volunteer hours at the hospital, choosing the acts of faith that were the core of her identity. But somehow it had spiraled out of her control. She had barely escaped from Xiu Li once, had barely saved Jake. And the price had been sudden insanity in people she had barely met, perhaps permanently. Alvara didn't know how to feel about that, about Selene twisting her honest prayer into a curse. But she and Jake had survived.

Now Isabella had them. After what Isabella had done, Alvara figured they could expect no better from her.

Fear was useless here. Alvara needed anger, and she needed patience, in order to figure out what her captors intended and what she could do about it.

"You okay?" Jake asked.

"Peachy." Alvara said, turning toward Jake's concerned gaze. "At least my burn is gone. And the bitch, as Ridge correctly named her, was right; no scar."

"Good to hear."

"Yeah." They sat for a while.

"So, we're in a car again."

"Yep." Alvara quipped, not in the mood for conversation. She adjusted her posture, trying to get comfortable even though the wing cuffs dug into her back. She hoped they arrived soon, just to relieve the boredom.

Their car turned off the main highway and followed a winding road through the trees and fog of the falling night. The road was well-maintained, though there were no turn-offs. It turned out to be a driveway, which led into a large facility.

"Jake, look. It seems like some sort of institute," she said.

"Just forest on my side," Jake replied. "What do you see?"

"There are huge windows on the buildings, most with lights on inside, with a bunch of people walking around. Business types. We've got to be headed somewhere secret."

"I guess we'll see." Jake said, and Alvara could hear his stomach rumble. She could use a bit of food as well.

The car passed into darkness, almost as if it had dived underwater. But soon they emerged from the tunnel, and regularly-spaced lights were visible out the window. Descending down a steep slope, the car followed the curve of the road before coming to a stop. A squat man wearing a black uniform with a sunburst on the front pocket helped Alvara out of the car, and another did the same for Jake on the opposite side. The young man met her eyes for a moment, then looked away guiltily. Alvara felt embarrassed to be in cuffs, which was ridiculous.

Xiu Li and Isabella walked in front of them and led the way down a hallway, up an empty elevator, and down another hallway. The walls were concrete, but the linoleum floor reminded Alvara of a hospital. Or a research facility. Alvara concentrated on breathing steadily, pushing away thoughts of unsanctioned human experimentation.

The group halted at a door, and the uniformed men forced Jake and Alvara inside.

A black bullet smacked into Alvara's chest, causing her to stumble. Jake shouted in alarm, but the bullet became Laerik, who pelted them with scolding caws.

"Hang on, Laerik," Alvara sighed.

When Laerik noticed Isabella in the hallway, she hissed and retreated to a perch in the corner, glaring at their captors.

At Isabella's nod, guards released their wings and hands. Jake winced and massaged his hands. Alvara smiled at Laerik; her presence, and her good treatment, gave her hope that she and Jake wouldn't be harmed. The room was the size of a small bedroom, with two beds and a door ajar leading to a bathroom. It was practically cozy after the cages.

"You will sleep here," Isabella stated. "We will talk in the morning. Robert joins us then."

"If you could bother yourselves, my friend and I are hungry and need food." Jake said dryly.

"It will be no trouble, I'll have someone bring you a meal," she replied, almost kindly. "Until tomorrow," she said, and shut the door. Laerik flew around the room and came to rest on Jake's shoulder, where she nuzzled his cheek.

"I can't stand that woman; she gives me the shivers. I'm so glad you're here! I haven't heard from you for days; I waited at the hotel for you! What were you doing? I missed you." Having finally completed the barrage of questions, she hopped down to rest on one of the beds, flexing her wings and waiting for answers.

"It's good to see you too, Laerik. How did they find you?" he asked.

"Nothing interesting," Laerik said with an embarrassed dip of her head. "I want to hear about you. Where were you?" she asked.

Jake explained all that had happened to them in the week since they had seen her last, meeting the old man who was their Caretaker, visiting Selene, and their capture by Isabella and Xiu Li. Occasionally, Alvara chimed in with details, though hearing the story made the events of the last few days feel strangely serene.

"You actually visited the Goddess?" Laerik gasped, and then made a pouting sound. "My flock will never believe me! But go on!"

When Jake finished the tale, she blinked. "Wow, I missed a lot. So I was right that the Children of the Sun are no good? And they are out to destroy the world," she shuddered. "And your wife may be alive? That's new," she said dryly.

"I guess those are the key pieces. It's hard for me to keep up with it all. We just need to figure out what the Children of the Sun want and try to convince them to stop what they are doing, somehow," Jake said with a yawn.

"Great plan," Laerik chirped. "All right, I'm tired. Good night." And with that, she shoved her head under a wing, instantly asleep. Jake mumbled a reply and turned over.

Alvara couldn't find sleep as easily. *It would help if we knew what they wanted*, she thought. The actions of the Sun's Children appeared random; sending them threatening letters, shooting at them, breaking Jake out of police custody, teaming up with a nutcase like Xiu Li, flying them all over the country, and now taking them to an underground facility for some unfathomable reason. Alvara couldn't decide what Isabella's role was: the person in charge, or just the strong arm? Her behavior was confusing, first claiming that Jake and Alvara had brought this upon themselves, then torturing Alvara for information. It made no sense.

A man showed up with a dinner of cold chicken and some mashed potatoes, but it tasted like a feast. Alvara got out of bed to grab her plate, rousing Jake so he could eat too. They got ready for bed as best they could. She managed to slip into a restless sleep.

Chapter 20

"So what's been happening on the Internet lately?" Jake asked. With no way to tell how long they'd slept, the hours passed slowly waiting for Isabella to return. A meal, maybe breakfast, had been the only external signpost. That and the disappearance of their wings. "I've been out of the loop for, I don't know, five years or so?"

"Five YEARS?" Alvara groaned. "Do you even know how much gets added to the Internet every day? How could you ever catch up?"

He shrugged and flashed a hopeful smile. "Indulge me. Summarize the highlights?"

"Not like I have any visual aids," she muttered, but dived into the task. "Well, Twitter is for ranting about things, and Pokemon is back—" Jake learned way more than he could hope to remember. Bands and blogs blended together. He promised Alvara that he'd check out Snapchat and Instagram, but Tumblr seemed way too complicated.

When she paused for breath, Jake shared some of his joyful memories, primarily of Rory. She was an opera singer, he said, and she hated to perform late at night, which limited her jobs. He used to travel with her to opera houses throughout Europe, and spend his free time in those places studying the local bird life. He traded Alvara for the music tips, convincing her to listen to the call of the nightingale and visit YouTube to see the strange mating dance of the blue-footed booby. She chuckled, and said that nothing could compel her to perform a search for 'booby' on YouTube. They both relaxed into friendly silence.

The door swung open, and Isabella entered with a young guard in a baseball cap. Jake tensed. "Follow me, please," she said. It was silly to refuse, so both Jake and Alvara made their way into the hallway, Laerik riding on Jake's shoulder. As they walked, stretching a bit, they passed more doors like their own.

"How many people like us do you have locked up in here?" Jake asked.

"No others like *you*," Isabella replied. "A fair amount of others, to answer your question; most do not heed our warning letters. We have to get through to them somehow."

"That's because your letters make no sense," Jake said, "What do you expect? They just talk about some mysterious balance of power."

"Mysterious, is it?" she replied. "I didn't expect you to claim to have no knowledge of the damage you do, but I didn't expect an apology, either. If you were so ignorant, why didn't you contact us for information?" Jake didn't know what to say to that, but Alvara stepped up.

"After those letters? We didn't trust you! When we're not running for our lives, all we try to do is help other people, and search for ways to prevent the damage *you* are doing! People like Ridge are probably dying, and you don't even care."

"Confusing the issue," Isabella replied, and kept walking. "Look, perhaps Robert will have the patience to get through to you." The man with her turned the key to a room that appeared a bit sturdier than the others, and held the door open for the three of them as they entered. Jake caught a glimpse of a room with desks and couches on one wall and cages on the other before a fist slammed into his head.

He fell to the ground with a groan, floating in and out of consciousness. He thought he heard Alvara yell, and tried to reach out a hand to help her, but someone held his hands behind his back. He felt himself being lifted and dragged, and tried to resist, but his eyes didn't seem to be working right; he couldn't see his assailant. There was an irregular thumping, clanging sound that he couldn't quite place.

He heard someone call his name, but the metal floor felt too wonderful against his skin. He heard it again, and this time a sharp pain on the side of his head accompanied the request. He managed to pull himself to a sitting position, blinking to try to take in the scene. Laerik stopped pecking him. His eyes focused on Alvara, who had a cut on her forehead, and called his name from a cage nearby. She was shaking. "Jake! Are you okay?" she whispered.

"I feel like a whale sat on me," Jake said, though where that image came from he didn't know. "Are you?"

"Yeah, but look around! What are we going to do?" she replied, and when he focused on her face he saw that it was pale with fear.

"What?" he said, but he peered around the room and began to comprehend the situation. In a cage nearby, Isabella rammed against the padlocked door to her cage in a blur and then slowed down to pull the bars with all her strength, but they weren't moving. The wheeled cages were secured to the walls with heavy chains. She was breathing harder than she had yesterday and muttering in a language with lots of consonants. She kept attacking her restraining bars until a coughing fit forced her to collapse to the floor. Jake stared past her to see a dark-skinned, middle-aged man just beginning to stir in a cage of his own, and out to the center of the room to see Xiu Li smiling at them all, not a hair out of place.

"I would not try so hard, my dear Isabella. These cages were meant to keep individuals like you in, yes?"

"Dra åt helvete!" she screamed at him, shaking the bars.

Three more men in simple black suits slid into the room, and from the deference they showed to Xiu Li, it was all according to plan. Jake's heart pounded a staccato rhythm. Xiu Li had never looked happier; he would get four sets of abilities rather than two. Panic started to take over, and Jake pounded his hands on the bars, searching the cage for a way out.

"Jake, calm down," Alvara said. Jake couldn't seem to stop pacing.

"Oh, an exciting day," Xiu Li trilled as his men prepared to cut the chains in order to transport the cages. "I am sure I do not know all that you two are capable of," he pointed with index and middle fingers toward Isabella and the man who must be Robert Noon, "but I am sure someone will pay big money for it. Life is good." And he laughed, disturbing because of how normal it sounded. He could have been delighted at a friend's joke.

"You'll never get any feathers from us!" Alvara yelled, but shrank back at Xiu Li's intensity as he put his hands on the bars of her cage.

"We shall see how often you grow bat wings when your friend is in danger of permanent harm, little Alvara. You will bend to me, and it will be soon." And he smiled again, that sweet poisonous smile Jake hated and had learned to fear. Laerik cowered behind Jake in the cage.

"Xiu Li, is it?" Robert asked. Despite the low, musical lilt of his accent, his voice was dry and emotionless. It was not a voice that inspired much confidence. "I will have to ask you to release us now, or suffer the consequences. We can even discuss those feathers you asked for, if our release is prompt."

"Just like that?" Xiu Li asked. "You and your female Hulk have no bartering power here. I have a better plan. How about I allow you to live, and you do exactly as I say?" he seemed less cocksure, but no less powerful.

"Remove them to the trucks," he directed the men. A few approached Jake's cage to cut the chains attaching him to the wall, but Jake kept his eyes on Robert. Xiu Li did as well. "Tranquilize him," he told one of his men.

The man pointed a gun at Robert through the bars of his cage, but Robert raised his hand and a thin burst of flame shot toward the man's gun. The man dropped it in surprise; the gun was a smoking lump of twisted metal and plastic.

With incredible aim, Robert dispatched the remaining four guns in the room, and turned to Xiu Li. Robert twisted his hand, and a burst of flame shot out, catching Xiu Li full in the face. Alvara and Xiu Li screamed together. His scream was cut off abruptly as his body collapsed to the floor, twitching spasmodically. The smell of burning flesh filled the room, and Jake gagged.

"Listen to me," Robert said, wiping his brow, which dripped with sweat. As he removed his other hand from the lock on his cage, the warped red-hot metal fell to the ground with a hiss and a clang. He stepped out of his cage with his hands at the ready in front of him, and walked toward Xiu Li's men. "Lie down on your stomach with your hands outstretched—"

One of the men reached to a leg holster and pulled out another gun. Robert extended his hand toward the man, but a shot rang out as the man's head burst into flames. Robert fell to a kneeling position in front of Jake's cage as the rest of the men dived to the ground with their hands outstretched in surrender. Robert put his hand on his chest, and when it came away it was drenched in blood. "Fader!" Isabella yelled. "No, Robert! Robert!"

Robert stared at Jake, his eyebrows lifted in surprise. He slid to the ground, and blood oozed out of the side of his mouth. Isabella shouted, hysterical. She was frantic. She loved this man.

Jake didn't know if that made him do it. He reached into his wallet and pulled out the soft downy feather he had gotten from Biyu ages ago. It was still a deep red, the color of blood. He stretched his arm through the bars of his cage, and could almost reach where Robert lay.

The movement must have caught Robert's attention, because his eyes flicked to Jake's hand. His body shuddered, and Robert blinked and focused again. Jake waited with his hand outstretched. "Give me your hand," he said.

Robert's hand twitched, and then extended to within his reach. Jake slipped the feather between two of Robert's bloody fingers, and then sat back.

Nothing happened. Robert took a few more struggling breaths, and let his last out in a sigh, staring at Jake as his eyes lost focus and closed. Jake couldn't even see the tiny feather in Robert's hand anymore; it was lost within his blood. *What about those kids at the hospital*, Jake thought in frustration. This feather stuff couldn't have been a coincidence. Their gifts had a purpose. He believed that with everything he had.

The moments passed. And suddenly, Robert took a shuddering breath. And he took another; it was working! A shiver passed over Jake as the recently dead man breathed deeply. There was a delighted squeal from Isabella's cage. Robert sat up, staring down at his bloody shirt. His first action was to get to his feet and push a button on the wall.

It must have released a deadbolt somewhere, because in stormed a dozen guards who supervised the removal of Xiu Li's disarmed men, as well as the bodies of Xiu Li and his bodyguard. A couple of his men tried to tend Robert, but he waved them away, only accepting a syringe for himself and Isabella that they each injected into their thighs. The room fell into silence once more.

Robert ripped his shirt open, wiping aside the blood, but his chest was undamaged. Where the bullet had torn through, a raised crescent-shaped scar had formed, stark white against his brown skin. His yellow eyes met Jake's, and Jake saw a mixture of awe and frustration playing across his features. "Why did you do that?" he asked angrily.

His question stunned Jake. "Are you kidding? I just saved your life," he said.

"Do you have any idea how much you have put us back?" Robert said, though he didn't seem angry anymore, just tired. "Every time you draw on your power like that, it's more of a losing battle. But I suppose thanks are in order."

"What are you talking about?!" Jake yelled, smacking his hand against the side of the cage. It made his head hurt again, which fueled his anger. "You have done *nothing* but speak to us in riddles since that first letter, not to mention teaming up with a man who beat me bloody and almost did it again! Why do we need to stop using our gifts? I mean, if anything, using them keeps people like you from getting too much power and destroying everything!" He tried to calm down. "Let us out of these damn cages. And maybe explain yourselves, for once."

Jake caught Alvara's eye. *Run,* he mouthed, but she shook her head, her eyes darting to Isabella and back again.

Robert waved to his men to release Jake and Alvara, all the while staring at Jake. It was an interesting expression, but Jake didn't like it directed at him.

Isabella, freed from her cage, ran toward Robert. She embraced him wordlessly, her body shaking. He patted her hair before releasing her.

Alvara walked toward Jake, and he hugged her tightly. She was fine, and Xiu Li was dead. *Xiu Li is dead,* Jake reminded himself. It didn't feel real.

But he and Alvara were still trapped.

"Where are you getting your information?" Robert asked Jake. The gentle tone caught Jake off guard. He released Alvara, and stepped between her and Robert and Isabella.

"We went to visit the Moon Goddess," Jake answered. "And she explained the situation between her and the Sun God, and with you both."

"You met her? In . . . person?" Robert asked, a note of disbelief coloring his words.

"It was weird, but we did, all right?" Alvara snapped. Robert shrugged. Jake continued.

"She pointed to global warming, and blamed you and the Sun both, saying you have ultimate plans for destroying the Earth. She said we should try to stop you at any cost."

"This is going to sound strange, Jake, Alvara," Robert began. "But please, now that we can see you were against us in profound ignorance, please sit down so we can talk." Jake still thought the words rude and cold, but at least they were getting somewhere.

Robert walked toward a doorway leading to an adjoining room, and Isabella followed him. Jake gave Alvara a small push in the opposite direction. "Get lost," he whispered.

Alvara managed to stroll past the line of guards before breaking into a run. Jake didn't wait to see what happened, but immediately sprinted toward the opposite doorway. He thanked whoever was listening that he couldn't hear gunfire, but otherwise ignored the commotion that erupted behind him. He nearly reached the exit.

The door in front of him exploded into flame with a wave of instant heat. Jake yelped and barely managed to stop before a collision with the wall of fire. He looked left, and right, but there was no other nearby exit.

Alvara stood struggling next to Isabella, who held her by a single wrist in an unbreakable grip. Robert stood facing Jake, his arm upraised.

"I did not miss, Jake," Robert said, breathing hard. "Neither Isabella nor I want you harmed. But I cannot allow you or Alvara to leave. You must understand why. Please come with me now."

"So you can cackle and reveal your master plan?" Alvara hissed. "I'd rather be in a cage," she said.

"Grow up, girl," Isabella said. "We just want to talk."

"Fine, but I want some answers," Jake said, still disoriented by what had just occurred.

Isabella released Alvara, but walked behind the two of them as they followed Robert to a smaller adjoining room.

It was a cross between a doctor's waiting room and a living room. Though couches were arranged in a semi-circle facing a blank screen, the room had a sterile quality. Jake and Alvara took a seat on one couch, with Laerik perched behind them.

Robert and Isabella sat facing them, a study in contrast. Isabella, young, blonde, and slim, wore a business suit only slightly crumpled from her attempts to escape her enclosure. She met Jake's eyes for a moment and looked away. He was surprised to notice that her eyes were amber, not brown.

Robert was much older, in his mid-forties Jake would guess, with short black hair, a trim beard, and thick brows framing his intense yellow eyes. Jake tried not to be discomfited by Robert's tattered, bloody shirt, but he looked like a civilian casualty of war.

"There have been a lot of accusations flying around, and we're tired of it," Jake said finally. "You won't let us leave, so at least tell us what you know. We'll judge your and Selene's words on their merits." Robert nodded, and began.

"I have never spoken directly with Sol," Robert said, "but he has left me messages, of a sort. When I was a young boy in Mumbai, I fell asleep once while writing in my journal. When I awoke, my hands were burned. I looked back on what I had written, and it was a list of instructions. It seemed nonsense to me at the time. I discovered that afternoon that it had been a warning." Isabella put a hand on Robert's shoulder. His face fell, but he otherwise didn't acknowledge the gesture.

"I was playing with my sister, a game that is much like tag, chasing her through the streets by our apartment. When I caught her, when I touched her, she burst into flames before I knew what had happened."

"Oh my God. I'm sorry," Jake said, horrified. Robert dismissed his apology with a wave of his hand.

"It was long ago. I knew I needed to fulfill the instructions, but I was only ten. It seemed impossible, and took me many years," he continued.

"You were ten? What were the instructions for?" Alvara asked.

"I'll get to that soon. I grew older, and my work continued. I felt like I was missing something, or someone, that I needed. So, maybe fifteen years ago, I picked up that old journal and began to write. As before, I fell asleep, and when I awoke I discovered a new list of instructions, but these consisted of a time and a place. The place was in Sweden. I lived in London at the time, and took the next flight to get there in time. I knew not to ignore the instructions this time," he added.

He was interrupted by the arrival of a thickset man and a short women, both in business attire. The man carried a fresh shirt for Robert, while the woman bore a tray containing a basket of rolls and pastries, a jug of juice, butter, and jam. As Robert unselfconsciously replaced the strips of cloth he wore with a fresh shirt, Isabella dug into the breakfast.

Jake was struck by the incongruity of the scene. He and Alvara were prisoners here, for no reason he yet understood. Yet for a moment, the habit of eating breakfast in company had nearly overwhelmed him. He waited a few minutes after Isabella had begun eating before taking a careful bite of his own.

Alvara wasn't eating. She was busy seething at their captors, her arms folded in front of her. Laerik flapped to the edge of the table to peck at a roll of her own. Isabella appeared poised to swat her away, but she refrained. Jake figured she probably saved herself a harsh peck.

Once Robert had finished his croissant, he continued. "I arrived in Sweden. The location turned out to be the front lawn of an orphanage in Stockholm. Young children played outside in a yard. One girl was older than the rest, and sat to one side, reading from a large book in her lap. I felt tied to her, and went to talk with her." He smiled at Isabella, and she beamed back at him. "She spoke barely any English then, but we could somehow understand each other perfectly. I filed for adoption that day."

Robert finished another roll, and helped himself to the juice. Jake wondered if Isabella, with her incredible strength and speed, had experienced her own tragedy at the appearance of her powers, but thought it impolite to ask. Less impolite than Robert, of course, who had recently thrown a fireball at his head.

Instead, Jake said, "Robert, you mentioned instructions."

"Ah," Robert nodded, "Yes, the instructions. When I was young, they explained about the balance of power between the Moon and the Sun, and how important it was for humanity that the balance is maintained. Later, when I was sent to Isabella, more instructions were added. They explained that while the Sun had slightly more power, the Moon was exerting more and more influence in what could only be a dangerous way."

"Your instructions make no sense," Alvara said. "How could the Moon exert more influence if she had less power?"

"I still do not know," Robert said, his brow furrowed. "But it meant we had work to do. With my new organization Legion of the Light, I spoke out against superstition and magic in favor of a reasonable interpretation of the world, and in an attempt to decrease the belief the Moon possessed. I championed scientific achievements and declaimed the video game culture, among other battles. With my effort, the imbalance dissipated.

But about ten years ago, the power struggle took a steep downward turn. It forced Isabella and me to take more drastic measures. We began to round up creatures that get power from the Moon, because when they use that power, they return power to her."

"Like Ridge," Jake challenged. "You expect us to get on board with this organization of yours when you keep an innocent boy locked in the back of your airplane. How can you justify this?"

"He is a special case," Isabella interjected. "We thought, since his connection to the moon is a direct link but of low power, we might be able to remove it entirely. We have tested a treatment, part of which is to keep him from the moon. With our help, he is losing his gift, though the process is not painless. I tell him this, but he does not believe me. This treatment has worked before," she added at Alvara's outraged expression.

"Your treatment sucks," Alvara said, her hands clenched into fists. "He is dying in that plane!"

White wings burst from her back, knocking Jake from his seat on the couch. Alvara screamed in pain. Isabella and Robert leapt from their couch in shock, knocking plates to shatter on the laminate floor.

When Jake looked at Alvara again, the wings were gone. Alvara sat breathing heavily, eyes closed. "What," she said, her voice pained, "was that."

"It is day," Isabella said to Robert, her eyes wide. "It is day."

"*Bakrichod*," Robert cursed. "Jake, you have had this gift for decades. Have you ever grown wings during the day?"

"Never," Jake replied. "Alvara, are you all right?"

"Fine now," she said. "But it was different from normal. It felt like my back was on fire."

"It is worse than I thought," Robert said, standing and beginning to pace the small room. "Even Isabella and I together have been losing this battle. The balance tips steadily farther in favor of the moon, and with your wings appearing during Sol's time, the balance must be dire indeed." Robert ran a hand through his hair. "I can hardly sleep some nights, the imbalance is so strong. You must have felt it." He stopped his pacing, and looked from Jake to Alvara.

"What does this mystical balance feel like?" Alvara asked, still rubbing her shoulder blades.

Isabella answered. "There is a curtain over your joy," she said with tired eyes. "Like the whole world will just get worse and worse unless you fix what is broken or find what is lost. I confused it with depression until Robert explained that he felt it too."

There was something very important about what Isabella had just said, and Jake tried to grasp the wisp of a thought before it escaped. He drifted through memory to the dark days after Rory fell, and braced himself for the pain he knew he would feel.

But in a flash he remembered what he had made himself forget. He had mourned her and missed her deeply, and had been inconsolable for months. But he had begun to heal; two years or so after her death, the support from his friends and colleagues, as well as his sister, had helped him to move on. He had continued his research, and had begun to heal for five years after her death. Ten years ago he had slipped back into depression and could not be roused.

He had attributed his incredible guilt and daily sorrow to the loss of his beloved wife, and his own part in her death. But with Isabella's explanation, he could finally separate them in his mind. He missed his wife, missed her more than he would have thought possible, but he could finally make sense of the way his life had seemed to stop just in the past decade. It was a gift he never expected.

"Ten years ago; that was the year my father died," Alvara said. "Life seemed to only go downhill, but I didn't want to just give up. Are you saying some of that was knowledge of the balance? You're not making this up, right? It matters a lot, you know, in how I think about my life."

"It sounds similar," Robert replied. "The timing is right. It affected Isabella and me in different ways; mine has always been insomnia."

"That really sucks, if you're right. This balance affects the whole world, but we're the ones who have to suffer when it's out of whack? For years?" Alvara fumed.

"It certainly forces us to pay attention," Robert said wryly.

"Jake, can you feel the imbalance?" Alvara asked.

"I think so," Jake said, still reveling in his discovery. He felt dazed.

"Like you said, Robert, the imbalance became worse," Isabella prompted.

"Yes," Robert continued, returning to his seat on the couch. "And then you, Jake, began to use your wings again," Robert said, his voice frustrated. "It was like a cascade of power flowed into the Moon; she has been growing stronger and stronger ever since, but we don't know what she plans to do with this power. Not even Sol's extra influence in us has helped in the slightest."

"What do you mean, his extra influence?" Alvara asked.

"You may have noticed," Isabella replied, "that Robert and I cannot use our abilities for long without becoming ill, and we regularly need injections. We have a medical scientist on staff, but he has no answers for us. We are both suffering from some sort of cancer, tied to the Sun. It is getting worse, but there is no alternative, no cure. The injections help us to keep going," she said. They sat in silence for a minute, as Jake and Alvara absorbed all that they had just heard.

"We have healing feathers," Alvara said after a while. "Has no one thought of this? This cancer thing shouldn't be a problem after what Robert just went through."

"While I appreciate Jake's quick thinking, and your offer," Robert said, "this is not a normal injury. It comes from our gifts, so I think it would not be affected by your feather cure."

"Look, I get it," Alvara continued, iron in her voice. "You've been selflessly struggling for years, trying to save the world, with everyone against you," she rolled her eyes. "I get why it feels good, OK? But Selene told us the complete opposite. Do you think she would just lie to people she claims are her children? You don't do that to family. And when I look at her, trying to do right by us, and you two, capturing and maybe torturing innocent people, it's not that hard to figure out who to trust."

"Alvara, she must be lying to you," Isabella said. "I am sorry we did not see your false information sooner, but we are just trying to restore the balance. You can feel it, now," she said, hand on her heart. Alvara snorted and shook her head.

"You should be able to feel us, too," Robert continued. "I can feel both of you from a hundred yards away." Alvara shot him a glare, but Jake began to see what he meant.

"I wondered about that," Jake mentioned. "It was like there was a pull on both of you, that some force drew us together."

"Yes, that is it, a pull. But who pulls harder?" Isabella said, tossing her ponytail. Jake then realized what she was talking about. He could feel the magnitude of the imbalance; even though it hadn't happened yet, he knew which side would win the game of tug-of-war.

"I guess that I, I mean Alvara and I, have the stronger pull," he said. "Is that what you both mean by the imbalance?" he asked.

"More or less, in addition to the depressive feelings that accompany it for all of us, no matter which way the imbalance lies," Robert replied.

"And so every time Alvara or I use our abilities, it gives us a stronger pull. But what are the other factors? And what does this imbalance allow either side to do?"

"We do not know that. We just know that Sol does not want it, and we have done everything in our power to prevent it. Though it has not done much good," Isabella finished bitterly. It was strange to hear her side, Jake thought. But she had hurt them out of fear and a belief that nothing else would work, so he couldn't really hate her for it. He didn't have to like her, though. And he sure as hell wasn't ready to sign up.

"So you're both working toward a goal that you don't understand," Jake stated. He hadn't heard any excellent arguments in favor of swearing off usage of his wings for good, nor for neglecting the warnings Selene had given them, though that feeling of the imbalance felt genuine.

"Look Jake, I will be frank with you," Robert said. "This is one of those situations where I have the power to prove myself right or wrong; I truly believe that the world will end if we do not find some way to fix the imbalance so if we do it, you can never have proof that there was a crisis. But we have evidence even now that this is the largest the imbalance has been in my lifetime; Alvara grew wings during the daytime," said Robert gravely. Despite himself, Jake worried that the situation really was dire.

"There will be signs that the imbalance cannot be stopped. Global signs," he clarified. "If nothing obvious happens in the next few days, then I was wrong, and Sol is misleading us," Robert said. "However, if we begin to see signs that Selene is out of control, we need to come up with a plan of action, because our actions so far have been too little to make an impact. Perhaps your involvement will make all the difference."

Jake thought for a moment, then spoke. "We are on the same page," he said. "We both want to preserve the world, and it seems that either one or the other of its deities is misleading us. I'll allow your test to discover if it's Selene; if it isn't, you have to be ready to face the fact that you could have been working for the bad guy all along, and take steps to make it right."

"Jake, are you serious?" Alvara asked. "Selene was a strange woman, but she lived alone for a long time. She helped me rescue you. And I believe that she was trapped there, maybe by Sol. How can you trust them after what they did to Ridge?" she asked.

Jake wished that Alvara had gotten away from them, just as she had managed to escape Xiu Li. But she was anything but frail, or in need of protection. Her eyes were steady, her jaw set in a determined frown. The memory of her burning flesh, after Isabella's treatment in the plane, made Jake ashamed of his scientific curiosity.

"I don't trust them," he said, his eyes meeting Robert's. "And you both have a lot to answer for. You haven't even met Sol, but he wasn't exactly friendly when I made a brief acquaintance." Jake showed the others his hand with its sunburst scar. They remained silent, and Jake had another realization.

"Where's the third one?" he asked.

"Excuse me?" Isabella asked.

"The third Child of the Sun. If your system works similarly to ours, there is one of you born in each generation of humans, meaning there are three at any given time. You guys are missing an older generation sibling, and if your names mean anything, you're missing a 'dawn' sibling as well."

"Sol never told us about a third child, so I guess that we are all," Isabella said. "That is strange about our names. My strength and speed are at their maximum right before the sun starts to set, and Robert's fire ability is most potent around midday, so we chose our last names as sort of an inside joke," Isabella mused. "What happened to the third Child of the Moon, then?"

"She lost her wings," Alvara said.

"What happened?" Isabella repeated.

"It's complicated, but Xiu Li was involved," Alvara continued, staring at Isabella. "After selling her feathers on the black market, he captured us and beat Jake nearly to death to get more. We barely escaped with our lives. And then met him here."

Isabella actually blushed. "I am sorry," she whispered. "I did not have good judgment with that man." Robert reached out to pat her on the shoulder, but she jerked away. They sat in silence.

"Robert," she said suddenly. "You still have blood on your face. I will get a towel."

"Isabella, you don't need–" Robert began, but she nearly ran from the room.

Jake took the opportunity afforded by her absence to state what had been bothering him. "Isabella hurt us," Jake told Robert. "When she first captured us. I'm telling you in good faith, because you don't seem to be the kind of man who likes to cause pain."

Robert rubbed at the side of his mouth with his thumb. "She is a true believer. It is hard to be objective when you have such conviction. I will talk with her later," he said. "It was her idea to start the literature campaign against fantasy for children, which was a brilliant idea." Jake remembered that strange quote he had read a few days ago in the paper. "The fewer kids believe in fantasy, the less power leaks out of either the Sun or the Moon to wreak havoc here on Earth. The campaign has helped, more than either of us thought." Robert sounded proud.

"Your 'daughter' branded me to try to get Jake to reveal information," Alvara snapped, "that doesn't sound like *protocol*."

"What?" Robert asked. "I never taught her that." He looked older after that remark. An awkward silence fell.

"Well, not permanently," Alvara eventually admitted.

"That is not an excuse. There is no reason for her to do what she did," Robert whispered, his hand covering his eyes. Jake felt sorry for him.

"You're right," Alvara said simply. *Even Alvara's compassion had limits*, Jake thought.

Alvara changed the subject. "About what you said though, both Jake and I had a problem with that article. Kids need to believe in fantasy to fully express themselves. It's essential. You want to take that away from them just because it might help this balance issue?"

"Maybe misguided, like so many of our actions these days," Robert bitterly replied. "How could I have missed what Isabella was doing?"

"It's easy to be blind to those closest to us, especially when we are busy," Jake said. "But doing what, exactly? What is the real goal of the Legion of the Light?"

Robert furrowed his brow. "I guess you could say it is a philosophical organization, first and foremost. The underlying purpose was to reduce belief in the moon and minimize the impact of moon-related individuals, only to remedy the balance, you understand," he paused. "But I was almost as proud of its overarching goal; the reduction of erroneous belief. If societies and individuals were to believe in themselves, rather than a mystical other that pulled all the strings, there would be less belief to go around to either side, reducing both the power of Sol and Selene as well as their influence on our world. We could be free to live our lives again, without this cosmic tug-of-war which plagues us. That is my theory, at least."

"Flawed, though," said Jake. "Belief is fundamentally human. It's how we figure out what the right questions are. Science can fill in some of the gaps, but belief is what charts the course for it to follow."

Alvara stared at him, head tilted to one side, then allowed herself a brief smile. "Jake. That was a pretty stirring defense of faith. I didn't know you had it in you."

Jake smiled back, and was about to come up with a retort when the screen to their left flared into life.

On the screen, a broad-shouldered man wore the now familiar black uniform and stood in front of a featureless white wall. The audio was full of whistles and crackling sounds. "Mr. Noon," he said formally.

Robert cleared his throat and addressed Jake. "You wished to know what we do. Unless I am mistaken, this will be an introduction. Go ahead, Mitchell," Robert said to the screen.

"Sir, we've apprehended the source of the outbreak in Ecuador,"

Mitchell said.

"What was it? Was it moon-related?" Robert asked.

"Bats, sir. An entire colony of vampire bats," Mitchell said, gesturing to someone behind the camera. The view shifted to show a series of small cages covered in black felt. Mitchell lifted the edge of one and dark shapes could be seen moving behind a Plexiglas exterior.

Mitchell faced the camera again. "It appears to be moon-related. The bats are behaving in unusual ways because of the force of the moon. They were attacking any humans or animals that neared their colony, very unusual for this species. We consulted with an expert at the University of Chicago, and with her help, we succeeded in rescuing the whole group for further observation. Unfortunately," he said, his expression grim, "we had a casualty. Saanvi had a gap in her protective gear, and was bitten. She's being observed in a hospital near her home in Seattle. We aren't sure what to expect."

"Saanvi?" Robert whispered. Then, louder, "I am very sorry to hear that. Please forward me all the details, I would like to check in on her." Robert said, and the screen went dark again.

"So," Jake said into the silence. "This Saanvi, she was bitten by a bat?"

Robert didn't answer at first. Then he stood, strode toward the wall, and slammed his hand into it with a frustrated yell. When Robert let his hand drop, Jake could see a charred handprint.

"The outbreak," Robert finally said, still facing away from them. "Was one of moon madness. In a small town in Ecuador, nearly half the population came down with it. I had Mitchell and his team investigate because the first case occurred on a full moon, and we could not determine the origin of the affliction." Robert said. "Saanvi and I grew up together. We are family. Nothing of value is safe from this cursed imbalance," he breathed. He sank onto the couch.

"I'm sorry," Jake said. "What is there to be done?"

"I am not a doctor," Robert snapped. "I know not."

"You should go to her," Alvara said. Her hands were folded on her lap. "I know a bit about hospitals," she said gently. "The worst part is being separated from the people you care about. She may be scared, but you being there might help. And this wouldn't hurt, either." She pulled out Biyu's feather from the pocket of her jeans and set it on the table in front of Robert.

"It cannot help," Robert said. "The feather and the bite are both related to the moon, why would one gift undo another? It does not—"

"Everything we have experienced seems to run on faith!" Alvara said. "You could try it, for once."

Robert sat, staring at the feather in deep thought, until Isabella returned with a towel. She had been gone a long time, but Robert didn't ask her where.

"I have to go, Issy," Robert said. "Saanvi is in the hospital. In Seattle."

"No," Isabella said, her hand rising to her mouth.

"I will go visit her now. I will be back later today, tonight at the latest. I will take one of the vans. In the meantime, please show these two around the facilities," Robert said.

"Wait," Alvara said. "I'm glad you're going to see your friend, that's the right thing to do. But you owe us, and me specifically, for how you've treated us."

"What do you want?" Robert asked, annoyed.

"I haven't forgotten about Ridge, not to mention the other people you probably have locked up here for no good reason. Before you leave, order them to let Ridge go."

Robert didn't consider it. "That is out of the question. You grew wings today! Can you not see that the balance is precarious?"

"Alvara's right," Jake added. "This 'every little bit helps' philosophy clearly hasn't worked for you in the past. And you said it yourself, his power is barely a blip on the balance tally. You need a new strategy. You want us to trust you. Maybe it all starts with doing the right thing."

Robert rubbed a hand through his dark hair. "Fine," he said. "I cannot debate this right now. Ridge will go free."

"Now. Please," Alvara said, her eyes hard. She wasn't backing down.

Robert sighed and placed a call. "Yes, the experimental subject on the plane. Number 248, yes. Released," he continued, listening for a moment. "Yes, drive him blind so he cannot locate the landing pad. Yes I'm sure," Robert snapped. "Give him some money while you do. Just drop him in town. My thanks," he bit out, and hung up.

"I pray we will not all suffer the consequences of this," Robert said to Alvara. She said nothing as he snatched up the feather and stormed out of the room.

Chapter 21

Isabella, towel in hand, glanced from Jake to Alvara. *At least Ridge was safe*, Alvara thought. She glared at Isabella, arms folded. There was no way Alvara would make this even a tiny bit easier for her.

"Well," Isabella said. She tossed the towel on the couch and straightened her blouse. "Can I take you back to your room?"

"Oh, you're asking now?" Alvara challenged.

Isabella squirmed. "Yes," she said. "I want you to feel like our guests."

"Since you guys seem to want this to be a fantasy-free zone, let's cut the crap," Alvara replied. "How about you let us go?"

"Robert explained why I cannot," Isabella said, her face earnest. "You two are central to the problems with the balance, and may be essential for solving them. And I cannot allow you to use your wings, or the problem may get much worse."

"That's pretty vague, Isabella," Jake interjected. "We're your prisoners, just tell it like it is. If we're forced to stay, you might as well show us around like Robert told you to."

"First, I need to make a call," Alvara said. Isabella opened her mouth to forbid it.

"I'm not going to call the cops," Alvara added, "Like you'd let that call get through anyway. But I need to call my Aunt and my friend; they think I've been kidnapped."

Isabella looked very confused. "But . . . you have been kidnapped."

"Well of course, but I'm not going to tell them that and freak them out, am I?" Alvara said, shaking her head. "As I'm pretty sure you're not about to murder us to fix the balance . . . that's not on the table, right?" Alvara asked suddenly. She meant it as a joke, but she didn't want to give Isabella any ideas. She certainly had the power to do it, at least during the day.

Isabella shook her head in horror.

Alvara tried to let her sudden burst of fear drain away and forced a laugh. "Then this situation is temporary. So I'd rather make up a story to reassure them than leave them worrying."

Isabella squinted at Alvara, as if trying to discern any hidden motives. "Fine," she said, and pulled out her cell phone. "I will wait."

Gingerly, Alvara took the phone. It made her uncomfortable to be so close to Isabella, so close she could smell her floral perfume. She gave herself a few paces before making her first call to Max.

"Hello?" Max said. It was so good to hear his voice, Alvara suddenly felt herself on the verge of tears. But she had to hold it together; there was nothing he could do for her. Besides, Isabella was watching.

"Max, it's Alvara. I hadn't checked in for a while, and—"

"Jeez, Alvara! Are you okay? I was so worried! Alicia was sure something happened to you."

"I'm fine," Alvara lied. "We were just off the beaten path for a while so couldn't check in. I can't talk for long, I just didn't want you to worry."

"Fat chance of that," Max breathed.

Isabella strode toward her, pointing at her watch.

"Sorry, have to go," Alvara said, and hung up on her friend. "One more," Alvara said, "And this should be well within your time limit."

Alicia picked up after the third ring. "Bueno," she said.

"Hola Tia, es Alvara, y estoy bien . . ." Alvara began.

Alicia had sounded pleased at first, but seemed a bit let down that Alvara hadn't been kidnapped. Alvara wondered if her aunt had been hoping for a good kidnapping to get some extra attention and sympathy from her neighbors. After Alvara hung up, she wondered why she even bothered.

Isabella snatched her phone back. "Are you coming, bird?" Isabella asked.

Laerik responded by tucking her beak under her wing and promptly falling asleep. Isabella shrugged.

She strode toward the door to the large holding room. Then she turned back to look at Alvara and Jake.

"I am showing the facilities to you," Isabella said. "Follow me please," she added as she walked out of the room.

"From a prison cell to a prison 'facility'," Alvara muttered to Jake, mimicking Isabella's pronunciation of 'facility'. They both followed her out of the room.

"Don't give up hope," Jake whispered. "We'll figure out a way out of this. And if Robert follows through, we'll have a friend on the outside when we do."

"A supervillain and her armed henchmen might make that difficult," Alvara whispered back, thinking of Ridge, praying that he really was safe. "But we'll see."

"All right," Isabella said brightly. Once they had joined her in the hall, she channeled her inner tour guide. "We shall start with our pharmaceutical branch."

"I don't think so," Jake replied.

"Excuse me?" Isabella retorted.

"You heard me," Jake said calmly. "I want to believe in you and Robert, and I hope you both desire and deserve our trust. But no PR or pharmaceutical visits will set me on that path; only one sort of tour can do that. Take us to see the people you are holding captive here. I want to hear all about them."

She shifted her weight and winced. "Jake, you are not a scientist. Some of our techniques may disturb–" she began.

"Jake's right," Alvara interrupted. "We want to see the other captives."

"Robert has shown a desire to change, to find a new way forward," Jake added. "Don't you share that desire? Nothing you've done with these people has proved enough to cure the problem. And anyway, after all you've done," he began, and Isabella frowned. "We have a right to know."

Isabella couldn't meet either of their eyes. She was ashamed, Alvara realized, of what she'd done. Too little, too late. The road to hell wasn't paved with bricks.

"I know," Isabella whispered. "I will show you where they are being held, but I will not promise to release them. Some of them are highly dangerous."

"Like Ridge is dangerous?" Jake asked mildly. Isabella made a frustrated sound, and gestured for them to follow. They entered an industrial elevator.

"No, not like him," Isabella said as she turned toward them. "Some of these cases are a moral grey area. They are malicious, and capable of harming others. It would be wrong to release them. You'll understand more when you see them."

Isabella reached down into her neckline to withdraw a tiny keycard that dangled on a long golden chain. She inserted the keycard into a thin slot on the number panel, but depressed no buttons. Though they had been on the ground floor to begin with, the elevator descended for over a minute before coming to a halt.

The elevator doors opened to reveal a cohort of security guards relaxing in a reception area, passing around white cartons of Chinese food. A burly man in a black uniform with a sunburst on one arm stood, brushing a noodle off his potbelly.

"This is a restricted–" the man began, but faltered as he noticed Isabella.

"Ms. Dusk, what a pleasant surprise," he finished, and the rest of the guards hastily stood to attention.

"What's she doing in the Loony Bin?" Alvara heard a short male guard whisper to his friend. The man at attention shot him a murderous stare over his shoulder.

"Ma'am, we weren't expecting you this afternoon," he continued. "And there is a strict no guests policy–"

Isabella cut him off with a firm hand gesture. "Mr. Noon and I created the policy for good reasons. I'm glad to see that such strict," here she glanced around to the littered cartons of Chinese food, "security is being maintained. Now, please return to your posts." The men quickly gathered the cartons and wiped down the tables, while the security guard behind the desk buzzed them through the sturdy metal door.

Lights flared into being in a long hallway containing heavy doors made of thick, transparent plastic. Alvara was at the wrong angle to see into any of them, so she walked toward the nearest one and peered inside.

There was a small child in white cloth curled up asleep in a corner. Alvara felt a slow rage begin to simmer. The boy had a thick head of black hair. He couldn't be more than five years old.

"How could you do this?" Jake whispered. His voice shook.

"Alvara, stay back. And Jake, we've tried everything. Our pharmaceuticals–"

Jake slammed Isabella's shoulders against the door to the boy's room. They glared at each other.

Alvara looked past them to see the boy only a foot or so away, staring intently at her. The black of his pupils had eclipsed his eyes, and the black holes drew Alvara in, slipping and sliding downward into despair and terror with no end.

"Alvara!" Isabella yelled, and Alvara was shoved across the hallway, breaking eye contact as her butt hit the floor and she skidded to a halt. Alvara blinked as Isabella slammed a hand down on a button by the door. An opaque panel slid down, blocking the boy from view.

Jake appeared at Alvara's side, shaking her shoulder. Isabella's hands gripped her face. Her eyes searched Alvara's, and she nodded with obvious relief. "Lucky," she breathed, and staggered, sitting on the ground across from Alvara. "I told you these people are dangerous! We call his disorder Moonstruck," she said between breaths. "He seems to have gone completely insane, and never makes a sound except for the screams. It's contagious, but you didn't get a large enough dose."

Alvara shuddered in the violent aftermath of adrenaline. "I felt hopeless," she admitted. "Like the despair would never end . . . Thank you."

Isabella met her eyes. "He's one of those I believe should never be free. I have no idea if the small child is still in there somewhere, but we've taken blood samples and tried a variety of drugs to affect his state, with no positive result. At least in here, he cannot harm anyone but himself, and it seems that his moon affinity is steadily decreasing." She shut her eyes. "I pray for the day that he'll wake up as himself again."

"Please," Jake said, "show us more."

Isabella proceeded to describe each of the cases before showing them the captives. There was a woman who looked like she was very pregnant, though Isabella said their doctor could find no biological evidence of a child. She was kept comfortable, though she claimed she wanted to go home. Another teenage girl felt whatever emotions anyone in her presence felt; she pleaded for her release with a strange relaxed expression that must reflect the calm emotions of her captor. They skipped one room altogether, and Isabella admitted that it housed a murderer with some small ability to read minds. On and on it went. Though all individuals being held were human, they all had some small quality that tied them to the moon.

There were even a few people with some affinity to the sun that Isabella and Robert had attempted to enhance, with some success. The only one Isabella would show them was an eighty-year-old woman who looked like a girl of fifteen. She was the first that seemed genuinely pleased to be part of the project, and returned to her television show when they moved on.

"Robert has a theory," Isabella explained as they shut out the sounds of the television. "While the deities' gifts to their Children are intentional, the rest are accidental fallout. It would explain why we have had such difficulty affecting the balance by working with these people."

No kidding, Alvara thought. It was like trying to get rid of a blazing forest fire by stamping out burning cinders.

"Then let them go free," Jake suggested, "And we'll find another way. All those you can," he clarified, and Alvara felt sorrow for the young Moonstruck boy.

"You need to give them a choice," Alvara added. She remembered something Selene had said. "That's probably what is so damaging to those you keep here against their will. It isn't that they can't see the moon, it's that they aren't free. A desire for freedom is at Selene's core, and it makes sense that it might transfer to those affected by the moon. You have to set them free."

"I'll think about it, and talk with Robert about it when he returns. This may be the time for some new ideas," Isabella said, smiling.

Alvara ignored her and led the way back to the elevator. Talk was easy, but despite Ridge's release, Alvara didn't believe for a second that Isabella would release the rest of the captives that easily. After Isabella inserted her key into the elevator, they rode up in silence.

When they reached the familiar ground floor, Alvara asked, "I'd like to use the restroom. Can you show me where the nearest one is?"

"Of course," Isabella said. "Down this corridor, make a left and you'll see a restroom at the end. When you get back I'll show you other aspects of our organization and answer any of your questions."

"Thanks," Alvara said, her heart pounding as she forced herself to walk at a measured pace to the restroom. At the end of the hall containing a restroom, she passed a guard who nodded in her direction.

She pushed the door open to reveal a tile floor, mirror, sink, and toilet. She was slightly disappointed that there wasn't a window. However, she noticed something else that might work.

Alvara smiled at the grate over the ceiling ducts and made sure that the door was locked. It wouldn't stop Isabella in full-blown strength mode, so Alvara would have to be as quiet as possible. She turned the fan on, and was grateful for the background hum.

She considered the grate.

It was about three feet square, and Alvara thought she'd be able to reach it by standing on the sink. Praying it would hold her weight, she scrambled up onto the white porcelain and braced one hand on the wall.

The panel was held in place by a bolt at each corner. Alvara tried them in quick succession, wishing for a quick burst of strength. Or perhaps a well-placed fireball.

The fourth one she tried wobbled. Alvara painstakingly unscrewed it with her fingers, wincing as a nail cracked under the strain. She braced her other hand on the ceiling, glad that her shoes still had some tread.

When it came loose, Alvara dropped it.

It clinked loudly on the tile. Alvara froze. But she couldn't hear anything over the roar of the fan.

Slowly, she wedged her fingers into the gap between the ceiling and the grate, and let it take more and more of her weight.

The grate slowly bent at one corner, revealing a dark hole in the ceiling. Alvara pushed as hard as she could, hanging off the grate with her entire weight, and the gap widened enough to admit her.

Her pulse sped with excitement. She might actually get away.

"Alvara?" she heard through the door. "Are you okay?" It was Isabella.

Alvara panicked. She was so close. Then she had an idea. A disgusting idea, but she would take it. "Ugh, this is so embarrassing," Alvara said. "It's my time of the month, and I don't have anything." Even though it was a lie, Alvara still blushed.

"What? Oh, I understand," Isabella said quickly. "I will get you what you need, I will be right back." Her steps retreated.

Alvara actually felt ashamed of lying to Isabella about this, then felt dumb for feeling that way. Isabella wasn't evil, Alvara would give her that.

But it was time to get out of here.

Alvara heaved herself up into the darkness of the crawl space, muffling a yell as the edge of the grate scratched across her belly. Her arms shook, but she managed to get a leg up and squirm into the space.

Alvara couldn't sit upright, as the space was barely large enough for her to crawl through. It hadn't been created for that purpose; an adult would never have fit.

On her hands and knees, she made out shapes in the dim light coming from her grate as well as a series of others into the distance. Periodic indentations into her space could be metal siding for building support beams, or exits. The floor was concrete, and rough on her palms.

The route ahead of her appeared slightly brighter than the one behind, and she didn't have time to test both. She set off at a crawl, immediately hating how the concrete dug into her kneecaps through her jeans.

Alvara ducked under a round duct that was wrapped in soft insulation. At a fork, she chose the left route and continued. The tunnel turned abruptly, and she followed.

And got stuck.

Alvara tried to reverse, but one shoulder was jammed into a metal wall, and another was braced on the ceiling. Her legs couldn't get purchase, and her arms were squished beneath her body.

"Dang it," she breathed, and worried, irrationally, that she was running out of air. She tried to calm her panic.

"So you're stuck," she said aloud. "What needs to move?" Alvara did a mental inventory and decided that her hips were not the problem; her shoulders were what halted her progress.

Alvara had an idea, but even the thought sickened her. The reality would be so much worse.

But she didn't have a choice. Not if she wanted to get out of this damn prison.

Alvara braced one leg on the lower outer corner of the turn. She checked the angles, gritted her teeth, and kicked out at the wall.

Pain shot through her shoulder, but it didn't budge. Alvara blinked the tears out of her eyes, took a few deep breaths, and slammed her heel into the corner with all her strength.

Her shoulder popped with an audible displacement, and she slid free of the corner, to a further and more extreme chorus of pain from her dislocated joint. Alvara's breathing came in hisses of pain and her eyes filled with tears. She wobbled and wriggled until she was free of the corner, then lowered herself down onto her opposite side.

Mercifully, after a minute or two, her body popped her joint back into place with another small burst of pain. Alvara tentatively moved the arm, but her shoulder was back to normal. *Thank you*, she thought, and for once she wasn't talking to God. A wave of shame coursed through her at the thought.

A distant shout behind her made her start. She didn't have time to waste. She had to find a way out of this duct.

After a few more minutes of crawling, Alvara peered through the first horizontal grate she'd seen. A stairwell. She squirmed around to get her feet on the grate and kicked it until it fell to the concrete stair with a clang. In the sudden light, Alvara saw a wrench to one side of the grate. She grabbed it before sliding into the stairwell, blinking at the bright fluorescent bulbs.

"Hey, who's there?" A voice called from below. Alvara saw a guard peer into the small gap between the stairwell levels.

"Stop!" he yelled. His face disappeared, and she could hear him sprinting up the stairs.

"Copy, North stairwell!" he shouted as he climbed.

Alvara wasted no more time, taking the stairs up two at a time for floor after floor. Adrenaline surged, pushing her to climb faster than she thought possible.

When the stairs ran out, Alvara came to a locked door. The wrench was still in her hand. Clangs rang out as Alvara brought the wrench down on the door handle as hard as she could, over and over again.

The handle broke off. Alvara slammed a shoulder into the door and stumbled out onto the roof.

The roof stretched into the distance, a vast flat plain of white silicate panels, air conditioners, and complex ducts. As Alvara jogged across it, she was confused. It was like a hundred other roofs she'd seen, so why did it seem so unfamiliar?

Daylight, she thought. She was on a roof during the day.

Crap.

She turned to see the guard, along with a few of his buddies, step through the broken door and fan out across the open roof. Alvara backed away, until they drew their guns. She stopped, frantically thinking. The edge of the forest, just visible in the distance, might as well be a million miles away without her wings.

"Yes, Ms. Dusk. She's on the roof. We have her," the first man said into his radio.

"Keep her there until I can join you," Alvara heard Isabella say through the crackle. The guard ended the call, weapon held steady in one hand.

A slow rage grew in Alvara. For Selene, strange as she was, trapped on her moon. For the hundreds of people that Robert and Isabella had kidnapped and imprisoned, as if it was their right.

And for Jake, imprisoned again. He must be getting tired of Alvara letting him down.

Alvara was done yielding, and done playing by the rules. She deserved to be free.

The guard must have sensed a shift in her posture. "Wait!" he said, as Alvara broke into a sprint. As she approached the edge of the roof, her body remembered what wings felt like, the sweet rush of her power, and the taste of her independence.

Alvara leapt from the roof, the sun on her face, and felt wings rip from her back. She beat her wings through the pain of this unnatural growth, not sure how long it would last, but hoping she could make it to the forest, and freedom.

Moss exploded around her as Alvara crashed into the forest floor. She rolled once and collided with the base of a tree. A branch snapped.

Got to keep moving, Alvara thought, though her head spun and her body felt like one continuous bruise. She reached down to push herself up, and nearly blacked out.

After a few moments and some deep breathing, Alvara looked down at her hand. It rested at an extreme angle to her wrist, but didn't hurt yet. Alvara thought that might be a problem, and that she might be in shock. But she staggered to her feet, bracing one wrist with the other, and stumbled further into the forest.

Soon, her head would clear, and her wrist would knit, and she would figure out what to do next.

Large, moss-covered deciduous trees loomed over her. Ferns and moss coated every available surface, so that the predominant color in every direction was a vibrant green. Though it was near to midday, the leafy canopy trapped most of the sun's light.

As Alvara stumbled over hidden obstacles beneath the moss, her head indeed cleared. She figured that she had gotten maybe a mile or two from the compound before her day wings disappeared, which was a blessing. Isabella would send someone after her, or come herself. But Isabella was unlikely to cover much ground in terrain like this, and the likelihood of catching a glimpse of Alvara through the trees from above was almost zero.

Once Alvara's wrist healed, she almost enjoyed the hike. The temperature skirted both warm and cold, and the dark boughs and the bright leaves and moss made a contrast that was stark and beautiful.

Remembering Jake took some of the peace from the afternoon. He was captive, yet again, and for the moment she had no way to free him.

Yet this time was different. Robert and Isabella were true believers, but they had also shown plenty of restraint. One could almost call their recent behavior civil. Other than the actual captivity, that is. Jake would be all right until she could get him out.

She had to believe that.

Shadows grew and stretched as midday became late afternoon. Alvara stopped to rest on a dry boulder, kicking herself that she hadn't eaten any food or had anything to drink this morning. She was paying for it now, as her throat felt as dry as cotton.

Her backup plan, if she couldn't make it to town on foot, was to wait for moonrise and simply fly. And then see what she could do to find Ridge.

As plans went, she had heard better ones.

At her next rest break, she heard a harsh sound that immediately ended her reverie. A dirt bike was coming closer, and fast.

Alvara scrambled to her feet and jogged in the opposite direction, prevented from going faster by the need to watch her footing on the slippery ground.

"Alvara, stop!" a voice called. Alvara put on a fresh burst of speed.

"It's me, Ridge! Jesus! Calm down, stop!" the voice continued. The motorcycle cut out, and Alvara halted.

Ridge, the boy from the plane, looked like the fresh air had done him good. Instead of the ratty clothes she had seen, he wore jeans, combat boots, a leather jacket, and a cocky grin.

"Miss me?" he asked slyly.

"Ridge, man is it good to see you!" Alvara said, breaking into a grin. "I thought you were Isabella. I didn't exactly get permission to leave."

"You broke out? Sick!" Ridge exclaimed, dismounting from his bike and taking off his helmet. "And you don't even have wings! Do you have other powers?" Alvara wondered if he was taking mental notes for a comic book series.

"I'm so glad Robert released you," she said, ignoring his question. "He said he would, but we didn't know what to think."

"That was you?" Ridge said, his eyes wide. "Thank you," he added, and surprised her by giving her a leathery hug.

"You're welcome. Wait," she said, pulling back. "How did you even find me?"

He looked nonchalant. "You know, I got mad skills."

"Ridge," Alvara sighed.

"Okay, okay," he said, "Even though I can only see visions at night, sometimes I get weird sensations during the day, like when something is going to happen. I somehow knew you needed help. This one was like that game kids play, hot or cold?" Ridge asked. Alvara nodded.

"So I followed it until I won," Ridge said, smiling. Alvara blushed. Was he flirting with her?

"Thanks Ridge. I'm really happy you're here. But I would be even happier if you had something to drink?" she asked hopefully.

"Sorry, no place for a water bottle on this bad boy," Ridge said, patting his bike appreciatively. "But I can take you to my Mum's place in town. She definitely has water," Ridge winked. "And I may have brought an extra helmet. Whaddaya say?

"If there's water, I'm so in," Alvara said.

Ridge put Alvara's helmet on before he swung up onto his bike and buckled his own helmet into place. Then he helped Alvara get situated behind him. She put her arms tentatively around his waist. He adjusted her grip so that it was a lot tighter.

"I've never been on a motorcycle before," Alvara confessed as Ridge revved the engine.

"Don't worry,' he said. "When we get to the open road, just lean the way I lean. Over this bumpy stuff, I'll go slow, just make sure you hold on tight."

They started off at a measured pace, but Alvara maintained a firm grip, as the bumps came out of nowhere. Once she relaxed into it, she realized how nice the leather felt beneath her hands. She could smell the oil of the motorcycle and the sharp crisp scent of Ridge's shampoo.

It became a bit too comfortable. Alvara tried to distract herself, since she couldn't exactly put distance between them.

"I'm really excited to meet your sister, too," Alvara said. The bike was crawling along through the forest, so she hoped Ridge could hear her over the engine.

"She's something else," Ridge said finally. "I haven't seen her yet since I got released, but I'm sure she'll help us. The past day or so I've gotten really twitchy, and I think it means there's a problem with the Moon. She would know," he added. "She's a bona-fide Seer, but unlike me she dreams the future. I thought it was a load of . . ." Ridge remembered who he was speaking to.

"That she was pulling a fast one on us. You know the feeling of déjà vu? Mine is like that, only ahead of time, about people I'm just meeting but will be friends with in the future, little flickers like that. Even with the bit of the gift in my family, what she was claiming was way impossible. But then she saw the drunk driver that was going to hit my Mum and warned her."

"How did you know it would have hit her?" Alvara asked, ducking with Ridge so they could pass under a low-hanging branch.

"I figured, you see, because he crashed into a tree about the time she would have been driving by. But there have been other times . . . I was an idiot this once and didn't listen to her."

"What happened?" Alvara asked.

"I was captured," Ridge said. Alvara felt the hairs on the back of her neck rise.

"Whoa. She can really tell the future then?" Alvara asked. "That's got to be insane. How does she handle it?"

"She tries not to see too many people, keeps her daily schedule predictable," Ridge said. "The psychologist suggested it, though what could he know about my family, right? I was kind of a jerk to my Sis about it, but she says it helps. She's not even sixteen yet. She's just a kid."

"Yeah," Alvara said, knowing she was barely sixteen and Ridge couldn't be much older, but she knew how the older brother thing worked. It would have been nice to have one like Ridge.

"At least you have a sister, a family. All I have is a self-centered aunt."

"What, but she's family! She can't be that bad?" Ridge asked.

Alvara suppressed her urge to rant and merely thought as they drove. She remembered nights when she would see her aunt's light on late into the night, and know that she was up trying to balance the budget or worrying about who knew what else.

"I don't know," she finally said. "She seems that bad, I mean she really makes it clear that she doesn't want me around, but I think it's because she doesn't really know what to do with me, that she's just as scared as I am about trying to make a family after all this time. She's probably just lost," Alvara said, almost in a whisper, realizing for the first time how weird it must be to get a kid mostly grown and have no idea how to cope with it.

"Well, that sounded deep," Ridge said, but reached back to poke her in the side so she knew he was kidding. "At least you have somebody." Alvara could only nod, but Max and Jake, not her misunderstood aunt, occupied her thoughts.

They rode on in silence. It was a small miracle to just travel through the forest with this strangely endearing young man. Alvara had always loved to hike with Max, and her mind slipped into the familiar rhythms like the straps of a favorite backpack. As the trees thinned, the forest was filled with the light of a late afternoon sun. The warmth invigorated her, and she chatted with a semi-interested Ridge about some of her favorite biblical passages and their complexities. A smile snuck onto her face and took up residence there, almost without Alvara noticing a thing.

When it was obvious that Ridge had tired of religious talk, Alvara asked him about his life, and what it was like to be a Seer. Ridge shrugged it off, not seeming to want to talk about it, but gradually he opened up to her.

"My Mum is pretty normal, even less of the gift than I have; Da left when I was about four so I don't remember him much. Then it's just Sheila and me that I know of with our gift. When I was about twelve I played on the playground and I saw a girl sitting off by herself, reading a book that made her laugh. Her hair was really red, and in the setting sun her ponytail looked like it was on fire. I started to walk over to where she leaned against a tree, and one of my eyes went blind. In it, I saw the girl all grown up, my Mum's age, and I knew that we were married. I could see both of her at the same time, the little kid in my left eye, and the grown woman in my right, both smiling at me."

"I can't imagine how scary that would be!" Alvara gasped. "What did you do?"

"What do you think I did? I ran for it! I didn't stop until I got home." Alvara laughed.

"My Mum found me there later, shaking, and told me about how

160

sometimes we can See things." He chuckled ruefully. "My Sis has never let me live it down. I haven't seen that girl since, but she's out there somewhere." He picked his way along the trail, his attention far away.

Alvara shook her head in disbelief. "I mean, I grew wings, but that didn't change who I was, or what I knew about my future. That's pretty crazy stuff, Ridge."

He shrugged. "It's never been that strong since."

They rode farther, and hit a track that sloped downhill. It was a welcome change from their bumpy ride through the deep forest. Ridge kept the speed down so they could still converse, and talked about the normal half of his life. He spoke of high school, and of working as a mechanic in the evenings and during weekends for a bit of extra money. Alvara tried not to notice those relics of his job, his comfortably solid abs, but they were right beneath her fingers under the leather.

"You know, Ridge; you're a pretty cool dude," Alvara finally said, and meant it. She tried to infuse it with a brotherly tone, despite the tenor of her thoughts.

"Well." Ridge replied, and tried to dismiss the comment, but she wondered if it was his turn to blush. She thought he sat up a bit straighter on his bike after that.

When they emerged from the forest they hopped a curb onto a suburban street. Ridge finally picked up speed, so they could no longer talk. The houses they passed sported paint in a variety of colors, with tans and light blues dominating, and there were no bars on the windows or fences around the yards. It was a nice neighborhood, full of perfect little families, Alvara thought, and the bitterness she expected didn't come.

Ridge followed signs through the city to get them to the town of Bremerton. Alvara watched for any signs of pursuit, but saw no one suspicious. They skirted what Ridge told her was not a lake, but Oyster Bay, before coming to a stop on a deserted street.

It wasn't a bad area, Alvara thought. Certainly no worse than where she lived in Torrance. The houses were in various states of worn-down, but the streets were clean. Ridge took off his own helmet and helped Alvara with hers. Once he had the helmets situated on his bike, he glanced toward Alvara. He seemed mildly embarrassed.

"So, I may not have visited my Mum yet. Which means she will flip. Take this as a definite. Just hang on and she'll chill, okay?"

"Your Mom doesn't know you're all right?! Ridge!" Alvara said, smacking him on the shoulder. "Why didn't you go to see her when you were released earlier today?"

"I wasn't sure it would stick," Ridge said, his face hardening. "When they said I was free to go I thought it was a trick. If those people came after me again, I wanted to be nowhere near my Mum or my sister. That way they would be safe," Ridge said. "But I need to let her know I'm all right. We'll head out for my sister's cabin in the woods as soon as the sun sets."

Alvara agreed, and they walked toward his mother's house.

Chapter 22

Jake couldn't stop grinning. Every time he pictured the expression on Isabella's face when she confronted him with a package of sanitary napkins, or the sight of the bent grate in the ceiling, the smile would catch him off guard, blossoming again. *Scrawny Latina my ass,* he thought. *Go Alvara.* He could tell his smile was driving Isabella crazy, but couldn't bring himself to care.

Through the back and forth over Isabella's radio, Jake had pieced together what had happened. Somehow, Alvara had made it to the roof and flown away. In broad daylight.

His smile finally faded. Robert's words about the imbalance surfaced, and despite himself Jake worried about what growing wings during the day might portend.

As he thought, Jake glanced up to the glass ceiling of Isabella's well-appointed private office, which he had been confined to, after the sudden breakdown of their guided tour. He leaned back in the office chair. It squeaked.

Isabella, who spoke into her cell phone and simultaneously smacked her desktop computer in frustration, glanced over at him and frowned. She ended the call.

"Jake, I will ask again," Isabella said, feigning patience. The set of her jaw and harsh frown made her frustration evident. "Where would Alvara go? Tell me."

Jake didn't appreciate her tone. "Isabella, I'm your prisoner. If you want cooperation, you could try torture."

Isabella's face crumpled, and she sprang up from her chair and strode across the room. Before she turned away, Jake thought her eyes might have glistened with tears. He stood, regretting his words. Isabella stared out the window toward the green of the forest, her back rigid.

"I was wrong," Isabella said, her musical accent nearly obscuring her words. She glanced at him, and her eyes were dry. "I was worried that Xiu Li was hiding something. I was worried that you would escape. I was worried that you would attack us. And I was correct in two of these, Jake," she added. "You must understand that I did not want to hurt either of you, but only to have you two under control, to force you if you would not come of your own choice, because the alternative is worse," Isabella said. "But what I did to Alvara was too much. I am sorry." She took a slow breath, and waited.

Jake still stood next to his chair. Only a few feet separated him from Isabella. He was struck by how young she really was, to have so much authority, and so much responsibility. Robert treated her as an equal, rather than a daughter. He wondered if she had ever had a real childhood at all.

"Thank you," Jake said. "But Alvara's the one who needs to hear it."

"I just want to reach her in time, to make sure she does not use her abilities," Isabella said, her features full of worry.

"Maybe you should stop treating her like an enemy," Jake suggested.

Isabella met his eyes. "I have to find her, Jake. If you will not help, my team will handle it. They managed to lose Ridge once, but it is likely he will return home at some point. If Alvara is with him, she will be apprehended." She noticed Jake's grimace, and nodded in acknowledgement. "If necessary, I will do it myself. I am sorry."

Jake felt a pang of dread, but hoped that if Alvara had managed to connect with Ridge, they would both be smart enough to stay away. "I can't stop you," Jake said, and growled, "But if you harm her, then you'll see what a real enemy looks like."

Isabella's fists clenched, but she was the first to look away. "I understand, Jake," she bit out. "Neither I, nor any of my team, will harm her. I owe her that and more."

"Actions speak louder than words," Jake said, and to his surprise his anger was gone. His voice came out gentle.

Isabella sank into her chair. "I have done enough," she whispered, her head bowed.

Jake laid a hand on her shoulder. He felt her flinch, but she didn't pull away. "Sometimes it's hard to chart the proper course. But you can't keep blaming yourself for what you've done in the past," Jake said, thinking of himself as much as Isabella. "You have to make amends. Release the prisoners who aren't a danger to themselves or others."

"I'm not sure what will happen," Isabella said into her hands.

"We'll find another way," Jake said. "There's got to be something we're missing about this imbalance. I can feel it."

"I hope you have a mystical feeling," Isabella said. Jake realized it was a joke, and offered a weak chuckle.

"I'm not sure," he said as she stood up. "Maybe some data would help. Do you have a plot of the imbalance across time, maybe with significant global events alongside?"

Isabella looked at him strangely. "Aren't you a shopkeeper?" she asked.

Jake chuckled wholeheartedly. "I wasn't always," he replied.

"I can get you something like that," Isabella said, her eyes on her computer screen as files opened and closed.

"Is there a quiet space I can sit and work? With a laptop and a pad of paper?" Jake asked.

Isabella thought for a moment, then pulled her radio out of her suit pocket. "Charlie, I need an escort for Mr. Coughlin to the dojo." Her radio stowed, she addressed Jake directly. "I would take you myself, but I have business elsewhere."

"What business?" he asked cautiously.

"I have an appointment with some long-term clients," she said, and smiled. Trust once lost had to be earned, but Jake decided to give her a chance.

The dojo was a marvel. Instead of the wooden columns and paper panels that decorated a traditional dojo, the walls alternated with floor to ceiling mirrors and shiny black panels. Against one wall was a pile of gray blocking pads, along with some black padded body armor. The floor was polished wood, and gleamed in the recessed lighting.

"Wow," Jake whispered.

"Totally," his guard, a young muscular black woman named Karen, replied. "I would love to be able to work out in here."

"You can't?" Jake asked. He spied a cluster of comfy chairs in one occluded corner. When he reached them, he saw that they faced a window, out of sight of the main floor of the dojo. He located a plug for the laptop and collapsed in a chair.

Karen leaned against the back of another, smoothing her hair. "Private," she said. "Though Ms. Dusk once asked me to spar with her, so I got one chance."

"How did that go?" Jake asked nonchalantly.

"She laid me out. I may have gotten a single hit in. Despite her figure in that suit, that lady can move. I don't know where she hides her muscles," Karen added, shaking her head.

Jake opened the laptop, and Karen moved to lean on a chair where she could see his screen. Jake turned and met her eyes.

"I'm to monitor your internet usage," Karen said, her features carefully neutral.

Jake shrugged. "Doesn't matter to me," he said. "Just researching conspiracy theories."

He turned his attention to the graph of sorts. It was more of a list, of dates and commentary on the imbalance, sprinkled in with potential events of importance. These events ranged from solar and lunar events like moon phases, eclipses, and seasonal shifts, to global outbreaks of moon-related phenomena or successful campaigns against 'belief'. This last category was the most nebulous, so he set it aside for now.

Jake worked at putting the rest of the data in a format he could use, creating a spreadsheet and putting numbers to the vague imbalance judgements as best he could. Shaky correlations emerged; the imbalance was worse when the moon was full, for example, or during the emergence of moon-related phenomena around the world. But he couldn't tell whether the imbalance caused the phenomena, or the other way around.

Despite small fluctuations, the imbalance had drifted steadily downwards for the past fifteen years, with a sudden dip about ten years ago. No global events or eclipses corresponded with either time point.

Jake ran his hand through his thinning hair, and focused on the past few weeks, which was filled with fluctuations. Robert must have typed a note before he left this morning, notating a relatively large increase in the imbalance with the curt words, "Feather cured mortal wound. Profound negative effect." Jake shook his head, wondering how the man could be so cold about his own near-death experience.

Jake's attention snagged on a large deflection from the week before. It, unlike most of the others, was positive, nearly halfway to normal. A question mark was the only notation.

That day was before Jake and Alvara had left for China, but after the night he had flown with her to the children's hospital. It was nothing that Jake, Alvara, Isabella or Robert had done.

Jake started in his chair, everything suddenly snapping into place.

Biyu.

I don't know why the imbalance started, Jake thought. *But I know why they can't fix it.*

The door to the dojo opened, and fire boiled through, slamming into one of the black plates. A mirror to one side cracked, and Robert strode into the room.

Jake glanced at Karen, but her eyes were wide and her hand had moved to the gun at her hip. He moved the laptop to the side of his chair and waited to see what Robert would do.

The man was in the grip of some strong emotion, and grunted as he expelled fire balls at the black wall panels. The bursts of flame had shrank, and Robert paused for longer between each one.

Finally he bent over, coughing. When he straightened, he noticed the two of them for the first time and jumped.

"Get out of here," he said to Karen, his accent much thicker than normal.

"I have orders from Ms. Dusk–" Karen began.

"Out," he enunciated, his hands smoldering.

Karen walked past him, turning back once to cast a worried look in Jake's direction.

"Why are you here?" Robert asked, staring at his hands.

"Isabella told me this would be a quiet place to work," Jake replied. *She was slightly mistaken*, Jake thought but did not say. Jake walked toward Robert, stopping some distance away.

Robert seemed not to have heard him. "The feather did not work," he said.

Jake paused, uncertain. "At least you tried," Jake replied.

"Yes," Robert said, his features steady but his voice a riot of emotion. "Even though I knew, had it worked, that it would add to the imbalance. With that knowledge, maybe I did not believe in it, and so caused it to fail. And when your borrowed gift failed," he added, "all I had left to offer a crazy girl and her family were ashes." Flame licked over Robert's hands and up to his elbows, and he shook it off like water droplets. Bits of fire hit the lacquered floor and disappeared.

"These are the rules we live with, Jake," Robert said. "Isabella and I were not graced with healing. We were given powers of control and intimidation, and failing that, execution." His voice had twisted into a bitter irony, and his hands shook.

Jake took a step back. "I'm sorry it didn't work," Jake began.

"Save your sympathy," Robert spat. "My daughter is dying of cancer so that you and that girl Alvara could fly around on your wings, does that make you sorry? Even once we explained what it meant, what it would cost, Alvara escaped using her wings, during the day. How could she?" Robert hissed.

"Your daughter branded her!" Jake yelled, his hands bunching to fists. "After kidnapping us and delivering us to Xiu Li! You're damn right Alvara escaped."

Robert threw a fireball at Jake's head.

Jake had time to be surprised before wings erupted from his shoulder blades in a burst of pain, wings more massive than he'd ever grown before. They curved in front of his body as if to protect him. Jake felt the impact as the fireball collided with his wings, but there was no explosion of heat. The flames dissipated, and the wings retracted as if they had never been.

Stunned, Jake reached back and felt two slits in his shirt where his wings had sliced through. Unlike his normal growth of wings, which could rip a shirt to pieces as they grew, these holes were precise, as if from daggers.

Robert looked stupefied. "I . . ." he began, but could not finish.

"Robert, you're back!" Isabella exclaimed as she strolled into the room. She slowly came to a stop, looking from one man to the other in confusion. "I smell smoke," she said.

"Robert, what the hell?" Jake finally said, the leftover adrenaline in his system making his voice shake.

"I can't believe I . . . I am sorry," Robert replied. "Are you all right?"

"Somehow my wings . . ." Jake began, shaking his head.

"Please, someone explain to me what happened," Isabella asked, tense.

"I attacked Jake," Robert said. "I was angry. But not that angry," he mused. "This will sound strange, but I do not think it was me. It felt like Sol was in charge."

"Convenient," Jake spat. "So this is how you avoid taking responsibility for your own actions? Your entire operation here makes more and more sense if someone else is always to blame."

"Jake," Robert pleaded. "Did you choose to use your wings like that, to block my attack? Or did it just happen, somehow, with you watching but not acting?"

Jake forced himself to calm his righteous anger. Once he considered, the answer was obvious.

"I wasn't in control of my wings," he said. "So you're saying Selene was? I didn't know that was possible."

"The situation is changing rapidly," Robert said. "And with Alvara loose and probably using her gift, the balance could be truly broken, beyond repair."

Jake recalled his epiphany. "I have some ideas about that. You can't fix the balance, not as things now stand. Let me show you," he said, walking back to the laptop. He flinched when Robert got too close.

Robert backed off a step, not meeting Jake's eyes.

Jake opened his graph, trying to calm down.

"Here's the last time there was a real uptick, or reduction, in the imbalance," Jake said, pointing to the change he had noticed from a couple weeks ago as Robert and Isabella crowded around to look. "Alvara and I weren't using our gifts, and you didn't have an idea of what it might be. But then I remembered; that's when Biyu, the third Child of the Moon, lost her wings forever." Jake let them process that.

"So without this woman's gift, there were only two of you. And we were closer to balance?" Isabella asked.

"It makes sense," Robert said, sitting down in one of the chairs. He looked exhausted, but interested. "But then why did the imbalance return soon after?"

"Selene mentioned that the gift passed to someone else," Jake replied. "And no, I have no idea who. A child, most likely," he added, seeing Robert's frown.

"So I came back to a question I had earlier today. What happened to the third Child of the Sun?" Jake said. "That's why nothing you do seems to make a difference. One of you is missing, and we just need to find out what happened, and why there has been no replacement."

Robert and Isabella stared at each other. "Another like us," Robert said. "I never thought to ask. When Sol brought me to Isabella, I believed that she was all there was," he said simply.

"This must be true," Isabella said. "It puts all our struggles in perspective." She frowned in thought.

"Share that document with me," Robert told Jake. "I will get to work to see whether we can track down what happened to this third child. This may be the key," he said. Then Robert smiled. It was like a sun barely peeking out of the clouds, and his parentage was visible for the first time. Robert jogged from the room, leaving Jake and Isabella.

"Did you release the prisoners?" Jake asked.

Isabella nodded. "I have not yet told Robert," she said. "He has a lot on his mind."

"Thank you. You did the right thing," Jake said. "Alvara will think so too," he added kindly.

Isabella nodded again, her eyes troubled. "After what you have discovered," she said, "I do not think it is necessary to recapture Alvara. I have decided to call off my team."

Jake smiled. "Before you do, I have an idea."

Chapter 23

Ridge and Alvara cautiously approached an off-white clapboard house with a rusted pickup parked out front. No one moved on the street, so they crunched through the dry grass to the front door. Ridge opened the screen door and knocked hard.

"Read the sign!" they heard a woman scream from the house. Alvara saw that there was a 'No Solicitors' sign next to the door, similar to those she had seen before. However, this one had a shotgun next to the words. A stronger message. The sound of footsteps receded.

"Mum it's me, Ridge!" Ridge yelled at the top of his lungs, causing Alvara to wince. Apparently, yelling ran in the family. She heard a clatter inside the house as if someone was running, and the door opened to reveal a severe woman in working boots and an orange floral dress. It was a striking combination.

"Jesus, Ridge!" she screamed at the same volume as before. "Where the hell did you go; it's been *a month!*" She ignored Alvara completely as she continued a barrage of harsh criticisms, crushing Ridge in a hug. Ridge attempted to get out explanations every other breath or so.

"Bitch woman kidnapped me . . . worried about the Moon . . . tried to escape before . . . cut it OUT . . . Alvara helped . . . I'm okay, for crying out . . ." Her hug became less frantic, and her accusations tapered into whispers. Ridge's mother broke into tears, and it somehow ended with them both kneeling on the dead lawn, Ridge's mother cradling him and mumbling about how blessed they were to have him home. Ridge glanced at Alvara over his mother's back and managed to wink. She could see that he was struggling a bit to catch his breath, but he beamed. Ridge's mother finally let him go, and blinked before turning to Alvara.

"You feel familiar," she said, wiping her brow on the sleeve of her dress. "What are you, exactly?" Before Alvara could answer that she was a person, thank you very much, Ridge answered for her, a note of smugness in his voice.

"*She* is a Child of the Moon Goddess. We met when we were both locked up, and she got me released so we could go talk with Sis. She's technically on the run, though," Ridge added.

Ridge's mother considered how to respond. "It's nice to meet you,

Child," she finally said. It was weird to be called a child with a capital 'C'. "I'm Martha."

"I'm Alvara, and it's great to meet you." Martha reached out to shake her hand, and Alvara could feel calluses on her strong palms.

"We haven't seen one of your kind around here for forty years," she continued.

"Yeah, yeah," Ridge said. "Alvara's famished, but we'll be heading to Sheila's place soon."

Martha smiled, but looked worried. "Why don't you both come inside, and I'll get you some beer."

"Um, just water please?" Alvara asked. Ridge rolled his eyes as he led the way into the house.

The house was sparse but clean. Black and white prints covered the walls, and cheap furniture decorated the living room. Alvara almost tripped over an enormous tool kit lying half-open next to the kitchen sink. Martha picked it up with no apparent effort and bid them take a seat. She grabbed two beers and a bottle of water out of the fridge and passed the water to Alvara. Alvara noticed that Martha pulled off the bottle caps of both beers with her hands, and wondered at her strength. The water tasted amazing, and Alvara had to stop herself from chugging the whole bottle in one go.

Martha grimaced as she took a seat. "I have a message for you, Alvara. A man in a black uniform gave it to me about an hour ago, to give to a girl named Alvara if she should show up at this house."

They were here, but they didn't wait to capture me, Alvara thought, and wondered why.

"Of course, the bastard lacked the decency to tell me my son would be with her," Martha nearly growled. She passed a handwritten note to Alvara.

Robert and Isabella agreed to stay off your back for now. They're all right once you get to know them. But situation is intensifying, and I found some new information that could change the game. Careful with your gift, mine has been unpredictable. Come back when you're ready. 'Works for you?' -Jake

Alvara looked up from the card to see Martha and Ridge staring at her. "My friend, Jake, is still a prisoner," she said. "But this note is definitely from him. I have to think about what it means, but for now I think they've decided not to chase us."

"Thank goodness for that," Martha said without conviction, and they returned to drinking in silence.

"Sheila isn't doing so well," Martha told Ridge after a while. "She's been asleep for days, now, longer than I've ever seen. I've gone to visit a bunch, as you'd guess, but she just mutters or screams nonsense when I try to wake her."

"Mum, she said never to wake her up," Ridge insisted.

"I know, I know, I just worry about her. It isn't natural, even for such a one as she is. But at least we know why."

"Yeah," Ridge replied, sipping his beer and running a hand through his uneven hair.

"Sorry, but why?" Alvara asked the silent table.

"The balance," Martha replied, taking a long draw from her beer. "Or imbalance, I suppose I should call it now. Sheila gets her Dreaming from the Moon. The balance is out of whack in favor of the Moon, and so her Dreaming is more powerful, and I guess deeper and longer, than it's ever been before."

"Wait," Alvara said. "So you can feel this balance thing too? I thought it was just us and the Sun's Children who felt it."

Martha frowned at her. "Figures a Child would assume that. Anyone with even a touch of the Moon or Sun in them should be able to feel a balance that's as far off as this one is, which means virtually every creature out there with a whiff of magic about them is worried, and with damn good reason."

Alvara sipped her water. So the issues with the balance were real, and Robert and Isabella were right about that, at least. Even with that confirmed, she couldn't tell whether it was the Sun or the Moon who wanted the imbalance to continue, or had plans for using it to their own advantage. Alvara needed to figure out exactly what had caused the imbalance, and hopefully find some way to fix it. She still knew so little.

"If we go and talk with Sheila . . . I mean, if she happens to wake up for us, she may be able to tell us what's going on with the balance?"

"Is that what Ridge said?" Martha replied. "Her gift isn't like that, where you ask a question and she gives you a nice easy fact sheet of the answer. Even if she knows what's going on, she may not be able to tell you, or explain it very well."

"That's why we both need to go," Ridge interrupted. "I've been listening to her crazy dreams since I was a kid. If anyone can figure out what the heck she's trying to say, it's me."

His mother considered for a moment, and then broke into a hesitant smile. "Maybe you can talk some sense into that girl, get her to eat a meal once in a while."

"Yeah, of course," Ridge answered, and Alvara could see it was a rote reply to a common question.

Alvara's stomach let out an audible grumble.

"You must be hungry," Martha said with a trace of irony. "I'll put in a frozen pizza for you both. When are you planning to visit Sheila?"

"After sunset," Ridge answered, nodding toward Alvara.

"Right," she muttered, stopping with her hand on the freezer handle. "It's good to have you back, Ridge," she said. Then she continued prepping the pizza as if she hadn't spoken.

Alvara had a lot to consider. As she smelled the garlic and tomato aromas of the cooking pizza, one thought solidified. She hoped Sheila would feel like waking up.

As they finished their pizza, the sun set. Alvara's white wings grew, blessedly free of pain, as they had every moon rise since she was a child. The moment felt unfamiliar, and she realized that she hadn't prayed to God for her wings. The guilt filled her with sadness, and she wished for a private moment to sort out her feelings.

"Wow," Ridge said, his eyes wide with appreciation. "Now those are some serious wings."

Martha, her left eye entirely blue, touched Alvara's wings in wonder. "They're beautiful, Child. Take care." Alvara still wasn't used to having her wings appraised, and blushed as she nodded.

Ridge led the way outside, carrying a backpack filled with food for Sheila over to his bike parked down the street. Ridge straddled the bike and held out his hand, "There's room on here for two, you know." He winked, his blue eye gleaming in the darkness.

Alvara laughed, and with a rustle of feathers she leapt into the air, her darker emotions melting away in the joy of flight. It would never be customary, or routine, or boring to feel her wings lift her into the night sky. Alvara smiled as her wings cupped the air, wishing she had borrowed a jacket on the cool evening. It would only be a few more days until the full moon, and it felt amazing. She felt the power coursing through her, and the night was alive with the thrill of possibilities.

After a few minutes of forceful beats to gain altitude, Alvara spotted Ridge through the trees, the sound of his bike a soft hum, his headlights illuminating the road in an arc before him. He was just leaving the highway for the dirt roads that led deeper into the forest.

The smells of car exhaust and French fries finally gave way to pine and damp cedar, and Alvara breathed them in as she worked to maintain altitude in the cool air. As it faded from dusk to full dark, Alvara savored the beauty of the night. Each moment was sharper and clearer in the dim light than it ever felt in the garish full light of day.

Ridge whooped as his bike shot over a small dirt jump, and understanding flooded her. It was like with Biyu, speaking Chinese, but even clearer, somehow; Ridge finally felt free under the open moon, and he was the happiest he had ever been.

As they moved away from city lights, it was harder to keep track of Ridge, as the branches tended to block most of the light reaching her altitude. Yet Alvara didn't want to risk a crash by ducking below the tree line to search. So she was left craning her eyes and ears and wishing for some heat-seeking goggles. They continued far into the dense forest, until Alvara wondered if perhaps Ridge could be lost. He had begun to slow at regular intervals, taking side trails and once circling back to take a different fork.

Alvara heard the bike sounds cease, which she took to mean that they had reached Sheila's place. From her vantage above the trees, there was no sign of habitation.

As she glided downward, she noticed a sturdy cabin nestled in a copse of trees. The lights were out, so it was difficult to see even when she knew it was there. Alvara banked her descending circles and stalled in order to land gently next to Ridge.

"Man, I could get used to this!" Ridge exclaimed. "I didn't realize how much I missed biking at night. Wanna go again?" he teased.

"Ridge, how old are you?" Alvara complained.

"Kidding, only kidding," he said. "I am of course fully focused on figuring out whether the world will end." They walked toward the small front door, and Ridge pushed the handle. The door creaked open, revealing darkness behind it.

They crossed the threshold on tiptoe, but the only sound was of breathing from the bed in the far corner. "No electricity," Ridge whispered, and struck a match to light the oil lamp beside the door. He moved around the room and lit two more lamps, before lighting the lamp next to his sister's bed. He pulled up a stool on one side of the bed for Alvara and knelt on the side closer to his sister. Sheila didn't rest easily, but twitched and murmured in her slumber. She had long, wavy brown hair, and it spread over her pillow and off the bed. She looked about Alvara's age.

"Hmm," Ridge whispered. "Staying asleep this long is pretty weird for her. I know I made a big deal about my Mum trying to wake her, but I think I should try."

"Whatever you think we should do," Alvara said. She felt weird, like her presence was an imposition on this boy and his sister. The feeling only got stronger as Ridge tried to wake her.

"Hey La-la . . . It's Ridge . . . Come on you lazy chick, time to get moving . . ." He shook her lightly at first, and then a bit harder. He turned to Alvara, clearly worried, but he managed a smile.

"Watch this. I hate to get to this point, but she can't help herself." He leaned over his sister and shouted, "Sheila, a spider!"

"Ahhh! Get it off me!" she screamed, springing up, throwing the blanket off herself, eyes darting frantically. Ridge huffed with suppressed laugher, and she oriented toward the sound. "Jeez, you're such a jerk!" she squealed, and smacked him hard on the shoulder. He winced and rubbed his shoulder, but he didn't stop smiling.

"Nice to see you again, Sis. I'm glad you're okay."

"Ridge!" she said, and a chill ran over Alvara as she saw Sheila's eyes: two bright blue, glistening orbs. She realized Sheila couldn't see them at all; at night she was blind. "I was so worried about you! Before I fell asleep this time, I told Mum you were trapped in a cage that moved, but somehow I still knew she couldn't find you." She leaned over from the bed and hugged him hard, and he patted her shoulder until she let him go.

"It's been crazy, but I'm okay now. Sheila, this is Alvara. She convinced them to let me go." Alvara was about to shake hands, but Sheila beckoned her into a fierce hug, looking the part of the little sister with her bouncy curls and her cow themed long-sleeved pajamas.

"Thank you for bringing my brother back. You've got wings," she said by way of greeting, having just run her fingers over them.

"Only at night," Alvara corrected. "It's a pleasure to meet you, Sheila."

"Before this goes any further you have to eat, or Mum will kill me. Do you know how long you've been asleep?" Ridge asked as he bent over the backpack he had brought.

"Is it four weeks now? Or maybe three?" Her brows drew up in worry. She shrieked and closed her eyes, wrapping her arms around herself and shaking.

"Don't worry, this happens every time she wakes up; it's like an aftershock," Ridge said to Alvara. He waited a minute or so until she had relaxed before replying. "Nah, you're overestimating again. You've been asleep for five days or so, Mum said."

Sheila peered at Alvara for a few seconds, and Alvara stared back at her, though she knew Sheila couldn't see her. She wondered if it would feel tingly if Sheila was using a supernatural ability to examine her, but she just seemed like a normal sixteen-year-old concentrating on a difficult math problem.

"You've got a fighting spirit," she replied, still shaking slightly, "and a stronger moon aura even than me, but I can't really see much past tonight. Don't worry, it's pretty normal not to see much, but what I can see is weird." She continued to examine Alvara, the puzzle not yet fully solved.

What was she supposed to do with that comment left hanging? "Um, what do you see?" Alvara asked.

"Oh, just lots of fire," Sheila said seriously. Before Alvara could respond, Sheila dived into the food her brother had brought her with an almost manic intensity, which consisted of bread, cheese and grapes, as well as a carton of apple juice. After Ridge guided her hands to the different foodstuffs he took a seat on the bed next to her.

In the five minutes Alvara and Ridge watched her, she managed to polish off a half a loaf of bread, a large hunk of cheese, a bunch of grapes, and about a half-gallon of apple juice. After licking her fingers, she burped.

"That was so tasty. Ridge," she said, "you better have a good reason for waking me up; I told you to only use the spiders thing when you really need to. If you use it too much it might not work at all. And I was in the middle of so many dreams . . ." she rubbed her temples with the gesture of a much older woman, but looked a lot healthier now that she had eaten.

Ridge nodded at Alvara, so Alvara explained as best she could. "I heard from Ridge that you're a Dreamer. The balance is way off; farther toward the moon side than anyone has ever seen it. We wanted to know if you understood what was going on and if you knew some way to fix the problem." She waited for Sheila to respond. Sheila tugged her hair with a troubled expression on her young face.

"There are layers within layers," she mused. "I've dreamed about this a lot lately; the image of a scale usually means I'm learning about the balance. I know, obvious right?" she smiled sardonically. "In the past couple of years, I've seen it continue to dip toward the side of the moon. In this past dream I saw it lying broken on the ground." Alvara felt cold. "And that was the present. The other vision from the present was," she frowned

173

with her eyes closed, "a woman singing." She peeked by opening one eye. "Mean anything to either of you?" Ridge shrugged and Alvara shook her head. "Okay, well, think about it. It's the big picture right now."

She sighed and cracked her fingers. "Talking about the future is going to take some effort," she said. "I found a prophesy, which is good, but I can never remember what I've seen. You two can watch during my trance and remember for me."

"You sure you need to be in a trance for this?" asked Ridge. "It's creepy."

"Course I'm sure. How do you think I feel, I'm the one who has to be in it," Sheila snapped. Alvara could see that while she was trying to be brave, what she was about to do terrified her.

"All right, whatever," he replied, crossing his legs on the end of the bed. He still seemed uncomfortable, and Alvara wondered what this trance would involve.

Sheila stood up from the bed and grabbed a stick that leaned against the wall nearby. She walked around the room, gathering three short white candles and a lighter. She only occasionally used the stick for guidance. Then she felt around with her feet for slip-on shoes by the door.

"Out we go," Sheila said. Ridge grabbed a shawl from a peg next to the door and wrapped it around her shoulders before they walked outside. Alvara followed.

"Sit with me in a triangle," Sheila said, and sank cross-legged onto a flat patch of ground covered in pine needles.

Alvara and Ridge joined her. Alvara noticed that though she was blind, Sheila had sat herself so that she directly faced the moon visible through the trees. Was it coincidence?

Sheila handed the candles to Ridge, who lit them with the lighter and distributed one each to Sheila and Alvara. Alvara stared at hers as it flickered.

"Goddess of the Moon," Sheila intoned, her voice sweet and pure, "You have been known by many names, and your light fills the night. God of the Sun, you have been known by many names, and your light, reflected and changed in form through the Moon your opposite, fills the night. Bless us with your presence as we attempt to see beyond."

Alvara felt a chill settle over her. The candle flames swelled to five times their size, then shrank again. It took a conscious effort not to panic. The flames left bright spots on Alvara's vision, so that the rest of the scene was shrouded in darkness.

Sheila spoke again, though her voice had changed. "What is taken away will also be given. What kills will also give birth. What pains will also soothe. What is to come will also be." Natural sounds blended to form her voice, as if the rustling of the trees and the yips of coyotes and the twittering of a thrush just happened to string together into speech. Her eyes glowed in the green reflective manner of feral forest animals.

Sheila hummed, increasing in volume until the whole forest glade vibrated at its frequency, and her head swayed back and forth to rises and falls in the intensity of the sound. Alvara's heartbeat began to match the pulses of Sheila's hum; it was the rhythm of the world. Alvara's wings suddenly extended out to either side of her, trying to rip themselves from her back. When the pain became unbearable, the humming stopped. Sheila said:

A pale child screams,
A pale child prays,
A pale child believes,
The moon sings to her children.
A bright child was lost,
A bright child was careful,
A bright child was faithful,
The sun calls to his children.
Unless a mother is betrayed by one of her children
And the sun dances with the moon once more
The earth will cry for the moon's folly
And bathe in her children's blood.

At its conclusion, Sheila let out a heart-wrenching scream that sent a shiver through Alvara's body. When the scream ended Sheila blinked a few times. The candles had been extinguished at some point. Smoke curled up from their wicks.

Sheila's eyes returned to bright blue, and she wept silently, tears streaming down her cheeks to mix with her hair.

"With harm to none, so shall it be. The circle is undone," Sheila whispered through her sobs.

Alvara reeled from the intensity of the vision. Ridge patted Sheila's shoulder awkwardly. Alvara wondered if she should try to comfort someone but didn't know what to say. The light of the lantern through the windows allowed them to see, but beyond the edges of the light, the darkness of the forest was complete.

Alvara turned away from the cabin, looking up toward the visible patches of the night sky. She wanted to see the light of the moon again; its gentle glow would help to dispel some of the worries that had settled around their shoulders. But when she saw the moon, her mouth went dry.

"You guys. Look," she murmured, standing.

Sheila and Ridge craned their necks to see. Sheila gasped, and staggered to her feet, so she must be able to sense what Alvara had seen. Ridge muttered a low, "No way," and stood as well.

The moon was clearly visible through the trees, but it had swollen in the sky to five times the size of normal. Alvara tried to remember what Jake had explained and thought of Selene when she looked at the moon. Glimpses of blonde waves of hair sweeping over the moon rewarded her efforts. But Selene's face wasn't visible. She wondered what it meant, and what they could possibly do now. What had changed?

"Let's go inside," Alvara suggested. They followed her, and Alvara was quietly relieved not to have to keep staring at the impossible moon.

Alvara sat on the stool, while Ridge helped his sister sit next to him on the bed. She had a sudden sense that even though Ridge was older than she was, he and his sister were waiting for her to tell them what to do. It was a humbling feeling. She took a breath and began.

"I know you both are probably scared. I'm a bit scared too." *Too true,* she thought, *but let's focus on something else.* "Let's look at what Sheila said, and see if we can figure out what any of it means." *Better,* she thought. She hoped the matter-of-fact way she addressed the problem would keep them from focusing too much on the darkness those words predicted.

"I don't remember," said Sheila, her voice small.

"I can write it down," Ridge suggested, and produced a paper and pen from a small cabinet on one wall. He copied out the words in jerky letters, and read it aloud a few times for Sheila's benefit. If anything, hearing it repeated over and over only increased Alvara's dread.

"She talked about the sun and the moon, so it has to do with the balance," Ridge suggested. "It doesn't sound good."

"I could see visions while I was talking," Sheila admitted. She was pale.

"What kind of visions?" Alvara probed.

She closed her eyes. "I saw people drowning, swallowing water as they screamed. The whole world cried out . . ." She opened them. "I don't want to talk about it; I don't think it'll help. It was bad."

"Hey, it's okay," Alvara said, patting Sheila on the shoulder. "Let me look at the prophesy again," she said, scanning it. "It looks to me like it's about the Children of the Sun and the Moon. I don't get what all the pieces mean, but that's the general picture." She read it over again. "According to this, it seems like there's a third Child of the Sun, unless I'm reading it wrong."

"You think there's only two?" Sheila asked.

"I know of two, and they believe they're the only ones," Alvara said, wondering.

"This is messed up," said Ridge. "Unless this kid betrays their mother, or whatever, the Earth is totally screwed."

"That's not all," Sheila replied. "The sun has to dance with the moon."

"Great," Ridge growled, "that sounds a hell of a lot more likely."

"These don't have to be literal, right Sheila?" Alvara asked. "At least, that's how prophesies usually happen in books and movies."

"Alvara, I'm no expert," she apologized. "I don't get told how to interpret what I see in dreams; I just try to figure it out. That's . . ." she paused, "how Ridge got captured in the first place."

Ridge scratched behind his ear, but said nothing, so Sheila continued. "I saw Ridge running, and the sun opened up and wrapped around him, dragging him away. I thought I needed to warn Ridge to stay away from the sun, so I did. He laughed, and asked if it was for his complexion, and I was embarrassed. I didn't know how he would stay away from the sun, or even what would happen if he didn't. The next afternoon, when he was out jogging, they took him. I'm so sorry Ridge," she ended.

"It's okay, I shoulda listened," he replied. He tried to smile but got stuck halfway. "We're forgetting about the prophesy Sheila just told us. Not to mention the moon having suddenly gotten way bigger." He gestured with one hand. "I mean, the moon and sun are way the hell out in the sky. What can we even do?"

Alvara thought of Jake's message. *Come back when you're ready.* She couldn't believe what she was considering. "I have to go back," she said.

"Like, to that bitch Isabella? Are you serious?" Ridge said, furious. "You escaped today! You're home free!"

"Sure, I'm free to go. But go where?" Alvara asked. "Jake is there, and I need to tell him what I know. He's great with stuff like this, he'll have ideas about what we can do. And even without all this, I can't leave him there."

Alvara flared her wings, smacking the prophesy in frustration. "And look at what you wrote, Ridge. Robert and Isabella are a part of this, too. I hate this, but Jake and I probably can't fix it on our own. We might have to work with them. I don't know."

"I do!" Ridge said. "They are kidnappers, Alvara! Don't put yourself in their hands again. Just don't," he repeated, his brow creased in worry.

"It's not just about me," Alvara said. "I have a responsibility to fix this, or it won't just be the moon growing in size. Global catastrophe, Robert said."

"And you believe this man? One who kept Ridge and you prisoner?" Sheila asked.

"I don't know," Alvara said. "Jake seems to. If he's right . . ." she didn't finish.

"Well, you're on your own," said Ridge, folding his arms stubbornly. "You helped me get away, and I'll always be grateful. But I brought you to Sheila. I've held up my end of the bargain."

"I'm not asking you to come," Alvara said. "I'm not exactly thrilled to be going." In fact, the idea of it filled her with a combination of anger and dread.

"I'll come with you," Sheila said. Alvara and Ridge turned to stare at her in confusion. "I might be able to help," she continued. "I do have a lot more experience with visions than either of you. Maybe I will be able to see something you don't." Her mouth quirked into a smile at her currently blind state.

"Sheila, they held me captive for weeks," Ridge began.

"And then they let you go, right?" Sheila replied. "Look, it sucks, but aside from this whole end-of-the-world vision, I don't sense any danger to me personally. I'll be fine."

"What about me, anything in the near future?" Ridge challenged.

"No, nothing specific," Sheila answered, confused.

"Great, then I'll keep you company on your little adventure."

"Wait, you're coming?" Sheila asked, bouncing slightly on the bed.

"I said I would, didn't I?" Ridge retorted defensively. "That means I'm coming. Though I don't know how much help we'll be."

"Well, if everything falls apart, you two can envision our way to a grand escape," Alvara said, mostly joking.

"This is a horrible plan," Ridge stated.

"I've never met Children of the Sun. What will their auras look like?" Sheila wondered aloud.

"I'll give you a hint: they suck," Ridge muttered.

Alvara smiled. "Thank you," she said to both of them. "I hope Robert and Isabella will listen to reason. Jake seems to think they might. And they need to know what we know. But right now," Alvara interrupted herself with a yawn. "I'm exhausted. Would it be all right if we crashed at your Mom's place, Ridge? Then we can call them for a ride in the morning."

"Oh no," Ridge said. "My Mom. I'm going back there. She'll kill me."

Sheila shrugged. "Just don't tell her where we're going."

Ridge massaged his brow. "Just let me do the explaining," he said. "But yes, you can stay." Ridge cracked his knuckles. "You can fly, and my motorcycle still seats two. She's just skin and bones anyway; it's basically one and a half people."

"Hey!" Sheila protested.

Ridge and Alvara waited outside as Sheila changed into warmer clothing. Then the door of the little cabin opened, and a girl with wings and two kids on a motorcycle melted into the forest night.

Chapter 24

Alvara's footsteps crunched on the gravel as she walked from the car to the front entrance of the headquarters of the Legion of the Light. She could see the roof where she had barely made her escape the day before. Sheila and Ridge walked a few steps behind.

Though her heart raced the closer she got to the front doors, Alvara forced her shoulders back and her features into a neutral expression. She remembered her Aunt Alicia, that time she had been fired from her job as a receptionist. She had been smoking, a vice Alvara rarely witnessed.

"Never let them know they can get inside your head," Alicia had said, almost to herself. Then, she patted Alvara's shoulder. "Or your heart," she added, eyes fierce behind a cloud of smoke. "Those belong to you."

In place of a line of men with weapons drawn, Alvara spotted a few employees in plain clothes loitering, waiting to see if they'd be needed. But she wasn't here for a fight. She was here for Jake.

And for answers.

Within the doors, Isabella waited alone. Alvara forced herself to keep walking, until she came to a stop a few feet away.

"Where's Jake?" Alvara asked.

"Oh," Isabella said. "He is with Robert. They are comparing notes."

"Truth," Sheila piped up from directly behind her.

Alvara jumped. "Truth?" she asked, "You can tell when someone's lying?"

"Not always," Sheila added helpfully. "Sometimes I can't tell. But I'm not wrong." She squinted at Isabella. "I wish it was night," she said, "then I could really get a good look at you." Sheila frowned and folded her arms. "My Mom and I were really worried. You are a huge jerk for keeping Ridge here."

Isabella didn't seem to know what to do with the girl. "Yes," Isabella said, darting glances at Ridge, whose eyes sparkled dangerously. "I have a lot to make up for. Would you please follow me?"

"Why should we," Ridge asked softly.

"Please," Isabella said. "I want to show that I, that we, are not the monsters you believe us to be." She walked across the atrium, and Alvara,

Ridge, and Sheila hesitantly followed.

Isabella led them to a tan door and preceded them inside a dimly lit room. Men and women squinted at computer terminals or inspected a wide bank of wall screens showing video of various sites inside and outside the compound.

A handsome man looked away from the screens as Isabella made her way through the workstations. "Anything I can do for you, Ms. Dusk?" he asked tiredly. "Discharge was completed early this morning."

"Thank you, Dan," Isabella said. "I want to show my guests feeds from containment. Current feeds. Cycle through them all."

"Yes ma'am," Dan said. "Not much to show," he muttered under his breath as he tapped keys next to the wall display.

Half of the wall feeds were replaced with concrete rooms that Alvara recognized immediately. 'Containment' was clearly code for the underground prison she and Jake had visited before her escape.

Almost all the cells were empty.

Alvara's eyes tracked across the different video feeds as they shifted, though as almost all showed featureless cells, it was difficult to see when one shifted to the next. She saw the young child, still sleeping on a bed in the corner, and one other occupied cell, but no others.

"Where are the others?" Alvara asked, hardly daring to believe.

"Released," Isabella said with a small smile. "Now please follow me, we will meet Jake and Robert now." She nearly jogged out of the security room and back into the hallway. Alvara was still processing her admission and struggled to keep up.

"Isabella, wait!" Alvara said in the hallway. Isabella stood before her, her expression guarded. "You set them free? After everything you said about how important it was for the balance, and the rest of your 'ends justify the means' crap? Why?" Alvara asked.

Isabella took a slow breath, but it didn't help her composure. "It was the best way I knew to show you both how sorry I am," Isabella said. "I was wrong. The imbalance is a huge problem, but this was not the way to solve it. Alvara," she added, her eyes vulnerable. "What I did to you was much too harsh. I am terribly sorry for all I have put you through."

Alvara nodded.

Isabella turned to Ridge, who stared at her stonily. "I would like to say," she began, "Well it seems the appropriate time to . . ." She began again. "I want to apologize for the way you were treated. The way I treated you," she emphasized. The tears in her hard eyes surprised Alvara. Her voice sounded raw. "It was cruel. And it was no excuse that I thought you were trying to disrupt the balance we worked so hard to maintain. I should have . . . cared more about you. About what captivity was doing to you. Treated you like a person." She swallowed and tried to maintain control, but she was failing. "I know you will probably never forgive me, and that I can live with. I just want you to know that we will not keep anyone else the way we kept you prisoner."

Ridge shifted uncomfortably. "I can't forgive you just yet," he admitted.

"But you did the right thing, releasing the others. That's a start, I guess." Isabella nodded, unspeaking. *It was enough to get by on*, Alvara thought.

As Isabella led them through the twists and turns of the building, Alvara considered her actions. Isabella and Robert's intentions had been good, but their methods were inhumane and horribly wrong.

And yet, Isabella had understood, and had taken steps to demonstrate her conviction. Alvara struggled to come to terms with these two conflicting aspects of her behavior, with the terror she had felt during her capture, her brief torture, and her harrowing escape, and with the flicker of compassion she now felt for a woman trying to navigate a complex situation, guided by half-understood mystical commands and her own crooked moral compass.

The Bible verse that came to mind was right after the Lord's Prayer. Matthew 6:14, 'For if you forgive other people when they sin against you, your heavenly Father will also forgive you.' Alvara struggled with her belief, after all that she had seen. But she still believed in the importance of forgiveness. Isabella was misguided, but she wasn't evil. Alvara could afford to give her one more chance.

Isabella led them through the room with the metal cages and opened the door to the room with the couches. Jake looked up from typing on a laptop. He grinned when he saw Alvara.

"Jake!" she said, and strode forward to give him a hug. He was warm, solid, and reassuring. Despite her concerns, she began to relax.

"I'm so glad you're all right," Jake said, gently rubbing her shoulder before releasing her. "I would say I was worried, but you proved you can handle anything. You went full superhero, Alvara."

Alvara blushed.

He turned to Ridge and Sheila. "Good to see you again, Ridge," Jake said, shaking his hand.

"You too," Ridge said, standing up a bit straighter.

"You must be the other Child," Sheila said, bouncing forward. "I'm Sheila, Ridge's sister. And we have bad news."

Robert, sitting with his own computer, looked up at that. "Bad news is everywhere," he said. "Come see what was broadcast this morning."

All of them gathered around Robert's computer to watch the video. Even Laerik swooped down from her perch in the corner to land on Alvara's shoulder and nuzzle her cheek.

"Missed you!" Alvara heard her say, but then her voice dissolved into little whistles and caws again. It was more evidence that powers and abilities from the night had bled into the day. Alvara worried about what it would portend. Scratching under Laerik's feathers, she watched the screen.

A man spoke, and the label at the bottom of the screen proclaimed him an astrophysicist. "Since the Apollo missions," the man began, "lunar distance has been measured by bouncing lasers off reflectors that were planted on the moon's surface. Lunar distance typically varies on the order of meters depending on where the moon is in its orbit of Earth," he added. "However, recent measurements have been far outside standard measurement deviations, suggesting that the moon is in a tightening orbit around the Earth. It will appear larger in the sky due to this change in course. Preliminary tests suggest that the orbit continues to tighten, though as yet no scientific explanation has been forthcoming." He smiled at the camera. "I better get back to my models," he joked nervously. The video ended.

"We saw that," Alvara said first. "The moon was much bigger than normal."

"It wasn't natural," Ridge agreed.

"Jake," Robert said. "This must be related to the imbalance. In only a day, it has left the previous scale behind."

Jake frowned. "It certainly spells trouble," he said, and took his original seat. Laerik flapped back to her perch and preened. Alvara and Ridge sat next to Jake, while Sheila claimed a comfy chair across from them. She sat cross-legged and watched Isabella take a seat next to Robert.

"We're not here to make friends," Alvara began. "I appreciate that you're changing your strategies," she added, nodding at Isabella, "but that doesn't mean we're necessarily on board. We're here to share information, because it's not just about us. The moon is closer to the earth, and that can't be good. We will share if you do," she said.

Robert nodded. "The imbalance is worsening," He said. "In addition to your wings, Alvara, Jake grew wings during the day and I had some disruption with my normal abilities. However, Jake had a breakthrough."

"I realized a pattern in the imbalance," Jake clarified, pulling a file up on his computer. He showed it to the newcomers. "When Biyu lost her wings, the imbalance actually improved, almost back to normal," Jake said, pointing to his screen. "Then, when the wings passed on to the next child, the imbalance was back. I think that the major problem is that we are missing the third Child of the Sun."

Alvara thought for a moment. "I hope you're not suggesting we cut off our wings, Jake," she said.

"No, that wouldn't work," Jake said. "Biyu's loss was a temporary measure at best, and we seem to be past the point where that would help now, anyway. What we need is to find the third Child of the Sun."

"It's worse than that," Sheila said. "Alvara asked for my help last night, and I made a prophesy. It's not a good one," she added.

Alvara pulled the paper from the night before out of a jeans pocket and passed it around to Jake, Robert, and Isabella. After staring at it all last night and this morning, Alvara knew it by heart.

A pale child screams,
A pale child prays,
A pale child believes,
The moon sings to her children.
A bright child was lost,
A bright child was careful,
A bright child was faithful,

The sun calls to his children.
Unless a mother is betrayed by one of her children
And the sun dances with the moon once more
The earth will cry for the moon's folly
And bathe in her children's blood.

"Two sets of three children," Jake said. "It's about us, the Children of the Sun and Moon."

"We were more worried about the end," Ridge said. "It sounds like an apocalypse. It's cryptic, but not that cryptic," he said.

"If the first part is about the Moon's Children, and the second about the Sun's Children, then who are the Earth's Children?" Jake mused.

"Humanity," Robert said bitterly. "That's how Sol referred to humans in my journals. It means global catastrophe, like Ridge said."

"We have to stop it, somehow," Alvara said.

"I've made notes on what we have so far," Isabella interjected. They were very sparse. "The beginning talks about the three Children of the Moon, then the three Children of the Sun, one lost, and then states the requirements; to avert disaster, the 'moon's folly' or something similar, a child has to betray his or her mother and the sun must dance with the moon."

"Wait a second. I think it's one of us," Jake observed.

"What do you mean?" asked Robert and Alvara in unison.

"The child that must betray its mother; I think it's you, me, or Biyu," Jake said, watching Alvara.

"I can't betray my mother, Jake," she declared. "Never."

"But could you betray Selene?" he asked.

"Oh," she said, feeling stupid.

"Jeez," muttered Ridge, "so you, or Jake, or a Chinese woman needs to betray this Selene, but none of you knows how to do it, or even if you would want to if you could."

"That about sums it up," Alvara said. How could they figure this out?

"How about if we take a break?" said a small voice. It was Sheila. Everyone turned to look at her, but she kept her chin up and met everyone's eyes. "I mean, we've been talking for a while now. Would it be too much to ask for some . . . food?"

"Excellent idea," said Robert. "The kitchen is down the hall, Isabella can take you all. But Jake, could I speak with you?"

"No problem," Jake replied, and everyone else wandered off, leaving him and Robert alone on the couches. Alvara could sense the tension, and realized that there was more going on between the two of them than Jake's relaxed demeanor had suggested. She hoped she would get a chance to talk with Jake later, but left with the group.

An uncomfortable silence settled over them. Jake waited.

"I spoke again with Isabella last night, like we talked about," Robert began. Jake nodded. "We talked about the release of many of the prisoners yesterday, but mostly about you and Alvara, and what you have been through, sometimes at our hands." He was silent for a moment, and Jake watched him. Robert looked more than uncomfortable; his reserved exterior brimmed with emotion. He rubbed his brow and stared off into the distance.

"I have spent my entire life creating this organization, Jake. Its purpose was the maintenance of the balance, but through our research we have learned so much about our power, as well as the forces inhabiting this world. I never had enough information, I never had enough resources, but I managed. We managed, Isabella and me. I couldn't have done it without her.

We couldn't share our gifts with the world at large, or we would be nothing but freaks. And only we two had the skill sets to do what we needed to do. To maintain the balance by preventing creatures of the moon from giving her too much power.

Or what we thought we needed to do. Jake, I can feel, in the balance, that we've made a difference. I shudder to consider how dire the situation would be without our intervention. But now that we know it wasn't enough, I feel the strangest thing . . ."

"What?" Jake asked.

"Relief," he said. "And guilt," he added dryly. "I was terrified that we would fail, that it would have some catastrophic effect on the world. I know I neglected to consider our methods. Kidnapping . . . even now I think that in some instances we couldn't have avoided it, not and also prevent that power from reaching her. But what happened with Alvara . . ." He couldn't finish for a moment, but Jake was silent.

"When Isabella laid a brand on Alvara, she had long past crossed the line. We finally talked about it this morning, and Isabella planned to show Alvara the empty cells and ask her for forgiveness. Jake, I know that many interactions we've had together have been negative, and I apologize for that and take full responsibility. And I have searched my heart for a better answer for why I attacked you yesterday, and found nothing. Jake, I bear you no ill will, and in fact I have great respect for you. I hope that over the past couple days you've begun to see that Isabella and I are not evil. But who's to say what may be forgiven? For the record, I am sorry."

Jake had been watching Robert's face throughout his speech, and the shine of his eyes and tense muscles in his jaw belied his thin voice. The man was genuine, honest by every measure Jake knew.

But it wouldn't be enough, Jake realized, to simply accept Robert's apology, to trust his sincerity. Jake didn't know what they would decide to do today, but did know that any plan would involve Robert and Isabella. If he and Alvara couldn't trust them wholeheartedly, then any action taken with them would have an obvious rift. It was a weakness they couldn't afford. After only a few days with them, Jake knew what he had to do; the act of doing it would be difficult.

"Robert, I can't tell you how much trouble you made for Alvara and me.

Your letter forced us to go to China, and your second letter forced us to find out how to visit Selene, as well as started us on our desperate and crazy flight into the sky. Even upon returning, you captured us, didn't explain yourselves, and kept us in cages. You used a brand on Alvara." Robert stared stoically back and didn't interrupt.

"I had no reason to trust you, nor Isabella, and plenty of reasons to hate you. But when you lay dying on the ground in front of me, Isabella called out your name. No evil person could be mourned in such a way. I had no choice, once I heard her, in saving you, in saving your life.

I've gotten to know you, at least a bit. We all make mistakes. I've made my share. I forgive you yours, and she hers. I'm not sure what we'll decide to do, the group of us, but we need to decide it together and trust each other if we have any hope of success.

Well, what do you say?" Jake finished, and extended his hand. One glance at Robert, at the smile that slowly crept onto his face, and Jake knew he had done the right thing, hard as it had been.

"I say, we're with you 100%," Robert said, beaming for the first time. He reached out and clapped Jake's hand with surprising force.

Jake's thoughts sobered. "Good, because we're going to need everyone to figure a way out of this mess."

Robert's eyes hardened. "There is a solution. I believe in that."

Jake followed him to join the others, his mind working to fit the pieces of their situation into a functional whole.

After lunch, the group reconvened, though no one was anxious to speak first. Alvara was trying to understand how Jake and Robert's relationship had changed, but she couldn't really figure it. They were more at ease, certainly, so they had probably talked out some of their issues. But she thought it was deeper than that; they were no longer wary of each other, even in the midst of this crisis. She was thankful for it, at least. Try as she might, and despite the awesome power within the group now present, she couldn't come up with a way the six of them could do anything to prevent Selene from getting closer and closer to Earth, whatever it was she planned to do when she got there.

"I think there's only one thing to do," Jake announced. He seemed excited, though he was trying to contain it.

"Don't make us ask," Isabella complained.

"What, Jake?" Ridge said in almost the same breath.

"We should pay a visit to the Sun God," he said triumphantly.

"Sol?" Alvara exclaimed.

"Are you crazy?" Ridge asked.

"Talk about drastic," Sheila muttered.

"It's the only way we can be in a position to have any large effect on the situation; we're not helping anyone sitting around here," Jake said. "With both the Children of the Sun and the Moon together we'd have some swaying power; maybe the sun has a plan, and we can help somehow. It's worth seeing if we can even do it."

"I've gone off the deep end. I just listened to someone say with all seriousness that 'maybe the sun has a plan'," Ridge groaned.

Alvara took a deep breath and spoke up. "Jake, I know you're probably right, but don't you think this might have a bit to do with . . ." She stopped speaking, and he glanced at her.

"With what?" Jake asked.

". . . With maybe being able to see your wife again," she finished. She hadn't forgotten Jake's expression when he had awoken from the vision.

"What do you mean, Alvara?" Robert asked.

Jake was defensive. "Look, I won't say I didn't think about it. Selene convinced me that my wife might not be dead, but that she might be held captive by Sol," he explained brusquely to Isabella and Robert, "but it's not the reason I thought we should pay him a visit. Not the only reason," he amended. "The main issue here is the danger facing everyone on Earth. I don't need you to point out my priorities, Alvara." He bit off his words coldly.

"Well I guess I can retire then," she snapped, her face burning.

"I have an idea, of sorts, though in all likelihood it will amount to nothing," Robert interjected. He seemed oblivious to the tension.

"Please, enlighten us. No pun intended," Jake said automatically.

Robert half smiled. "I could attempt to write another journal entry, and we could see if Sol contacts us again. I should warn you I've tried many times over the years, with only those two successes."

Jake shrugged. "If there was ever a good time for your mystic connection to work, it would be now. Give it a shot."

"I'll come back with the journal," Robert replied, standing to leave. All present watched as he shuffled out the door. It shut with a soft click.

"What is Robert going to do, exactly?" Sheila asked the room.

"He's going to try to get a message from the Sun God," Alvara replied. "By writing in his journal, somehow."

"Should I have offered to help? I know about trances." She bit her lip.

"You can ask when he gets back, but he probably knows what he's doing," Alvara answered. Jake held a cup of iced tea and stared into space. She grabbed a cup for herself, and tried to sort through her thoughts.

She had conquered her fear, coming back to this place. This time, Jake hadn't needed rescuing. But she had showed up for him, and always would.

It was still hard to believe she wasn't alone anymore. After all the insanity of the past few weeks, Jake had still somehow kept her sane with his steady confidence and dorky humor. They had the same secrets, the same guilt to shoulder. He was like a father to her, a real one, and the realization shook her. Their eyes met.

"Look, Alvara, I'm sorry about snapping at you earlier—"

"It's okay, Jake," she said. "I was out of line to doubt your priorities. And if part of solving this problem lets you see your wife again, then that would be awesome."

"Thanks Alvara," Jake said. The tension between them eased, and she was glad. Even though, once it was over, Jake might prefer to catch up with his wife without some kid messing around in his life. She might be back to taking care of herself again. She hoped that Jake would still want to hang out with her, at least.

Robert strode into the room carrying a spiral bound journal, burn cream, and a roll of bandages. The journal was purple, with a picture of a sprig of lavender on the back, but Alvara didn't think it was the time to comment.

"I actually have some expertise with trances–" Sheila began.

"That won't be necessary, miss," Robert replied, staring down at his journal. "I have never done this with an audience," he continued. "Nothing may happen. Please remain silent."

Alvara watched as Robert opened the journal to a blank page, rested his pointer finger on the page, and closed his eyes. Alvara wondered if he'd forgotten a pen, but didn't ask. His breathing slowed, and his posture relaxed, as if he had fallen asleep.

Robert's eyes snapped open, and Alvara smothered a yelp as she quickly closed her eyes. Sunbursts appeared behind her closed lids. Robert's eyes had been entirely white, and as bright as the sun.

Alvara squinted through the glare to focus on the journal, careful not to look directly toward Robert's face. His fingers smoldered, his pointer finger dragging across the pages of the journal. Alvara smelled burning paper and the sickly sweet smell of burning flesh.

Robert blinked, his eyes returned to their strange yellow halos. He winced, and Isabella treated the burns on his hands.

"It worked," Robert said, completely unnecessarily.

"Pyrography, fascinating," Jake said.

"Whoa," Ridge said. "Man. That was crazier than one of your trances, Sheila, no offense."

Sheila's eyes were wide. "That wasn't Robert," she whispered. "That wasn't him. I've never felt anything like it."

"What does it say?" Alvara asked, if no one else would.

Isabella finished with Robert's hand, and Alvara inspected the journal. The writing on the page was scorched and blackened, burned through the page on particular points of emphasis. Robert cleared his throat and read.

"Noon; there isn't much time. Walk into the sunset, Dusk leading the way. Bring Her winged Children with you. Will yourself into it, as you will yourself to direct your inner flame. I cannot promise your safety. I will come for you. Dawn awaits." Instead of a signature, Alvara saw the same image of a sunburst as Jake carried on his hand. The symbol had burned through all the pages beneath, stopping partway through the back cover.

"Dawn awaits," Isabella said, wondering. "Maybe this is that third Child of the Sun."

"Maybe. But I don't like the way he said 'I cannot promise your safety'," Alvara broke in. "He didn't even say what could happen."

"We don't have a choice," Robert insisted. "This is the fulfillment of our destiny, and ours is tied to yours now."

"We do have a choice," Alvara retorted. "But I still think we should *choose* to go."

"Fine," said Robert. He turned to Ridge and Sheila. "It was nice meeting you both, but you won't be coming with us. Neither will that bird. We must keep to the letter of the instructions."

"No freaking interest, anyway, in meeting the sun," Ridge said, and shuddered. Sheila nodded thoughtfully, but didn't speak. Laerik couldn't speak, as it was still daytime, but her flared wings conveyed the sense of a shrug. The excitement in the room was palpable.

Jake smiled, a gleam of humor in his eyes. "I think we have a sunset to catch."

Chapter 25

Two hours had passed, and Alvara had spent most of the time worrying. Laerik had left, ostensibly to carry their story to her flock. Ridge and Sheila had gone, after promising to stay in touch. As they left, Alvara noticed that Sheila was crying. Sheila wouldn't say what was wrong, but Alvara couldn't get it out of her mind.

"Alvara, question," Robert said. He and Isabella hunched over her computer, brainstorming equipment to take on the journey. "On your trip to visit Selene, were you on the near side or the dark side of the moon? It may change our estimates of what we need."

Alvara shrugged. "No idea," she said. "It seemed more like the inside of the moon, because the horizon curved upward."

"And did you feel tired, cold, or hungry?" Isabella asked.

"Sure," Alvara said, remembering the campfire on the beach and the strange sequence in the pool chairs.

"Thanks. Non-perishable food, medical supplies . . ." Robert said as Isabella typed.

Planning for different possible scenarios made the whole expedition seem more legitimate, but Alvara knew how much help these items were likely to be. If Sol was anything like Selene, it would be impossible to plan ahead for what was in store.

Alvara found Jake in the large room with the movable cages. He leaned with his back against the bars, hands in his pockets, staring into space. His brows were furrowed, whether in frustration or some other emotion she did not know.

"Jake," Alvara said. "Are you okay?"

"I'm . . ." He began, then shook his head. "This situation is more complicated than we ever imagined. It's hard for me to see a solution. What do we *know*?" he asked, as she leaned against the cage next to him. "Selene has put something into motion that may have devastating consequences, but we don't know what. Sol has his own motives and plans, but we don't know what those are either. Sheila seemed like a nice girl, but how do we know this prophesy of hers will come to pass?" He rubbed the side of his mouth. "We take an awful lot on faith."

Alvara frowned. "Maybe we shouldn't," she said. Then, "I don't really mean that. But when I talked with Selene alone up there, I asked her what happened to the Gods that people still believe in, and where they were."

"I remember you were upset about that. What did she say?" Jake asked.

"She said that God was long gone, Jake. She said God, as well as some other good entities, sacrificed themselves to guard Satan's prison. Far away from here, and that they are never coming back. Jake, everything in my faith tells me that He wouldn't just leave Earth like that."

"You're worried that she's right," Jake stated. Alvara didn't answer, but her silence was answer enough.

"I get the feeling," Jake said gently, "that Selene is not the most trustworthy source for information. She lied to us about Sol and his Children, remember?"

"But why would she lie to me about this?" Alvara asked. "It doesn't help her. If she wanted to lie she could say they were buddies, to get me to be on her side, but she didn't. And that means that God is really gone." Alvara stared at her shoes, the full implications of her words falling like lead across her shoulders. She desperately wanted to have faith, but had trouble remembering what it really felt like.

Jake's hand rested on her shoulder. "Don't count on it," Jake said. "There is a lot we still don't understand; you should leave God in that category until we know more."

She surprised herself by laughing at that. "I think He created that category," she agreed, and sighed. "I guess it doesn't hurt to give Him the benefit of the doubt." Alvara pushed a strand of dark hair behind one ear. "So I guess it's almost sunset. Do we even have an idea of what we're supposed to do?"

"Do?" Jake asked. "Other than find some way to avert catastrophe? No clue."

"I'm not talking about that. I mean for the whole walking into the sunset thing."

"It can't be harder than flying to the moon," Jake replied innocently.

"Yeah, right," said Alvara. "It most definitely could be."

Isabella entered the room, and Alvara gasped. Isabella had dressed as a firefighter, complete with helmet, oxygen tank, and combat boots, in addition to a backpacking pack hanging off one shoulder. She looked like a post-apocalyptic firefighter refugee.

"So did I miss the second journal message? Where in Sol's message did it say to dress like . . . that?" Alvara asked, chuckling. Isabella managed to look dignified, though the coverall was too big for her and the helmet kept slipping down over her eyes.

"Robert and I seem to value our lives a little more highly than you two. We are visiting the sun. It may be hot," she sniffed.

"Where did you get that?" Jake asked.

"Borrowed, with interest, from the local fire department," Isabella replied. "They are not just for us; we got one for each of you as well."

"I don't think that will be necessary," Jake managed, and Alvara let out a full-throated laugh. "We were fine visiting Selene in just what we were wearing. The rules were a bit different for her, and she could change our clothing with a wave of her hand. I figure Sol might have similar abilities," he explained.

"Your *figuring* is simply not enough to keep us from being careful," Isabella replied.

"Thanks for thinking of us, but we'll be fine," Jake affirmed.

"You can heal, after all. You two should be all right up to a certain point." A chill passed over Alvara at the thought of how much damage they would have to take to not be all right if a single feather could bring someone else back from the brink of death.

"Right," Jake said. "So where's Robert? Isn't it about time we head outside?"

"He is waiting for us up on the street, thinking through our plan," Isabella made a sweeping gesture. "Not that there is much left to figure out; we just have to take a little walk." Alvara could see that she was nervous, because those large gloves kept dancing from one activity to the next; pulling on her ponytail, straightening her coverall. "Shall we?" Isabella said, and her voice sounded a little higher than normal.

"Let's go," said Jake, and he followed Isabella and Alvara.

They trooped out into the waning sunshine. After being underground for most of the day, it took a bit of blinking to acclimate to even this moderate brightness. The forest leaned into the campus, the trees casting long shadows across the manicured grass. The front lawn and streets were deserted, as the staff had been told to leave early that day. Alvara spotted Robert, standing alone on a street that stretched west into the setting sun. He too had donned firefighter attire. Alvara somehow no longer felt like laughing.

"Robert," Isabella said, and Robert nodded curtly. He turned to speak with the rest of them.

"Isabella, you will lead the way," Robert said without preamble.

She nodded, unspeaking.

"Jake, you and Alvara stay close to her. Grow wings, as we discussed. I'll bring up the rear."

"Right," Jake said.

Alvara stretched unfamiliar mental muscles and wings sprouted from her shoulder blades. The pain was excruciating, but brief; it faded after a few tight breaths. Alvara stared at one wing, and reached out to feel the softness of the downy feathers, complementing the sharp, strong flight feathers. The setting sun cast a golden sheen across her white wings, so that they seemed to glow.

Isabella and Robert connected up their suit air supply and double-checked each other's equipment, as Alvara waited to visit the sun. It had been strange enough, visiting the moon. But somehow, the fact that other humans had done so made it a little less strange. They were heading into the sun this time, and without some sort of supernatural intervention, they wouldn't survive the trip. What if, while they had been visiting Selene, Alvara had stopped believing in it? Would the air have exploded from her lungs on a barren and empty rock? The story of Icarus came back to her with the force of a memory, and she knew her wings would not be enough to protect her in the face of that terrible, scorching heat.

Isabella, fully covered in her borrowed equipment, beckoned with one glove. Jake and Alvara joined her and Robert. The four of them stood around awkwardly: two in street clothes, two in firefighter equipment, two women, two men, two former captors, two former captives; four people unsure of what the future would hold.

Isabella strode down the road as if she wasn't carrying over a hundred pounds of equipment. She slowed down when she realized Robert couldn't keep that pace. Jake walked behind Isabella, with Alvara following behind and Robert's boots crunching on the pavement a few steps behind her. Trees lined both sides of the straight industrial road, and the patch of sky above was bright and clear. Alvara squinted and looked into the sun.

Little grey spots danced before her eyes. Hoping she wasn't doing permanent damage, she stared until even the dots faded. The third of the sun still visible over the horizon was her whole focus, and she saw that it wasn't uniformly bright. Opalescent whites and harsh yellows swam across its surface. She realized that the shapes were faces; dozens, maybe hundreds of faces, appearing and shifting in a kaleidoscope of light.

Out of the corner of her eye, she could see Isabella begin to glow, and the air around her developed a mirage haze that rippled as she walked. Alvara's walking pace was steady, but the procession of trees to either side raced past in a blur. Each step appeared to cover more and more distance, impossibly more. Then, the constant trees that had marked their road leaned away to either side like a warped camera lens so that their path was clear.

The sun froze in its path toward the horizon, and grew bigger with each step they took. Alvara felt warm, with the sun on her skin bringing to mind days in childhood spent lying on the beach, soaking up the hot, satisfying rays. Her steps were the steps a giant, the ground a blur beneath her feet, the road a broad, flat, featureless brown plain that stretched infinitely far to either side.

The partially set sun filled her field of vision, and she couldn't look away. It was . . . like Selene's wine. Intoxicating. No one could see the true glory of the sun. It was larger and more powerful than anything she had known. She had to stop herself from leaping from the ground to fly straight into it. Frightened by the strength of the desire, she tried to turn away, or slow her steps. She could not.

"Jake, I can't stop," Alvara said. She felt the temperature rise.

Jake continued his slow trudge ahead, his wings drooping lifelessly. "Me neither," he said through gritted teeth. His arms continued in the steady rhythm of swinging back and forth.

Sweat poured down her face, and she couldn't reach a hand up to wipe it away. The heat around them spiked, and she had trouble breathing. Jake mumbled words, but Alvara couldn't make them out. Then Jake's wings disappeared, and he screamed in pain.

"Jake!" she yelled, but there was no answer. Her throat was too dry to even whisper afterward. Through it all, the sun grew in size and intensity. The sweat disappeared from her skin with a sizzling sound, and in its place the real heat descended. Her legs carried her forward, and her eyes could no longer make out Jake or Isabella. She couldn't hear anything but the ringing of her ears, nor smell anything but the acrid aroma of the hairs on her exposed arms and cheeks and eyelids burning up with little puffs.

Fear coursed through her, though it barely distracted her from the sweltering crushing impossible heat. They would die soon, and there was nothing any of them could do. They were staggering marionettes with eyes painted open, and their macabre dance carried them ever forward into a place no human could survive. Alvara could no longer see the sun, nor hear nor sense the others.

Alvara couldn't move her arms or her legs, but her wings were her own. She strained her muscles to wrap her wings across her body, shielding her face and blanketing her body in cool feathers. Fire surrounded her, ravaging what places it could touch. But it could not pass the barrier of her wings.

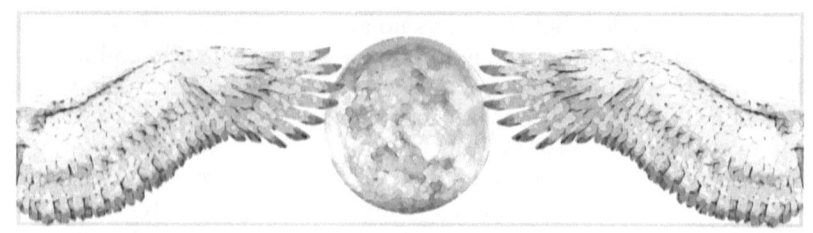

Chapter 26

Somewhere soft between dreaming and waking, Jake's mind drifted, devoid of intention. Yet somehow, with the inevitability of water flowing downhill, his thoughts settled on Rory. Jake used to dust off memories of her to keep him company, their edges now smooth by the countless passes and repetitions. In comparison, the conversation with her in the forest, and the hasty connection through Selene, were almost too sharp and vibrant to bear. But with masochistic regularity Jake would fall back into the memories again and again, gouging and gorging himself on the color of her eyes and the angle of her smile.

Jake's head ached, but the throbbing was less than it had been the last time he had fully awoken. His skin felt tender, an improvement from the sheer agony of his previous burns. He remembered a woman's face, and a cruel smile, before his wings disappeared and he was engulfed in flames.

Jake remembered it all. They had been walking into the sun, and Isabella had begun to glow . . .

Selene had appeared next to Jake, keeping pace, seemingly unaffected by the heat. "Hello Jake," she said sweetly. "I see you chose not to kill the Children of the Sun. Indeed, you are assisting them in their task," she daintily chose her steps, fingers lifting her trailing dress to keep it out of the dust. "Why have you, my Child, betrayed me?"

Jake had tried to respond, but the heat left his throat parched and dry.

"I did not expect much," Selene said, pouting. "But an apology might have been nice."

"Don't . . . hurt . . ." Jake managed.

"Oh, Alvara?" Selene smiled wickedly. "The poor dear was led astray by you, her friend, someone who should have known better. I can't take your gift, not now, not when I'm so close. But a temporary lapse, shall we say, might make you a bit more apologetic. It is daytime, after all," Selene said, and laughed.

Jake's wings disappeared, and his world had become flame.

He shuddered at the memory. Selene's vindictiveness had temporarily removed his wings, and with them his ability to heal. Selene had done this, had hurt him and made him weak. He hoped that Selene had told the truth, and had left Alvara alone.

Jake summoned the strength to finally open his eyes, but there were no lights, so the darkness was unchanged. He sat up, trying to get his bearings.

He reached down to feel the IV; that must be the reason he kept falling asleep. The bed seemed like a standard hospital assignment, complete with thin sheets and hard pillows. Jake much preferred it to his arrival to the moon, and his fall into that strange internal ocean.

Jake didn't think keeping him in complete darkness was an accident. Perhaps his eyes needed time to heal, and if so, he'd let them keep him in the dark as long as necessary.

A door opened in the wall. Jake could sense someone standing there in the dark. "Hello?" he called.

He heard a woman exhale, and the sound was unforgettable. "You're really here," he said, his voice rough with emotion. He felt her approach.

"Jake. Finally," Rory whispered gruffly, and then she was in his arms.

"Ah," Jake yelped involuntarily, as she rubbed his tender skin.

"Crap. Sorry," she said from his right. He reached his hand out, searching for her face, and her hands found his and guided him to her cheek.

"There's my girl," Jake said softly. Wrinkles framed the edges of her eyes. In the dream in his mind she had been the age he had last seen her, but now she felt like she had aged with him. "Is this real?" he asked.

"As real as it gets," she laughed, and he could hear tears in her voice. "Jake, you really made it."

"I really did." Jake smiled. "So when do I get to turn the lights on so I can see you? I swear it'll be a balm for my eyes."

"Jake." As she spoke, the anguish in her voice flared up. "I'm so sorry. The lights are on."

For a moment he said nothing; he couldn't breathe. "Come here," Jake whispered. "I want to hold you. Nothing else matters." He felt tears leak out of his useless eyes, and held Rory as tightly as he could. She was real, and she was in his arms, and he was kissing her, and he could smell her hair and feel her shoulder blades through her shirt. He experienced her with smell and taste and touch, and a ragged hole inside himself began to mend. Each detail was a stitch.

Yet he was blind. Rory touched his eyelids, kissed them, but her touch couldn't restore them. Jake would have believed anything was possible, with the magic and feeling of destiny it had taken to get him here. But if his sight was the price required for being with her again, then he would give it up willingly.

She simply rested her head against his shoulder, and he stroked her hair. It was shorter and thinner, but his fingertips remembered.

"Jake," she said without moving from his shoulder. "I want to tell you why I'm here. Why I didn't really die back then."

"I'm not sure I care so much about the 'why', Rory," Jake replied.

"Try," she said curtly, "or how about this: why I never came back to you if I wasn't gone."

Jake went suddenly cold. She must have seen the look on his face, because she added, "It was nothing like that. I just want to make sure you listen to me, because it's important."

"All right, go ahead," Jake said. The lightness of their banter had dissipated, but his arm still encircled Rory.

"Right. Before I tell you about this, I just want to say that I'm sorry. Since I was a little girl, I've been a singing prodigy. No one could believe it, least of all my parents. Especially my father; you know what a jealous man he was. At least, you know what I've told you of him." She paused.

"Right," he said. Her muscles seemed tense, so Jake rubbed her arm.

"One day, when I was about 12, he beat me, yelling." Jake nodded, knowing from her what her father was like. "He yelled, 'so you think you're better'n us, do ya?' I'd say no, over and over, but it didn't matter, and so he kept hitting me. Eventually he stopped, leaving me lying on the kitchen floor as he sat down to read the newspaper at the table. I couldn't move. I started to sing. I didn't know what I was doing, didn't know what I was singing, but it helped me feel better, and I stopped crying. I sang about . . ." she stopped again, and continued in a dead voice. "I sang about how my father was the lowest creature on the planet, and that he should just kill himself. The words were just nonsense, but I sang the emotion. When he stood up from the table, I cringed, thinking that the bastard was going to come hit me again. He went into the other room and blew his brains out with his shotgun."

"He . . . you just told me he killed himself," Jake said. "You don't think—"

She lifted her head from his shoulder, but took his hands. "I don't think, Jake. I know. It wasn't the last time. I can make things happen when I sing. Make people feel whatever I want them to feel. It didn't matter that I didn't really want my dad to kill himself; I wanted it then, and I got it. The feeling scared the crap out of me, Jake. I didn't know what to do. I loved singing, I had to sing, but what if I lost control again?"

He could almost feel her watching his face, searching for signs of his understanding. He didn't know what she could see there, much less how he felt. "How come you never told me, Rory? I grow wings every night; the least I could have done was empathize with you about being more than ordinary."

"Jake! Your wings were beautiful, they were fun; my singing was nothing but a curse. Even now you can't think of the reason why I would be ashamed of this, why I wouldn't tell you. Think of how we met, if that helps."

"I heard you singing . . ." he said, and it finally clicked. The reason she had never told him, for all those years. The reason she felt ashamed. The reason she pulled away from him now. It filled him with dread.

He tried to remember the words to her song, the one she sang that day. "What are you saying?" Jake asked.

"Jake, what does a young girl sing about?" She couldn't really believe this. Why was she saying it? "I'll tell you. A young girl gets up early in the morning and goes out to the mountains so she can be free to sing, at least once, what's really on her mind and in her heart. I sang about how I wanted love, Jake. It's what everyone sings of, sooner or later. You *walked* into it." It was cruel, that one sentence, as if something fragile and precious had become a shovel for gravediggers. But she didn't stop.

"I love you, Jake, and I always will, but I never deserved you. I learned to control my gift as I got older, but the damage was already done. That's why I want you to know the truth, whatever difference it makes."

He moved to pull her toward himself again, but she pulled away to arm's length and said relentlessly, frantically, "Two more secrets, Jake, just two: when I was dangling from that root, that's the only other time I used my gift on you. You needed to get the rope, I couldn't hold on, so I sang to you and you jumped up to get the rope, but it was too little, too late, and I fell anyway. I didn't learn the last secret until I woke up here and couldn't ever leave."

It hit Jake like a revelation. *Dawn awaits*, he remembered. Her full name was Aurora. *The Dawn.*

"I'm the third, mysterious, awe-inspiring, Child of the Sun," Rory spat. "Fat lot of good it did me." She leaned forward to get up off the bed, but Jake held her arm. "Let go, Jake. Our love is a fantasy."

"Rory, shut up. And sit down. I'm not through with you yet." She sighed, but didn't leave. He knew the truth, but he would have to convince her.

"Listen to me. And stop rolling your eyes; I may be blind, but I'm not an idiot." A sharp intake in breath let him know he succeeded in guessing her customary response. "I hate to break it to you, pumpkin, but there are a few reasons your little theory is hogwash. First, in no way can you compare my love for you with your father's crime of passion. Sure, your gift is all kinds of powerful, but nothing I've encountered so far, and I've seen a lot, mind you, has got anything on love. Second, when you made me leave to get the rope? I wanted to do that anyway; just couldn't think of a way to leave you, so thanks for helping me out there. And third, and this is my favorite," Jake inhaled, "your song was pretty that day, but no more than that. I didn't fall in love with you then."

"What do you mean?" Rory asked, "You always told me it was love at first sight, and that made my blood run cold."

"Look, honey. I knew very early on that you were the woman for me. But love grows over time. Hell, I didn't tell you I loved you for months."

"Not 'till I poured that ice water on your sister," she said. It sounded like hope in her voice, and Jake grabbed at it.

"It was the funniest damn thing I'd ever seen; she just stood there breathing in and out in fluttering breaths as the water dripped off her nose. And the way you laughed, it wasn't malicious at all, it was just revelatory, like it was your duty to turn the world on its head so that it would see for itself how beautiful life was." Please let her understand, Jake thought: a silent prayer to an absent God. He couldn't see her reaction, and it was killing him to feel the heartbeat in her wrist and have no idea what she was thinking.

"Rory, believe in me, please. It's the truth; my heart belongs to you, but not because you bewitched me. I gave it up freely, and it was the best thing I ever did." He squeezed her hand, and he felt her squeeze back.

"I can't believe it. I don't deserve it," she said, but her tone belied her words. Jake felt like crying with relief, and couldn't hold back his tears when she broke down again, sobbing into his shoulder.

"Rory, Rory, my Rory," he whispered into her hair.

Chapter 27

Alvara awoke to soft light, clean sheets, and dull pain. She blinked, and the room came into focus. White walls curved around her bed, which was nestled into an alcove. A dull stone floor shone in the light beams from the three open windows. She was alone, and her wings were gone.

Moments from the journey drifted back, and Alvara shuddered with the fear of it. She remembered the incredible, overwhelming heat. The impossibility of stopping. Jake's scream.

Alvara was unwilling to wait for someone, or something, to come looking for her. She would have to go searching for Jake, Isabella, Robert, and perhaps Sol, on her own. Wincing slightly, she sat up, only then noticing the IV in her arm.

She gritted her teeth in disgust and tried to pull the needle from her vein. She discovered that if she sort of held the skin down around it, it came out smoothly, with only a small drop of blood to mark its passage. The tiny hole closed up and healed in front of her eyes, a reassuring sight.

Alvara slid her legs off the bed and tried to stand. The first dizzy spell passed quickly, and she staggered around the room. She wore a white T-shirt and loose white pants with deep pockets; while her outfit wouldn't win any fashion contests, it was substantial enough that she could wander without the fear of offending anyone she met. What's more, it reminded her of her guardian angel outfit. The welcome familiarity helped her to focus.

She walked on bare feet to the door. It was unlocked. She turned the handle, pushed the door open, and nearly fell. Beyond her small room, a substance flowed.

It moved like water, like a river, but glowed and crackled softly as it streamed past. Though she had never seen any up close, it looked like lava. She stepped back in fear, but couldn't feel any heat emanating from the substance. Cautiously, she approached and leaned out over the lava, but still felt nothing but a slight warmth on her cheeks. After a moment's hesitation, she reached out her hand and touched the top of the river.

It was like reaching her hand into warm apple cobbler; past the slight crust on the surface she felt a gooey, chunky material that stuck to her fingers. When she pulled her hand back, it glowed with a vivid red light.

After a moment, she worried that it would somehow revert to real lava, and hastily wiped it on the edge of the doorframe. She heard a crackling sound above the normal crunching of the moving surface of the lava, and glanced around.

The river of lava passed by her door, but other doors lined the 'lane'. It reminded her of Venice, or that town they had visited in China, with a canal of lava separating the buildings from each other. She looked up, and the absence of the sky, akin to when they had visited Selene, disturbed her. Instead of sky, here the lava and buildings curved upward, disappearing into a bright fog above. Right on cue, she noticed the source of the crackling sound.

To her right, a boat approached through the lava. It reminded her of a kayak, and it floated on its own; there was no driver and no means of propulsion that she could see. The boat floated straight to her door and bumped against the frame, and she grabbed the edge so it wouldn't continue crackling along.

The arrival of the boat couldn't be random. It was just too perfect; there was even an oar. She took a seat in the center of the boat, careful not to capsize it. She gripped the oar in one hand and pushed off her doorframe with the other.

Alvara navigated the canal. The lava flowed ponderously, and with each pull of the oar she crunched her way to the next doorway in the line. There was a sign on this door; it said, "Human Food." That second word was enough to pique her interest, and by holding on to the edge of the door, she reached the handle and push it open. She could see, in the dim light coming from the canal, lines of crates stretching back into the darkness.

However, she had a problem. If she got out of the boat, she might lose it down the canal. There didn't seem to be any way to secure the boat to the door, but she dragged the boat over the edge of the doorframe to keep it more or less stable. Her way out secure, she investigated the crates. There was writing on them, but it was too dark to read the labels. With a small smile, she returned to the river and scooped up some of the glowing slop in her left hand to use as a lantern.

She found a crate labeled 'Apples'. When she touched the lava to the wood, it crackled and caught fire, dissolving the bar of the crate and making an opening. She grabbed a bunch of apples in her shirt with her clean right hand, shoving one into each pocket and dumping the rest into the bottom of the boat. After devouring her first apple while sitting on the doorframe, she returned to her search for the others.

She guided the boat to the next open doorway, grabbing the edge again and steadying herself to open it. The sign on this one read 'Recovery'. She fiddled with the door, and it opened into a curved white room very similar to her own. Alvara could see a woman with her back to the door leaning over a bed. When the door opened, the woman turned to face her. She had dark brown eyes and brown and gray hair, and looked to be in her sixties. She wore a white casual dress and sandals.

"Alvara, right?" she asked with a half-smile. At Alvara's nod, the woman reached out her hand and said, "I'm Aurora. Jake probably called me Rory."

"Nice to meet you! Then Jake's here!" Alvara ran across the room and discovered the man in the bed was indeed Jake, still asleep on top of the covers, wearing the same white shirt and white pants that she was.

"I wouldn't—" Aurora began, but Alvara was already shaking him.

Jake rubbed his eyes, and Alvara wrapped him in a hug. "God, I'm so glad you're all right. I was so worried about you. We're both fine. And Aurora's here!" To her surprise, Alvara felt her eyes tearing up.

"I'm glad you're all right, Alvara," Jake said with a sigh, hugging her tightly. "I'm pretty good too, but got a bit unlucky there." She heard a hitch in his voice and pulled back to inspect him again. He stared intently as he spoke, but his gaze was a bit to her right. Fear seized her.

"Jake, I'm right here," she said. "You can still see, right?"

But he shook his head, and panic seized her. "It's not so bad," Jake explained wearily. "We made it here. And Aurora's here. We'll figure out the rest as it comes."

"Jake, that's just not fair," Alvara whispered. "After everything! We followed all of his stupid instructions, and Sol makes you blind!" A tear leaked out of her eye, but she brushed it away.

"It wasn't his fault. Not really," Jake said. "I saw Selene, as we were walking into the Sun. She took away my wings, and my ability to heal, at just the wrong moment."

"Hey, it'll be okay, kid," Aurora said kindly. "We can go talk with the old man about it, see what he can do. I wouldn't worry too much right now, it could still be temporary."

Alvara ignored her. "Why would she do that?" Alvara asked. "She's never tried to hurt us before."

Jake shrugged. "She said it was because we failed to kill the Children of the Sun. She said she felt betrayed."

"She said she cared about us," Alvara said dumbly. "Maybe she lied. And now you're blind," she finished. "Does it hurt?"

"No, it doesn't feel like anything," he replied, seeming to stare into the distance. "So do you know if the others are all right?"

"Robert and Isabella?" she asked. "I'm not sure; yours was the first room I found. You know there's lava outside the door?"

"Lava. I guess anything is possible," Jake replied.

"It's not lava, it's a hallway," Aurora said, staring at Alvara as if she were crazy.

"Didn't you see me get here on a boat? I also brought us some apples. I'll show you," and she walked back to the door, which had shut behind her. She opened it to reveal a field.

"Whoa," she gasped. "That wasn't here before." It gave her the creeps; she had gotten used to the idea of lava. To all appearances, the field had always been there. If their surroundings could keep changing, how would they find their way around?

"What's out there?" Jake asked, and Alvara hastily explained that it was a field of green clover, stretching out to a large Victorian house on a graded hill. She also told Jake about the fact that the sky far above wasn't really sky, but ruffled like water in a breeze. A sun shone brightly from near the undulating ceiling, but Alvara could guess that it wasn't the real sun. The strangeness in comparison to the world they knew, as well as the similarity to their visit to Selene decided the issue. They had really made it to Sol's domain.

Alvara turned to Aurora, and noticed that she looked worried. "What's wrong?" Alvara asked.

"Oh, the world is just usually less in flux than this. The old man must be having a bad day."

"Maybe you should tell us a bit about him before we go searching for him or the others," Alvara suggested. "What do you call him?"

"It's a bit of a soft spot with him, actually," Aurora confided. "He doesn't go by any name that I know of, but if you have to refer to him as anything, I guess Sol works well enough. That's a large part of who he is."

"Why did he tell us to come here?" Alvara asked. "I'm so frustrated with everyone leading us around and not telling us anything!"

"He should probably explain," Aurora answered gently. "We'll go talk with him soon."

"Really, that's all you're going to say?" Alvara exclaimed in disbelief. Aurora shrugged, and instead of answering, helped Jake out of bed. He seemed weak, but proved capable of walking, Aurora's arm steady in his.

Alvara did her best to ignore the twinge of jealousy. She held her impatience in as best she could, and allowed them to walk for a bit while she investigated the clover now poking over the edge of the doorframe. It was normal clover, tickling her palm as she ran her hands over the tops of the heart-like leaves.

"Ready?" Jake asked, and Alvara craned her neck to see him standing behind her. Jake looked flushed, but happy. The creases had disappeared from his forehead and migrated to the space around his eyes, crinkling with amusement as he smiled. He was blind, but he was coping somehow. Alvara swallowed her aggravation as well as she could.

"Sure," Alvara replied, and lead the way across the field. The clover felt wonderful on her bare feet, which just made her distrust this place even more. It wasn't Earth. The thought of what had brought them here sobered her, and fed her simmering frustration. The world was in terrible danger, and here was this lovely patch of field that stood as a mockery to what she knew to be true. All her life she had wanted to be of service; she wouldn't let anything distract her and cause her to miss her chance.

She slowed her brisk walk to keep pace with Aurora and Jake, who strolled across the field toward the large house. "So Aurora, I'm sorry we didn't get to meet properly; this place is so strange, and Jake distracted me."

"Don't feel bad Alvara, I'm distracting to her too," Jake said, winking in Alvara's general direction.

"Distracting only in the surprise one feels that a man so bent on his own destruction manages to still be alive," Aurora retorted.

"Sorry to disappoint," Jake said, smiling contentedly even as his wife ruffled his hair affectionately.

"Anyway, Alvara, don't worry about it," Aurora continued. "Jake's told me a bunch about you; you're a pretty tough kid, putting up with this lug throughout everything. It's a pleasure," she said, and stopped to give Alvara a brief hug. She smelled like lemon and cinnamon, and felt real.

"So I was wondering," asked Alvara, "how you came to be here. Jake thought you were dead. If you survived all those years ago, why didn't you ever come back to be with him?" Alvara asked, not softening the question. After all Jake had been through, Alvara had to know the truth.

"It's okay, it's a fair question," Aurora replied sadly, as they continued across the endless field. At least the house was getting somewhat closer. "Turns out some strange singing abilities I've had since I was a kid marked me as one of the Sun's Children, which enabled him to snatch me up in the nick of time."

"*You're* the last Child of the Sun?" Alvara asked, dumbfounded.

"Seems to be the case," Aurora said lightly. "I've got to say, my first name should have been a dead giveaway. And Jake told me that he missed the old man's message that 'Dawn awaits'."

"Wow," Alvara said. She stopped herself from asking if Jake had known, because he would have told them if he had. Why had Aurora kept it a secret? "So why did you stay here?" Alvara asked instead.

Aurora's face fell, and such pain filled it that Alvara felt her own heart break. "I would have returned if I could," Aurora whispered, "in a heartbeat." A tear glistened in her eye, but she brushed it hastily away. "I couldn't come back to Earth because I didn't have a body," she continued in a stronger voice. "The old man saved I guess what you could call my soul, but back then he didn't know much about bringing people here, and my body burned up en route. Lucky for you, he's fixed most of the kinks, and your ability to heal took care of the rest." She glanced toward Jake's sightless eyes, and her brow creased with worry. Alvara could see Jake give her arm a squeeze, as if he could feel her gaze.

"So you're actually . . . dead?" Alvara asked. She hastily added, "Not to be rude, you know, I'm just trying to figure it out. What have you been doing all these years?"

"Nosy, aren't ya?" Aurora grumbled without heat. "A bunch of singing and making this place habitable, and once in a while I visited the Earth in my dreams. I was bored out of my mind before you two showed up."

Alvara muttered that she was sorry.

Jake snorted. "Don't worry, Alvara, she's just an old grump."

"And you're the picture of civility, is that it?" Aurora retorted, kissing Jake on the patch of skin above his ear. Alvara decided that she liked Aurora very much.

When she felt a shadow pass over her, she looked up in alarm. They had reached the front steps of the house.

Chapter 28

It was larger than it had appeared at a distance. At first the dwelling resembled a Roman villa, as the sloped roofs melted down into columns, between which could be seen a garden or courtyard of some sort. But when Alvara blinked it had taken on a more modern aesthetic, with large sheets of glass instead of walls and hard angles replacing the curved archways. Aurora laid a hand on her shoulder when Alvara staggered.

"Something's up," Aurora said. "Even the house is in flux."

"Why does he even have a house?" Alvara asked.

Aurora shrugged. "Humanity seems to bleed into him, now more than ever. When I first came here, he had most of this landscape made for me, so that it would be familiar. He appeared in a body, so that we could talk. Nowadays, though, he lives in it full time." Alvara wasn't sure if she meant the body or the house.

"He's in here somewhere," Aurora continued, squinting at the house. "Just try not to move when your eyes are shut, or it can shift without warning."

"I'll just take my cues from you, then," Jake said.

"Don't worry. I'm not letting you out of my sight," Aurora said. Her smile was fierce. She pushed open the ordinary, wooden front door of a clapboard New England beach house and led them inside.

Alvara discovered in the entranceway that if she glanced around as she walked, that was when the house changed shape. When she kept her eyes fixed on where she was headed, the passage wouldn't make any sudden shifts. Why did Sol play games with them like this? She wondered if it appeared the same to Aurora and Jake. *Well, not to Jake*, she amended. *Not being able to see, he's the only one who could think this place is normal.* Aurora pushed aside a woven curtain, led them through a curved mud room with a thatch roof, and to a surreal frosted sliding glass door at the other end. Alvara didn't know what to expect beyond it, but it wasn't what she saw.

Steam filled the air, along with aromas that made Alvara realize she had only eaten an apple in as long as she could remember. She could smell curries and roasted meat and squash, cinnamon and chilies, and the yeasty smell of baked bread, as well as other smells she couldn't name. She walked through the door, noticing stainless steel appliances and a marble countertop. Steam filled the room, preventing her from seeing the far end.

"Come in," a deep voice boomed from within the steam. "I don't bite." Alvara approached with caution. Behind her, she could hear Jake making his way with Aurora. The steam rolled away to reveal a large black man in jeans and a T-shirt, who leaned over a pot of some kind of stew on the stovetop. He ran one hand around the base of the pot, leaving a trail of red-hot metal in his wake that quickly cooled back to black. He inhaled deeply. Seeming satisfied, he picked up the pot and set it on the countertop. Then he ladled the stew onto plates covered in spongey, sour-smelling pancakes. He smiled as he distributed the food. Alvara knew it was cheesy, but she couldn't get out of her head the way his face lit up like sunlight when he smiled.

"So, are you—" she began.

"Alvara, I do not need any more names," he said, but with good humor. "Call me Sol, if you must." He extended his hand, and she shook it, blinking as she did so. At the end of her blink, he was tall, fair, and skinny, with hair tending to grey. She released her hand in shock.

"What, I mean, you're worse than she was," Alvara said, confused. He looked . . . hurt.

He only replied, "It may have seemed that way." Sol glanced over her shoulder. "And you must be Jake. It is a pleasure to meet you both." Sol walked toward Jake, transforming as he went to a young Indian man, with thick black hair and a strong nose.

He reached out a hand to shake Jake's. Alvara wondered how Jake could shake the hand of the man who nearly killed them both.

After a beat, Jake extended his hand, clasping Sol's warmly. "Thank you for saving Rory," he said simply.

"I did what I could," Sol replied. That was about the lamest answer Alvara had ever heard.

"Is that why we nearly burned to death on the way here? Because you did what you could? Did Isabella and Robert even make it here alive? And how about Jake; it wasn't enough to take his wife from him, you also reward him for visiting you by *blinding him?*" she yelled. The way Jake was just going to forgive all wrongs now that he had Aurora back just snapped something inside of her. "*Everyone* we meet uses us, no one tells us anything, and no one lets us decide for ourselves. It's always 'you didn't know this', or 'you have to do that'. I'm done with being ordered around! You owe both of us an apology and a damn good explanation, or I'm leaving. With or without your help!"

She was done with the mystery, the intrigue, and the deceit. She was no one's prisoner. She was no one's warrior. She would decide for herself whether to trust Sol, and would not take his words on faith alone. And she'd find some way out of here, with Jake, if it came to that.

Sol stared at her, and she shivered. He looked incredibly old, and tired, and sad. How could someone appear so strong, and at the same time, so beaten?

"There is no excuse for what you have been through, what my orders and my mistakes have cost both of you. I beg your forgiveness. Alvara, please do not go before I have the chance to explain everything. I promise, once I finish, you are free to do as you please, including leaving if you wish. I have been a terrible host; Isabella and Robert will be here soon. Will you do me the honor of dining at my table?"

It was strange, thought Alvara as she used the spongey pancake to scoop up the spiced stews and curries. As they sat around the table, she had had an overwhelming feeling of déjà vu. She realized this was not the first food she and Jake had shared with gods, and thought back to the campfire on the beach, and Selene in her long flowing dress. Alvara's anger was gone, as rapidly as it had flared, but she did not trust Sol. She would give him the benefit of the doubt though, which was more than she had thought she could afford.

Isabella and Robert had fully recovered, and said their injuries hadn't been too extensive. Robert droned on about his theories concerning the successful passage through the Outer Layers of the Sun's corona, but Alvara couldn't follow the technical explanations and so tuned it out.

Alvara made up her mind to like Isabella; there hadn't been even a hint of smugness in Isabella's voice after hearing that Jake and Alvara had had the worst of it. The other two had spent their time, which had been about a day, exploring the grounds. They had met Sol the day before, but he had claimed that he would only explain once.

The two of them were a bit in awe of the whole situation. Aurora's entry into their exclusive club particularly discomfited them. Aurora was clearly an outsider, though to their credit, the other Children of the Sun worked hard to include her in conversation.

Sol didn't say much, but instead soaked up the words of the rest of the table with obvious interest. Alvara supposed that it must get lonely here too, even with Aurora for company. She only asked him one direct question.

"Why does your body keep changing?"

"You are what you eat," he replied cryptically.

"That wasn't an answer," Alvara pushed.

Sol sighed and shrugged. "I will explain what I can after dinner," he said apologetically. The conversation halted at that, but Isabella valiantly picked up the loose end, and everyone was soon chatting again. Alvara played with her food as she waited for his explanation.

Once everyone had finished eating, they sat sipping a creamy, iced coffee beverage that complemented the spicy food perfectly. The people around the table all seemed relaxed, but as soon as Sol leaned forward in his chair, he had everyone's full attention. He brushed his waves of blonde hair out of his face, and stared around the table with deep green eyes.

"Well," he said. "I know you all have many questions, but if you would let me tell the story of her and me from the very beginning, it might answer some of them, and the rest can come at the end. I need to get the flow of this right, if this is to be our story." He waited for a response, but none was forthcoming, so he took a deep breath and began.

"Let me tell it to you the way it was, and is, and will be."

"When the Earth was new, we slept in the minds of men and women, emerging in a moment, fully formed and delighting in existence. I was one, and she was the other, my sister and mother and daughter and lover and friend. She was mine; she balanced me completely. Others came, but none like us, whole and apart from the tumultuous battles our peer gods waged on the Earth below. And they fought such battles, for the belief and energy that sustained us in this precarious, infinite existence. We were unique; our presence in the sky made us ubiquitous, noticed and fed by every culture on Earth, so our quarrels were few and our power great.

"In thanks for the blessing of our creation, we decided together to gift humanity and make of some of them our daughters and sons. She decided upon wings, as it was her deepest joy, and I think greatest sorrow, that they had the freedom to live and breathe and die and we did not. I decided upon a variety of gifts, each suiting the individual receiving it, as I felt that would be best. We hoped that our Children would be two halves of a continuous whole, enjoying the gifts we gave them as they acted to keep the world in a peaceful balance of energies.

"And so each generation of humanity receives a gift from each of us; a son and a daughter, yin and yang, dark and light. There are so many words for what we unknowingly created when we created those first Children of ours. For they were more than just gifts; our Children are inextricably tied to us and to our fate in ways we have yet to understand and cannot fully describe.

"As the number and variety of people worshipping us grew, we reflected those differences in belief. No longer stable in our bodies, or even occasionally in our gender, we felt the blessing and curse of our existence; eternal life, but living apart from other beings, and with our identities in constant flux. I was a creature of the light, and I accepted the multiplicity of identity while attempting to keep my 'own' intact; it was in my nature to face hard truths, and I have learned to live with it.

"She could not. She was of the two-sided self, dark and light holding equal sway. I will never know why she could not live with this chaos of identity, but it was so. She became obsessed with returning to the body she thought of as her true form. Though I warned her against it, she didn't listen, and she attempted to freeze herself in that single form. When she froze her body, her mind splintered, and the cracks have only continued to fissure.

"Throughout this time, ages of humanity rose and fell, and gods dwindled and their descendants replaced them, until those too were obsolete. Very few remained. At that time, the entities you associate with goodness had grown very powerful; it is in my nature not to name them, but I believe you can guess. These were the entities fed by the major world religions, and they each had hundreds of thousands or even millions of believers.

"It is in this that you can see the curse of ours most succinctly: they were exactly as good and as selfless as people believed them to be, though they personally chose to be the greatest and best of that belief. They agreed to give themselves to destroy the evil that was all around, the singular individual fed by the darkness in all humans, and who only sought to destroy. You know of whom I speak. These entities approached her and me in order that we might assist them in their task of crafting a permanent prison for Evil, knowing that to join them would cost us our lives.

"I cannot forget the laugh she uttered, though only a millennium before we would have agreed to join them without question. She said, "Is He so certain we should not be caged with that other?" I feared that the cracks had finally shattered her, and declined as well, in order that I might take care of her. And then, after an indefinable span, they were all gone. Only we two remained.

"Suddenly the battle had arrived, but instead of coming from outside our union it erupted between us. I attempted to quell her fears, but they had no grounds and so there was no debate. She became delusional, insane. She lost her grip on the balance we maintained, on our responsibilities, and even on the reality of our love for one another. In time, she stopped speaking with me, screaming that it was all a dream any time I tried, and blaming me for all that she had lost. She poured energy into her Children, and maintenance of the balance indicated that I must do the same. In my naïve rescue of Aurora from certain death I removed her gift from the world, tipping the balance irrevocably toward my other. But instead of mitigating this imbalance, she increased the power she gave to her Children. She threatened everything with her excess.

"Until a few of the Earth's rotations ago, I had no idea that she had any motive behind her madness, but I think this vision must have sustained her. I saw it in a dream she had, though it has become rare for thoughts of that type to pass between us. The Earth, as she saw it, was the Mother of us both. She somehow feels that if she could be reunited with her mother, she might too be reunited with her Children, and with me. She feels it will make her whole again, and will end her terrible loneliness. She has become obsessed. I saw her pursued by the wolves of her madness, crying out into the night, and wished to hold her again. But she has shut me out completely, and it breaks my heart.

"She is growing closer and closer to the Earth, and will destroy all in her folly. I cannot let her destroy humanity; humans are the creators, and without them nothing can come into being. All would be darkness; an unconscionable waste.

"I know I have to stop her, but there is only one way left I can see, and it is with her death. Being creatures of balance, the way to bring about her death is to offer my own. I have come to terms with this, and accept it. But it requires an act more potent. She has still blocked me out, and I cannot kill her unless I can embrace her. The cost will be paid, but not just by me; it must also be paid by you."

It took a few moments for Alvara to realize he was done speaking. He sat back in his chair, awaiting their questions. Thoughts spun themselves in and out of meaning as Alvara tried to grasp the enormity of what Sol had just told them. Selene was insane, and thought she could save herself by destroying the world. God was really gone . . . somewhere. What was left to be done? What could they possibly do to stop Selene?

"That's . . . a lot to take in," Isabella breathed. "I'm sorry," she continued, her expression showing she knew it was inadequate in response to Sol's tale, to his commitment to sacrifice.

"It makes sense," Jake added. "That Selene has lost her mind. There has been fallout from the excess energy from the Moon, and often it makes people crazy in one form or another."

"She made men crazy, or I did, when I asked for her help once," Alvara agreed. "We should have seen the connection," she added bitterly.

"There's more," said Robert gravely. "We met a young girl with prophetic knowledge, and she conveyed to Alvara what was to come, which was the reason we attempted to come speak with you in the first place. Alvara?" he asked. Alvara recited the prophesy by memory.

A pale child screams,
A pale child prays,
A pale child believes,
The moon sings to her children.
A bright child was lost,
A bright child was careful,
A bright child was faithful,
The sun calls to his children.
Unless a mother is betrayed by one of her children
And the sun dances with the moon once more
The earth will cry for the moon's folly
And bathe in her children's blood.

Its violent imagery disturbed her, juxtaposed on this friendly dinner. She wondered if it could be true, if it would change the story Sol told them at all, and if it would somehow alter the price to be paid.

"It feels real. And it fits," Sol whispered.

"I'd love to hear how it does, as we've puzzled over it until our heads spun," Alvara retorted.

"Well, the three children at the top are you three, her Children; Alvara, Jake, and a crying baby who will one day be the new child."

"So soon there will be three of us again, but the last one is still just a baby," Alvara clarified. Sol nodded, his attention elsewhere.

"And we've got my three Children, Aurora included, and the crux of the problem. If we do not stop her from colliding the Moon with the Earth—"

"—most of humanity will die," Alvara surprised herself by saying. A small planet was on a collision course with the Earth, and a lunatic sat in the driver's seat. The enormity of the problem they faced threatened to overwhelm her.

A child's betrayal was the only hope. It was the one part of the prophesy that suggested something could be done to avert the last two lines. But Alvara still had no idea who the child was that it referred to, and what he or she could possibly do to save the Earth from destruction.

"What do you think the part about the betrayal means?" Jake said into the stillness, giving voice to Alvara's thoughts.

"I know what it means," Sol said, and his face twisted in pain. "I just don't know the best way to ask you all. I have already expected, and circumstances have already taken, so much from you. Whatever you may think, I care about you," he said, glancing at Robert and Isabella, "as well as you two, Jake and Alvara, as if you were my own children. We meant it as a blessing," he whispered, a hand on his temple.

"Sol, please just tell us," Alvara said. "We have a right to know and decide for ourselves."

Sol raised his head, his eyes bright under dark brows. His changes were disconcerting at first, thought Alvara, but no matter how often his body changed, he was the same person inside. "You are absolutely right," he agreed, and explained.

"I can make myself go supernova; only once, mind you, and it is not reversible. There will be a partial solar eclipse in less than a rotation. If I can get close to her and hold her in an embrace, I can go, and take her with me."

"A supernova of our sun does not seem much of an improvement for humanity's survival," Robert interjected, frowning.

Sol waved a hand in dismissal. "The entity and the physical structure are not one. I will be gone, but your nearest star will remain. Empty," he said, his face falling.

"I cannot do it alone," he added, "and that is where that line of the prophesy fits. She is too powerful to entrap; she must embrace me of her own accord. The only way I can think of, and the prophesy seems to support this, is if our Children reminded us of our love. It would return her to me again."

"How are we supposed to do that?" Isabella asked, but Alvara thought she knew.

"Jake and Aurora," Sol said. "Your love is the strongest tie she and I share. If you were to agree to open yourselves to us both, it would be a conduit for both our power and would draw us together again."

Alvara watched them from across the table. Jake had Aurora's hand resting in two of his own. She didn't think they had once been apart since they had found each other again. Theirs would be a perfect conduit for Sol's idea. But it didn't seem like a hopeful resolution; what suddenly filled her with dread?

"Don't ask this of them," Robert said quickly. Alvara didn't know what he meant, but he didn't explain. "Jake and Aurora just found each other again. I volunteer; I know what I'm doing. Use me instead."

"Robert?" Isabella asked, and he met her eyes. "Me too," she said quickly. "I'll do it with Robert. We are a family. We, also, can remind you both of love. Let us help."

"It cannot be you two, or you, Alvara," Sol said before she could speak up. "You cannot bridge the divide between Selene and me. It has to be Jake and Aurora, or no one."

Robert let out his breath in a sigh, and Isabella's face fell.

"Jake and Aurora? What will they have to do?" Alvara asked, finding it hard to breathe. Why wasn't anyone saying what they meant?

"The catch, Sol," Aurora said gently, "what you've withheld. The same bond that would allow you to entrap Selene would bind us to your fates. As you went up in flames, so would we."

The anxiety Alvara had felt overwhelmed her in a sudden wave. "What? That can't be right!" she said. She knew she was shouting, but she didn't care. "Jake, Sol? That's not what will happen; there's got to be a better way? You're a god!" The others stared at her, but didn't say anything. "What's the point of being a god if you just have to give up?" No one answered her.

"Jake?" she pleaded. "You wouldn't do that; you just got Aurora back!"

"I know," Jake said in a small voice, his stare fixed over her shoulder. "I don't know what—"

"Say you won't do it! Stand up for yourself, Jake!" Tears welled in her eyes, and she needed to be anywhere but in the midst of all those sympathetic faces. How dare they feel bad for her, when it was Jake and Rory who would suffer the real price? It was so far from fair, worse than anything since her father had gone to get her those stupid balloons. She stumbled from the room, and thankfully, no one got up to follow her.

Chapter 29

The walls felt smooth and cool under Jake's fingertips. Like polished stone. He found if he stepped carefully with one hand extended, it wasn't too difficult to navigate. Sol had crafted a creature to follow him to make sure he didn't get hurt, and he could smell the brimstone fumes of the thing and hear its crunching gait. Jake imagined a smoldering version of Selene's golem. He tried to ignore the creature. He just wanted to be alone.

He needed to think.

Jake was still getting used to 'living in the dark', as he referred to it in his head. Blind was too final. Suddenly, he didn't want to be alone; he wanted to talk with Alvara. Maybe she could help him begin to straighten out his thoughts.

As he felt his way to the front door, the creature behind him grunted when he found the correct handle. A soft whiff of flowers and the freshness of the air told him he had made it outside. As he emerged from under the overhang of the building, he could feel the sun on his skin, though to him, it seemed the darkest night. Jake felt, somewhat foolishly, that if he could just blink and open his eyes the right way, with the right amount of squinting, he'd be able to see again. He knew it was absurd, but the thought persisted.

"Alvara?" he called, but only the breeze answered. He tried again, louder, "Alvara!" and waited for a reply.

"Over here, Jake," her voice answered. "I'll come get you, just stay there."

"You can leave," he said to the creature, and the burning smell dissipated. Jake stood still, feeling the grass and fresh earth seep between his toes.

He felt her slight arm slip into his, and they walked across the field. Jake didn't say anything, just treasured the silence between them. There was trust there, and respect. Jake knew he wanted to protect her from what was to come, and hated to see her hurting. He didn't know what to think about anything else.

"Did you and Aurora decide?" Alvara whispered.

"No, we haven't really discussed it yet. I don't know what to do," Jake confessed.

"Oh," she replied. They stopped moving. Alvara guided him to sit, keeping her arm in his. He was glad that she did. The ground was damp, but he relished in the feel of the soil beneath his free hand, and the smell of the generations of plant life that had died and lived in this field. Unless that too was an illusion.

"Of course, I want to help save humanity," Jake spoke into the silence. "We made it clear at the beginning of this whole adventure that we wanted to help our people." His whole body tensed.

"But this damned situation doesn't make any sense. I mean, what are the odds? That I'd meet Rory? That I'd fall in love? That she'd fall at sunset? That she wouldn't die? That she'd be the daughter of the sun, and I'd be the son of the moon, and we'd both make it to this moment and be the particular recipe required to avert otherwise certain disaster, a horrible, terrifying tragedy for everyone on Earth? If these *children* who call themselves gods didn't make this happen, then who the hell did? It's too big to be coincidence. And tell me this, Alvara," Jake said, breathing hard with the force of his feeling. "Why us? Why were we chosen?"

"Jake, I don't know," she said, and he could hear the tears in her voice.

"Because I can do what I want," Jake said fiercely, standing up. "I have control over my own life, maybe not over who I meet or fall in love with or lose or find again, but damn it, I have control over my decision right now! You hear that!" he yelled out over the field, "It's *my* choice, mine." He could feel tears leaking out of his eyes, and he was shaking.

"Oh Jake," Alvara said, and stood to put her arm around his shoulder. "I'm so sorry, but I don't want you to go. I just found you," she whispered, and cried into his shoulder. He stroked her hair.

What did he want?

He wanted his life back. After so many years alone, and after so much inner torment, he had Rory, at last and completely and forever.

Yet she could never leave here, as she no longer had a body; she wasn't alive, not really. They could never go back and have a life together, though he had been trying not to think about that. But he could be with her here, indefinitely, and that was a gift he had never been foolish enough to hope for until now.

And Alvara. He didn't want to leave her; he couldn't just abandon her now. Not to an aunt who wished she were gone; Alvara deserved to be treated like the wonderful and amazing woman she was growing up to be. He knew he could do that, could be the father she needed, could have in her the daughter he always wished for and never had.

But what about those people down below, those countless millions whose lives rested in his hands? To betray Selene wouldn't be so hard, though he felt nothing but pity for her destructive madness. It was the thought of the aftermath that left him weak. He was afraid to die. A reasonable thought, to be afraid of death. That didn't bother him very much.

But nothing else about the situation was reasonable. Why would he even consider putting his life above that of so many others? The fact that only one person would have to die was a great blessing. Was his happiness worth more than the world? To him, it was close.

He couldn't shake the feeling of despair of walking to his own death. He would prefer some sort of all-out battle; isn't that how one normally conquered the forces of darkness? The thought didn't make him smile. It just left him feeling cold. It felt so weak, to just lay down his life in quiet resignation.

But Rory would be there, with him. That alone might be enough.

Alvara had stopped crying, and he could hear her wiping her nose on fabric, her breath still ragged. "I wish there was something I could do," she raged. "The whole world in danger, and me always wishing for something I could do. And there's nothing now."

"I know, honey. I was just wishing that we could prevent this whole drama from playing out. But as far as we know, there's nothing else to be done." *Just a quiet walk to a quiet death*, Jake thought.

"But you don't *deserve* it, Jake," she said, her voice angry. "It should be people like Xiu Li who need to die to make things right. I know I sound like a kid, but that's the way it should work."

Jake's heart swelled. He wished he could see her now, facing down fate with her back straight. "You make the world the next time around," he said. He thought he could hear her smile, and she chuckled through her tears to let him know.

"Jake, I don't want you to do this," she said, her voice quavering. He wished he could look into her eyes and tell her it would be all right, but he couldn't do either one. Instead, he pulled her into a hug, where she cried into his shirt.

They stayed like that for a while. Jake thought of everything they had overcome together, the dumb jokes they had shared. She was such a strong girl, fierce and true. He put a hand on her head and held her while she came to grips with the wrongness of the world, and realized he wouldn't trade one minute of the time they had together.

"I know, Alvara. Shh," he said. "I'm not sure of my decision, and it's Rory's decision too. We have to talk it through together. There may be alternatives we haven't considered," he said, not really believing it. "And besides, I've had a good, long life, you know, and you've got most of that still ahead of you. I don't know what I would do if it was you and not me that had to give all that up."

"You're not *that* old, Jake," Alvara scoffed, and Jake had to laugh.

"Thanks, kid," he said, releasing his hold. "Let's get back. I think Sol wants to talk with each of us alone. And I need to speak with Rory."

"Okay," she said, though it wasn't, and they both knew it. "But don't leave without saying goodbye."

"You can count on it."

"Sol," Jake called. Rory held his hand. Alvara had gone off to talk with Robert and Isabella. She hadn't been willing to leave until Jake had made it clear that he wanted a bit of privacy. He hoped she would forgive him that.

Jake could sense Sol's presence in front of him; he wondered that he'd never before been able to feel the power of the sun and the moon like he could now. Standing near Sol was like facing a furnace.

"Jake," Sol boomed back. "I will answer any questions that I can, to help you make your decision."

"Here's one, just for kicks. Why us? Why did you give us gifts, while others were passed by? How do you and Selene choose?"

"Why ask that?" Sol asked. "It does not seem relevant."

"On the contrary, it's at the heart of everything I can think of. Rory and I could have led a normal life without our 'gifts', and we'd still be living it as far as we can tell. So we have to know why you and she chose us. It will help us make sense of it all."

"You cannot tease threads apart like this, Jake," he replied. "The paths of fate cannot be reasoned into new trajectories through supposition, there are—"

"I'm sure there are all kinds of intricacies, but please spare us your crap, Sol, and just answer the question. Why were we chosen?"

Sol took a deep breath, and sighed. "I do not know."

"What?" Rory asked.

"I do not know," Sol repeated. "I have never known. Why this crisis? Why this moment? Why you two? Why me? Why her? And my favorite, why do I have such power when I cannot even use it to save the goddess, the woman, I love? *Why.* This is the heart of the matter, Jake: I am no different from you in all the ways that count. I have a fixed duration, shorter now than it has ever been. I have a lost love. And I have no idea in hell or heaven why I was put above this Earth and whether or not I have fulfilled my purpose. Much less tell you whether or not you are fulfilling some damnable grander purpose of your own."

He slammed his palm into the wall and strode off. Jake didn't know what to say. It was disappointing, almost pathetic that Sol should have no answers for them, like a parent confiding his or her weaknesses to a child. He'd existed for millennia with a perfect view of the world and power to shape it, and he didn't have any idea what it was all for. *Makes you wonder how much hope the rest of us could have,* Jake thought. He was surprisingly happy with the answer he found.

Some.

Chapter 30

My child, Sol thought. The experience, as it had always done, left him with a feeling of awe. He gazed down at a young girl of perhaps thirteen, on her way to fetch water from a nearby stream. She was dressed in little more than rags, and lugged an old bucket made of bamboo. It would be the last time she would feel so normal.

He was excited, but patient, knowing from the sense of his power building how soon her life would change. She picked her steps down the riverbank, pushing rushes aside until she could reach the water. With her bucket filled, she was breathing hard by the time she could set it atop the steep rise surrounding the river. She was tired, and didn't want to carry the water, and put her hand in for a sip.

And the water wobbled into the air above her outstretched fingers.

She pulled her hand back in alarm, and the water fell back into the bucket with a splash. But with a child's curiosity, she reached for it again. This time, the water left the bucket and made its way to her hand. As the water flowed over her hands without wetting them, she broke into a grin.

He couldn't help it. As the vision faded, he smiled too. He tried to keep her joy in his mind's eye, ignoring for the moment the price she would pay for her gift. He found himself back in his study, no longer alone.

An old man was seated in the armchair across from him. Though His image shifted subtly at each moment, His strength and compassion were constants, like gravity, which pulled others toward Him. The old man smiled, and he smiled in return.

"Hello, Father," he said.

"Though I am not your father, I appreciate the compliment."

"You always say that, Father."

"I hope I did not interrupt. Whom were you observing?"

"My newest little girl," he glowed. "Her name is Apsara, and she just discovered that she could manipulate water."

"How precious," the Father spoke, and Sol knew that it was so.

"You are always welcome, of course," said Sol, "but what is the occasion of your journeying here?"

"I am here for you, child," the Father intoned. "How does she fare?"

Sol's face must have shown his thoughts, because the Father rose from His chair and walked across the room to pull him into a fierce embrace. "I feel for you," the Father said, and Sol lost what little composure he had gained in observing his child, and wept. No words were spoken, but much passed between them.

Finally, Sol relaxed, and the Father knelt before his chair. Sol met His eyes, and saw compassion there, and resolution. "We are planning a paradigm shift," He said, "so that Evil will not only halt in its advance; Evil will never wreak havoc on the world again."

"I should have been there, I left her alone and He fed her His words, I should have . . ." Sol mumbled, staring into the fire in the hearth. It had the tenor of a mantra that he had repeated so often it had lost much of its sting. He looked back at the Father. "What are you planning?"

"There is nothing you could have done for her. But there is something you can do now. All of Us have agreed to spend Our essences in order to build a prison for Him. Join with us, and you will protect those you love from His influence for the rest of time."

Sol couldn't believe it. "All of You agreed? You cannot be thinking of taking Yourselves out of the equation forever! How will humanity fare?"

"Child," said the Father, "If you love someone, as I love My Children, you must allow them to decide their fates for themselves." His face was lined with pain, and with the ache that comes from love. He watched Sol, and Sol wanted to believe he could give up his existence to protect his Children, and the countless more Earth's Children at the mercy of their own evil desires.

She chose at that moment to enter his mind. It wasn't like the carefree joy he remembered; she forced her way into the conversation. At once she knew the dilemma, though not his thoughts on the manner. This method had limits.

And she laughed, in his head. It was not a nice laugh. "Is He so certain we should not be caged with Him?" she cackled, and left his mind as violently as she had entered it.

Tears leaked from his eyes again, though he tried to wipe them away. They weren't healing tears. They were poisonous, hopeless tears. And he knew his decision.

"I am sorry, but I cannot," Sol admitted. "I could not go without her. I cannot leave her."

The Father nodded, and it was a weary nod. "I had feared you would say that." He returned to his seat.

The two beings were silent for a while, as the fire crackled and wound down. "Father?" Sol asked.

"Yes, my Child," He answered.

Sol felt foolish, but pressed on. "Is this in Your plan? For You to die? For what happened to her? Are we just unwinding the thread You picked, its weavings all planned out long before? Are we free to decide things for ourselves? Or is there really no point to any of it?"

The Father chuckled, but it wasn't a mean sound. It was delighted.

"Oh, there is a point," He said. "But it is like a punch line."

Sol was confused. "But what—"

"It does not make sense out of context. I could not do it justice. But do not worry." The Father smiled as He stood and stretched. "When you get it, it will not disappoint. Watch over them, Child. Farewell."

Sol found himself alone in his room. He moved to build up the fire once more.

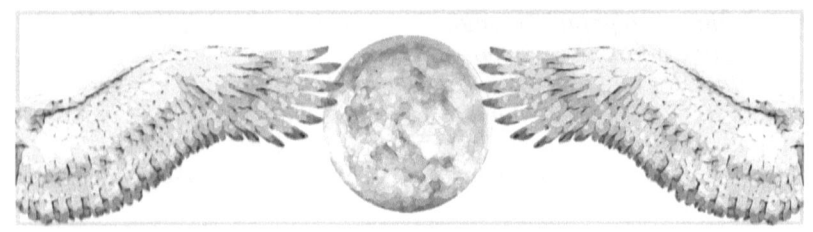

Chapter 31

Jake and Rory skirted the murmuring surf as they strolled along the sand, arm in arm. Rory described how the ocean continued for about a mile to their left before curving upward and smoothly transitioning to evening sky. Sol had built it for her, of course. The beach had always been their favorite place.

The false sun in that evening sky dimmed rather than set. It was not the Earth, but they took pleasure in each other's company just the same. Rory occasionally bent down to grab a seashell, as she had used to do in their youth, but her hand remained firmly on Jake's forearm. There was so much he still needed to say to her, but he let the companionable silence persist. He focused on the crunch of the sand beneath their feet and the sound of her breathing beside him for another few minutes.

"I left Alvara with Sol. He should be sending her home now," Jake said finally.

"Jake, you promised her you'd say goodbye. She might not forgive you for that."

"I know. I couldn't tell her. I left a note in her pocket, and we basically said our goodbyes anyhow. Sol didn't have much time to send them all home before the eclipse, and I needed time with you." The first pang struck his heart, but he let it hit.

"Jake," she chided, but didn't finish the thought. They walked some more. "She really cares about you," she said instead.

"I care about her too," Jake said, his voice soft. "I wish you could have had time to know her, Rory. Hell, I wish I could have had more time to know her. She has such a clear vision for a young girl; she believes the best in others, always. I'm going to miss her." Rory squeezed his hand, and it was enough to know she understood.

"After you left, Sol showed us a video feed of what's going on down on Earth. It was horrible," Rory shuddered. "People beginning to evacuate from shore regions; some waves reaching beachside homes. Some kids were saying it was the Apocalypse, end of the world. As I watched, a newscaster on a beach in Thailand stopped speaking and tried to run, and the camera went dead. I don't know what happened to her."

"It was like that vision I had of the future, that the old man showed me inside myself. When you saved me . . . that was you, right? I wasn't just seeing things?"

"That was me," Rory said, and the warmth in her voice made him smile. "Whenever I could, I got Sol to try to allow me to contact you. Do you remember the cemetery too, when I spoke to you? Sorry that got cut off."

"It's all right! I thought I was crazy. It helped, Rory. And you know, I was thinking about how you would react to the tombstone I picked out for you." Jake explained.

She surprised him by giving a full-throated belly laugh, so hard that they needed to stop walking until she recovered. "Ha, whoo! It probably is a swell rock, Jakey," she said, and kissed him on the cheek.

They felt a deep rumble beneath the beach, and the sand made a whispering noise as it shifted. Jake ran a hand through her hair and said, "That wasn't the only future I saw, you know. There were also futures with the sun shining brightly and people going about their lives as if nothing had ever happened to change them."

"Sol believes that he and she will just be gone, but the physical sun and moon will still be around; the objects were around before, and should be there after their tenants have vacated. But he isn't sure." Rory chuckled, though Jake could hear her fear. "He's not a bad sort, that old man. You would have liked him too, and I'm sorry to see him go." She rubbed Jake's arm. "Jake, you're glowing."

"What?"

"You're glowing, a kind of blue light. Hell, I'm glowing yellow." She pulled him into a fierce embrace, running her fingers through his hair over and over.

"Rory, you know that—"

"I know, Jake. Me too."

There was silence, and pain, but they held on.

"Don't you dare leave me again."

"We'll go together."

And they did.

Alvara awoke on the bluff by her house, where she found herself dumped by a dwindling ray of light. She blinked twice; it was day time, but the sun was absent. A black shape filled the sky, ominously drawing closer through the dim light.

"Wait, no! Where's Jake? You said I would have more time! Jake!" she screamed into the empty air. Jake had promised he would say goodbye. "No," she exhaled, feeling helpless and hating it.

She fell to the ground as a shock wave shook the Earth. She dusted herself off and peered up at the sky. A full solar eclipse.

But she knew how to see the truth beyond her expectations. When she looked up with this knowledge in the front of her mind, the placid scene shifted.

Sol and Selene wrapped each other in a fierce embrace. Selene's hair sometimes hid them from view, and sometimes whipped out to snake among the stars and blend into the darkness of the void. Her eyes were almost entirely pupil, and her skin was a pasty white as she screamed and reached out for the Earth.

Every muscle in Sol's body strained in his determination to hold her back. He held her close, whispering into her ear as she writhed and tried to escape his grasp. His strong arms flexed as he kept her from the Earth below, and Alvara was somehow able to read the words on his lips. Then she understood.

I love you, he said. Over and over. *I love you.*

Selene wept, large tears that left trails of moon dust on her cheeks and spun off on comet trails into the night. Still she struggled, but her struggling grew less intense, and her arms that tore at Sol began to cling to him instead. Sol cradled her face in his hands, wiping her tears away and smiling. She reached up and pulled his mouth down for a kiss.

When their lips touched, a spark erupted and Alvara's vision went white.

Alvara sat up from where she lay on the ground, her ears ringing as if from an explosion. Wings had sprouted from her shoulders, their pure white coated in a layer of dust. They glowed, and then slowly faded and disappeared.

Alvara looked up at the sky, and could see through her tears that the eclipse was ending, the sun peeking out from behind the small, white, familiar orb of the moon. Both the moon and the sun had survived their dance, but Alvara knew that the man and woman who gave them form and life were gone.

Epilogue

Major news networks capitalized on the hype of the strange celestial phenomena witnessed by many across the globe. The day turned night was dubbed simply, "The Eclipse". Scientists called it 'astounding'; voters, 'weird', 'frightening' or 'alarming'; and politicians 'no great cause for alarm'. As the eclipse began, the people of the world traveled inland and awaited what would befall them in a surprising universal darkness, longer and more complete than any eclipse in recorded history. Yet strangely, as the eclipse ended, it seemed that the moon had returned to its original size and orbit, and had shown no further deviations in the days since, though astrophysicists still had no explanation for its disturbed orbit or the strange collision course of its alignment just days before. Aid was sent to developing countries for coastal rebuilding amid great fanfare.

Across the globe, apocalyptic cults which had gained surprising power in the previous days melted back into the woodwork, muttering excuses, as the majority of humanity returned to business as usual. Scattered psychics and mediums, as well as members of the Aputna'a and Shovem indigenous tribes, experienced widespread depression, and were able to articulate to varying degrees that a power had left the world, but this unity of feeling never received widespread attention. The average person might or might not notice that the sun's brightness had diminished by a minute amount; astronomers did, though again, no one placed very much importance on the information. Some journal articles were published and then forgotten.

With all the excitement, as well as some coastal repairs of their own, few in the cities of the South Bay even noticed the small segment in The Argonaut on a long-time Venice Beach resident, owner of A Siren Symphony, who passed away at the age of sixty-five during the eclipse of the previous week. A service for the individual, Jacob Coughlin, was held in the chapel of a cemetery some miles north. The only family member in attendance was his sister, though a group of other eclectic guests arrived as well. At the end of the ceremony, a teenage girl approached the youngest attendee and slipped the child a lacquer-painted bird figurine. The girl gripped her mother's hand, and attempted unsuccessfully to use the figurine as a tissue. The teenager then held out her hand to the boy she had been sitting with, and they wandered into the cemetery.

Alvara kicked at the loose gravel with her sneakers as she crunched along the path toward Jake's grave. Even though dusk had settled over the cemetery, Laerik rode her shoulder in silence. Hummingbird wings made a small lump under her dress.

Alvara didn't know how to feel. It was strange, because she still grew wings every night, so her life was almost back to normal. She even led Bible Study again, and avoided calls from the hospital to come visit the children in her 'angel costume'. She had grown tired of the gift of her wings, and in low moments they seemed more a curse than a blessing.

True normality was a ruse, because people who should have been a part of her life were absent. The crisis was averted, but Jake was really and truly gone. At least he was finally with Rory.

Alvara struggled to come to grips with how much she had lost. She and Jake had been through so much. And now she was alone, without even a God she could still believe in to keep the loneliness at bay.

Well, she wasn't entirely alone. She glanced at Max, who held her hand as he walked with an ease she hadn't known was possible. She had told him everything, and he had understood how hard it had been, and offered his support without question or judgment. It was then that she had understood how much that had meant to her. He had helped her plan and survive the funeral, her hand firmly in his.

After the eclipse had passed, Alvara had paid for the funeral with the small amount Jake had set aside for his passing, though she didn't tell the guests who was responsible. In addition, she read and re-read the letter Jake had slipped into her pocket, apologizing for his absence, thanking her for everything, and instructing her on what he wanted her to do. The note explained how she should donate the rest of his savings to the children's hospital they had visited together, and she proceeded to do so, anonymously, by her own choice. She couldn't bear to explain to his sister the choice he had made. Jake had said that his sister had never seen his wings, and that they hadn't stayed in touch. It was too much of a burden, so Alvara had stayed silent. At least it had been a lovely ceremony.

Alvara and Max didn't speak as they reached Jake's grave. "Farewell Fluff," Laerik whispered. "We don't do this sort of thing in my flock, but this was a good funeral. See you soon, Alvara." Laerik nuzzled her before taking to the dusky air. Alvara was sorry to see her go, but the bird had promised to visit as often as she could.

Alvara looked at the grave and half-smiled; she had known Jake would want to be buried next to Rory, so made sure to place his grave there. She knew he would also enjoy the irony of his grave site; neither he nor his wife was actually buried in the cemetery. Alvara pulled out a feather she had saved from the night before, and planted it in the fresh soil as if it were a flower. It stood straight and white, a testament to his sacrifice, or so she thought. It was a lovely decoration, and waved slightly in the crisp breeze. *You won't be able to help me figure out how to use my feathers*, she thought. *Or find the baby. I'll have to figure it all out for myself. Jake . . .* She fought to hold it together.

"Hey, you certainly ran off," Ridge called. She turned, and saw that Isabella and Robert, Sheila and Ridge were all walking down the path toward them. She had debated inviting them, but was glad they had flown down for the funeral. It was lovely to see Sheila and Ridge again, though Alvara couldn't decide how she felt about Robert and Isabella.

"We wanted to come see his grave, even though he is not there," Isabella said.

"Yeah, Jake was a hero, a thousand times over," Ridge said solemnly. Sheila nodded her agreement. They were silent for a few minutes, out of respect.

"He asked me to find and take care of the baby, who will be the last Child of the Moon," Alvara said suddenly. It was important that they understand. "I won't let him down."

"You'll find him. Or her," Ridge said, "No sweat. Look at all the crazy stuff you've already done." Alvara smiled, and punched him gently on the shoulder.

Alvara slipped her hand back into Max's again. He turned and pulled her into a hug, and they stood that way for a while. Alvara began to cry into his suit jacket, and found that she couldn't stop. She wept for Jake, for the sad and lonely Selene, for the frustrated and heartbroken Sol, and for herself, and what it had all cost her. Max put a hand on her hair and whispered soothing sounds into her ear, and her sobs eventually calmed.

"Whoa," he said suddenly, and Alvara wiped her eyes to see what he meant.

From the tree a few yards away, a huge bird peered down at them. It had the graceful neck and curved beak of a seabird, with a white body and grey wings, and had some difficulty keeping its footing on the branch. It flapped a couple times before settling down, and it had the biggest wingspan she had ever seen. She and the bird just stared at each other for a second, and a wave of recognition washed over her.

Jake, she wondered. Why would she think that? He was gone.

The bird let out a call between a clatter and a trumpet blast, tipping its head back so its beak was high in the air. Alvara glanced to the west and saw another of the birds come and land next to the first one, clattering as well. After the second bird landed, they rattled their beaks together. *Jake and Rory*, she thought, and it felt right. Their lives had ended, but somehow a new life had begun; one in which they could finally be together.

"Alvara, those are albatrosses!" Max said. "Freaking awesome birds. I've never seen one this far inland. Hey, did you know they can fly from the North to the South Pole almost without stopping, and they are one of the few species that mate for life?" Max approached the birds on tiptoe. But before he could get close, they leapt from the tree. "Aw, dang." They spread their massive wings, flapping a few times and then gliding out of sight.

"I might have guessed," said Alvara. At Max's confused expression, she laughed and took his hand once more. "Let's head back." They waved goodbye to the others, who wandered off to their respective homes and lives and futures. Isabella looked like she wanted to speak to them, but Robert took her by the shoulder and led her away, conversing with her in muted tones. And Alvara and Max didn't notice. Together they walked along the path, hand in hand, leaving the empty graves to keep each other company.

Dear Reader,

It may not surprise you to learn that I used to dream of wings. They were huge, wider than my outstretched arms, and beat the air with powerful strokes. Only rarely could I manage to get off the ground in these dreams, but when I did, I felt exhilaration and peace in equal measure.

In Alvara and Jake's story, I wanted to explore the rapturous joy of that freedom, coupled with the inevitable sorrow, heartache, and regret that life can bring. In an instant, you can grow wings for the first time, or a tragedy can occur. Either way, life is never the same. For a while, you simply feel the utter difference between one moment and the next. But often, with the help of those you care for, life goes on, in all its tiny details.

I had so much fun watching Isabella and Robert grow up throughout the events of The Night's Gift. It took me a while (and many edits) to find their voices. But once I understood Robert's slightly befuddled social style and Isabella's oddly maternal instincts, both in strange opposition to their gifts, the two sprang to life. Also, I could hang out with Ridge all day. He is probably my spirit animal.

If I am haunted by anything I have written, it is the character of Selene. Just her, standing alone, gazing out toward her curved oceanic prison. Loneliness has always seemed to fit with the moon, as those lonely ones among us gaze up at the cold, distant, reflected sunlight and try to take some warmth from it. She is sweetness, even kindness, and also pettiness and sudden rages and self-delusion. She is the picture of mental illness, but thanks to a twist of fate, she is too powerful to respond to soothing words. She must be stopped, and it breaks my heart every time.

This novel would be nothing without the feedback and encouragement of my readers. Some write with suggestions, some with questions, and others write to tell me what they loved about the book. You, reader, can help me to go deeper, to question my own assumptions, and may even take Alvara's future adventures in a new direction. Feel free to reach out to me, as I'd love to hear your thoughts. You can reach me at Robert.b.noon@gmail.com. And please, if you have a moment, write a review. Reviews help books to find their way to the exact people who need them – those people are counting on you to make that magic happen!

Writing The Night's Gift felt like a quest in its own right. I could go back to those nights spent staring out my bathroom window at my Southern California suburb, feeling the cool breeze on my face, and I could follow that what if out the window and into the starlit night. And best of all, I could take you all with me.

Yours,
Sarah Hersman

Acknowledgements

I wrote this book in a burst of fiendish activity between the end of college and the beginning of graduate school, a curious in-between moment in my life in which anything seemed possible. But Alvara and Jake wouldn't be who they are today without so many wonderful, intelligent, and supportive people. Thank you to my sister Megan and her friend Taylor, who egged me on after the first few chapters, and believed in the story almost as soon as I did. Thank you to Josh Essoe, for editing advice, to Jeff Blyth, for his honest suggestions, and to Romy Sutherland, for her delighted feedback on the manuscript. To my Muses, Cat and Gineve, who took a chance on a new author, and whose edits re-shaped the novel into a focused and suspenseful narrative, without sacrificing one iota of the sheer wonder. Most of all, to my mother Nancy, who was editor-in-chief and marketing executive and cheerleader, all when I needed it most. Finally, to you, who picked up this book. Many thanks – hope you enjoy it!

ABOUT THE AUTHOR

Sarah Hersman is a graduate of Brown University, with a PhD in Neuroscience from UCLA. Though she has multiple scientific papers to her name, The Night's Gift is her first novel.

In her spare time (such as it is), she reads voraciously, sings opera, writes constantly, and very occasionally delights in falconry. She lives in Boston with her husband JJ and two dogs, Dante and Jackson.